Prologue

JERSEY

Koa once told me he didn't believe in god, heaven, or the afterlife. He claimed organized religion was nonsense since in his opinion, our existence on the earth was about as special as the algae in the ocean or of allergy-inducing dust mites found in most peoples' homes.

"Life is meaningless," he'd said. "Whatever we do, however we act, none of it matters in the end. It makes no difference." A bold statement from a preteen, and one I was too young to fully dissect and understand at the time. But Koa had always been beyond his years. When most boys were catching frogs and having races on their BMXs, Koa's childhood had imploded, altering the course of his entire life.

His best friend called him morose.

But who might he have been without tragedy?

My convictions about god, religion, and the afterlife were more ambiguous and obscure. A constantly changing ideology, morphing with my ever-fluctuating mood. A seed of doubt prevented me from classifying myself as an atheist, yet most days, I didn't feel the presence of a higher power in my heart. The few years I'd spent as an altar boy at my parents' church had left an impression, and there were days when I yearned for a stronger faith, for the certainty and naivety of those childhood beliefs.

So, I waffled, knowing the answers to those universal, cosmic questions could only be discovered at the end of a lifetime.

On days like today, with frost coating the landscape, the sun warming our cold cheeks, and as we shared coffee on the back fence, faith or something akin to faith burned in my heart.

Koa and I had been brought back together by forces I couldn't explain. Be it fate, destiny, or chance, I didn't know. Be it a god who was tired of seeing two middle-aged men alone in their suffering. It didn't matter. What mattered was we made it out of the darkness and into the light. Koa had trudged through the toils and despair of an unforgiving life and found a way to smile again.

To enjoy each day.

He had found serenity.

Meaning.

Purpose.

Peace.

Koa might never believe in a higher power, but I didn't think he continued to dwell on the pointlessness of his existence. He had found a reason to live.

A reason to smile.

A reason to go on.

But I'm getting ahead of myself.

Our story started many years ago.

1

Jersey

The tick and ping of a cooling engine filled the cab of the Gladiator, joining chorus with the accelerated drum beat of my heart. I'd driven her long and hard from Toronto several times that week, the all-season tires eating up the road and chewing a path through the morbid conversations that had been playing on repeat in my brain since I'd received the dreaded call five days ago.

Had it been five days?

"Jersey Reid? This is Constable Everett from Lakefield OPP. I regret to inform you..."

Squeezing the leather steering wheel, I stuffed those life-altering words into a mental steel box and slammed the lid.

The funeral was already lost in the haze. As if I didn't already feel guilty enough, dozens of people had felt the need to remind me how much my absence over the years had hurt them.

The two-story country-style house at the end of the driveway sat weary and haggard in the fading daylight. My perspective could have been tainted by the recent news, but I hadn't been home in almost fifteen years, so it was possible the house's disrepair was caused by nothing more than the dreaded passing of time that plagued us all.

Fifteen years. Had it really been fifteen years?

Derby was seventeen next month, and Christine had left when he was shy of two. Yep. Christmas of 2008. I'd been on crutches still, fresh out of my second surgery, chewing oxy like they were candy. The following March, officially addicted to painkillers, miserable from injury, and caustic with the world because my career had ended abruptly, my wife announced our marriage was over too.

Fifteen years.

How many hits could a person take?

It didn't take much to derail a life. A teen accepting drugs in a back alley. A man stepping out on his wife. A mother taking her eyes off her rambunctious toddler for two seconds to admire a sundress in a store window.

Bam.

In an instant, life could become something entirely different. I knew all about it.

Twice I'd experienced life-altering events.

Early December, not long into our 2008 season, I'd taken a bad hit on the ice and torn my ACL. Because of the injury, I'd lost my career, marriage, son, and parents. I wasn't blameless. Apart from the physical hit and subsequent injury, the rest of the tragedy was on me. An addiction to painkillers was not something anyone had anticipated, and it had changed me.

By the time I'd gotten clean, it was too late.

Then, five days ago, a distracted teenage driver in an SUV crossed the center line and hit my parents' compact Honda Civic head-on, killing them both instantly—or so I was told. I hoped they hadn't suffered.

Ever since the phone call, a fog had descended on my life as I tried to pick up the pieces and make sense of what was left, as I learned to mourn parents I hadn't seen or conversed with in more than a decade.

Guilt had burrowed a hole in my chest and wouldn't leave. I deserved it.

Moving robotically, I exited the Jeep, stretched my aching knee, and aimed for the front door. A false spring had settled over my hometown, typical for March. It wouldn't last. At some point, the balmy temperatures would dip, and snow would return. It happened every year.

A few flyers and envelopes stuck out the top of the mailbox. More jobs to add to the list—canceling subscriptions, phoning the utility companies, informing the lawn boy he wouldn't be needed this summer.

I gathered the mail, peeked inside the box to ensure I hadn't missed anything, then wedged the few envelopes under an arm as I dug keys from my bomber jacket. The coat was overkill, but I hadn't listened to the weather before leaving the house that morning.

Grant Maurier, my parents' elderly lawyer, had met with me not fifteen minutes earlier at his ramshackle office in central Lakefield. *"I'm an old family friend,"* he'd informed me. I didn't know him, and he didn't know me either, outside the stories my dad had shared. Offering his condolences, Mr. Maurier had gone over a few legal aspects, had me sign the paperwork, and handed over the keys to my parents' house, shed, garage, and safety deposit box. *"If you need anything or have any questions, don't hesitate to call,"* he'd said.

Fifteen years.

How had it been fifteen years?

Lakefield was the same, but wasn't that the joke? *"Gotta get outta this shit town. Nothing ever happens here."* How many times had my buddies and I said that in high school?

I unlocked the front door, hesitated, then reluctantly stepped inside. The stagnant, oppressive air made it hard to breathe. The furnace pumped scads of heat into the empty house, unaware its services were no longer needed since the occupants would never return.

I grew roots in the front hallway, unable to move forward yet incapable of reversing time. The house emitted a special type of silence unique to the dead. I had felt it at the funeral home and again in the cemetery. Life contained substance. A soul? Maybe. I wasn't sure I believed in souls. When you died, you died. It would be nice to imagine my parents living it up in heaven, but my conflicting beliefs about the afterlife had been put to the test lately. If there was a god, he was cruel.

Either way, no one could argue that a living person projected an unmistakable presence into the atmosphere. In the absence of that soul or whatever you wanted to call it, the rooms were like dark, empty voids, sucking all remaining hopes and dreams into the abyss.

I shivered, momentarily ready to reverse course and hire a random company to take care of this part.

Accosted by memories, crippled by grief, I lingered in the hallway, getting a hold of myself before I kicked my shoes onto a mat, hung my coat on a hook, and wandered beyond the foyer.

The furniture had changed—modern couch, classy end tables, no more TV stand since the flatscreen hung on the wall—but the decorations were the same, right down to the ceramic vase I'd broken as a kid. Dad had glued it back together, promising he wouldn't tattle. Mom had always displayed dried flowers from her garden within. Dusty roses occupied the vase now.

As I stood in the archway to the living room, gaze skipping about, more of the past unfolded. An indent in the plaster, low to the ground next to the window where I'd ridden my skateboard into the wall. A faint wine stain on the carpet from a New Year's Eve spill. Mom had gotten tipsy, and Dad had danced with her until she was too dizzy to control the glass. The afghan my grandmother had knitted. Whenever I was sick, Mom would wrap it around me, tucking in the sides so I was snug as a bug in a rug. She would pet my sweaty hair off my fevered forehead and tell me stories, feeding me chicken noodle soup and flat ginger ale until I felt better.

It was too much. How was I supposed to deconstruct an entire lifetime of memories? How was I supposed to sell or donate their possessions like they meant nothing?

Fifteen years.

I aimed for the kitchen—a new table, upgraded counters and cabinets, a fancy KitchenAid mixer—and opened the fridge. Grimacing at the rotting scent of spoiled food, I closed it again. In a high cupboard, I found Dad's not-so-secret stash of booze. He wasn't a big drinker but enjoyed the odd glass of whisky when the mood was right. Mom preferred chardonnay.

I stilled with a half empty bottle of Forty Creek in hand.

Had preferred. *Had* enjoyed. Those indulgences were no more. They were gone.

Forever.

Gut-punched, I twisted the cap off the bottle and rooted around until I found a clean tumbler. Two fingers, no ice, exactly how Dad drank it. I held the glass in a toast and spoke to his ghost.

"To you, old man. I wish you could be here to enjoy it with me. I wish... I wish I'd gotten my shit together sooner. I wish I'd not been so goddamn stubborn." It burned, but I drained the liquor, leaving the tumbler on the counter as I continued to reacquaint myself with my childhood home and all I'd left behind.

Fifteen fucking years.

I'd never hated myself more.

I climbed the staircase with the wobbly banister. *"I'll have Dublin come fix it next week, hun. Don't you worry."* Like hell you would, Dad. At ten, I'd taken into my head I could do the banister slide. Eleven and a half hours later, after a trip to the emergency room for stitches in my forehead and a long wait at the dentist's office for a shattered tooth, I swore I would never play daredevil with the staircase again.

The oath had lasted one year and six months. On my twelfth birthday, using an empty cardboard box from a present as a sled, I tackled them anew, earning a scolding.

The third and seventh steps from the bottom creaked underfoot as I climbed, the same as they had done all those years before. A teenager noted those imperfections when planning a midnight escape to be with his girlfriend. One had to be wise when evading the parents, especially when the goal involved losing one's virginity. It should be noted, said virginity was not lost that night.

The upstairs hallway veered in both directions, and I stood at the top, undecided and queasy. My childhood bedroom was to the right. A bathroom, a spare room, and my parents' domain were to the left.

Which would hurt less?

I veered left, remembering how my first hockey coach had nicknamed me the Wrecking Ball since I rarely waited for an opening on the ice and plowed through the heaviest congestion, leveling anyone and everyone in my path.

"It's like you live for pain, Reid. I hope your parents have good insurance."

A pained chuckle rose with the memory as I placed a hand on the cool metal doorknob leading into my parents' bedroom. I'd skipped two doors along the hallway, determined to take the biggest hit first, knowing the damage it caused would make the rest of the tour seem like a cakewalk.

I didn't make it past the threshold. Caught in a vice, my heart squeezed and ached. I gritted my teeth against the pain and clung to the doorframe when my bad knee threatened to buckle. It had never been the same after the hit. All the physiotherapy in the world hadn't helped. The pain was constant. Drugs had been my saving grace, but I didn't touch them anymore. Tylenol was all I allowed myself, and even then, I used it sparingly.

In the end, understanding the impact such an injury could have on a person's life helped me excel at my new job. I could empathize and commiserate. I could help other young men and women come to terms with their future.

Fifteen years, yet the scent of my mother's laundry detergent and perfume hit me hard. The woodsy aroma embedded in Dad's flannel coat hanging less than three feet away was a one-two punch to the gut.

Before tears could burn my eyes, I closed the door like a coward. I would deal with their room another day when I had more strength.

The bathroom was functional and didn't tug as hard at the past. The spare room, intended long ago for a sibling who never arrived, sat stark and austere in the slanted sunlight shining through the window. The bed and dresser weren't familiar. The wallpaper was new and tacky. Who put up wallpaper in this day and age?

I closed the door and continued down the hall toward my old bedroom, convinced it wouldn't be the same, prepared to witness how effectively my parents had erased their only son from their memory. I wouldn't blame them. The shrine of my life had remained long after I'd signed with Hamilton and the Ontario Hockey League at seventeen. It was still there when I'd gone pro at twenty and moved to Edmonton. The switch to Vancouver had come seven years into my career, and Mom had made a point of giving my then-pregnant wife a tour, indulging her in fantasies of how her first grandson might play hockey too.

Derby hated sports as a child. If that had changed, I hadn't been told. I wasn't privy to updates.

Fifteen years had passed. Fifteen years of failed communication. I was the stubborn son and husband who had fallen into the pits of despair after a freak accident had ended his career, turning to oxy for comfort, shunning the support Christine had offered because she couldn't understand.

Fifteen years since the argument.

Fifteen years since she'd walked.

My parents had chosen Christine and Derby over me. They couldn't let go of their grandson, and I'd obstinately refused to listen to reason and seek help. They had rightfully left me to drown in a pit of despair.

The five stages of grief weren't reserved for death. I'd experienced them all after surgery. Denial—I would so play hockey again and fuck any doctor who said I wouldn't. Anger—at the situation, at the guy who'd hit me, at my wife, parents, and life in general. Grief—which had coupled nicely with depression. And, years down the road, acceptance. By then, I'd made a mess of my life and didn't know how to go back.

Fifteen years.

The heat was getting to me. I considered retracing my steps and finding the thermostat. No one said I had to fully evaluate the house on the first day. I could rip the Band-Aid off little by little. There was no hurry.

"Coward."

I opened the door, and my breath caught. The shrine hadn't vanished. It had blossomed and grown, immortalizing my failed career. The haze of tears I'd been holding at bay filled my eyes.

Posters of a nineteen-year-old, a twenty-one-year-old, a twenty-five-year-old, and a twenty-seven-year-old hockey hero lined the wall—my second year playing in the OHL with Hamilton, my first year playing pro with Edmonton, the short switch I'd made to Philly, then my first year with Vancouver. The ignorant man smiling from the glossy print of the last poster was unaware that it would all be over three years down the road.

A signed hockey stick hung from two pegs. Above it, a signed jersey from my OHL days, number nine like Gordie Howe. Despite his career being over before I'd learned to walk, I had idolized him. Other jerseys lined the wall, all of them signed.

A glass-fronted cabinet showed several framed pictures going back decades. A timeline of a glorified son's hockey career. Each showed me geared up, grinning wildly and proudly for the camera.

I stared at the chronology of photographs with a pang in my chest. My father had laced my first pair of skates when I was three. He'd gone to every practice, clapping, cheering, and fighting with the refs until he was red in the face. He'd endured early mornings and long car rides when I'd joined the travel team as a teenager. My father was—*had been*—my biggest and loudest fan.

In a neat row, a few inches in front of the photographs, lay a handful of hockey pucks, the date and my initials written in silver permanent marker on their surfaces. I chuckled. As a defenseman, I didn't shoot often on net, but when I did, and if I scored, my parents had made a point of taking possession of those pucks. At least until I'd gone pro, and it wasn't feasible.

The double bed and its themed covers were the same. The trophy shelf, ribbons, and medals remained. A pinboard over the desk was littered with newspaper clippings—their central focus was my career-ending injury. I turned away, not interested in reliving the fatalistic past.

Exhaustion settled into my bones, and I sat on the edge of the bed. Same creaking springs. Same lumpy mattress. The past five days since the phone call had been brutal. I'd barely slept, couldn't remember eating much, and moved through each minute by rote.

How many times had I driven from Toronto to Lakefield?

I scrubbed my face, my short beard rasping under my palms. What did I have left to do?

Go through the house, pack it up, and donate what I could.

Cancel utilities.

Call a Realtor.

Sell the house.

I tallied the furniture in each room, considering how many boxes and bags and trips to Goodwill were in my future. The basement. I hadn't gone into the basement.

Another thought struck, and I craned my neck, peering at the covered hole in the ceiling leading into the attic. Growing up, I had always hated how it was in my bedroom. Its presence was creepy, especially to a highly imaginative young boy. The number of nightmares I'd had about monsters emerging from the hole was innumerable.

In retrospect, my fear was comical.

I never found out if my parents used the space. With my luck, it was full of junk I would need to dispose of.

My knees creaked as I got to my feet to inspect the opening. The panel pushed inward, and I had no clue if there was a built-in pull-down ladder or not. Using the wooden desk chair, I maneuvered the panel out of the way and was greeted with a shower of dust and a dark abyss. Feeling around and discovering there was no means of climbing up, I went in search of assistance in the form of a ladder and flashlight.

The garage caught me off guard. It was a horrifying mess. My father was a bigger pack rat than I realized, and I noted the umpteen boxes and shelves littered with junk. The task of cleaning out the house grew exponentially the more I looked around, and a headache bloomed to life behind my eyes.

"Great."

With an A-frame ladder and an electric camping lantern hooked over my arm, I returned to the second floor and my bedroom. The entrance to the attic was a narrow hole. It did not provide much in the way of wiggle room. I wasn't as bulky as in my hockey days, but I was not a small guy either. Middle age was taking its toll, but I hit the gym as often as possible.

Ascending, squeezing through the slight opening in the ceiling, I chanted a plea to the hoarder gods that the space above was empty. Propped on the edge of the hole, feet dangling into the room below, I maneuvered the lantern around the attic, unveiling a dusty, cob-web-littered loft. The slanting roofline perpetuated a crawling claus-trophobia. Relief washed over me when I sighted scant handful of boxes, some ancient Christmas decorations, and the GT Snow Racer I'd loved as a kid on the far side of the room.

Hunched, unable to stand fully erect, I cautiously crossed toward them, stepping on the long cross beams, unsure if the spaces between were able to hold my weight. The last thing I needed was to crash through the ceiling and break a leg.

Dust tickled my nose, and the scent of mildew made me wonder if anything in those boxes would be salvageable. I didn't remember the house having a leaking roof, but to be fair, those grown-up concerns had not registered when I'd lived at home.

I inspected the items but didn't see any water damage. The boxes looked intact—if not brittle and crumbling—taped and labeled with their contents. Most of them seemed to contain Christmas decorations. A few had my name in bold print across the side. *Jersey's Stuff*, they said in my mom's distinguishable handwriting. Those interested me.

I found a place to plant my ass on the dirty floor and dragged one closer, picking at the fragments of remaining packing tape. It had long ago lost its stickiness and came apart under the assault.

The first box contained school mementos. Notebooks with doodles. Assignments with grades worthy of getting pinned on the fridge. Art projects I couldn't remember making. Old board games, a baseball mitt, VHS tapes—I paused and smiled, reminiscing over the dated titles. My first cassette Walkman, a vibrant yellow, lay at the bottom, a well-played Mr. Big tape still inside.

"Oh god." I chuckled, pushing the box aside and grabbing another.

The second one was full of outdated clothes and hockey gear. I had no idea why my mother had felt the need to keep them. They were so worn I could hardly see the point in donating them. Maybe the skates. Poverty was rampant, and hockey was expensive.

The final box was mostly empty. It contained novels. Dozens of *Hardy Boys*, a collection of *Goosebumps*, and a few thrillers by Christopher Pike. I couldn't remember having indulged in any of those stories. Academics came second to hockey. If I wasn't on the homemade rink my dad made in the winter, I was tearing up the road, playing street hockey in the summer.

I hated reading.

I set the books aside in a pile but paused when I encountered a roughed-up copy of *The Adventures of Tom Sawyer*. A wave of un-expected memories pummeled me, and I froze. The years peeled away, and I was flung back in time.

I flipped through the yellowed pages as the face of a forgotten boy, someone who had unbalanced my life when I was fourteen years old, took form inside my mind.

"Shit."

Three times. Not two.

Three times, my life had been permanently altered.

My parents' sudden death.

The career-ending injury I'd sustained on the ice.

And meeting Koa Burgard at summer camp.

2

Jersey

CAMP KAWARTHA 1989

"Dad, go. I'm fine."

My skin buzzed, both warmed by the noonday sun and blistering with excitement. Before long, its pasty winter pigment would grow bronze with the mark of summer.

One month of freedom. One whole month. No parents to nag about chores or bedtime. No teachers breathing down my neck. No homework. Camp Kawartha was the best part of every year—after hockey. The second school let out at the end of June the countdown was on.

We'd arrived twenty minutes ago, and I couldn't get rid of Dad fast enough. He liked to linger, ensuring I had my sleeping bag arranged on the right bunk, checking with the counselors to confirm my emergency contacts were up to date, and Mom had logged my recent immunization records. It was so annoying. When he joined a group of parents and started with the embarrassing camp jokes he'd invented on our drive, I wanted to die.

"Just leave!" I shoved him toward the car and endured another minute of lectures, reminding me to "behave, don't start any fights, and use your manners."

"I never fight. Go."

The kid whose tooth I'd knocked out on the ice this past winter didn't count. Fighting was par for the course on the rink, even if Coach Stevens disagreed. How else were we supposed to get ready for pro?

"Watch your mouth, too, or your mother will have your head. None of that colorful shit you use on the ice."

"Shit is a bad word too, you know."

Dad glared and raised a finger in warning.

"I won't. Gooooo. Please."

When Dad finally drove off, I waved, bouncing on my feet, eager to race away and see who had come this year. I'd seen Peter and Daniel, but I wasn't sure if Bruce and Justin had arrived yet. Those four guys were my clan. We'd been attending Camp Kawartha since we were six years old and were glued at the hip every summer.

The minute Dad's station wagon vanished in a cloud of dust around a bend in the dirt road, I was off like a shot, howling my excitement to the woodlands, my voice echoing across the field.

Since it was registration day, there were no organized activities. Counselors roamed, ensuring everyone knew where to be. Kids would be dropped off periodically throughout the day, and much of the fuss was dedicated to cabin assignments, tours for the new campers, and saying goodbye to clingy parents. By evening, we would sit around a massive bonfire, and the counselors would put on a welcome skit. We would stay up late, stuff our faces with roasted marshmallows, play games, and get to know one another.

At age ten, I was becoming one of the top dogs. By age fourteen, the cut-off age for Camp Kawartha, the counselors let us run part of the program and help with the younger kids. I had a few years to go, but since I was an old pro, it wasn't unusual to be assigned important jobs.

Peter and Daniel were with their parents, so I wandered about, noting who had returned and who was missing. It was early in the day, so things were quiet. Eager to reacquaint myself with my old stomping grounds, I took a beaten path through a forest of spruce and white pine. I weaved among birch trees with their white paper bark and skirted around ancient maples as I picked my way toward the lake. Fern and ivy snuck across the path in places, snagging my ankles. I kicked pinecones aside and collected half-eaten acorns, launching them at tree trunks.

I knew the area like the back of my hand but returning after a long winter always brought feelings of rejuvenated interest. I had to be sure our favorite climbing tree, a crooked and twisted elm with low and accessible branches, hadn't fallen during a random winter storm. I had to check on the secret cave, sheltered by a deadfall in the heart of a clump of cedars, to be sure it was still there. We used it for club meetings during our free time. The boulder at the lake's edge, marking the best fishing spot, was important too, and even though it was enormous, I had to be sure no one had rolled it away. Was the dock still standing? Had the canoes been brought out of storage? Were there fish in the reedy part of the pond?

Partway along the trail, a scuttling noise under the dense trees stopped me in my tracks. The sun slanted through the leafy canopy overhead, dappling the ground in prisms of light but providing decent shade from the scorching heat of the day. Was someone there?

I crouched low in the brush and cocked an ear. The noise continued. It was too big to be an animal unless I'd encountered a deer, but the chances were slim. Deer were nervous creatures and rarely ventured near camp. Too many rambunctious boys to contend with, my mother would say. The low murmur of a voice caught on a gentle breeze and wove between the trees until it tickled my ears.

"The treasure's not under this tree either, Huck. Any luck over there?"

I waited for an answer, but none came—none I could hear—but the boy with the light and airy voice responded as though a companion had replied.

"Darn it. How deep did you dig? Are you sure?"

No audible response. Perhaps his friend was farther away.

"That's pretty deep. I guess we should move on. We'll find it. Chin up, Huck. Let's not give up yet. We're on their trail. I know it."

The crunch of branches and dried leaves retreated deeper into the woods, but I was invested, curious, and eager for adventure.

I followed the noisy explorer as he trudged away like a two-ton elephant through the brush, branches snapping under his shoes. I kept hidden and maneuvered on silent feet, my skills unmatched. Spying was the name of the game, and I was the master. At a vague clearing, I caught my first sight of the boy.

He and I appeared to be the same age. The boy was lankier. Bony arms and knobby knees stuck out of tan-colored shorts and a red T-shirt. Messy, sandy-brown hair fell into his eyes, touching the bridge of a pointy nose, currently aimed at the ground. A delicate mouth with parted lips sat below it. His forehead was crunched like he was deep in thought. His cheeks were dotted with freckles and sported round pink smears. I looked like that when I got off the ice, and Mom always said it was because I played hard.

This boy must have been playing hard too. Unless it was a sunburn already, but the rest of his face was white.

He searched the ground for something, one fist clasped around an imaginary tool. A shovel, I thought, considering the conversation I'd overheard.

But where was the other boy?

Frowning and narrowing my eyes, I picked apart the clearing and scanned the tree line, seeking his companion.

Then the boy spoke. "Over here, Huck. This spot looks suspicious. See how the dirt's loose? I bet they buried it here. I told you. We're on the right path."

Dropping to his knees, he pretended to dig in the earth with his imaginary shovel. No one joined him, but he kept right on talking as though someone had.

"No. You dig on that side. We can go faster that way. It's called teamwork." He giggled. "You're a goof, Huck."

The boy abandoned his invisible shovel and used his hands, shoving dirt, dried leaves, and debris aside, raking his nails in the dirt to make the hole deeper. After a time, he sat back on his heels and pushed a sweaty mop of hair off his forehead, leaving a smear of dirt behind.

"It's no use. What should we do? It must be here somewhere. The clues aren't wrong."

A pause, and the boy let out a long, drawn-out sigh. "You're right. We'll go tonight. I'll sneak out when Aunt Polly goes to bed, but we have to be careful."

Who was he talking to?

Curiosity piqued, I emerged from my hiding spot, startling the boy to his feet. Wide, frightened eyes the color of golden honey watched my approach. His knees were scuffed and grimy with dirt. His nails and fingers were black from digging.

"Hi. Who're you talking to?" I glanced among the trees but knew there was no one around.

The boy didn't answer and retreated another step as if preparing to run off.

"Who's Huck?" I asked, examining the shallow hole he'd made under a tree.

"My friend. He's... invisible."

I snorted. "You have an imaginary friend? How old are you?"

"I turned ten two weeks ago."

"Me too." A lie. My birthday wasn't until August, but Camp Kawartha considered me ten and put me in the ten-year-old cabin. "Aren't you kinda old for baby games?"

The boy shrugged and glanced at the spot where he'd been digging. "We were looking for the pirate's treasure. They were here not long ago. We've been tracking them. Huck thinks they might have hidden it in a haunted house on the other side of the forest. We're going tonight after dark, and if we find it, we'll be rich."

The kid was weird. "There are no haunted houses around here. I would know. I've been coming to this camp since I was six. I've explored everything. I'm Jersey. Jersey Reid. What's your name?"

"Tom Sawyer."

Something felt off about his answer, but I couldn't figure out what. I narrowed my eyes. "Is that your real name? Sounds like a fake."

"I'm pretending. Tom Sawyer's from a book my grandfather made me read. Tom's best friend is Huck Finn. My real name is Koa. Koa Burgard. Do you wanna play with us?"

I chuffed. "No. I don't play baby games. Wanna hunt for frogs at the pond? Last year, I found a fat one and put it in Garrett's sleeping bag. Garrett was my cabin leader. I don't know if he's here this year, but we can pull a good prank on someone else. It was so funny. Bruce almost peed himself laughing when Garrett screamed."

"The pond?"

"Yeah. It's over there. Not too far." I pointed.

"Okay. We can do that." Koa glanced at the ground where he'd been digging, then at the empty space beside him, mumbling, "I'll meet you tonight, Huck. I gotta go hunt for frogs now."

I tried not to snort, but one snuck out. Wait until I told the guys about this.

The new boy followed me through the dense foliage toward the pond. He slapped at a few mosquitoes feasting on his arms as I shooed the swarming gnats from my face. Cicadas buzzed in the trees overhead, and a few twittering birds sang. Their songs echoed through the canopy of green fluttering leaves.

"Is this your first year?" I asked as Koa scratched at a lump on his elbow.

"Yes. My doctor told Grandfather it would be good for me, and I was ready."

"Ready for what?"

"To... be with other kids my own age. It was time. I'm better now."

"What was wrong with you?"

Koa didn't answer right away. He chewed his lip with a funny-looking scowl on his face. When he glanced up, he shrugged. "Head stuff. No big deal."

"Wanna race?"

"Okay."

I ran, bouncing over fallen branches and avoiding tangles of bramble. Agility was my forte, and I crossed the forest floor effortlessly. Koa struggled to keep up until he was red-faced and sweating.

When I got too far ahead, I stopped and waited for him to catch up. Once we were trudging along side by side again, I asked, "What about your mom and dad?"

"What?"

"You said your doctor told your grandfather you should go to camp. Why not your mom or dad?"

"Oh. I live with my grandfather now."

"How come?"

Koa remained silent, thin lips pursed. As we walked, he picked a leaf from a low bush, twisting it around his finger. A distant look hung in his eyes. His pace slowed.

"Hey," I smacked his shoulder. "Did you hear me?"

Koa flinched and stopped walking. He shifted his weight, absently rubbing the spot where I'd whacked him.

"Please don't hit me," he mumbled.

"You didn't answer my question."

"I'm not allowed to talk about it."

I stared at the strange boy as he studied the ground. Something about his answer didn't sit right. "I'm sorry I asked."

"It's okay." Peering ahead, a glazed expression in his golden honey eyes, Koa said, "I wonder if there's piranha in the pond."

I frowned, intrigued but confused. "What's piranha?"

"Fish with teeth. They'll eat you if you're not careful."

I snorted. "There's no such thing."

"Yes, there are. I saw them on a nature show. I don't like them."

"Well, there's none in the pond. I've been in it before, and the only thing that bit me was a minnow, and they don't hurt."

"You sure?"

"I promise."

"Okay."

We continued walking and arrived a short time later. The sun gleamed off the water's murky surface. Swarms of bugs hovered in the air, zipping along the low grass and landing on lily pads. We removed our shoes and socks, wading into the grimy water to midcalf. The slimy muck on the pond bed oozed between my toes, cool, slick, and inviting. I loved how gross it felt.

Koa laughed and made a face. "It's disgusting."

"It's awesome."

Koa and I searched the thick reeds and algae-covered rocks for frogs. Koa spotted two dragonflies doing the nasty, and we laughed and tried to interrupt their fun time by splashing them with water. A school of minnows tickled our calves. We tried and failed to catch them in our palms. Our frog hunt, however, was successful. Koa caught the first and carefully put it into his pocket. When he chased and caught a second, he let me have it.

"Look!" Koa shouted, pointing across to the other embankment. "A turtle. Two of them."

"Where?" I stilled and followed his finger. Sure enough, two baby turtles sunned themselves on a branch where it protruded from the water.

"Think we can catch them?" I asked. "That would be way cooler than frogs."

"We'll need a plan."

"I'm listening."

But before we could discuss a strategy, a storm of running feet and shouts rumbled from a path in the woods. It grew closer and louder, and our turtle friends dove back into the pond. Peter, Daniel, Bruce, and Justin appeared, laughing and shoving each other, tripping over rotting logs and bumping into trees as they advanced.

"Jersey!" Daniel howled at the top of his voice. "What are you doing?"

"Catching frogs." I pulled the one Koa had caught for me from my pocket and displayed it. "Thought we'd play a prank on one of the counselors. Wanna help?"

"Forget it. Grady said if we get some people together, he'll organize touch football in the field."

I was torn. I loved touch football at camp, and Grady was one of the coolest counselors. Glancing at Koa, I registered sadness swelling in his eyes. "Wanna come play with us?"

He shook his head and backed up a step, but he must have stumbled over something under the water and went down on his ass in the pond.

The other boys howled. "Smooooooth," Justin yelled. "You're gonna smell like pond all day now."

More laughter.

I helped Koa back to his feet, but by then, my buddies were shouting for me to hurry up. I asked, once again, for Koa to join us, but he was adamant about staying behind.

I gave him my frog, and he cradled it in his hands. "Save him for me. I'll see you later, Tom Sawyer."

He grinned, wide and toothy, and I smiled back.

I shoved through the calf-deep water as I made my way to shore.

"Hurry up. Last one there has to share a bunk with fee-fi-fo-fum. Remember the kid who sucks his thumb?" Daniel demonstrated, goo-goo gaw-gawing like a baby.

Bruce, Peter, and Justin broke into peals of laughter, while I scrambled to find my shoes and socks. "Oh man. He's back?" I asked. "Tell me he's not in our cabin."

"Yep," Daniel said. "We got a few newbies. Hurry up. We need to make sure we're on the same team, and Grady's not gonna wait for us."

I didn't take time to dry off or put my socks back on, but I did wave goodbye to the new kid I'd found in the woods. Then I ran with my old friends, crashing through bushes and dodging the backward swing of more than a few tree branches, eager to start my summer off on the right foot.

We shouted and howled and beat our chests like the crazed boys we were.

Little did I know at the time, Koa was one of the new kids in our cabin, and he'd claimed the bunk beneath me.

3

Jersey

PRESENT DAY

I couldn't let go of the book. *The Adventures of Tom Sawyer* continued to profoundly affect me after my first year at camp with Koa. His piracy days with imaginary Huck had continued, and I spent a long time watching him play. He'd been oblivious to the teasing remarks from the other boys his age.

Koa, as Tom, had hunted for treasure, explored the haunted woods, and used a piece of driftwood as a boat to cast off to places unknown with a friend only he could see.

Something about Koa had drawn me in. He was mysterious and shy.

My insides jittered with old nerves, and I set the book carefully on my lap as I removed the last item from the cardboard box—a dull and battered cookie tin, warped from the passing years. I remembered how the butter cookies inside melted in my mouth. An annual Christmas treat gifted by my grandparents.

The lid stuck, and I had to wiggle it free. When it popped off with a squeaky protest and clattered to the floor, I puzzled at the contents. The cookies were long gone. Dozens of tightly folded papers filled the inside. I plucked one from the top and unfolded it, skimming the childlike writing inside until it dawned on me what I held.

"No." My breath caught. "She didn't."

I removed another, unfolded it to check its contents, then a third, and a fourth. My hands shook progressively worse as each discovery confirmed my suspicion.

She had.

My mother kept every single letter of correspondence I'd exchanged with Koa over the five years of our friendship.

Every. Single. One.

Koa, the strange boy I'd encountered in the woods as he'd sought buried treasure, had returned to Camp Kawartha every year until we aged out at fourteen. Our friendship had been complicated by many variables. Primarily, our vastly different social circles. As a preteen, popularity was the be-all and end-all of life. Koa and his uninhibited ways were peculiar, and he hadn't fit in. His character quirks had mounted to such a degree most kids wouldn't talk to him. On the other hand, I hung out with the cool kids who went out of their way to knock Koa down.

But somehow, among the teasing and bullying, I'd been drawn to the odd boy I'd met in the woods, and we'd spent time together in secret when the other boys were occupied. Our friendship had grown to unfathomable levels until it had been incinerated in an instant.

I thumbed one of the brittle pieces of lined paper containing Koa's juvenile handwriting. It had been his idea to become pen pals.

For four winters, we had exchanged letters, and for five summers, we had secretly bonded under the watchful eyes of the forest animals.

Five summers.

My cruelty had driven us apart during our last year at camp. Had I known then what I knew now, it might never have happened.

I hadn't expected to ever see the letters again, but my mother, in the nostalgic way she had, kept them all.

For twenty minutes, I remained in the attic, too stunned to move, too tight in the chest to take in more than shallow breaths.

When was the last time I'd thought about Koa?

It had been decades. I'd ejected him from my mind for self-preservation. What an idiot I'd been.

I returned the lid to the container and took it and the classic story of Tom Sawyer back down the ladder. In the kitchen, I poured another two fingers of whisky and sat at the table, thumbing through the yellowed pages of the book and stealing sideways glances at the cookie tin.

Its discovery disrupted my plan. Gone was the notion of tidying my parents' house. Gone were my plans of packing boxes and shipping them off to Goodwill. Koa and his letters, like he'd done from the day I'd met him, derailed my life.

Decades had passed, yet the return of those long-forgotten memories birthed an urgency I never expected. I owed him an apology. If he only knew...

Finishing the drink, I set the empty glass aside and headed out to the Gladiator to retrieve my overnight bag and laptop. At the table once more, I opened a search engine and typed Koa's name into the bar.

In seconds, a mature version of the boy I'd once known filled the screen, and I couldn't move. Numb, ripe with a sadness I couldn't contain, burning with old guilt, I stared at the face of a man I'd hurt long ago. He was all grown up and more handsome than ever, and my heart pulled to him like it had decades ago.

Returning to my parents' house had been painful, but discovering the letters was like taking a slash to the knee once more. It leveled me in a way my parents' death hadn't.

Koa, my sweet, troubled Koa. What has your life been like?

Clicking the link attached to the image took me to a website for an elite boarding school for gifted children. Dr. Koa Burgard, teacher of classic literature and philosophy.

I smiled to myself. "Fitting. You always wanted to be a teacher."

I stared at the man's face for a long time, seeking the boy I'd once known. His honey-colored eyes had hardened to amber. The faint lines beside his mouth and along his forehead showed his forty-four years the same way mine did. His slender nose and brush of freckles were the same. His fine lips were less curious and sterner than I remembered. But the chin dimple remained.

Koa had taught me more about myself at fourteen than I'd learned in all the years that had gone before or since.

Regret tightened my chest. We had been children. Blaming myself was hardly fair, but I did. I always would. If he only knew why I'd done it.

Without a second thought, I dug through the kitchen drawers until I found a notebook with enough blank pages to spare and a pen.

Maybe it was stupid. Maybe it would amount to nothing, but for old time's sake, and because it was my fault we'd stopped communicating all those years ago, I wrote Koa a letter.

4

Koa

"All right, settle down. We still have ten minutes before the bell, and if you don't listen, you'll miss your weekend assignment."

Groans rippled through the classroom. Even the most brilliant students turned to mindless sloths on a Friday afternoon, hanging off their desks, bodies melting slowly toward the floor with lethargy.

"Next week, we will start a new unit and explore the wonders of existentialism. We will touch on the relationship between nature and god, transcendentals, causality, substance, the soul, freedom, morality, etcetera, etcetera. I could go on and on, but you aren't listening and have already checked out for the weekend."

A few giggles rippled through the room.

"As always, we will couple this unit of study with some classic literature. We will explore the works of Nietzsche, Dostoevsky, Sartre, Kierkegaard, and Kaufmann, among others. We will—"

"What about Camus?" Katie Woolsey asked from the front row. A bright spark in a dreary Friday afternoon. She was one of my top students, always ready to engage in debate and never afraid to express her opinions.

Grinning at her eagerness, I nodded. "Yes, we should definitely add Camus to our list. Who can tell me what Camus is known for? Not you, Miss Woolsey," I said when her hand darted into the air. "You've likely read all his work."

"Not *The Fall*, but it's on my list. My favorite was *The Plague*. Riveting, especially since we just lived through a pandemic. Most people like *The Stranger*, but I found it boring."

I dramatically clutched my chest and gasped. "Boring? Boring? You wound me. We'll have to thoroughly discuss your reasoning at a later date. I'm officially adding it to the curriculum." I addressed the class. "Anyone? What is Camus known for?"

Blank-eyed faces stared back. A few students ducked their chins to avoid being called on. In the back row, Nathaniel Frost shouted, "Didn't he coin the absurdist philosophy?"

"Yes. Thank you, Mr. Frost. Please raise your hand next time. Not all has been lost. There is hope for the minds of our youth. Camus did coin the absurdist philosophy. And what can you tell me about absurdism?"

Nathaniel gawped like a fish and darted a panicked look at his neighboring classmates who were not coming to his aid.

The bell rang, effectively halting the conversation, and the relief on Nathaniel's face was striking.

"Give me your answer Monday, Mr. Frost."

The room burst into a flurry of activity as eighteen students scrambled to pack their bags and vanish before I could assign them homework on a Friday.

I shouted over the commotion. "Take a look at pages two-seventeen to two-thirty-one in your textbooks. There will be a pop quiz on

Monday morning to commence our new unit of study. No one should be surprised."

Students filed out of the room, pushing and shoving, disappearing into a blur of navy and white uniforms. I wasn't sure anyone heard, but it didn't matter. A scheduled email would go out later that day, clarifying the assignment so no one showed up unprepared.

Miley Prism, a quiet girl who always sat three rows back, waited until the stampede calmed as she adjusted her knee socks and retied a shoe. On her way out, she shyly smiled and ducked her head, muttering, "See you next week, Dr. Burgard."

"Goodbye, Miss Prism. Don't forget about your overdue report. Your extension cutoff is Wednesday."

"I won't."

Timber Creek Academy was in an isolated wood near Chemong Lake, a short drive southwest of Lakefield and a stone's throw from Peterborough. The private boarding school housed some of the most brilliant, youthful minds across the province, and I'd been lucky enough to secure a position on their staff twelve years ago.

The transition from high school remedial English to literary classics and philosophy was a dream come true. I taught what I loved most to students who appreciated and absorbed the true essence of my passion. It didn't hurt that their parents paid astronomical fees to send their teenagers to our academy. Our standards were high, and the dean didn't flinch at dismissing troublemakers from our form. So, for the most part, we housed a decent bunch of kids and had few issues.

Although the academy stayed current with society's technological advances, we were housed in a century-old brick building in dire need of upgrades. The high ceilings and intricately sculpted woodwork gave it class but also made it echoey and hard to heat. The double-pane windows rattled, and drafts poured into the room when the wind blew.

My classroom was north-facing, so I often donned a knitted cardigan over my standard tweed vest, shirt, and tie. Today was no exception. The dated building also meant each classroom was fitted with a chalkboard, and although some teachers had long ago retired the antiquated equipment for projectors and PowerPoints, I used mine frequently. I believed that when students copied notes longhand, they retained more information.

I erased the day's lesson, brushing chalk dust from my hands when I finished, then tidied my desk. Numerous books littered its surface, examples I often used during lessons. My classroom contained a wall-length bookshelf filled with an innumerable number of classics. I'd bought most at thrift stores over the years, but some had been gifted by eager parents. My personal collection lived at home. The odd copy traveled with me in my briefcase. My books were heavily annotated and tabbed so I could find what I needed in a pinch. The students always got a kick out of the fact that I wrote in my books. The horror.

I tucked my reading glasses away in their case and organized what I needed to bring home for the weekend before heading out.

A handful of teachers at Timber Creek lived in private cottages on the perimeter of school property. The structures were quaint, if not small. I'd chosen to keep my accommodations private and had recently bought a house in nearby Peterborough. It suited my more introverted personality, plus having students show up at my doorsteps at all hours looking for help with their homework grew thin after a few years.

Two dormitories housed the one hundred and twelve students enrolled at Timber Creek. One for boys. One for girls. A common building sat between the two, separate from the main schoolhouse. It offered a minor library, a vast lounge, and a dining hall.

I made my way down the fast-emptying corridor to the staffroom on the second floor. Several students called out greetings or wished me a good weekend. I smiled and continued, not inviting conversation. Outside the classroom, I kept to myself, rarely engaging with others. In my mind's eye, I was already home, feeding Rask his dinner and collapsing with a drink and a book in the cushy chair I kept by the fireplace.

Every teacher had a cubby slot for mail, and I usually collected mine once a day. Typically, the contents were the same. Notices about staff meetings. Pamphlets advertising professional development in the area. The odd request from fellow teachers, seeking second opinions on lectures or magazine articles.

That day was no different, but as I tugged the handful of papers from the tight slot I'd been assigned, an envelope fell. It landed face down on the tiled floor. I squatted to pick it up, turning it over and finding my name and the school's address scrawled across the front in an unfamiliar hand. The postmark in the corner told me it had arrived by mail, which struck me as odd. No return address.

I stuffed the rest of the junk mail under my arm and wedged a finger under the envelope's seal, curious what this was about. Inside, I discovered a single slip of lined paper and a handwritten note—bizarre in the age of emails and text messages. When was the last time I'd received a handwritten letter in the mail? I couldn't honestly remember.

I started at the top, but the simple greeting sent a jolt through my system. Icy fingers tickled up my spine, and I froze.

To my dearest friend, Tom Sawyer (aka Koa),

Confused, certain I was misunderstanding, I skipped the body of the letter and read who it was from.

Yours truly, Huck Finn (aka Jersey).

"No," I whispered on an exhale. "This has to be a mistake."

The ground beneath me shifted, and I stumbled backward and sat on the edge of the staffroom table before my legs gave out. Jersey? How was it possible? I hadn't heard from him in... "over thirty years," I mumbled under my breath.

Was it a mistake? But his name was beside the monicker I'd used with him hundreds of times as children. No one else knew I'd called him that.

The single sheet of lined paper trembled in my hand. Before embarking on the rest of the message, I glanced around to be sure I was alone. Dr. Colbert and Dr. Madison, the art and history teachers respectively, were conversing near the coffee station, but they were thoroughly engaged, and my presence went unnoticed.

Short of breath, heart racing, I refocused on the letter and read.

Surprise! Hi, Koa. I'm unsure how to start this letter, but I figured a nostalgic greeting might get your attention. You were always my Tom Sawyer, and I was always your Huck Finn. It's been so long, maybe you've forgotten all about me. I hope not. I certainly remember you.

Circumstances, which I won't get into, brought me home after several years of being away. While going through some old boxes I found in storage, I came across your old letters from when we were pen pals. Turns out, my mother kept each one. Reading them again after all this time brought back so many memories... both good and bad. We didn't part on good terms, and I regret that to this day. I have so many things I want to say, but a letter isn't the place to do it.

I looked you up (I hope that's not creepy) and discovered you're teaching at a school not far away. An elite boarding school! Wow. Good for you. It didn't shock me to hear you'd become a teacher of literary classics. Fitting.

I know this is a wild, far-fetched idea, but I was wondering if you'd like to meet for coffee or something. I'd happily come your way. We could

take a walk down memory lane. I'll understand if you don't want to.
Time has likely erased me from your mind, or maybe you'd rather not
revisit the past. Anyhow, if coffee (or a beer) sounds like something you'd
like, drop me a line. I'd love to see you again.

Jersey had written his phone number and address on the bottom
before closing the letter with the signature *Huck Finn* like he used to
when we were kids.

I read the letter again, and a third time, before stuffing it back into
the envelope and stacking it with the rest of my mail. Numb from
top to toe, I couldn't make my feet work. The letter had disrupted my
Friday momentum. My goal of heading home and nesting in a chair
by the fire with some proper literature, a drink, and Rask had been
disturbed. I trembled inside as a swarm of long-suppressed memories
pummeled me, not solely regarding Jersey, camp, and the mischievous
games of Huck and Tom, but the nightmare that had brought me to
Grandfather and Camp Kawartha to begin with.

I closed my eyes and refused to open the door. I wouldn't go there.
Couldn't.

He doesn't matter, I said to myself. *None of it matters. It's history*
and has no influence on today or tomorrow. Let it go.

But the sermon was no use. My complex and ever-changing
philosophies held no water if the dam broke. I wouldn't allow that
to happen. Damn Jersey for muddying my day. I was finally living a
somewhat stable existence. I didn't need this or him.

Jersey's letter unearthed far more than a fanciful trip down memory
lane. It grated rusty nails over my skin. It bubbled poison in my gut. It
threaded inky toxins through my veins. His letter picked the scab on a
wound that decades of therapy had barely managed to heal.

Burying the past had been essential.

Off-balance, I got to my feet. Instead of aiming for the staff parking lot and my car, I mindlessly wandered the halls of Timber Creek Academy, futilely seeking stability, waging war with the maelstrom wreaking havoc on my brain.

I didn't have to respond to the letter. I could shred the words and Jersey's attempt to reconnect and never think about it again. Inviting old hurts back into my life was not healthy. After thirty-six years of hell, the ground beneath my feet was solid. Why introduce new fissures?

But the boy I'd known years ago was not easily forgotten. Jersey had been my savior once—until he tore the rug from under my feet and left me alone once again to face a world that hated me.

For reasons I couldn't explain, I found myself outside the music room on the first floor. The music department was secreted away in a far corner of the academy where its constant clamor wouldn't disturb other classes. It shared a wing with the physical education department and gymnasium. Niles Edwidge, Timber Creek's music teacher, interminably moaned about his irritant neighbor.

The cacophony of instruments, all practicing on their own, bled through the poorly insulated double doors. After-school rehearsal was in session. Horns resonated with held notes as flutes and clarinets tiptoed daintily over their staccato refrains. The slide of a trombone was followed by the bleating of a tuba. But it was seventeen-year-old Damian Werner, beating on the drums and crashing the cymbals, who outshone them all—I didn't have to see him to know his style.

Damian was one of Niles's protégées and loved to show off. He could play drums, timpani, French horn, saxophone, or oboe with equal skill. He wrote his own music and had formed a punk band, earning gigs at school dances and special events. If he played his cards right, Damian could go far.

Entering the music room, I witnessed the discordance firsthand, cringing at the chaos and wondering, not for the first time, how Niles put up with the noise. The students were practicing individually, warming up, I assumed, since after-school rehearsal would have only recently begun.

The man himself was conversing with a doe-eyed piccolo player, clapping a rhythm she tried desperately to emulate on her instrument. The time signature was challenging—seven eight—and she stumbled more than once, unable to find the beat.

"You'll get it. Stacey, come and give Nora a hand," Niles said, calling over a flutist when he caught me standing at the door. "Clap it out while she plays. Emphasize the fourth and seventh beat. Like this." He demonstrated before leaving them on their own.

Niles strolled toward me with a cocksure grin and swagger common to artsy folk. Those qualities had once lured me in, but the relationship hadn't lasted more than a year. My cynical view on life, indifferent attitude, and frosty demeanor weren't for everyone, but we'd remained close friends, and Niles was the one person who knew me best. Although he didn't know all of me, which was another problem. Secrets of the magnitude I held didn't bode well for forming bonds, and Niles had claimed numerous times I was too distant and closed off.

"Dr. Burgard." Niles used a syrupy tone as he sidled up beside me.

"Master Edwidge." Niles hated that he'd never acquired a Ph.D, but unlike the other staff members who insisted on using the title *mister*, I gave Niles the more standup designation of *master* since he'd gone so far in school as to acquire his master's degree. He appreciated it, and it had been a long-standing joke between us.

The appellation made Niles's sunny smile appear as he leaned against the wall beside me, lowering his voice so it was barely audible over the ruckus of his afterschool practice session. "To what do I owe the pleasure of your company on a Friday afternoon at"—Niles checked his nonexistent watch and gasped—"almost three thirty? Don't you have a cat to pet, a drink to pour, and a book to read?"

"Am I that predictable?"

"Sweetheart, it's half the reason we broke up."

"We broke up, and I quote, because"—I adopted Niles's haughty tone—"'Your indifferent attitude is exhausting. How can you be so wearisome and formulaic all the time? Doesn't it get tedious?'"

"Did I use those words?"

"You did. I distinctly remember commending you on the creativity."

"That's because you didn't think my vocabulary extended beyond two syllables. I should be insulted. Wearisome," he said thoughtfully. "Yes, I can see how that might have come across as shocking."

"I think it was the word formulaic that surprised me."

"I'm a music teacher, for god's sake. Give me some credit. Math and formulas are all part of the musical equation. Ha! See what I did there?"

"Clever."

"Are we going to banter, or are you going to tell me why you're here?"

I didn't know why I was there. Niles knew nothing of Jersey or my childhood. In retrospect, my unconscious detour was senseless. An act meant solely as a distraction. Avoidance, perhaps. My brain did the strangest things sometimes. Niles wouldn't have answers, even if I were inclined to share my woes. Whatever forces had driven me to visit were unknown. Diversion? Distraction? None of it mattered. The problem remained, and Niles couldn't fix it.

Jersey had reached out after thirty years, and I had to decide what I was going to do about it.

"Koa?"

"Mm?"

"You're doing that thing where you have conversations inside your head I'm not privy to. I've told you before how unhelpful it is. What's on your mind?"

I scanned the classroom, listening to various sections of disconnected music, trying and failing to interpret it. "What's on the agenda for the spring concert?"

Niles huffed. "Vivaldi, of course."

"How utterly predictable."

"Have you been practicing?"

"On occasion. I don't enjoy it." In truth, I had a love-hate relationship with playing the piano.

Niles huffed again. "You're better than all these kids combined. I wish they had half your skill."

"You're too kind."

"You're too modest."

My grandfather had insisted on giving me piano and violin lessons growing up, but after several years of struggle, a tutor, aggravated beyond measure, had thrown her hands up and announced I would never be a musician. *"He's tone deaf,"* she'd said. Grandfather had fired her and found someone else to torture me. It was the same nonsense, year after year.

I'd put up with it, but I'd never wanted to play.

"You like playing, Koa."

"I'm tone deaf, and unless my grandfather is smacking my hands with a ruler every time I make a mistake, I don't hear it. It's embarrassing."

"Excuses. Beethoven was all deaf. Didn't stop him. He wrote his most famous symphony after losing his hearing completely."

"Why do you bother me with this?"

"Because you love music, and deep down, you enjoy playing. I've seen your face when you sit at the piano. Why you're so damn stubborn, I'll never know. Don't discredit what gives you joy. That's all I'm saying. You're always welcome to join us. Not one of these kids will be offended if you make a mistake. Good lord, are you listening to this screeching?"

I was, but a stone had landed in the pit of my stomach, and its ripples radiated dissonance to every extremity. "Music doesn't bring me joy. Stop pushing me. Happiness is an illusion, and you know it."

"Ah, there's the attitude I hate. You're far too old to be this emo."

"You sound like you're sixteen."

"Keep it up, and you'll be alone forever."

"Maybe I'm happier alone."

"But happiness is an illusion, sweetheart, remember?"

"You drive me crazy."

Niles rolled his shoulder on the wall, bringing himself closer. He snagged the knot of my tie and gave it a gentle shake. "You drive *me* crazy."

Our proximity was intimate, and the curious attention of a few teenagers drifted in our direction.

"We have an audience," I warned.

"So? We battled the rumors before. We can battle them again. Listen to me. I'm going to use big words so that literary brain of yours takes me seriously. I'm starting to think the small ones don't compute."

I smirked. I couldn't help it. "Don't hurt yourself."

"Your fatalistic attitude toward life is exasperating. Everything doesn't have to be tragic to have merit. Joy exists if you let it."

"Your understanding of fatalism is concerning. I beg you to sit in on a few of my classes. Fatalism is about inevitability. Believing and accepting life is a series of predetermined events we cannot control. Besides, I'm not a fatalist."

Niles chuckled. "Whatever you want to call yourself, your complete indifference to life makes you unapproachable and miserable. What do you have against happiness?"

"Nothing."

"Don't you want companionship and love?"

"To what end? What difference does it make?"

"My god, Koa."

"There is no god."

Niles playfully yanked my tie. "You're infuriating. What I'm saying is it's okay to be joyful on occasion. You're allowed to feel pleasure." Again, he lowered his voice. "And not just in the bedroom. Not everything in life is pointless or meaningless. Sometimes, you have to create meaning. Find things that make you feel alive. Take control of your happiness. Why are you smirking?"

"Because I can't believe you read it. You said you wouldn't, and you did."

Niles let go of my tie and repositioned himself so his back was against the wall again, arms crossed as he surveyed his students. "Of course I read it. I would read anything you wrote. I told you that. I want to understand you better, Koa."

"Was it terrible?"

"No, but your convoluted philosophy leaves much to be desired. If you would believe in something, anything, maybe you would be less... less..."

"I believe the words you're looking for are wearisome and formulaic, and since we've gone full circle, I should go. I have a cat to feed, a drink to pour, and a book to read."

"You haven't told me why you came."

And I still didn't know.

"I was looking for something."

"Did you find it?"

"I don't know. I'll let you get back to your rehearsal."

I left, the weight of Niles's concern pressing in on me.

The drive home was quiet, but my thoughts were loud. Every attempt to dismiss Jersey's letter from my mind didn't work. Its presence in the car upset my equilibrium. In the self-torturous way I had, I almost dropped in on my grandfather at the nursing home but thought better of it. My past was a deep well of pain. The bottom was the worst, the stuff I tried hard to forget. On top of it was my grandfather and growing up in his house. Then Jersey. He too lived in the well of pain but near the top, within reach. Could I save him from the well? Did I want to? I'd convinced myself for decades that anything that fell into the darkness never came out again.

For my peace of mind.

Rask greeted me at the door. I bent to pet him as he weaved between my legs, purring. Rask was a ten-year-old Persian, smoky gray with a cloud-white belly. I'd gotten him as a kitten on the advice of my therapist. Brilliant Dr. Kent thought to pull the wool over my eyes as she tested a theory, but I'd seen through the ruse, and she had succeeded in her quest to discover if I was capable of emotionally connecting with anyone or anything.

I loved my cat. Rask played an important role in my life—in my healing.

"It's Friday," I told my furry friend. "You know what that means. Shall we? I'm thinking of ordering out tonight." Rask meowed. "Yes, I know. I never order out, but I need it. What about Italian? Thoughts?"

Rask arched into my touch but offered no opinion.

My house was a refined century home of the same era as the academy. The previous owners had done a lot of work on the inside, reinsulating the walls and refurbishing all the woodwork. The leaded windowpanes had all been replaced, and the roof sported new shingles. The two-story monstrosity was more than a single man needed, but I'd fallen in love with it, mostly because it was similar to many of the wealthy English dwellings I read about in books.

I'd chosen it specifically for its library. Built-in floor-to-ceiling shelves lined every wall. A rolling ladder provided access to the ones I couldn't reach. A fireplace offered the perfect reading nook on a chilly winter night, and I'd adorned it with plush chairs and warm rugs.

The staircase creaked, and it cost a fortune to heat, but I wouldn't have traded it for the world.

I ordered food and poured a glass of pinot noir before browsing my collection for a book. I was a mood reader with a constantly fluctuating mood, so I often read several books at once. The short table by my chair contained a new translation of *The Brothers Karamazov,* a battered and crumbling copy of Forester's *Maurice*—the same copy I had owned and loved since I was a teenager—and Sartre's *Existentialism is a Humanism.*

After the suggestion from Katie, I removed my heavily annotated copy of *The Stranger* from the shelf, determined to revisit the modern classic and work it into my upcoming curriculum.

Rask sat by my feet as I sipped wine and paged through forgotten notes, waiting for my dinner to arrive. Unsettled, my mind quickly drifted to Jersey's letter, and I found myself interminably distracted.

Frustrated, I set the book aside and faced the problem. Rask took my distraction as an invitation to hop onto my lap. Since Huck Finn—not Jersey but the imaginary friend I'd created as a child who had persisted into my late teenage years—was no longer in my life, I tended to voice my issues aloud to Rask instead. Commiserating with a cat was not the same, but conversing with imaginary friends at forty-four was grounds for a straitjacket. Rask's nonverbal opinions were always sound, if not wholly dictated by my unconscious will. I'd always imagined Huck having a mind of his own, and as a child, I took his advice to heart.

"Where will reconnecting with Jersey get me?" I mused aloud for Rask's sake. "Is there a point in rehashing the past? Meeting with him objectively changes nothing. I don't need apologies, and I'm sure that's what he's after. Besides, a rendezvous risks stirring more problems. I was a mess back then. Everyone knew it. Everyone saw it."

Rask purred and lifted his head so I would scratch under his chin.

"There is no reason to respond. Right?"

Closure was the word that flashed through my mind. It was a therapy word, and I did not appreciate its implication. Closure for what? I didn't need closure. What had happened between Jersey and me was a childhood misunderstanding. It had been thirty years. How pointless to rehash bygone hurts. A waste of time and energy.

But no matter how hard I tried to refocus my thoughts, adorn the attitude of indifference I'd written about in my convoluted philosophy—as Niles had so bluntly put it—I couldn't.

After dinner arrived, I ate and returned to my book, but the words blurred. Jersey had packed his bags and moved into my mind without invitation or notice. Worse, the unwanted guest didn't seem to plan on leaving until I took action.

Inevitably, at ten o'clock that evening, I landed at my desk, awash in a pool of amber light cast from a shaded lamp. Strewn with countless notebooks, journals, essays, and failed poetry, it took a moment to uncover a crisp notepad and pen.

An hour later, I sealed a handwritten response in an envelope and wrote Jersey's name and address across the front. On Monday, I would stop by the post office, buy a stamp, and mail it. If he expected a phone call or text response, he would be disappointed. I wasn't sure I was ready to reconnect so intimately. Correspondence through the written word provided a much-needed separation and offered time and space to decide how I wanted this connection to play out.

5

Jersey

Boxes littered the living room and kitchen floor, most packed to the gills and waiting to be taken to the donation bins. I'd kept precious few of my parents' belongings: a handful of framed photographs, the knitted afghan my long-dead grandmother had made, and a box of my dad's dated sports magazines.

He'd collected ones featuring his son at the peak of his career. I hadn't taken the time to read them when they were published. Mom had spent a great deal of my later teen years lecturing me about ego and vanity and not letting stardom go to my head, so I hadn't. Mostly. My sole focus had always been on the game. Besides, sitting for photoshoots and interviews was a rarity. I hadn't been the most sought-after player. History books would never mention my name. In my professional career, side by side with the best the world had to offer, I'd been mediocre at best.

No one had missed me when I'd been permanently taken out of the game. A brief headline one day, forgotten the next. Easily replaceable.

The late afternoon sun angled through the blinds, cutting bright lines across the kitchen table and floor, highlighting floating dust motes. I'd spent the past week traveling between Toronto and Lakefield, working reduced hours at the clinic so I could take care of my parents' affairs.

Grief lingered like an unpleasant bruise in an especially tender spot, and no matter how careful I was, I banged it often, lancing a new ache through my heart. Memories surfaced unexpectedly. Some were so profound they cut me off at the knees and left me grappling for a drink to soothe the pain.

If I wasn't wallowing in sadness and self-pity, I was bitterly angry for the years of stubbornness that had kept me away from my home and family. I'd gotten clean of oxy five years after the accident—around the same time I'd decided to return to school—but I'd refused to make amends with the people who'd tossed me out like last week's trash.

On a particularly rough evening a few days into my task and tipsy from too much drink, I'd called Christine, insisting she let me talk to my son. We'd argued, and Derby had refused to come to the phone. In his mind, he had no father. A court order had rescinded my rights years ago, and I'd never fought back when I'd managed to come off the drugs. The scant visits were dictated by my ex-wife and had dwindled in recent years. Derby had become a surly teenager with his own thoughts and opinions, and he opted to pretend I didn't exist.

The morning following the drunken phone call, my mountain of regrets grew.

I didn't call Christine again. She and Derby had attended the funeral, and what condolences she'd offered, what tenderness she'd displayed at my situation, had been put to rest. I was back to being the irresponsible one. The guy she'd grown to hate.

While wrapping my mother's fine china in newspaper, a tea set I subconsciously knew was a family heirloom, a noise outside broke my concentration—the familiar squeak and clattering of the metal mailbox lid lifting and falling shut.

I poked my head into the living room in time to see the postal carrier cross in front of the house, scurrying off to his next destination.

All week, I'd been making phone calls, informing people of my parents' death. All week, I'd been submersed in condolences I didn't feel I deserved.

More mail meant more phone calls.

Abandoning the china teacups, saucers, and newsprint, I aimed for the front door. It was a cool afternoon, chilly enough that my breath fogged the air. A dusting of snow had fallen overnight, and the fresh, glimmering remains coated the front lawn. Spears of grass poked through in places, but as I'd predicted, winter had returned, snuffing out the attempt of an early spring.

Inspecting the contents of the mailbox, I found a single envelope. It wasn't for my parents. It was addressed to Jersey Reid, and the calligraphic scrawl on the front could only have belonged to one person.

He'd responded. When I'd written to Koa, I'd half expected to never hear back, but I was wrong. Three decades of silence had officially been broken.

I returned to the kitchen and moved a partly full box off the chair to the floor so I could sit. The table was strewn with newsprint and other debris, so I shuffled the delicate dishes out of the way, giving myself ample space.

My fingers were blackened with ink, leaving imprints on the white envelope as I turned it over in my hands, too eager to bother washing.

Koa had responded. Not a text. Not an email or a phone call. He'd written back like old times. I'd given the address in Lakefield for nostalgic purposes, hoping he'd recognize it.

The return address in the corner belonged to the academy. Koa had gone out of his way to ensure I wouldn't learn where he lived. I didn't take the time to evaluate his decision for discretion. He'd written back, so it barely mattered, and my stomach fluttered unexpectedly with excitement. Three decades hadn't erased the way I'd once felt.

I tore into the envelope and unveiled a single sheet of lined notepaper. Tightly uniform cursive filled the page. Koa didn't use the same playful greeting. He stuck to formality. It stabbed, but I let it go. We were adults, not children. Tom and Huck were part of the past. As were old feelings. I needed to remember that.

Leaning back, I read.

Jersey,

I would appreciate it if you could forgive what I'm about to write in advance. I fear it may come across as rambling and disjointed, but I assure you, I've sat with it for many hours, compiling my thoughts as cohesively as possible in order to respond to your letter.

To say hearing from you was a shock is an understatement. I considered letting sleeping dogs lie (ugh, I'm resorting to ancient proverbs. How cliché. I would rip my students apart for such things), but like always, your presence in my mind is demanding and won't be ignored.

It's been a long time, Jersey. Three decades.

I'm forty-four, and ignoring your letter seemed entirely unfair and immature, so here we are. I wish I could say you've barely crossed my mind in three decades, but that would be a lie. Don't fear I lingered on your memory. I didn't do that either. I don't intend this to be a slight, but life goes on, and so did I. Childhood is nothing more than a passing phase, and we've moved beyond it.

You allude to old hurts and seem to feel it necessary to make amends. I assure you, time has erased any need for apologies. Not only are they unnecessary, but they would be meaningless in the grand scheme of things. What happened happened. If it's forgiveness you seek, consider it given.

I hope life has treated you well. Although the notion of reconnecting for nostalgic purposes might seem inviting or exciting to some people, I fear it could open old wounds (and before you selfishly think this has anything to do with you, it doesn't.)

If you feel compelled to continue corresponding, I would prefer we do it through letters, the formality suits me better, but as for coffee or beer, I must decline.

Koa

The paper fell from my hand onto the table. A numbness crept through my limbs as I absorbed Koa's words—biting, formal, and achingly distant.

What had I expected? Our parting had been brutal.

His response didn't quell my guilt and suffering. It amplified it. Brushing the past aside and facing forward might be easy in theory, but ever since I'd found our childhood correspondence in the attic, I'd been unable to get Koa off my mind. Every moment we'd spent together was etched into my memory until that last day when it had all fallen apart.

I opened a cold beer and paced the kitchen, considering my next step. Koa had insisted on keeping things formal and distant. Despite suggesting it, the notion of exchanging letters didn't sound like something he desired, but he'd drawn a hard line at meeting face-to-face.

That stung. What I wouldn't give to see him in the flesh.

I checked the time on my phone. It was after four on a Friday afternoon. Even if I decided to drive to Timber Creek Academy on the off chance of running into Koa on school premises, he would likely have left for the day.

Monday then.

How angry would he be?

An influx of new patients at the clinic meant I didn't get to seek out Koa until Wednesday afternoon. I was one of three physiotherapists at Olympus Medical Center, a facility specializing in sports medicine, so taking extended time off to deal with my parents' affairs wasn't feasible. When Chevy St. John, a longtime buddy and fellow coworker, had called Saturday morning to say they were swamped, I'd headed home for a couple of days of work and to reorganize a few appointments.

Timber Creek Academy was roughly the same distance from home as my parents' house. Once I hit Peterborough, I headed northwest instead of northeast for the remaining fifteen minutes of the drive.

A few minutes before three, unsure when classes got out, I pulled into the isolated property and parked in the lot beside a stately, late nineteenth or early twentieth-century four-story brick institute. After browsing the school's website, I learned the students and many staff lived on the premises in dormitories or cottages respectively. The handful of cars in the parking lot suggested several teachers commuted.

Not having a clue what category Koa claimed, I parked the Gladiator at the edge of the lot, aiming her nose in such a way that I had a decent view of what seemed to be a much-used courtyard, thick with an abundance of healthy cedars and wooden benches, and the back exit of the academy.

The teasing spring temperatures had returned, typical of our fluctuating weather. A pale sun shone through a thin veil of clouds. A breeze from the south brought balmy warmth. I powered the window down, inhaling the crisp cedar-scented air. The fragrances of a rejuvenating earth filled my nostrils, and I savored it. Nothing was so crisp and clean in the city.

The courtyard and surrounding fields were quiet. Not a single soul wandered. Birds chittered and bounced from perch to perch, and if I strained, the churning waters of Chemong Lake whispered on the wind.

At precisely three fifteen, an obnoxious bell sounded, invading the tranquility of the day and sending the wildlife to scatter. It was another seven minutes before the school hemorrhaged students like a fatal wound. Nothing would stop their escape. Once given freedom, they wouldn't offer it back.

I remembered those days, racing from class as though another minute of suffering would mean imminent death.

I scanned the student body, faces glowing with youth and excitement, eyes alight with evening plans. Their trill voices echoed and carried as they joined friends and scattered in several directions; some moved to the recreation hall I'd tagged when driving in, and others aimed for the football field. A few, slower in pace, headed to the dormitories, overfull backpacks giving them a sideways lean.

I had yet to spot an adult. Before leaving home that morning, I'd studied Koa's staff photo on the website. In my mind's eye, he was still a fourteen-year-old boy with freckles and secrets and a special smile he reserved for me alone.

Those days were gone.

The man on the registry was older. The sandy brown hair I remembered had darkened to a rich mahogany and was threaded with silver. Koa wore it longer now, or at least he had when the photograph was taken. It curled some with the new length, escaping any order. Youth might have packed her bags and gone, but the maturity that had replaced her suited him better. He was stunningly gorgeous, which didn't help my quest to forget old feelings.

The crystallized amber color of his eyes still held unimaginable secrets in their depths. As a stubborn child, those secrets had nagged me. I'd hated Koa's refusal to share, especially when I unburdened my heart almost daily.

Time, as it did to us all, had stolen Koa's radiant glow, and the man on the Timber Creek Academy website had developed a handsomeness unique to middle age instead.

And how would Koa react if he heard me think of him as handsome?

The outflux of exiting students calmed to a trickle. When the first adult appeared at the back door, I sat up straighter. Two female teachers chatted as they moved toward a different building across the parking lot. I hadn't determined its purpose, but the structure was more modern, possibly administrative in purpose.

A tall, slender man with a cell phone pressed to his ear headed to a nearby Coupe and got in, starting it up but sitting as he finished his conversation.

All was quiet after that, and a swell of disappointment pressed against my sternum. It made sense that teachers would linger after hours, but I had been riding an eager wave of adrenaline all afternoon, and it was slowly petering off.

At ten to four, two more men left through the parking lot exit, both similarly built and dressed semi-professionally. They paused a few steps from the door to converse. The man facing me wore his hair in a messy man bun, loose strands framing his face. He had his shirt sleeves pushed to his elbows and carried a leather satchel over one arm and a case for a moderate-sized musical instrument of some kind in the other. The devil-may-care glimmered in his eyes, and he wore a coy smile for his friend. A smile that spoke of familiarity.

The second man had his back to me. He wore dark jeans and a cable-knit beige cardigan wrapped protectively around his middle as though the balmy spring air was a brisk arctic wind. He too carried a satchel, fat with whatever it was teachers lugged around. The second man had the same color hair as Koa on the website—same length, controlled disarray, and soft curl—but I resisted getting my hopes up until he turned to face me.

I observed the conversation, and it went on for a long time. With the Gladiator's window down, I caught snippets, but not enough to piece together what was being said. They exchanged a handful of smiles and a few arm touches—initiated by the man carrying the instrument. The intimacy between the two was apparent, and for the first time since I'd discovered the tin of letters in the attic, I considered the fact that Koa might be married or in a relationship. All this time, my mind had considered him the awkward, outcast youth I'd left behind at Camp Kawartha.

A surprising knot of jealousy cinched tighter under my ribs, and I picked at a thumbnail, shunning the perplexing and unexpected emotion the idea had stirred.

I'd never consciously considered my purpose for contacting Koa, but a small part of me was undeniably and unfairly disappointed at the thought that he was, possibly—probably—involved with someone else. How stupid. I had childhood love on the brain and needed to get with the program.

Their conversation ended, and they continued their stroll through the parking lot, shoulder to shoulder, bumping on occasion. At a silver

Audi, they stopped. The man with the instrument pivoted to face his friend. He brushed a stray curl off the other man's forehead and cupped his cheek. Definitely familiar. His final words were unclear, but after a time, Instrument Man dropped his hand and backed away with a grin.

Then he was off. He aimed for the courtyard and took a path among the cedars. Before long, he was out of sight.

The second man, seemingly lost in thought, followed his friend's retreat as he remained beside the newer model Audi, keys in hand. Although he'd turned in my direction, he was oblivious to my presence.

But it was him.

It was Koa.

He was in front of me for the first time in thirty years.

And I couldn't bring myself to get out of the Gladiator and say hi.

Under the cardigan, he wore a tweed vest over a collared shirt and tie. The thick layers and his insistence on hugging the knitted sweater around his body gave the impression not of someone cold but of someone like the boy I'd known, who was perpetually trying to hold himself together and using the only thing he had on hand.

Koa's dazed expression persisted long after his friend vanished, and I was hurled back in time to an archery field where I'd first experienced a similar disconnect. How many times had I caught Koa locked in a trance, staring vacantly into thin air, trapped and unable to escape whatever he saw in his mind? How many times had the other boys teased him and called him retarded, as preteen boys are wont to do with someone who doesn't fit in or acts strange?

The blank fits—as I called them—would sometimes persist for several long minutes. At first, they had scared me, but I learned how to dispel them on my own with sharp kicks and vigorous shakes, screaming in his face like the unsympathetic boy I was.

Only then would the snare set him free. Koa would blink and return to the present—often confused and moody—wipe drool from his mouth, and abandon whatever he had been doing at the time. In the aftermath, he generally wanted to be alone. When asked what had happened, he would shake his head. If I persisted, he would get angry.

The only person he talked to during those times was Huck.

The blank fit accosting him that afternoon in the parking lot lasted less than a minute, and Koa seemed to shake free on his own without difficulty. He glanced around once before ducking his head and maneuvering the keys in his fingers. An audible click announced his doors were unlocked.

The moment for a reunion was fast slipping away, and I let it, jarred by the recollection of things I'd forgotten and unsure how to approach the man who was once a troubled boy who had put his full trust in me.

And I had failed him.

I put the Gladiator in gear as Koa pulled out of the lot. Following him was shameful, and I knew better, but I wanted to know where he lived, so when I was ready to face the past, I could do so in a more private location.

I'd thought today was the day, but I was wrong.

6

Jersey

CAMP KAWARTHA 1989

Lukas Innis, our cabin's leader, announced the after-breakfast plans as the twelve of us stuffed our faces with banana chocolate chip pancakes drenched in syrup and washed them down with tall glasses of milk. Each cabin had a separate schedule to prevent overlapping activities and congestion. The exceptions included afternoon swim time at the lake, meals, and the evening bonfire.

"We're starting with arts and crafts"—a ripple of groans leaked from behind overfull mouths—"at which time you can either do your own thing or help with set design for the end-of-season play. Next, we have archery"—whoops and cheers—"then free time in the woods. I was thinking we could arrange a game of capture the flag. In the afternoon..."

Lukas's voice vanished into the rise of boyish chatter as we made our capture the flag teams. Peter, Daniel, Bruce, Justin, and me. That was five. We needed a sixth since we were a group of twelve.

"What about Arty?" Bruce whispered with his mouthful, spraying bits of chewed pancake onto the table.

Justin was already shaking his head, wearing a thin line of milk residue on his upper lip. "No good. He won't want to be separated from Glen, and Glen will have Sam glued to his side, so that's three no-goes."

"Come on. We have to pick fast. Who?" Panic leaked into Daniel's voice as he darted his gaze between the others.

I stared at the boy at the end of the table. Koa rarely interacted with anyone. During free time, he wandered into the woods to play with his imaginary friend, Huck. All the boys knew, and he was the laughingstock of our cabin. Unlike the kids I'd seen teased at school, Koa seemed oblivious to the taunts and torments of others.

We'd barely spoken since the first day of camp, but I watched him often when he wasn't looking.

"Ollie." Peter shouted at a redheaded boy on the far side of the table. "Wanna be on our team for capture the flag?"

Hair flopping over his eyes, Ollie shook his head. "Too late. They already snagged me."

He'd joined ranks with Glen, Sam, and Arty. And before we could ask Robby or Kel, they had joined the opposition.

"Shit," grumbled Bruce under his breath so Lukas wouldn't hear. He smacked Peter's shoulder, who was sitting beside him, and pointed at Koa before twirling a finger around his ear.

Peter giggle-snorted. "We'll lose for sure now."

Justin and Daniel commiserated.

Koa stared into the middle distance, oblivious, drawing absent lines with a fork through the puddle of syrup on his plate as he talked under his breath to the empty place beside him. To Huck.

Why did he do that? Did he know how babyish and weird he was acting? If he stopped, maybe people wouldn't make fun of him.

As my friends continued lancing rude comments in Koa's direction and inventing as many insults as possible, I finished my pancakes. Only once did I burst out laughing. Insults toward Koa had turned to banter among my friends; a string of "Yo mama" jokes, and they got worse and worse as we tried to one-up each other.

Daniel had a way of miming the actions along with his jokes, and when he stood on the bench and performed a particularly auditory and vulgar rendition of someone having sex, our ten-year-old brains broke.

Lukas put an end to the fun, telling us to clean up and get outside.

Koa didn't once crack a smile.

During archery, I ended up in the lane beside Koa. A long line of straw-backed targets stood over twenty yards away, the papers so torn with holes they looked like Swiss cheese. It was our first-time having archery that season, but I'd been shooting a bow and arrow since my first year at camp when I was six. Like most sports, I caught on fast, and it went to my head.

Lukas gave a quick tutorial and explained the rules, then let us have fun as he supervised.

Eager to begin, I let fly my first arrow without remembering all the tricks I'd learned in the past, and it went wide of the target, landing somewhere in the long grass on the other side. Embarrassed, I glanced around quickly to see if anyone noticed, but my friends were too occupied with their own tasks.

My second arrow settled with a thunk on the edge of the straw barrier but outside the perimeter of the paper target. The next one pierced the third ring in. I was regaining the feel for the bow and its function, awakening muscle memory. My fourth arrow landed a few inches from the center, and I whooped and cheered, pumping a fist in the air.

"Nice one, Jersey," Lukas shouted. "Bullseye next time."

I aimed and fired, but my ego got in the way, and the arrow flew wide.

I glanced at my neighbor to see how Koa was doing. He struggled to nock his arrow. The few times he got it in place and lifted his gangly arms to aim, it fell.

Checking over my shoulder to be sure my friends were still busy, I moved in behind Koa to give him some pointers. God forbid I get caught talking to the weird kid, but I couldn't help feeling sympathy toward him.

Koa flashed an inquisitive, wary-eyed glance in my direction but returned to his task, likely thinking I was there to make fun of him.

He fumbled again, and the arrow fell to the grass. "Dammit."

I picked it up and handed it back. "Hook your finger loosely over the shaft when it's resting on the shelf. It will stay in place when you pull the bowstring."

Taking my advice, Koa managed to get the arrow nocked and retracted the string without losing it.

"See? It helps. Now hang on. Hold it like that for a second."

Koa's twig-thin arms trembled with the tension, but he waited, dashing a glance at me as I moved to his other side. Several beads of sweat ran from his temple to his cheek. His hair was damp with more. Standing as close as I was, I could smell the heat blistering his skin.

The hot July sun was unforgiving, even at ten in the morning. The archery field was in the wide open without the benefit of trees or shade. Our T-shirts clung to our bodies, and dirt and grass stuck to our knees. No one was immune.

Koa's running shoe was untied, the lace coiling like a snake in the grass, but I didn't tell him since it wouldn't affect his shooting. On a soccer field or baseball diamond, I might have had the forethought to warn him lest he trip and fall, but archery didn't involve running, so it slipped my mind to worry as I concentrated on the task at hand.

"Now, see this spot here?" I touched an area on his bow above the shelf where his arrow rested. "This is the spot you use to aim, but there's a trick, and I'll tell you in a minute. Try to hold the bow as steady as you can, and when you're ready to release the arrow, move your hooked finger down with the rest of your fingers so it's out of the way. If you don't, it will catch the fletching."

Koa did as I said, and his first arrow whizzed away at an angle, landing in the grass ten feet short of the target.

"You did it. See?"

Koa's shoulders slumped. "I did. Poorly. It's definitely harder than it looks."

"That wasn't bad for a first try. At least you didn't drop the arrow that time. Try another, and I'll tell you how to aim better."

Koa nocked another arrow, keeping his finger hooked on the shaft like I'd taught him. Before he retracted the string, I touched his arm. "Wait. Lemme explain how to hit your target first, so you don't get so tired holding it."

Koa relaxed and held the nocked bow aimed at the ground. I used mine to demonstrate and prepared an arrow. My strength was greater, so when I retracted the string and held it, my arms didn't shake the same.

"Archery isn't like shooting a gun." I said this like I had the knowledge required for the comparison when I didn't. "It's trickier because of gravity. A bullet flies fast outta the barrel and stays true to its target. So, with a gun, if you aim at someone's head, you'll probably hit someone's head. Boom, brains everywhere, and they're dead. With an arrow, you have to account for the curve, which changes depending on your target's distance. It arcs through the air. So, from here, I try to aim at the top of the straw. That way, when the arrow comes down, it's pretty close to where I want it to hit. Takes practice, but that's the trick."

My arrow flew, and it landed with a thunk on the third ring from the center. "For me, it helps if I pretend I'm killing the enemy. I want to aim for their guts since it's the biggest target and a solid spot for a kill."

I stole one of Koa's arrows, nocked it, and aimed. "Adios amigos." I let it fly. When it landed dead center, I pumped a fist and whooped. "Kill shot!"

Turning to Koa to share my glee, I found the odd boy staring catatonically across the field, his nocked bow still dangling in front of him, a glazed expression in his eyes.

My excitement simmered. "What's wrong?"

Koa didn't respond.

I waved a hand in front of his eyes, but he didn't blink or acknowledge the action.

Panicked, I glanced around, concerned Lukas would see and think I'd done something when I hadn't. Our cabin counselor was busy assisting Sam restring a bow. All my cabinmates were busy nocking and shooting over and over.

I turned back to Koa, who hadn't moved. His lips were parted, and a string of drool escaped the corner of his mouth, trickling toward his chin. Part of me wanted to race back to my lane and pretend I hadn't noticed, but a bigger part of me was scared he was having a seizure or something. A boy on my hockey team had seizures, and sometimes they made him stare into space and drool.

"Koa?" I shook his shoulder and called his name again and again.

No response.

I jostled him harder and told him to snap out of it. Panic turned to anger, and I knew, *I just knew* this boy was going to get me in trouble when I hadn't done anything wrong.

I tore his bow and arrow from his hand, and he didn't react. I shoved him. He compensated by stepping back so he wouldn't fall. Otherwise, I got no reaction. His face remained blank. The saliva ran down his chin. It took a solid kick to the shin before Koa blinked his eyes clear and met my gaze.

"What the hell is wrong with you? What happened?"

Koa, confusion and terror in his eyes, backed away. "I... I don't want to play this game anymore. Now I know why Huck said we shouldn't."

"Huck's not real, you idiot. What is wrong with you?"

Koa turned and ran across the field toward the outhouses. Halfway to his destination, he tripped over his laces and fell hard. Getting up, he brushed grit from his palms and examined his legs. He hobbled the rest of the way to the bathrooms and disappeared inside.

Later that night, I noticed Band-Aids on both his knees. Guilt swamped me, and I wanted to apologize. I hadn't meant to be mean like the rest of the boys, but he'd scared me.

Koa never played archery again.

That day was the first time I witnessed one of Koa's *blank fits*, but it wasn't the last. When they happened, if the counselors saw, they usually took Koa somewhere else until he was better. The adults seemed to share an understanding we campers didn't.

More often than not, the fits occurred randomly during free play, away from the safety of grown-ups. Shouting and shaking him usually set Koa free from the trance, but whatever caused them lingered behind Koa's eyes, dark, haunting, and secretive.

Koa never shared those miseries with anyone.

And it was just one more thing the other kids used as ammunition to tease him.

7

Koa

PRESENT DAY

I felt no sadness for the dying man in the hospital bed. No pity, no guilt, no remorse. Death was inevitable for all of us, and his was no more significant than the millions who had traveled the road first or those who would follow.

Our time on earth was short. We were born, we lived, we died. Humans served no great purpose to the universe. Our successes and failures meant nothing in the end. One man's life was no different than another. It was something I'd come to realize as an adult. A belief that infuriated Niles and had caused many arguments.

As I stood a silent sentinel in the doorway, the man in the bed had yet to ascertain he wasn't alone. Blind in both eyes, thanks to the cancer eating him alive, my grandfather peered blankly into a void, ear cocked as a radio announcer broadcasted the news. The ancient machine, with its dial knobs and clunky rolling-digit display, had come from the house—a house I had yet to deal with. A house where I refused to venture under any circumstances.

At eighty-nine, Grandfather's skin, a victim of time and gravity, pulled in an unsightly manner away from the once strong and prominent bone structure of his face, disfiguring him and weakening the threat that had once tormented my nights and days in equal measure.

He trembled, insubstantial earthquakes on the surface, but ones that stole his fine motor control, leaving him feeble and inept. He loathed the nursing home and all it represented. He despised the nurses who fed him pills and helped him dress, who stole his dignity when he couldn't toilet himself without help. He abhorred the cancer eating him alive yet had refused all treatment, telling the doctors he'd lived long enough and was ready to be with his god.

But the majority of the black, oily hatred that seeped out of his rotting soul was reserved for me. His grandson. The boy he'd willingly raised from the time he was eight years old to save him from a life in foster care.

I entered the room on soft feet, making enough noise to call his attention from the radio but not stepping loudly like the staff. A marked difference existed, and Grandfather picked it out.

I offered no greeting. It was unnecessary. His body may have given up, but Grandfather's mind was as sharp as ever.

The dying man's attention shifted. He blinked milk-hazy eyes in my direction. Lips like wrinkled worms parted, and wattles of skin undulated with the relentless tremors of old age and sickness.

"'Bout time you got here. It's gotta be going on five."

"It's five after four. If it were five, Darnel would be delivering your dinner. You know that."

Grandfather harrumphed. "Don't get smart with me. You're still late."

"There was traffic, and I had to stay after class to help a few students."

"Excuses. Turn that shit off." He waved a bony arm in the direction of the radio.

I obliged and rotated the knob until it clicked. A heavy silence settled into the austere room, with its dull white walls and the scent of oppression stinging my lungs.

We had a routine, and like the loyal grandson I was, I fulfilled my duty without complaint. Anticipating my grandfather's next command, I moved to the bedside table and retrieved what we literary fanatics had coined "the quintessential long book" from the drawer.

I fully respected Tolstoy and thoroughly enjoyed *The Death of Ivan Ilyich* and *Anna Karenina*. *War and Peace* was, indisputably, a masterpiece on every level, but any book force-fed to a person repeatedly grew wearisome. The tome had long ago lost its spark.

Books had saved my life growing up, but they'd also been a curse and punishment. I had therefore learned to use words as weapons. A wonderful thing for an English teacher. I'd taught my students year after year how any battle fought with words and intellect was a battle worth fighting. Once they learned to wield knowledge as a weapon, they would have no need for violence.

Every Tuesday and Thursday afternoon, through an inexplicable sense of obligation, I visited my grandfather in the nursing home and read to him as he'd done for me in my youth.

Giving credit where it was due, my grandfather and his love for literature had set me on the path to my career. The endless hours I had spent absorbed in books as a child helped dim the pain and black out the horrors of my past. My knowledge was frequently tested, as was my grandfather's way, and if I didn't fully grasp a concept or accurately relate a theory when asked, I earned a smack and was told to read it again.

My grandfather was a fan of corporal punishment. It was how he was raised, and if it was good enough for him, it was good enough for me too. How different life might have been had my grandmother been alive when I'd been sent to his house.

Reading glasses on, I read *War and Peace* like I always did, careful not to stumble on the Russian names or mess up the flow of the prose. I paused to allow for proper rumination and participated in thought-provoking conversation when Grandfather insisted. Upsetting the dying man beside me would earn a demeaning reprimand, mirroring those I'd heard as a child, and at forty-four, I knew better how to avoid them. Arguing was pointless.

Maybe he couldn't hit me any longer, but words cut like a knife, and I was not immune to pain.

Our visit was perfunctory, neither pleasant nor unpleasant.

At five, Darnel arrived with dinner, marking the end of my visit. I replaced the thick novel in the drawer and waited until the evening nurse had departed before sitting again in the chair beside the hospital bed.

Grandfather held out his bony hand, and I took it. He ducked his chin, closed his blind eyes, and prayed to his god. I watched his wormy lips move over empty words, wondering, not for the first time, what it felt like to have faith. I'd stopped believing in god when I was eight years old, and no matter how many times Grandfather had yelled and screamed and beat me with the Bible, no matter how many times he had dragged me to church and forced me to pray, he couldn't rekindle a fire that had gone out.

As an adult, I humored him, like I did with my visits. It was cold and superficial, but I had nothing else to give.

The man in the bed was no different than a stranger on the street. I had no love for him.

One day, Grandfather would die, my routine would change, and life would go on.

⚜

Back home, I fed Rask, telling him about my visit with Grandfather, and filled a glass with pinot noir before retreating into the library to mark papers and organize the following day's lecture.

Before settling, I shuffled through a music app on my phone and selected the playlist Niles had recently shared. *"For your moodier days,"* he'd said. A joke since every day was a moody day, according to him. I'd said as much, and he'd laughed. *"Precisely."*

Soft classical bled through hidden speakers on the bookshelves, filling the air with relatable, melancholic compositions that touched my heart and soul and called to my creative, introspective side.

I found reading glasses in my briefcase and fit them on. Settled at the desk, I found the moleskin journal I'd been using recently and opened it to a clean page, smoothing a hand down the crease so it sat flat.

Closing my eyes, I let the music flow through me as I found the words I wanted to write. Sometimes, I wrote lyrical poetry. Other times, I let the hidden wound bleed and wrote about the encapsulating darkness that never let me go. Most times, I journaled. On a few rare occasions, the words that found their way onto the page turned into novellas or essays, too personal to share with the world.

Apart from Rask, who acted as my unpaid second therapist, Niles was the only person who had been privy enough to see my thoughts on paper, and even with him, I was selective. The piece I'd recently shared dealt with an exploration of my underdeveloped philosophy. Niles and I had spent endless hours discussing our theories so he would understand its disjointedness and be able to navigate the muddle of mixed messages I couldn't quite express clearly or concisely enough to have it make sense.

Every day before embarking on schoolwork, I allowed myself thirty minutes of free writing.

Music helped purge my soul. Sipping wine, petting Rask, who had deposited himself on my lap, I let my mind inosculate with the melody.

Words came.

I put pen to paper, and the doorbell rang.

Wrenched from the moment, I startled. Rask verbally protested the interruption to his nap and scattered. Launched so abruptly back into reality, my softly flowing thoughts also fled. Getting them back would be an impossibility. Sighing, I abandoned wine and serenity both and headed to the front door.

As an introvert, I'd socially distanced myself from neighbors and coworkers. Apart from Niles, I had no friends, so I couldn't guess who it might be.

Standing on the threshold was a gentleman near my age wearing an expensive bomber jacket and trendy blue jeans. Although the quality of his outfit claimed one thing, his rugged features said another. The man's broad shoulders and stance reminded me of the sports-addicted fathers who came to watch their teenage sons play rugby or football at the academy. Old high school athletes who lived vicariously through their children and thought they knew more than the coach or referees. The man at the door had a similar presence.

Dark brown hair, windblown and laced with the odd strand of silver, shone in the late afternoon sunlight. He wore a trimmed beard flecked with more gray. It surrounded a generous mouth and chapped lips. Sorrowful eyes, the color of faded denim, locked onto me, staring with an intensity that made me shift my weight.

"Can I help you?"

The man hadn't spoken, but his demeanor suggested familiarity, putting me at a disadvantage.

"Hey, Koa. It's been a long time."

All the pieces clicked, and I froze.

The threads of remaining winter that had spent all week teasing the spring air and threatening to return found their way into my bones, eviscerating what warmth I'd gathered by the fireplace, and I shivered, wishing I hadn't shed my cardigan.

I should have known or guessed this might happen. How naive to think the problem might blow away as easily as it had blown in.

The man was no longer a stranger, and his greeting effectively transformed his mature features into those I remembered from boyhood. I should have recognized his faded denim eyes and the freckle standing guard high on his left cheekbone. Had I been looking for it, I'd have known right away that Jersey Reid, the first boy I'd ever loved and trusted and the first boy who'd ever broken my heart, was standing on the doorstep.

So this was how my day was going to go. So much for writing and grading work. So much for a peaceful glass of wine and a bit of reading. I closed my eyes as whisps of words flowed through my head.

The road of life is ever-weaving, ever-winding.

Cast all faith aside and ride.

Go blindly into a future of unknown paradoxes, where pleasantries and banalities await.

For on this road, the only certainty is death.

I needed to write that down.

Instead, I opened my eyes and faced the newest obstacle in my path.

"Jersey."

He smiled, and I was a child again, yearning for the attention of a boy who couldn't give me what I needed.

"You recognize me."

Over the man's shoulder, parked on the side of the road, was a hydro-blue Jeep Gladiator with black rims and tinted windows. It was a beast of a vehicle, overstated and showy, and one that stood out in a crowd of the mundane. It had been at the school the previous Wednesday. I'd seen it parked in the lot when Niles and I had strolled outside after class.

I'd paid it little mind, assuming it belonged to a visiting parent, but I had been wrong, and the dots connected, telling me the truth of the matter.

"You found me at school on Wednesday and followed me home." I met his gaze, daring him to deny the truth.

Instead of shame, Jersey smirked. "Guilty. I thought about getting out of the truck then and there and saying hi, but this felt like a reunion that required more privacy. I didn't want you stuck having to explain anything to coworkers, so... here I am. Surprise."

I crossed my arms, partly to fend off the chills wracking my system but also from irritation. "Help me sort this out. You got my response to your letter?"

"Yes." He pulled it from an inside pocket of his jacket, displaying it with pride.

"And you read the letter?"

He frowned. "Of course."

"Hmm." I didn't mean to treat him like one of my students, but his complete ignorance of where I was going with this line of questioning baffled me. "Were my instructions unclear?"

"Oh." He chuckled, tucking the letter away. "No, I just thought—"

"You thought you would do what suited you best and disregard my request?"

Any humor he carried fell away. Sobering, recognizing I wasn't as pleased with the situation as he'd likely hoped, he tried again. "I wanted to see you. There's too much to say. I can't write it all down. It's been thirty years, Koa. A lifetime. I... Okay, I see this wasn't the right decision. Forgive me for assuming, but... I would really love to take you out for coffee or a beer. Catch up, you know?"

"This isn't a good time."

"Tomorrow? Next week?"

It would all be the same. I pinched the bridge of my nose. The timing didn't matter. Jersey would say what he needed to say, and I would listen. He would go his own way, and I'd go mine. Years down the road, the conversation Jersey was so desperate to have would change nothing. Such was life.

So whether I agreed to a reunion today, tomorrow, next week, or next year, it didn't matter.

"Why is this important to you?" I asked.

Jersey tucked his hands into his coat pockets, his bravado gone. "You were a special person in my life all those years ago, and I would love to know what happened to that man. I would love to hear how his life is going and, with his permission, discover who he's become." Jersey shifted his weight and added, "I'd also like to apologize for how we parted."

"I've already addressed that in my letter."

"I know. But a proper apology would make me feel better."

"So it's for selfish reasons?"

Jersey sighed. "You say you forgive me, but it's clear you're still hurt, so no, it's not selfish. It's authentic. Saying sorry in a letter isn't the same thing."

I couldn't look at him and stared at his ostentatious truck, wondering at the life Jersey had lived. For self-preservation, I'd never kept track of him in the intervening years. His story was a mystery. His life undefined.

I wanted to be alone with my thoughts. I wanted him to vanish like he had when we were fourteen. I wanted to climb inside a book, pet my cat, drink wine, and forget the past. All of it. But it was a blister on my brain, and time and therapy had taught me that deep wounds rarely fully healed.

"Fine. Not today. Be here Saturday morning at six. You get one hour. I'll make coffee. You can say what you need to say. From there, we part ways."

"Saturday?"

"Take it or leave it."

"I'll take it."

"I have to go. I'm busy."

"Koa—"

"Six a.m. Don't be late."

I closed the door, but I did not return to my desk. I couldn't. My mind spun between the past and the present. Memories assaulted me out of nowhere. How could I focus on anything now? Jersey's presence took over like it had always done, throwing me off-balance, and messing with my head.

An ornate wooden container no bigger than a jewelry box occupied an inconspicuous spot on the bookshelf. It was a wartime piece I'd found at the junk store, made of burnished wood and creaky hinges.

I took it to my reading chair and sat with it on my lap for a long time. It was a box of insignificant physical weight, but its conceptual weight was cumbersome. Unlatching the hook, I opened the chest, unveiling a treasure trove of items that would be meaningless to most people. Tom and Huck had discovered these valuables on their quest to hunt for pirate treasure at Camp Kawartha. The Huck who had helped me plunder the shores of Clear Lake was not the one from my imagination but his stand-in, Jersey.

Dented bottle caps; pop tabs by the dozens; three plastic butterfly charms; a dozen pieces of sand glass; fossils; dingy pennies, nickels, and dimes; colorful beads we'd stolen from the craft supplies, pirate jewels all of them; a baby turtle shell—we'd found it empty by the pond—an animal skull of unknown origin; three robin eggs; and an arrowhead we were convinced was used by natives on a bison hunting expedition long ago.

Near the bottom of the box was a hand-drawn treasure map, Jersey's artwork, marked with all our favorite hunting spots. He'd made it during craft time and presented it to me in secret so his friends wouldn't know what we'd been up to.

I removed the last item from the box. The most prized possession of my camp days. A soft velvet bag with purple ties. Inside, a treasure more important than all the pirate riches combined. I held the pouch in my palm, feeling the lumpy form between my fingers, unsure why I'd kept it, why I'd kept any of it after all these years.

Carefully undoing the ties, I upended the bag, dumping a colorful knotted bracelet into my hand. Time and wear had faded its vibrance, but nothing could dim its significance.

Echoes of the past surrounded me; two young boys making promises they could never keep.

8

Koa

CAMP KAWARTHA 1989

Free time was my favorite time at camp. Huck and I could get lost in the woods and continue our adventures. After having a few daytime nightmares where my brain took over and made me see things I didn't want to see and think things I didn't want to think, the lead counselor had called my grandfather. I didn't know what was shared, but everyone treated me differently after. If I wanted to be alone, they let me wander off. If I didn't want to participate in cooperative games, I didn't have to, but I wasn't stupid. Someone was always keeping an eye on me.

When the lead counselor asked if I wanted to go home, I told him no. Camp was better than Grandfather's house. Besides, I was getting better and didn't have to see the doctor as much anymore, and since I didn't get to go to school, camp was the best fun I'd had in a long time. Huck and I were free to explore a real forest with a real lake and have real adventures. At home, I had to read and practice music. I had to be quiet and not run around. If Grandfather heard me talking to Huck, he yelled.

Camp was better, even if the daytime nightmares had followed me.

Alone in the woods, with a chorus of birds singing overhead and fresh cedar in my nose, I wandered, kicking the scrub and pine needles out of the way so I could search underneath. Dried leaves and brittle twigs crunched under my running shoes. Fungus hung like roof shingles on rotten logs, some of it colorful like a turkey tail. Lukas said that was what it was called, and it was a fitting name.

Huck walked ahead of me, scanning for clues, peeking around trees, and waving a stick around like a sword. He knew I hated swords, but he insisted it was necessary to keep me safe, so I let it go. The pirates had come through the area during the night, and we'd discovered signs of their invasion, so Huck wasn't taking chances. During the daytime, we thought the pirates took their boat onto the lake and hid on an out-of-sight island. It was the only explanation of why we couldn't find them.

Huck and I had plans to build a raft and explore, but driftwood along the beach was scarce, so collecting enough was a daunting task. Plus, the other boys kept stealing the best pieces when I wasn't guarding them.

Near the base of a mossy tree, a few empty snail shells caught my eye. "Huck! Huck, get over here. I found a clue."

Huck raced back, sheathing his sword, dropping to his knees, where I examined my findings. "Pirates eat snails. I think they stopped here for a snack."

Huck agreed, and we collected them in our pockets.

An explosion of running feet nearby drew me up short, and I pressed a finger to my lips, urging Huck to be quiet. "I think it's them."

Huck shook his head. He knew better.

Ducking behind a tree, we peered into the forest where a shirt-less, sweaty Jersey appeared, rosy-cheeked from exertion. He slowed, glancing over his shoulder as he wedged himself under a picked-over raspberry bush, making himself as small as possible. His legs stuck out, so it wasn't a great hiding place. Lying on his stomach, his back rose and fell with his labored breathing.

Scratches, likely from stray tree branches and foliage, marked his calves. Raised welts from mosquitoes speckled his back and arms, and his skin was bronze from too much sun. His dark hair was sweaty and matted, sticking to his forehead. Of all the boys, Jersey was the only one who showed an ounce of kindness. He wasn't always nice, but he wasn't outwardly cruel either. He laughed at the mean jokes and went along with the teasing, but he never added his voice to the crowd who bullied me.

Once or twice, he even seemed ashamed.

The boys from my cabin had been using their free time for a game of hide-and-seek. I had not been invited to join, not that I wanted to play. I didn't. Huck and I had things to do. But Jersey's legs sticking out from under the raspberry bush bothered me. He sure didn't know how to hide. At this rate, he'd be captured for sure.

"*Psst.* Over here." My hissing caught Jersey's attention.

He whipped his head around, a branch catching in his hair, a star-tled look in his eyes. He didn't see me at first. The oblivious boy had had no clue I was right behind him, huddled next to a nearby tree. Amateur.

I revealed myself and waved him over, pressing a finger to my lips like I'd done with Huck.

Jersey frowned, rescanned the area beyond the raspberry bush, then seemed to consider. For a moment, I thought he might ignore me, but he wiggled his way out from under the bush and approached in a waddled crouch, staying low to the ground.

"What are you doing out here?" he whispered.

"Playing. Your hiding place sucks. Your legs were sticking out. They would have found you for sure. Follow me." I turned to Huck. "You stay here and keep your eyes peeled for pirates. I'll be back."

Jersey gave me a weird look, but he followed as I moved into the forest. A short distance away, I showed him the rotted hollow log I'd discovered earlier in the day. A prolific red oak had been uprooted, possibly during a storm. The interior was big enough to fit an average grown-up, so Jersey would fit inside with no problem. With the tangle of roots and vegetation on the outside, he would be more or less hidden, but I could help make it even better.

"Get in, and I'll put some branches in front, so they don't see you."

I earned another confused glance, but Jersey followed my instructions, worming his way inside the hole backward so his head was at the opening. I searched the area for a few broken branches and piled them around the log so he was covered.

No sooner had I finished then a stampede of feet closed in on us. Bruce appeared, followed by Justin. They shoved their way through the brush and jumped over fallen tree branches.

Both boys paused when they saw me. "Hey, loser," Bruce shouted. "Have you seen anyone?"

"No."

"He's lying. I know Jersey came this way. I saw him." Justin crossed his gangly arms over his bare chest.

"What are you doing?" Bruce asked.

"Looking for pirate treasure."

"You're so gay."

Justin snorted, agreeing, calling me a homo under his breath.

I didn't know what those terms meant at ten, and since I'd spent two years being homeschooled by my Grandfather, I had only recently learned they were a common insult tossed around among boys my age.

I didn't care if they liked me, but I wanted to get rid of Bruce, so I told a fib, despite knowing how much Grandfather hated fibs and would smack my mouth for saying them. "I saw Jersey running toward the lake. He's probably hiding under the dock or inside one of the canoes. He told me not to tell he was here."

Bruce smacked Justin's shoulder. "Let's go." And they took off, shouting more insults, not once thanking me for my help, even though it was a diversion and no real help at all.

When they were gone, Jersey fumbled the branches out of the way and grinned from within the log with a wide, toothy smile. Dirt smeared his cheeks, and pieces of the rotting trunk dusted his hair. His skin glowed in the low light. "Thanks, Koa. That was awesome."

I shrugged. "I have to go find Huck. He's probably wondering where I am."

Jersey's smile fell. He looked like he was about to say more, but a war cry coming from the direction of the beach cut it off. It sounded like Bruce and Justin had found several more of their friends, and they were racing down the beach path in our direction.

"Quick. Get in." Jersey waved frantically. "They'll hound you again if they find you. They'll know you lied."

Without thinking, I scrambled inside the log next to Jersey, and together, we worked to cover the opening. It was a tight fit. Two child-sized bodies side by side were wider than a single, average grown-up. Wedged against one another, the scent of moldering wood surrounding us, we stayed quiet and listened as a thunderous herd of boys clomped through the woods.

Jersey's sweaty scent filled my nose. He smelled like sunshine and hot summer days, like the lake and the trees. I liked it.

When the boys got close, Jersey wrapped a bare arm around me and forced my head down. Nose to nose, he hissed, "Don't move."

I didn't. In the shadowy space of the hollow log, I stared at the excitement in Jersey's eyes.

At one point, two of the boys jumped over the log, oblivious to us hiding inside. They howled and yelled, calling Jersey's name so loud it echoed in the tree branches overhead. In no time, they were gone, off to another area of the forest in search of their clever comrade who had thus far eluded them.

As the thunderous commotion quieted with distance, Justin's faint voice announced, "Forget Jersey. Let's get a field hockey game going. He'll give up eventually and come back on his own."

Then they were gone.

The forest reawakened. Birds, cicadas, and the occasional chittering of squirrels filled the air.

"Screw that. I'm not going back yet," Jersey announced. "It's a trick."

His breath ghosted my lips, his peeling, sunburned nose brushed mine, and something funny tickled inside my belly. The shadowy inside of the log gave the atmosphere an otherworldly tranquility and seclusion. We were far, far away. Alone. We were hermits on the mire, hiding from hideous giants. We were elves in the forest, aliens exploring another planet, or prehistoric men living inside a cave.

We were not two boys at summer camp who barely knew each other and talked to each other less, lying nose to nose inside a hollow log.

"I have an idea," Jersey whispered, wiggling, and moving a few inches away.

I listened.

"You don't need Huck anymore. I'll help you find your lost pirate treasure."

"But..." A queasy sensation stirred my guts. "Huck is Tom's best friend, and I'm Tom. I can't abandon him."

"He's not real. Don't you get it? That's why those guys think you're weird. Only babies have imaginary friends."

"Huck isn't imaginary. He's part of the story. Don't you know it?"

"No."

"*The Adventures of Tom Sawyer*. It's a book. My grandfather made me read it when I went to live with him. In the book, Tom and Huck go hunting for pirate's treasure."

Jersey sighed. "Okay. But books aren't real."

"They are inside my head."

"How about this? You be Tom, and I'll be Huck. That way, you don't need to make him up and look stupid."

"I'm not stupid. My grandfather says I'm intelligent. And you don't know the story. How can you be Huck when you've never read it."

"Do you want to find that treasure or not?"

I did, desperately, but what about the other Huck?

"Okay. You can be Huck for now, but if you're Huck, you have to be my friend. That means no making fun of me."

"Deal."

"Do you swear?"

Jersey held out his baby finger between us. There wasn't much room. "Pinky swear. The girls at school say it's the strongest promise you can make."

I hooked my little finger with Jersey's, and we shook them twice up and down. "Promises are for forever, so you can't take it back now."

"I won't."

"And now I have to lend you my book so you can read the story."

Jersey groaned. "I hate reading."

"But how can you be Huck without knowing the story?"

"Fine. But I don't read fast."

"That's okay. Give it back when you're done."

Jersey didn't seem pleased about the book part, but he didn't argue.

"So we're friends now?" I asked. It seemed too easy.

"We're friends."

He must have seen the mistrust in my eyes.

"Hang on." Jersey wormed and wiggled, doing all he could to maneuver in the tight space as he dug something from the pocket of his shorts. It was a colorful, knotted bracelet.

"Give me your arm."

I did, staring from the clumsily made band to Jersey. His tongue poked out the side of his mouth as he tied it around my wrist. He used his teeth to tighten the knot, leaving a wet impression on my skin.

"There. I made it during craft time. Lukas got mad because Bruce and I were horsing around too much, so he made us sit down and taught us how to knot them with this cool design. It's a friendship bracelet. So, if I give it to you, it means I promise to be your friend for life. But you can't take it off, or it breaks the bond."

"What bond?"

"The friendship bond. You have to wear it forever."

"Even in the shower?"

"In the shower, the lake, and even when you leave camp and go back to school."

"I don't go to school."

Jersey flinched, looking gobsmacked. "You don't go to school?"

"No. My grandfather teaches me at home."

"Why? And how come you live with him?"

I shrugged and examined the bracelet.

"Okaaay," Jersey said, drawing out the word. "You're so weird. Should we go treasure hunting, *Tom*?"

He said it mockingly, but I grinned, staring from the knotted bracelet to Jersey. "Sure thing, *Huck*. Let's do it."

We wiggled our way free of the log and set off on an adventure.

9

Jersey

PRESENT DAY

The streets were bare in the predawn hours of Saturday morning. The sun remained hidden below the horizon as the moon hovered on the opposite side of the sky, preparing for slumber. Darkness retreated on one side as faint vestiges of the coming day lightened the other from black to an inky bruise.

In another hour, the world would wake up.

I parked on the road outside Koa's house at quarter to six, adamant I was on time for our coffee date. The early hour didn't faze me. Waking to the alarm in the dark of night had reminded me of all the years I'd laced my skates for practice while Dad hugged a thermos of coffee, looking as half-awake as the rest of the parents. A couple of hours on the ice before school was customary and expected. I'd dreamed of going pro, which meant hard work was non-negotiable.

Koa's classic Victorian dominated the street, dwarfing the neighboring houses. The two-story structure was majestic, with its scroll-cut cornice brackets, pierced balusters, and sawtooth siding. Far too much house for one man.

A light in an upstairs window glowed around a heavy curtain. Another shone at the back of the house on the first floor, streaming from a distance and illuminating the dark front room, where the silhouette of a cat perched on the sill stared back at me.

Someone was awake and active. Did Koa live alone? Was he married? I hadn't thought to check for a ring. The guy he'd been with, was he a lover? A boyfriend?

Did it matter?

Who was Koa to me except a child I'd known a lifetime ago. I'd lived a hundred lives since then. I couldn't expect to show up out of the blue, wipe the slate clean, and revert back to our innocent days of camp.

I shut off the engine and reached for the Mark Twain book on the seat beside me, flicking through the brittle yellow pages, unable to read the words in the shadowy interior of the Jeep. After confronting Koa the other day, I'd gone home and reread it, captivated by the nostalgia it unearthed. For one night, I was Huckleberry Finn again, chasing after Tom through the woods, hunting for pirates, and stuffing my pockets with treasures.

The dash clock read five fifty-five, and a second silhouette, that of a man, joined the cat at the window. The pair watched the Jeep with blank faces I couldn't see. It was my cue.

I got out of the truck and tucked the book into the inside pocket of my jacket as I headed to the front door. Koa opened it as I followed the flagstone path to the house. He leaned on the doorframe and crossed his arms over his chest, inexpressive and unreadable. He wore the same beige knitted cardigan over an unbuttoned plaid, a plain white T-shirt underneath, jeans, and slippers. His hair was mussed, and his scruff was dense. Even with casual weekend attire, I saw the teacher inside him, scrutinizing and studying my every step.

"You made it."

"You doubted me?" I stopped at the bottom step leading to the porch, waiting for a proper invitation.

The cat I'd seen at the window appeared, and Koa picked it up, snuggling it in his arms. "You get one hour."

"So you said."

Koa hesitated before sighing. "Come in, I guess."

He retreated into the house, and I followed.

Koa led me into a quaint kitchen, modernly renovated yet fitting to the house's era, with wood-fronted cupboards, a stone slab floor, and various textures and patterns that worked to create a vintage theme. The granite countertops, range stove, workspace island, and high-topped table stood out. The atmosphere was warm and close, private and serene. Candles burned on various surfaces, bathing the room in a soft glow. The overhead lights were not illuminated. Books littered the island and filled the most inconspicuous nooks and crannies. Everywhere I looked, there were more. The embellishments of an artist's life gave it a feverish pitch I couldn't quite explain.

The air was perfumed with cinnamon, coffee, and a hint of melancholy. Despite its vastness, it gave the impression of a single man's dwelling, a home not often shared with the outside world. The kitchen alone was immensely personal, and I felt like an intruder, trespassing somewhere I shouldn't. I could only imagine what the rest of the house might be like.

Koa moved to an elaborate coffee machine in the corner. The cat prowled around his legs, but Koa didn't seem to notice. "How do you take your coffee?" he asked as he rooted through an assortment of bagged beans.

"If it's good coffee, black."

"Why ever would you drink coffee that wasn't good?"

I chuckled. Koa had no clue what it was like growing up in an arena. I'd had my fair share of vending machine coffee that burned your tongue and stuck like tar to your ribs. The only way to make it palatable was to dump half a cow's worth of cream and six or eight packets of sugar into it. All that mattered in those days was being awake enough to play.

Koa ground the beans he selected, fiddled with buttons and knobs on a fancy machine with more bells and whistles than my Gladiator, and stuck a mug under a drip arm. It gurgled and spat as it worked. When the mug was full, Koa placed it carefully on the island where I assumed I was supposed to pull up a seat.

"There are few things that bring me pleasure in life," he said, gaze locked on the mug. "Coffee is one of them. Let me know what you think." He backed up, turned around, sidestepped his cat without thought, and returned to the machine.

I sat on a stool and held the mug between my palms, letting it warm my hands. Steam licked my cheeks as I brought it to my nose and inhaled. Complex, understated floral notes blossomed in my nostrils. Smooth and delicate with a whisper of something nutty. "It smells amazing."

"It tastes even better." Koa started the machine a second time and waited for his mug to fill.

I sipped, and holy shit, did it ever. I'd had good coffee over the years, but this was above and beyond. Koa glanced over his shoulder when I made an audible noise of pleasure. A self-satisfied smirk touched the corner of his mouth.

"Told you."

"I need to know your secret."

"Get in line. If I won't tell Niles, I certainly won't share with you."

Koa's back was turned when he made the comment, so he didn't see my reaction. Niles? Was he the man in the parking lot? The sudden urge to know everything about Koa's life was ferocious. But who was I to make such demands?

Koa retrieved his full mug and joined me, taking a stool on the other side of the work island, shifting a stack of books and papers aside to make room. The clutter on top had nothing to do with cooking and was the anarchy of an English teacher's life.

For a long time, we drank our coffee and stared at one another. The intervening years had erected a barrier I wasn't sure how to disassemble. We were strangers, yet not. Old friends, yet current nobodies. As I examined the man in front of me, searching for hints of the boy I'd once known, I scrabbled for remnants of the easy nature we'd once shared. The banter, the adventure, and the creative ramblings of uninhibited youth.

It was gone.

"You look different," I said into the silence.

"I should hope so. It's been thirty years."

I chuckled at my ineptitude when it came to breaking the ice. "Fair enough. What I meant was you look good. Time certainly favored you."

Koa sipped his coffee, unreadable gaze never leaving my face.

I spun the mug between my palms and tried again. Something told me Koa would hold me to the one-hour mark, and if I didn't get to the point, I would lose my chance to make amends.

From the inside pocket of my jacket, I retrieved the book and placed it carefully on the island between us. "I believe this is yours."

Koa glanced at the tattered Mark Twain novel, and something passed across his face.

"You asked me to return it when I finished reading it. I'm sorry it took so long, but in my defense, I told you I wasn't much of a reader."

He reached for the book and dragged it in front of him, fingers dancing delicately over the worn cover, a complicated look on his face. "You read it?"

"Twice. It took me over three years the first time and two nights the second, which was recently. I thought you might want it back. I get the feeling it was special to you."

Koa stared at the book but said nothing. He wasn't going to make this easy.

"Look, Koa, I know you don't want me here, and I know you don't want to listen to what I have to say, but I'm going to say it anyway. Then I'll leave, and you can go on with your life and forget about me again."

I didn't expect a response but paused to allow one. Koa sat motionless, fingers spread on the table, bracketing the book, coffee forgotten. An indent marked the pointer finger of his right hand near the base knuckle. Smudges of ink speckled his fingers. Marks of a writer, one who used pen and paper and not a computer to compose. How long had he been up? What had he been writing?

What was he thinking?

He remained quiet and unresponsive, pensive yet alert.

I continued. "I wasn't very nice to you on the last day of camp when we were fourteen. I said things I never should have said. Things I didn't mean. Things I regret. I was frightened and confused. When you—"

"When I kissed you," he interrupted, "you weren't expecting it and reacted the only way you knew how. You used words as weapons, the same as your friends always did. You pushed me away and acted like you hadn't invited it to happen in the first place."

"Koa—"

"It's fine. In the same way I wasn't in control of my raging fourteen-year-old hormones and clearly misread the signs, you weren't in control of your responses in the face of the potential demise of your reputation—which wasn't at risk, by the way, since no one saw the kiss happen. We were children. I learned a valuable lesson that summer. Now, since we're adults, and I assume this incessant need to apologize means you didn't grow up to be a bigoted adult, you're forgiven. Water under the bridge. Let's move on."

He picked up the paperback and tossed it aside with the rest of the books like it had no great value and hadn't impacted his youth on a level I had never understood.

"Can I talk now?"

Koa drank his coffee, but the look in his eyes urged me to proceed. Still impassive and impenetrable despite all he'd said.

"When you kissed me, I was frightened and confused because I had yet to sort out what it meant to be bisexual. At fourteen, I couldn't explain, even to myself, why I felt the way I did about you. I knew I liked girls, but you... it was different. All I knew was the idea of liking boys too was a terrifying notion because the kids at camp and at school and in my neighborhood and on my hockey team all made it into a big ugly thing. I didn't want to be a faggot or a homo. I didn't want to be an outcast. I didn't want to invoke teasing or violence. So yes, I reacted wrong. I hurt you in a way I never wanted to be hurt, but it wasn't for the reasons you thought. So for that, I'm sorry."

My coffee wasn't gone, and I was hard-pressed to leave it since it was truly one of the best coffees I'd had in my life, but I stood and rapped knuckles on the table. "For what it's worth, I wish I could go back in time and change things. I'd have kissed you back, and we could have continued to be pen pals. Who knows what might have happened. I'm sorry."

I found my way to the front door and slipped on my shoes. A rock sat in the pit of my stomach. The sun had barely crested the horizon, and morning dew saturated the grass and budding trees, glistening like diamonds. I got in the Jeep and started it up, cranking the heat to fight off the bone-deep chill that had arisen inside Koa's house. I was such an idiot. What the hell had I expected?

The stench of regret filled the cab. Never more had the passing years weighed so heavily on my soul. In the fifteen years since my career-ending injury, divorce, addiction, and recent accident that had taken my estranged parents from my life, I had always felt like I was living in a fog. Discovering Koa's letters had kindled a low-burning fire in my core, clearing my vision for the first time in over a decade. I had hoped to regain something I'd lost. I'd hoped to find purpose. A friend. Serenity. Maybe a small part of me had hoped we could rekindle those old feelings.

But I was wrong.

I was about to pull away when I caught sight of Koa standing at the front door, hugging his cardigan around his body. The protective swaddle had nothing to do with the morning chill.

We stared at one another for a long time before he hitched his chin in a "come back" motion.

I didn't have to think about it. Thirty years ago, Koa had held a quiet power over me. The strange boy with the imaginary friend who lived with his grandfather and had occasional blank fits had captivated me in a way that would take another decade to properly understand.

I shut off the engine, unbuckled my seat belt, and got out of the truck.

10

Koa

The complexity of thoughts and emotions brought on by Jersey's statement would take a while to unpack and process. The span of time between his revelation and exit was not sufficient for such a task, so my best bet was to let him walk away while I reflected and formed conclusions.

In the end, what did Jersey's disclosure matter? How did it change my life? It didn't. It certainly didn't change the past. All it did was answer long-dead questions that had no impact on the present.

He was bisexual. Good for him. It didn't matter.

So why did his sudden departure fester under my skin? Why did I want to yank him back into the house and tell him to stay?

I'd spent a great deal of my adult life coming to terms with the events from my past, finding ways to diminish their significance until the effect became negligible. Irrelevant. I'd studied endless philoso-phies, trying to discover the meaning of life because there had to be answers out there for why I'd been made to suffer. I'd asked countless questions about the existence of good and evil. I'd debated with professors and fellow students while in university, staying up long into the night, writing papers in a desperate effort to prove how utterly irrelevant humans were to the universe. Over time, I'd adapted various theories into something I could live with, something that painted me with a brush dipped less in insanity and more in abstract thinking.

Why the sudden urge to chase after Jersey surfaced so profoundly at that moment was something I could ponder later. All I knew was I didn't want him to leave, so I followed his escape, hoping I wasn't too late.

A wash of hazy morning light reflected off the shiny paint of his Gladiator, where it idled on the other side of the road. Behind the tinted windows, I could make out Jersey in the front seat, but his face and expression were shadowed. When he caught me staring, I almost changed my mind. What would I say to this man I no longer knew? I wasn't a skilled socializer on a good day. Reunions of this sort were uncharted territory. The notion of small talk made my skin itch.

Fearing he would drive off, I hitched my chin, inviting him to return.

Jersey shut off the truck and hopped out without a second thought it seemed, crossing the street with a look of relief.

Inside again, I encouraged him to bring his coffee into the library. It was there I was most comfortable. It was there where my brain functioned on a level that might save our awkward encounter. The library was my haven.

I sat in my favorite reading chair by the fireplace, tucking my legs under my bottom and wrapping my cardigan in a tight swaddle. I'd lit the fire that morning to chase away the cold. Sleep never came easily, and I was up most days by four, reading, writing, or marking papers. Tucked in my chair, I felt protected. Secure. In control.

Jersey spent a few minutes looking around, unashamedly scanning the bookshelves, and admiring the priceless artifacts I'd collected over the years. The library was a congested reflection of all the things I valued. Words, music, and art.

He stopped at the upright piano and lifted the fallboard, tinkling his fingers over the ivories and making them sing. "You still play?" he asked, gesturing to the sheet music spread across the stand.

"Yes." *Poorly*, I wanted to add but heard Niles's reprimand in my head.

My violin sat in its case nearby, along with a mountain of compositions tucked into leather folders, books organized by composers, and loose scraps of paper that hadn't been refiled after use. Sheet music covered three more stands and filled a shelf in the corner.

Jersey didn't seem to notice.

A few select pieces of framed artwork hung on the walls. He briefly admired them, but I could tell he didn't understand their deeper meaning. Artists were of a different breed, and Jersey was not a member of the right-brain thinkers club. His mind didn't work creatively. Be it poetry, watercolors, or complex arias, I had a hunch he viewed them all on a superficial level.

How did I know this at a glance? Because creative souls got a look in their eyes they couldn't hide. Left-brain thinkers, those controlled by logic and analytical processes, didn't. I could scan a classroom of students on the first day of school in September and know who would do well based on the look alone.

Jersey wandered to a bookshelf—a faint limp made him favor his left side—and browsed the titles, head tilted to the side so he could read the spines. "You're a classics nut, huh?"

"It's what I teach."

"I saw that on the school website." He stood straighter, craned his neck to peer at the upper shelves, then turned to me. "Classic literature and philosophy, right?"

"Yes."

"Impressive. I don't know the first thing about philosophy, and I can honestly say the only classic I've read is the one you gave me about Tom Sawyer."

"How is that possible? There are several classics used as required reading in school. I thought we all read *Lord of the Flies*, *Of Mice and Men*, and *The Catcher in the Rye*."

Jersey smiled and shrugged. "Nope. Couldn't be bothered. I found ways around it. Mostly by schmoozing the cute girls in my English classes and having them give me a rundown of the basic plot and whatnot so I could pass the tests."

"Crafty."

"My mother didn't think so."

Jersey found a seat on the chair across from me, one I rarely used but had bought strictly to offset the symmetry of the room. He didn't sit back but rested his elbows on his knees, legs splayed, coffee hugged between his hands.

"So." Jersey's smile was warm and inviting, not all that different than the smile he'd turned on me in childhood. It touched me on a personal level I wasn't expecting, and I turned away. "I want to ask about your life, but I hardly know where to begin."

"There's not much to tell."

"Humor me?"

I tried not to fidget. I wanted to be alone, not wading into the past. "I finished high school, and—"

"Wait. Homeschooled, right? I remember you telling me you were homeschooled."

I hesitated. "I was, but no. Grandfather sent me to private school for my last two years. It was easier to apply to university that way. From there, I went to Western and got my degree. Taught remedial English in a public school for several years out in London while I worked on my Ph.D."

"Jesus. You have a Ph.D? Smarty pants."

"I, um... considered teaching at the college level, but then I was offered a position at Timber Creek twelve years ago and took it instead. It was a better atmosphere."

"Impressive."

It didn't feel impressive. My career's evolution was simply a natural progression from childhood to adulthood. Wasn't that the expectation?

"What about you?" I didn't like the conversation centering on me. Jersey had asked a hundred questions about my life as a boy, and I had avoided every one of them. I had no doubt, with our reunion, they would surface again, and I was no more inclined to answer now than I had been as a child.

"You don't know?"

"Know what?"

Jersey chuckled and set his mug aside on an end table. His broad shoulders and relaxed stance spoke of confidence. Tattoos decorated the length of his right arm, but I tried not to stare. He subconsciously rubbed his knee. "My life was public for so long, it's hard to believe you haven't heard."

"Public? Enlighten me."

"You don't follow sports, do you?"

"No interest."

"And you really didn't keep tabs on me after that summer?"

That hurt. Did he think I would have?

"I did everything in my power to forget you, Jersey."

His smile dimmed, and he washed a hand over his trim beard. "I deserve that."

"I remember you enjoyed sports. You played hockey and baseball and were on every team under the sun."

"Not quite."

"So? I ask again. Enlighten me." I didn't mean to add a snap to my tone, but I was uncomfortable.

"I was recruited to the OHL at seventeen, then drafted to the NHL three years later. Played pro for ten years and"—more knee rubbing—"an injury took me out of the game in oh eight."

Jersey paused, and I was sure I was meant to react. He was likely used to people being wowed by his professional career and swooning at his feet. I'd never watched a single hockey game in my life, so it meant nothing. "Sounds like you lived your dream."

Hurt flashed through his eyes before he ducked his head and stared at the wooden floorboards. "It was everything I wanted, then it was gone overnight."

I wasn't sure if I was meant to ask about the injury or not. I wasn't excited to share my painful past, so I respected that maybe Jersey wasn't either. "What do you do now?"

"I went back to school and trained to be a physiotherapist. I joined a team in Toronto who had recently opened a medical center specifically designed to treat athletes. It's a good job. Rewarding. I can empathize with my clients, and they appreciate that."

"So you live in Toronto?"

"Mimico."

I nodded. I hated the city, but I knew the area. Silence invaded the room, unpleasant and uncomfortable. I knew I should say more, but every road forward was one I didn't want to take. What was I supposed to say to the boy who'd rejected me, successfully driving the final nail to my coffin when I was barely fourteen.

The quiet continued until Jersey broke it, speaking softly to the floor, still not lifting his gaze. "I was married for six years. I met Christine at a party shortly after signing with Edmonton. She was a well-known puck bunny at the time, but we clicked and ended up dating. We got married, had a kid, and then she left me in 2009, not long after I was injured. I umm... struggled a lot back then. Pushed a lot of people away."

"I see. Sounds familiar." How was I meant to respond? "So... you have a teenager?"

"Yes. His name's Derby. He's..." Jersey paused and thought for a second. "He'll be seventeen next week. I rarely see him. He doesn't care much for his dad." Jersey peeked up and offered a weighted shrug. "It is what it is."

The awkward quiet returned. Convention dictated it was my turn to share, but I had nothing to contribute. Who I was and who I'd been was irrelevant. I couldn't comprehend why it was so important for some people to unload things that no longer mattered. Why couldn't we stay in the present?

"I've never married," I said into the void, instantly wishing I hadn't. I was scrambling. Floundering. I wanted to be alone, not doing this. I shouldn't have gone after him. What was I doing?

"No?"

"No. I'm not the marrying kind. It doesn't interest me."

"Are you the dating kind?" I must have looked shocked because Jersey added, "You can't have been alone your whole life."

"And why not? Is there something wrong with living a life of solitude?"

"I guess not. It sounds lonely. Don't you desire companionship?"

"No." And it was true. I didn't. Alone was better. I didn't have to answer to anyone. I didn't have to force a mood because my partner expected me to be happy all the time when the very nature of happiness confounded me.

Jersey didn't seem to know what to say in the face of such a definitive response.

I could have elaborated and told him that, yes, I'd dated a few times. I could have told him how those relationships had failed to go anywhere and how my lovers had all thought I was cold and disconnected, but what was the point?

Jersey rubbed his hands together and sat more upright. "Well, I guess my time is probably up. I should go. Don't want to overstay my welcome. Thank you for the coffee. It was truly amazing."

When I didn't try to stop him, Jersey stood. He radiated disappointment. I recognized it but couldn't address it. I followed him to the front door, where he put on his shoes and coat before facing me, hands in his jacket pockets, worry creasing the skin beside his faded denim eyes.

"You really wanted nothing to do with this reunion. I can tell. That's fine. I'm grown up enough to know when to cut my losses, but I won't lie and say I'm not disappointed. I was really hoping we could... reconnect."

It wasn't that I was against it, but I didn't know how to fit Jersey into my carefully constructed life. The walls were too fragile and keeping them standing already took a herculean effort. Besides, people tended to move on a different plane of existence than me. I was a shadow, a grain of sand on a beach, a raindrop in a thunderstorm. The ability to flow fluidly, to combine our two worlds, seemed impossible. I would always remain too far out of reach. People grew frustrated and left.

And I was so tired of hurting. I couldn't risk bringing more pain into my life.

Jersey scrubbed a hand over his beard, shaking his head. "You know, I've spent the last fifteen years trying to rediscover my purpose. After losing my career, it upended everything I thought I knew. I became bitter and angry. I ended up addicted to painkillers. Spiraling. I lost my wife, my kid, and my parents. I didn't know who I was without hockey, and I hated everyone's attempts at telling me it wasn't the end of the world. To me it was. I've cleaned up my act. Kicked the drugs. But for fifteen years, I've coasted, lost in a haze, detached from life. A couple of weeks ago, I got a call from the Lakefield OPP, informing me my parents had been killed in an accident."

My lips parted on a silent gasp.

He held up a staying hand. "I'm not looking for sympathy. That's not why I bring it up. We hadn't spoken in fifteen years, and that's my fault. But I came back to my childhood home to arrange their funeral and get their affairs in order. Their death forced me to reconnect with life. Being in that house again... It made me reflect on the past. On who I was and where I wanted to be. When I found out my mother had kept all your letters, it awoke something inside me, something I'd thought was long dead. Christ, Koa, you had no idea what I felt for you back then, and I didn't have the words or understanding to tell you. I think I was halfway in love with you and fucked it all up. And yeah, we were kids, and feelings are bigger and bolder in our youths, but it doesn't excuse what I did."

He shuffled. "I'm not poetic or literary like you, so bear with me as I fumble and try to explain. Since my injury, I've been stuck in a state of depression. Every happy memory I was able to conjure involved hockey, and I couldn't have those days back, so I was certain I was destined to remain miserable for the rest of my life."

Jersey peered at the front door, his forehead crinkled, but his mind seemed elsewhere. "When I found the letters and read them, I was reminded of a time long ago when I was happy without hockey. When a quiet boy at camp drew my eye. I spent a whole evening reminiscing about those years and never felt lighter. I thought, naively, I could get some of that back by finding you and seeing you again. We parted on bad terms, but I thought it was forgivable. Maybe I was wrong."

Jersey lifted his head and faced me, studying my stolid expression as though looking for something deep beneath the surface. "I don't know a thing about your childhood, Koa. What I've pieced together is based on faded memories from thirty years ago, and they're not good. I know whatever you went through must have been brutal. I remember the blank fits you would have. I remember the nightmares that made you scream some nights. I remember you wetting the bed at camp more than once as a result. I remember the disconnection you had with other children. The crazy fits no one knew how to handle. And Huck, the imaginary boy who was your friend before me."

It took every bit of strength to stay present, to not cover my ears like a child and tell him to stop. This was why I didn't want to see him. I didn't want to go back there. I didn't want to remember.

"Something happened to you, and you never told a soul. I respect that, and I'm not asking now and never will again, but you were sent to camp a severely disturbed child. Looking back, I see it plain. I was too young to understand the seriousness back then. I think, and maybe I'm giving myself too much credit, but I hope I helped to shoo some of those demons away. I think for those few short weeks every summer, despite whatever haunted you, you were able to be a kid. Being pen pals in the intervening months gave you an outlet, didn't it?"

The answer was yes, but I didn't respond. Couldn't.

"Before I was an idiotic, hormonal, and confused four-teen-year-old, I think we had a lot of fun. Maybe it's stupid to cling to a time long dead, but my god, I miss being happy and innocent. Don't you?"

I didn't know the definition of happy and innocent.

"I miss the days before hockey ruled my life and became my identity. I guess I was hoping for a taste of those years again. I wondered if maybe the boy I was so fond of thirty years ago might have missed me a bit too. I'm sorry if reaching out unsettled you. I can tell you're upset. It wasn't my intent."

He touched my face and lifted my chin so I would look at him and not the floor. His thumb stroked my cheek. I wanted to pull away and lean into it at the same time. I wanted to crawl into a hollow log where magic and fantasies were real, and life wasn't cruel. I remained motionless, staring at his faded denim eyes, wiser, older, and sadder than they'd ever been.

"Thank you for giving me an opportunity to apologize, Koa."

Speech complete, Jersey dropped his hand and stepped back, pausing as though waiting for a response. I couldn't give him one. There was too much to unpack, and I wasn't one to make snap decisions. It was unclear what he expected or wanted from me, so I remained silent. Jersey didn't realize that happiness and innocence had been taken away from me when I was eight years old.

But he was the only real friend I'd had as a child. He was the boy who didn't run away from my trauma. He'd stayed beside me through the nightmares and screaming fits. He'd sheltered me from his mean friends as best he could.

He was the boy who kept his promise... until he didn't.

My silence must have been answer enough.

"Take care, Koa. You have my number." He wandered from the dark, closed-in hallway of my house into the bright, expansive world beyond. Out of the shadows and into the light. The symbology wasn't lost on me.

Jersey drove away without a second glance, and I stayed in the doorway, peering out into the complicated world beyond my haven as I groped and analyzed his final words, as I tumbled back in time to Camp Kawartha and into the arms of a boy who had been my salvation.

He wasn't wrong. Despite my issues, those few weeks I spent at camp every year offered the only respite I'd known in my entire life. Jersey had played a huge role in that contentment.

And although I distanced myself from life and people in general, I couldn't understand why dismissing Jersey stung. Why did I have the sudden urge to hang on to this one thing I'd lost so long ago?

11

Koa

CAMP KAWARTHA 1990

I'd had a rough year, and Grandfather didn't want to send me to camp. My doctor insisted I needed to be with other children, so he caved. In truth, I thought Grandfather would be happier not having to deal with me for a month. He could resume his regular routine, the one he'd had before I'd disrupted his life.

After Grandfather dropped me off, lectured the counselors about my problems, delivered my medication to the person in charge, and departed, I found my new cabin and set up my sleeping bag on a bottom bunk in the corner. When no one was looking, I put down the mattress pad my grandfather had sent because peeing the bed had become a problem. I saved the top bunk for Jersey. We'd talked about it in our letters. I liked having him nearby. He was the only kid who didn't make fun of me when I had nightmares and woke up crying. I secretly hoped having him around would stop the nightmares from coming.

The cabin leader was Randy, a boisterous guy with a booming voice and a laugh that made me jumpy. I didn't know Randy because he had been in charge of the eleven-year-olds the previous year. Since I was eleven now, he was in charge of me. He slapped me on the back and welcomed me to cabin eight. I smiled and ducked out of his reach. I wasn't a fan of loud people.

Once my gear was unpacked, I wandered around the outdoor buildings to see if I recognized any returning children. The younger kids ran around, screaming and laughing. The teenagers—the fourteen-year-olds—were sitting in the grass by the equipment building and talking quietly. The kids my age were spread out in small groups. Bruce and Justin were there, and when they saw me emerge from the cabin, they nudged each other, whispered, and pointed. I waved and smiled, but they didn't wave back.

I didn't see Peter or Daniel, but in Jersey's last letter, he'd said they return every year, so they would show up eventually. Those boys were Jersey's friends, not mine. Unless Jersey was there to divert their attention, they were mean, so I stayed out of their way.

When Jersey arrived a short time later, he acknowledged me with a sneaky wave but never came to say hi. In a flash, dumping his gear on the ground outside our cabin, he was surrounded by his friends. They pushed and shoved and roughhoused until Randy told them to calm down. Then they raced off to the woods like a herd of wild animals, shouting and howling.

Other children paired off, reconnecting with old friends.

My stomach turned to fire, and I sat alone in the grass. Sometimes, my insides grew hot and angry. Sometimes, my blood felt like it was bubbling inside my veins. My doctor told me to talk about it. She said if I let my guts burn, I would never heal. But who was I supposed to talk to? At home, if I talked to Huck, Grandfather smacked me in the mouth and told me to stop. Since Grandfather wasn't around, it was probably okay to acknowledge Huck, except I'd learned that make-believe was for babies, and I was eleven. Huck had to be a secret, and there were too many people around.

With no Huck and my doctor far away, I guessed my guts were going to burn.

Jersey and I had written letters back and forth for a whole winter. He told me about school, and I told him about the books I read. He told me about his friends, and I told him about things I did with Huck—the secret play times my grandfather didn't know about. Jersey thought having an imaginary friend was weird, but he didn't make fun of me or call me a baby anymore, so telling him was safe.

Jersey had been mostly nice to me the previous summer. We didn't always play together since he had his friends, and they didn't like me, but we'd gone on many adventures. He'd given me a bracelet—which I still wore—and promised he would never be mean. And he hadn't been.

I stared at the bracelet now. It was frayed on the ends and smelled funky, but I didn't care.

Running off with his friends wasn't mean, but the hotness in my gut didn't feel good. Randy eyed me. I knew he'd had a talk with Grandfather and knew about my pee accidents and head problems. It was embarrassing. I didn't want him to ask me if I was okay. I hated it when people asked me that. Lying wasn't allowed, but sometimes it was necessary. Randy definitely wasn't someone I wanted to talk to about the hotness in my gut.

Before my cabin leader could wander over and ask questions, I headed alone into the forest, weaving along a worn path, kicking at acorns left over from the fall and scraping my running shoes through mounds of pine needles and dirt. I whistled at the birds and chittered at the chipmunks, laughing when they responded. The whole time, I kept my ears alert to pirates or evil forest creatures. I imagined Huck walking beside me, sword drawn, but I didn't talk to him. I wondered what Jersey and his friends were doing, but thinking about Jersey made the hotness return, so I put those thoughts away.

I veered off the trail when I got to a place I recognized and searched the area until I found the rotting red oak lying on its side. The inside was musty and damp, the decay worse than the previous year. Tiny white mushrooms grew in the powdered bark, and a mass of stinky wet leaves had blown inside. I scraped them out and inspected the interior of the log. Ants and potato bugs crawled in and out of crevices, but otherwise, it looked the same as before. I wedged myself inside feetfirst and lay on my stomach, balanced on my elbows, chin rested on my upturned palms as I watched the forest from my secret cave.

I imagined Huck guarding the entrance with his sword in hand, ready to attack the enemy if they should approach. He stalked back and forth. He beat at the bushes. He peered far into the distance. When he looked at me, I giggled and pressed a finger to my mouth, telling him to be quiet.

I wasn't sure how long I stayed inside the log, but the sunlight changed and moved, angling through the trees and highlighting different parts of the undergrowth. I watched a squirrel eat a nut and listened to a woodpecker high above in a place I couldn't see. I thought about the bad stuff until my heart raced, and I had to sing a song and squeeze my eyes closed to make it go away.

I wanted to shout at Huck to join me inside the log so we could have a chat, but even alone, it felt silly, so I didn't. Seeing him in my head was enough. He was there. He was keeping me safe. I was hidden.

Much later, I heard someone approach. Someone real who wasn't Huck. Twigs snapped. Leaves crunched under someone's feet. They got closer and closer, and I held my breath, envisioning pirates, then a bear, then something far worse with a name and familiar face. For a brief, scary moment, I was back in the nightmare as he hunted me down, shouting for me to *"come out, come out wherever you are."* But I forced the thoughts away.

I stayed perfectly still and pretended I was invisible like I'd done on the day the bad stuff had happened. But the sounds grew closer, and my skin crawled. The pictures inside my head kept coming back no matter how many times I shook them free, and I wanted to cry.

With a startling "Gotcha!" a boy jumped in front of the opening to the log, and I screamed.

I screamed and screamed and screamed until my throat hurt and tears burned my eyes. I buried my head in my arms and covered my ears as my heart beat ninety to nothing, and the hotness burned me up. But the boy's riotous laughter took some of the fear away, and I lifted my head, coming face to face with Jersey. Not a monster. Not a bandit. Not a pirate.

Not *him.*

Jersey plunked down on his knees and sat back on his heels, still giggling as my terror receded. "I scared the crap out of you."

"No you didn't."

"Liar. You almost cried. Your eyes are wet."

"Well, I didn't."

"Move over."

I moved over, and Jersey wedged himself inside the log beside me until we were shoulder to shoulder. It was a tighter fit than the previous year. We'd grown. He smelled like the windy outdoors and summertime. When the sun warmed his skin, it always made it smell good. In the closeness of the log, those memories returned, and I wanted to lean in close and inhale all that was Jersey because I knew it would make me feel better.

I didn't. He would think I was weird.

"What are you doing here?" he asked, brushing an ant off his arm.

"Thinking."

"About what?"

I shrugged. "Nothing much. Stuff."

"It's the first day of camp. Why aren't you out there with everyone else?"

"I don't know. I like it here. It's quiet."

Jersey's presence washed away my turmoil. Maybe he still wanted to be my friend. He'd found me in the woods, which meant he'd gone looking for me. He willingly shared my log, and that meant lying close together. Unlike his friends, he didn't think I was too gross to touch. He didn't think I had cooties or homo germs—whatever they'd called it.

"I thought you were with the guys."

"I was, but Randy said it was time to make our cabin banner. No one knew where you went, so I said I would find you."

The heat of Jersey's gaze warmed my face. I examined him, looking for differences since it had been a whole year since we'd been together. He looked the same. Same soft denim-colored eyes. Same round face and fat lips. Same shaggy brown hair tangled with sweat. In my books, boys like Jersey were called brawny. The sweet scent of grape bubble gum filled the space between us. He munched a thick wad as he grinned and stared back.

He touched my wrist and the knotted bracelet. "Still have it, huh?"

"Promises are for forever. You said I can't take it off or we won't be friends anymore." So I hadn't, even when Grandfather had called me a sissy for wearing it.

"Cool. Want some gum?"

"Sure."

Jersey took the purple wad from his mouth and stretched it until it snapped in two, offering me half his chewed piece. "It still has flavor."

"Thanks."

We chewed and made bubbles, popping them with obnoxious snaps. When Jersey tried to make his bubble enormous, he blew too hard, and his gum flew into the dirt. We lost ourselves in a fit of giggles that made my stomach ache and tears leak from the corners of my eyes.

"Oh man. That was my last piece."

When the laughing fit calmed, I shared half of what was left with Jersey, and he wasn't afraid of my germs, taking it happily. But the wads of gum were too small now to make bubbles, so we chewed them silently as we peered into the forest beyond our hideout.

"I forgot your book at home," Jersey said.

"It's okay. Did you read it?"

"A couple of chapters. It's kind of boring. Is Huck even in it? I thought you said they went on adventures. So far, Tom painted a fence and went to church. Boring."

"You don't meet Huck until later. It gets better."

Jersey sighed. "Man, I hate reading."

"You promised."

"I know, I know. I'll finish it. We should probably go back."

"I don't want to make a banner."

"But Randy will get mad."

"He won't even find us here. No one will. It's too secret. We could play explorers."

Jersey gasped and shuffled sideways to face me better. Our knees knocked and settled halfway intertwined. His body was pressed tight to mine, and it felt warm and safe. "I have the awesomest idea! We should sneak out of the cabin one night and sleep here."

"In the forest?"

"In the log. How cool would that be? We could have midnight adventures. We'd find the pirates for sure. You said they only sneak around at night."

That was true.

"Won't Randy know we're gone? We could get in trouble."

"Not if we stuff our sleeping bags and make it look like we're inside them."

It was exactly the kind of thing Tom and Huck would do, so I agreed.

We made plans to sneak away, deciding to wait three nights to ensure Randy didn't have a weird nighttime ritual we didn't know about. Then Jersey convinced me to head back to camp and help with the banner.

When I asked if he was going to ignore me, he promised he wouldn't with a pinky swear.

"Promises are for forever," I reminded him.

"I know."

⚜

Three nights later, we snuck out. Bedtime at camp was ten thirty, but we waited until after twelve before stealing away into the night, slipping out from under the nose of our cabin leader. Randy was twenty years old and slept like the dead, his rattling snores a telltale sign we were safe to move.

Jersey hadn't told any of his friends, and I thrilled at the prospect of us having a secret even his buddies knew nothing about. We filled our sleeping bags with extra clothes and stepped cautiously to the door, unlatching the handle with care and closing it behind us with a silent *snick*.

We were free. The sky above was a blanket of stars as Jersey and I ran toward the forest path and our secret hideout in the woods. In July, the nights were sticky and hot, only slightly better than daytime when the sun's blistering heat was so strong it softened the tar that glued together the crumbling asphalt on the basketball court.

We were both dripping sweat when we reached our secret log. My eyes had adjusted to the dark. The forest, although shadowy and nondescript, untouched by the moon and stars, was familiar enough that I recognized certain landmarks.

Jersey tugged his T-shirt off and wiped his face. Mimicking, I did the same. My chest was scrawnier. His ribs didn't stick out, hiding under a fleshier midsection. We were both pale. Three days hadn't been enough time to bronze our skin, so we glowed in the dark.

Jersey didn't move to the log and instead wandered the perimeter, peering into the surrounding forest.

"What are you doing?" I asked.

"Checking for bad guys. They haunt these woods at night, looking for little boys like us. I want to make sure we're alone."

The hairs on my neck rose, and my skin prickled with goose bumps as I dashed a look in every direction. Bad guys were here?

"Listen, Tom. I think we should set traps before we fall asleep. We don't want to chance anything."

Tom. Which meant Jersey was being Huck. Which meant he was playing, and there weren't real bad guys. I calmed and moved in beside him, absorbing the sense of safety I felt in Jersey's presence. "Okay, but let's do it together."

Jersey's teeth glowed with his smile. "Are you scared?"

"No."

"Are you lying?"

"No," I said firmer. But my insides jittered.

"Come on."

Jersey took my arm, and we moved through the dense trees, pretending to set traps using sticks and stray pinecones. I collected acorn hats and stuffed them into a pocket. Jersey found a piece of wire and bent it at an angle, calling it the detonator.

We were working on the last trap when Jersey's head snapped up, and he grabbed my arm. "Did you hear that?"

I hadn't, but I peered wide-eyed into the forest. "No."

"They're coming."

"Who?"

"The bad guys. They have guns, so if they see us, they'll shoot us dead. We have to stay quiet."

Guns? *It's not real,* I told myself. *He's pretending.*

Jersey wrapped an arm around me and forced me to duck behind a bush. My heart raced, and the air grew stickier and hotter. My guts were on fire, and I couldn't stop the burning.

"I don't want to play anymore." Thin as a reed, my voice barely traveled.

"Shh. They're getting close," Jersey hissed. "Do you hear that? They're coming."

He's pretending. It's not real. I knew that in my mind, but the sense of urgency, the flood of fear, and the imminent danger hit me all at once. The bad times came back, and I wasn't in the forest. I was trapped inside the house with a real bad guy hunting me down, screaming my name.

The floorboards creaked. I could smell the burning air. My pants were wet, and I was shaking, holding my hands over my mouth so he wouldn't hear me crying. Sickness swirled in my belly and wanted to come out, but if I barfed, he would find me.

Jersey, smacking my face and screaming my name, brought me back to the forest. My body moved like a rag doll, head flopping as he shook me back and forth. A long whine of fear sang inside my head, and the fire inside me hurt so much I wanted to cry.

"Koa! Koa! What's wrong with you?"

It took me a second to get my bearings. I was in the woods, not the house. It was nighttime, not daytime. Jersey looked as terrified as I felt. The first thing I did was feel my pants to be sure I hadn't peed for real. I hadn't.

Words failed me. Breathing was still a challenge. I blinked away from the past and clung to the present, trying to be brave so Jersey wouldn't think I was some loser kid.

He stopped shouting when he realized I was with him again. Lowering his voice, he said, "You can't do that. I thought I'd have to get Randy, and then we'd be in huge trouble."

"I c-can't help it. I'm... I'm sorry."

"Don't cry."

"Okay."

"Why does it happen?"

I shook my head, shivering, teeth chattering despite the midsummer heat.

"We should go back," he said.

"No." If we went back, Jersey wouldn't be my friend anymore. I knew it. He would tell his buddies about this, and I'd be alone at camp with no real Huck and no fake Huck. I needed him. "Let's go inside the log now. The traps are good enough."

"Are you sure you're okay?"

I nodded, but my teeth wouldn't stop clacking together.

We went inside our secret log. Shoulder to shoulder, we peered out into the void of forest beyond. Neither of us spoke for a long time.

"Huck?" I asked after a while. My insides weren't as hot anymore, and I felt braver for five seconds. The doctor said to talk about it, but there were too many things to say.

"Yeah?"

"I'm scared."

Jersey wrapped his arm around me and drew me close, just like the other Huck would have done, except Jersey's body and comfort were real. "It's okay. I'll protect you from the bad guys."

But no one had protected me from the real bad guy. I'd protected myself.

Comforted and warm in the safety of Jersey's arms, I lay my head on my folded arms and fell asleep.

Shortly before dawn, Jersey shook me awake, and we returned to the cabin unseen. It was our first full night under the stars, but it wouldn't be our last, and I didn't have any more fits on later journeys. Jersey was careful how he played from then on. He never pretended bad guys were after us again. We looked for treasures and counted the stars. Once, we went for a nighttime swim in the lake.

We were Huck and Tom. Jersey gave me back something I'd lost that summer, and our friendship grew deeper.

12

Koa

PRESENT DAY

"All I asked was for you to explore your creative minds. Exercise your brain. To think deeply about what you believe in here"—I tapped my chest—"and to write a reflective essay on what you discovered. We've studied dozens of philosophies this year, and I'm honestly disappointed in over half of these papers. They were lazily written."

I tossed the stack of essays I'd been waving in the air onto my desk as I peered out at a classroom of seventeen-year-olds, all averting their eyes and looking shameful. Year after year, in midspring, I requested one thing of my grade twelve class. I asked the same question philosophers had been asking since the dawn of time and told them to write a minimum three-thousand-word essay. Three thousand words wasn't a lot to ask. I'd barely been able to introduce the topic of my thesis in less than five. Besides, there was no right or wrong answer. I wanted them to perform an internal search, reflect on how they connected to the universe, and decide, in their minds, what it all meant.

"What is the meaning of life?" I paced, arms crossed over my chest. No one raised their hand.

"Anyone?"

Silence.

"Each of you wrote three thousand words claiming to have answered this question already, yet I can't get a single person to speak up?"

Shelby Danbury half lifted her hand, then lowered it again. I nodded in her direction. "What do you think, Miss Danbury?"

"To find happiness."

"Okay. Explain."

She was a bright girl, and her essay was one of the better ones. At least she'd put some effort in.

"I mean... unless you believe in god and eternal life and that your purpose on earth is to eventually earn a place in heaven, then happiness is about all you've got left, right?"

I rolled a hand, urging her to continue.

She shifted in her seat, tucking a blonde lock behind her ear. "Without happiness, your time on earth just... sucks. Why would you want to live miserably? So, like, you have to figure out how to make your time here worthwhile or else—"

"Or else you might as well kill yourself," Joseph Miller added, earning a few laughs from his classmates.

"Thank you, Mr. Miller. Very insightful, but Miss Danbury is talking, albeit a little less succinctly than she writes, but I think she's fumbling her way to a point. No need to interject."

More titters.

"Go on, Miss Danbury."

Shelby shrugged. "That's basically my point. We have to attribute meaning to our lives, find happiness, or create it. Otherwise, life isn't worth living."

I smiled and stopped pacing. "Someone took my Camus lessons to heart."

Shelby's cheeks reddened as though having done so was wrong. Of all the classics I'd taught that semester, Camus was one of the easier ones to digest. The meaning behind his text wasn't always as clear cut, but Shelby seemed to have done her homework.

"It wasn't an insult, Miss Danbury. It was a compliment. It's nice to know someone pays attention when I speak. I, too, ascribe to many of Camus's philosophical ideas." And although I agreed about the absurdities of life, I struggled to imagine Sisyphus happy. Hence, I resisted the idea that happiness was the key to a meaningful life.

But I wasn't willing to get into a personal philosophical debate with a teenager. It was challenging enough with Niles, who managed to keep up for the most part.

I addressed the class. "Miss Danbury has made a good observation, and after reading her essay, I know she can back it up. Mr. Miller, your paper was interesting. Talk to us about it."

Joseph Miller squirmed, sitting straighter. "Um..."

A knock at the door interrupted, and the look of relief on Joseph's face was all-consuming. I glanced at the clock. "The bell is about to ring. Miss Butler, can you hand back these essays? If your grade was below a C plus, you can do rewrites, and I will look at it again. I suggest you stop trying to find the right answer and instead find the meaningful one, and that doesn't mean you're looking for what you think I believe to be the meaning of life. This is a *personal* reflection, folks. I can't stress that enough. Don't forget, our Monday discussion group will be based on *The Grand Inquisitor* chapter from Dostoyevsky's *The Brothers Karamazov*. Your participation is expected."

Amanda Butler retrieved the essays and started handing them out as I went to see who had come knocking. It was Annette Mandel, Timber Creek's head secretary, and she offered an apologetic smile as she handed me a slip of paper, whispering. "Sorry to interrupt. The nursing home called and asked that you call back as soon as possible. I told them you were teaching, but she claimed it was important."

"Thank you." I took the paper with the nursing home's number—a number I already had—and stared at it momentarily before stuffing it into a pocket. Grandfather had a full medical plan arranged with the doctors at the home, including a DNR if his health failed, so what they needed from me was a mystery. I did not have power of attorney, and I did not make medical decisions on my grandfather's behalf. Hence, I couldn't understand why it was an emergency. If he'd died, my rushing to the phone wouldn't change anything. He would still be dead when I got there.

The bell rang, and my students fled like the building was on fire. I stood in the empty classroom, ten degrees of separation keeping me from being present as my thoughts stirred. My mind had been especially unsettled lately, and it had nothing to do with the dying man in the home and everything to do with the unexpected return of Jersey into my life.

It had been two weeks since his visit, and not a day passed when thoughts of him didn't upset my routine. I'd mentally ventured back to Camp Kawartha a dozen or more times and had gotten stuck there. Tucking Jersey away into a little box with the rest of my past wasn't working. He kept finding his way out and disturbing my days.

I closed the windows along the far wall, latching their rusty locks. The balmy spring air was nice, but the classroom would be frigid by morning.

May was around the corner, and the cooler days were fewer and further apart, but the temperature dropped at night enough to make the earlier part of the day nippy. I lived in my cardigan, layering it over my usual tweed vests and shirts. Lately, it served a dual purpose, and I couldn't seem to go without it. I donned it like a shield. Without it, I felt unsafe.

At the window, I peered across the academy lawn. Budding trees dotted the landscape and perfumed the air. In the distance, the lake rushed with a swollen belly, thanks to recent rains. The earth was reawakening after a winter slumber, yet I felt more detached than ever. The darkness was swallowing me up, and I couldn't connect with the present. Days passed in a mundane blur, each the same as the last. I went through the motions, but my insides were numb.

I thought of Shelby Danbury and her belief that a meaningful life began with the discovery of happiness. She wasn't the first student to back Camus, but I couldn't tap into such claims. And if she was right, if Camus was right, what *was* happiness? How did one define its state of being? It was subjective. Music made Niles happy. It made me miserable. Nothing gave me that sense of euphoria. Reading, perhaps, but it was such an insignificant thing.

Sighing, I left the window, cleaned the chalkboards, and tidied my desk when another knock sounded, a softer rap of a single knuckle on the doorframe.

I peered up and found Niles, hair tied in a messy bun, shirt sleeves rolled to his elbows, and a smile on his face. "Dr. Burgard."

"Hey." I continued packing my briefcase, solemn and fighting the current, wanting to take me away.

"No official greeting? I'm wounded."

"You're not."

He wandered in and sat on the corner of a nearby desk. "You've been especially melancholy lately. I've barely seen you."

"The end of the year is always crazier. Wrapping up units, preparing for exams, and marking painfully bad papers that make me question our future generation keeps me busy."

Niles grinned. "Aw, yes. Let me guess. The Dr. Burgard spring special where he expects a bunch of juvenile delinquents to explain to him the meaning of life."

"It's meant to be a reflective essay. I'm not asking them to be the next Socrates or Voltaire. I'm asking them to meditate on the idea of our existence."

"That's a big ask for seventeen-year-olds. The only things these children ruminate on are relationships and food. They're driven by hormones and their stomachs. The end. Nothing else. Complex philosophies are beyond them."

"I disagree, and they aren't delinquents. They have above-average intelligence, or they wouldn't be here. Hence, requiring them to con-template deeply meaningful questions is not too much to ask. Why are you here?"

"Isn't it obvious? To annoy you. I haven't suffered a dose of glacial indifference this week. I needed it."

"Don't you have rehearsal?"

"No. It's Wednesday, and I have a coffee date with a friend who has clearly forgotten he made such an appointment."

I frowned and glanced at the open planner on my desk. Sure enough, I had made a notation about meeting with Niles after class today.

"It's not like you to be so scattered, Koa."

"It slipped my mind. Give me a minute. I have to call the nursing home." I found my cell and pulled up the number, connecting the call.

Once I was redirected to the right person, I listened as a head nurse explained my grandfather's particularly bad night; he'd required sedation to help him sleep. She kept pausing as though waiting for me to respond. I acknowledged her more than once, but it wasn't good enough. She seemed to expect something I wasn't providing, and by the time we hung up, I sensed she wasn't happy.

"Everything okay?" Niles asked.

Niles knew about my grandfather's poor health. He knew the old man had raised me from a young age—not why—and my indifference to him as a parental figure.

"He had a bad night, I guess. They had to sedate him to calm him down."

"Do you need to visit?"

"Why?"

"You just said he isn't doing well."

"And my being there won't change that. He'll either improve or he won't. Let's have coffee."

Niles shook his head and aimed for the door. I got the sense he was thinking much the same thing as the head nurse on the phone.

We drove to Peterborough and my house since I wouldn't subject myself to inferior coffee, and Niles knew it. He was about the only person I felt comfortable having in my home. We'd dated for a year, and although it hadn't worked out, it hadn't been terrible. Our love of art and ability to debate amiably had strengthened our connection. My inability to open up and love Niles back was where it had failed. Niles deserved someone who could return the feelings he so freely expressed. Someone who wasn't cold and cynical.

We stayed in the kitchen, Niles occupying the stool where Jersey had sat two weeks prior. The quiet atmosphere between us was soothing. I wasn't much for idle chitchat, and Niles knew that about me. We listened to a concerto he pulled up on his phone, and Niles hummed along on occasion, tapping rhythms on his coffee mug.

"I love Tchaikovsky," he said.

"I'm partial to Russian artists as well."

Niles smirked. "Yes, the maudlin sort are always fans of Dostoevsky. Most people outgrow their emo phases in adulthood. Not you."

"Are you insulting my taste in literature?"

"Never."

We listened to one of the numbered symphonies for a while, neither of us saying a thing.

I had a worn copy of *Meditations* on the table, and Niles pulled it forward and leafed through it, reading short passages and screwing up his brow. "This doesn't suit you," he said after a time.

"Marcus Aurelias is powerful. He has a lot of good things to say."

"Wasn't he a religious sort? Forgive me, I'm out of my league."

"You should be ashamed."

"Enlighten me."

"He believed in divine providence. His writing is representative of a stoic philosophy. It's speculated he wasn't fond of Christianity. In fact, they were persecuting Christians at the time of his reign."

Niles gave me an odd look.

"What? Being an atheist doesn't mean I refuse to educate myself in other areas. I'm a philosophy teacher. Give me some credit. Would you like to discuss stoicism?"

"No. Save your breath." Niles chuckled and continued flipping through the book, stopping on a page and reading a highlighted passage. "*Never let the future disturb you. You will meet it, if you have to, with the same weapons of reason which today arm you against the present.'"*

He glanced up, brow quirked.

I shrugged. "Self-explanatory. Do you need help understanding it?"

"No." He turned to another page and read another marked section. "*'You have power over your mind—not outside events. Realize this, and you will find strength.'*" He feathered through more pages, shaking his head. "You're a complicated man, Koa."

"I'm neither complicated nor straightforward. I am simply one insignificant being on a planet of many. I don't ask anyone to understand me."

"And you don't allow yourself to be understood."

"Not true."

Niles tossed the book aside and picked up *The Adventures of Tom Sawyer* I had yet to put away. A stray sheet of paper marked a page. I'd been thumbing through it since Jersey had delivered it. Niles tugged the page out and opened it. He never had any compunction about invading another's personal space. Only as he skimmed the message scrawled on the front did I realize what he held.

I tore it from his hands, folded it, and tucked it away. "That's private."

"Who's Jersey?"

"Someone I knew a long time ago."

"Someone who wrote you a letter? By hand?"

"Clearly." I couldn't control the snap in my tone. "And it's private." My insides burned at the thought of Niles knowing anything about Jersey.

"Did you respond?"

"Why?"

"Did you?"

"Yes."

"And?"

"And we had coffee. That's it. End of story."

Niles scrutinized me in a way that was disconcerting. He'd spent our entire relationship telling me I was closed off, but he had a unique ability, nonetheless, to see things I didn't want him to see, so I avoided eye contact.

When Rask wandered into the room, I picked him up and paid him some attention, hoping the moment would pass.

It didn't.

"Is he an old lover?"

"No."

"Childhood crush?"

"We were friends a long time ago. Drop it."

"Something happened. There's a story there."

"Excuse me?"

"Something happened. Discussing him makes you snappy and un-comfortable."

"It doesn't."

It did.

"When did you have coffee?"

"I don't think it's your business."

"When did you have coffee?"

I sighed. "Two weeks ago."

"Ahh, it's all coming together. You've been especially distant lately, and it started precisely two weeks ago."

"A coincidence, nothing more."

"No. I don't buy it. Not a lover. A childhood friend. You didn't deny him being an old crush. How young are we talking? Teens? Children?"

"Children." And early teens, but I didn't say as much. Niles was far too astute.

"Pre or post?"

My stomach soured.

Although my colleague didn't know the specifics about my past, he knew there was an event that had profoundly affected me as a child. He'd poked and prodded the wound, but I wouldn't reveal anything. Some things were best to remain buried.

"Post. Can we talk about something else?"

"No. What did he want?"

"It doesn't matter. You're awfully nosy."

"Are you seeing him again?"

"Why would I?"

"Why not? You said he was a friend. I suspect he might have been a childhood crush, but I'm sure it would take a skilled dentist to extract that particular confession."

"Jersey is no one. We don't know each other anymore. Time has since erased any bond that may have existed. Please drop it." I closed my eyes and nuzzled Rask's fur. "Besides, we are two very different people. Worlds apart. There's no point in—"

"Stop. Christ. Spare me the 'everything is pointless' bullshit for five seconds."

I glared across the island. "You're overstepping, Niles. Kindly stay out of it."

"Kindly kiss my ass. News flash. I don't tiptoe around you anymore. If you want to be mad at me for speaking honestly, so be it. You are a cold, closed-off man, Koa. I spent a year trying to chip away at the ice around your heart. You gave me nothing. All I did was touch that letter, and it fired you up. Whoever this Jersey is, he's not nobody. That man has a hold on you."

"He doesn't."

He did. I didn't want him to, and I'd spend two weeks trying to extract him from my mind. If I could return to my bubble of indifference, that would be great.

Niles helped himself to the letter again. I didn't protest and jerk it away that time. What did it matter? There was nothing overly revealing inside. Jersey alluded to us parting on bad terms, nothing more.

"Call him."

"To what purpose? We've reconnected and gone our separate ways again."

"I want to meet him."

I frowned and worked at wrapping my head around Niles's request. "I don't understand."

"How many friends do you have? Answer honestly. Don't include me."

Niles knew the answer. "I don't want or need friends. I'm perfectly content in solitude."

"It's unhealthy. Your views on life are damaging to your mental health."

That was laughable. My past had damaged my mental health.

"Call him. Plan a lunch date for this Saturday. I'll go with you and act as a buffer. How incredible that an old friend reached out after all this time. Who does that? It tells me you two had something special."

"We had nothing. We are nothing. I don't want to entertain this any longer. Please move the conversation forward or listen to your music in silence while I pet my cat and enjoy this coffee while it's hot."

Niles humored me. We discussed his spring concert and retired to the library when our coffee was gone. Niles played the piano, while I curled up in my reading chair and listened. The unsettled feelings I had about Jersey remained. Like a prelude to the flu, it upset my body on a cellular level, messing with my system enough to make me uncomfortable.

The music kept drawing me into unwanted memories of the past, and more than once, I found myself back at Camp Kawartha, nestled inside a log, shoulder to shoulder with a boy whose heat and scent wrapped pleasantly around me, giving off a sense of peace and safety I hadn't known in a long time.

After an odd rendition of a Chopin concerto, Niles spun on the piano bench to face me, a devious smirk I knew all too well curling his lips. "I've been watching you."

I said nothing. What was he getting at now?

"My music moves you."

I still didn't respond. It wasn't the music, but I had a feeling Niles knew that well enough.

"Why didn't you visit your grandfather today?"

I frowned at the non sequitur. "Because there was no reason."

"Because it didn't matter?"

"Precisely. I could go or not go. The outcome wouldn't change."

Niles rolled his eyes to the ceiling and chuckled. "Okay," he said, redirecting his attention. "Correct me if I'm wrong. As someone who shared your bed, I think I know some of your philosophies in life. Even when you struggle to explain them coherently, I have a vague notion of your beliefs."

"Incredible. Yet somehow, I remain perpetually in the dark."

Niles didn't take the bait and plowed on. "You believe life is inherently meaningless. You don't identify as a nihilist, absurdist, or fatalist. Fine. It's neither here nor there. To you, we are insignificant beings that serve no purpose in the universe. Our daily interactions, our laws, good versus evil, none of it means a damn thing. Am I close?"

"Why do I get the feeling your essay on the meaning of life would be as superficial as my students'?"

"I resent that. Shut up and listen. If those things stand true in your mind, then, and hear me out, there is no reason you can't meet with this Jersey guy again."

"Except that I don't want to."

"Meeting with him should, in theory, make no difference to your grand outlook on life—which is miserable, by the way. But"—Niles held up a finger before I could interject—"it makes a difference to mine. So, as your only friend and ex-lover, I think you should humor me in this."

"You're exhausting. Give me one good reason why you want to meet him."

"And if I do, will you consider it?"

"Yes."

Niles rose from the piano bench and approached, standing before my cushy chair, forcing me to crane my neck to look up at him. He brushed the hair off my forehead, his piano-fine fingers cool against my overheated skin. The action was tender and loving, much like he'd always touched me when we were dating. It evoked no reciprocal feelings, and he knew it.

Niles bent and whispered in my ear. "Because, Koa, in all the years we've been friends, not a single person has ever sparked any emotion in you. God help me I tried."

"There is no god."

"Shut up and listen." He pulled back and looked me square in the eye. Niles wasn't often so serious, so I knew what he was trying to say meant something to him. "In the few minutes we discussed Jersey in the kitchen, you came alive. You were hot-tempered. Defensive. His presence, if only in conversation, burned you from the inside out. It was triggering. This man isn't nobody, and I want to meet him because, somehow, in a single letter, on a single coffee date, he accomplished something I worked at for over a year. He succeeded where I failed. You might not be able to admit it, but this guy is important to you."

With that, Niles kissed my forehead. "I have to run. See you tomorrow."

13

Jersey

The first day of May had come and gone. The air was fresh and pungently scented with blossoming spring. Cleaning out my parents' house was taking longer than expected. My ambition faltered two weeks ago when I considered what closing this chapter in my life, selling the house, and leaving the town where I grew up meant. So when work insisted they needed me at the office, I was more than happy to oblige, prolonging the inevitable end to this story.

The furniture was gone, the boxes and bags I'd set aside for donation had been picked up, and the dumpster I'd rented was full. I'd kept a few things, mementos mostly, that reminded me of my childhood. Memories enough to fill three boxes, a shamefully scant collection considering how desperately I clung to this old life. I'd given my mother's family heirlooms to Christine—they'd stayed close through the years—and my grandfather's war medals to my son. I had no need for them, and my apartment in the city wasn't roomy enough to store items I cared little about. Dad's tools went to charity. Their clothes were outdated and worn, but someone short on funds might appreciate them.

The house needed a few repairs, some landscaping, and a fresh coat of paint before it would be ready to sell. I'd considered hiring a couple of kids from town to do the job, but there was something therapeutic about painting that called to me, so I'd been making my way, room by room, freshening it up. I took my time, absorbing the past clinging to the walls and had long ago soaked into the floor.

On the first Saturday in May, after masking my old bedroom, trimming the windows, and cutting along the baseboards, I retired to the backyard for a break with a cold beer. The creaky patio ensemble needed to go into the dumpster too. The endless cold winters had cracked the brittle plastic, and they'd lost their lustrous shine. Years of dirt were engrained into their surfaces, and no amount of scrubbing got them clean again.

They sufficed for beer breaks and contemplative time-outs when the house's ghosts wouldn't leave me alone. I'd spent many hours in the backyard over the past few weeks, alone with my thoughts, stuck in a cloud, wishing to shrug it off and simultaneously wrap myself up until it absorbed me completely.

From where I sat, the future looked bleak, worse than before the OPP had called with the news of my parents' death. Where would I be when the house was sold and I returned home for good?

With the warmer weather, Mom's gardens were coming back to life. Tiny buds decorated the bushes. Curling arms of new growth broke through the soil, reaching for the bright spring sun, and basking in its warmth. Tulips and daisies stood proud, a bursting array of purples, whites, and yellows. They marched across the lawn, defiant and unwilling to be restrained. I didn't miss the irony. Their gardener, the careful hands that had nurtured them year after year, ensuring they thrived, was decaying underground.

A knot pulled tighter in my gut, and I swigged a mouthful of ale, banishing those painful thoughts from my mind. My knee ached from climbing up and down the ladder all week, and I considered retrieving the ice pack from the freezer but couldn't convince myself to move.

The twisted branches of a prolific maple stretched its arms toward the pale blue sky. It was a colossal deciduous, ancient, and powerful. I suspected it was more than a century old. The chips and gouges in its bark had dulled with the passing years, no longer as stark as they had been in my childhood.

Every winter, Dad spent hours sawing and nailing a framework before taking the hose and flooding the backyard, making a rink for all the neighborhood boys to skate and play hockey. On days when I didn't have practice at the arena, I would spend hours on the rink, smacking pucks into a net, skating back and forth, and practicing my turns and stops. For a challenge, Dad would hang a target on the maple tree, much the same as the targets we shot at during archery at camp, and I would aim for the center, dashing pucks against the maple's thick bark until chunks flew off into the snow and the paper hung in shreds.

The maple had survived my abuse. My parents had not. And there was no going back in time to repair the damage.

My pocket vibrated, drawing me from the reverie. An unknown number had sent a text. I opened it with a frown and read. *I'll be at Pestle & Mortar this afternoon at 2. Their coffee isn't nearly as good as mine, but they make a decent Reuben. If you wanted to join me, I wouldn't object.*

A second text came through as I finished reading the first. *It's Koa, by the way.*

Cold and perfunctory, a reflection of the man I'd met a few weeks back.

Stunned and moderately confused, I stared at the messages, my beer forgotten on the plastic side table. It had been weeks since my meeting with Koa. For as much as I'd wanted to rekindle a friendship, I hadn't gotten the same vibe in return. The years had been too numerous to transcend. Cutting my losses, I had not contacted Koa again.

It was after one. Searching up Pestle & Mortar, I discovered it was in Peterborough. Was Koa's last-minute invitation a test? If I had been in Toronto, I would never have made it on time. Perhaps that was his hope. Reaching out with impossible standards only to say he'd tried and I'd failed. Would he do that?

I didn't have time to contemplate if I wanted to get there on time.

I typed a quick *OMW* and glanced at my paint-speckled shirt and jeans. My hands were the same, and I didn't have time to clean up. If he wanted me presentable, he should have given me a heads-up. I darted inside to grab the keys to the Gladiator and took off.

Lakefield to Peterborough was a fifteen to twenty-minute drive. It gave me time to examine the purpose behind Koa's invitation and what I hoped to achieve in pursuing a friendship he didn't seem interested in. Unless he'd changed his mind.

Everything I'd said during our last visit was true. He awoke a long-dormant part of my soul. I craved the innocence of childhood and those blissfully happy years at camp before the game had dominated my life. Before I'd forgotten how to live for me and started living for everyone else.

But then why Koa? Why not look up Bruce or Justin? Logically, they should grant me the same sense of serenity, shouldn't they?

Was it the feelings of affection that had surfaced upon finding those letters? Was it that Koa had been a catalyst to discovering who I was—even when it had taken several more years to put a name to it?

I couldn't answer any of those questions. Whatever had driven me to seek out Koa, whatever had made me leap at the chance to see him again despite his adamancy we let the past go, was beyond my ability to understand.

The fact was, Koa had texted, and I'd jumped.

Pestle & Mortar was a quaint coffee and bistro on Lansdown Street in the southwest corner of Peterborough. Koa's Audi was in the parking lot, so I hadn't missed him despite being ten minutes late.

At two in the afternoon, the bistro was quiet. Soft sunlight filtered through the sheer curtains lining the front windows. The decor had a homey feel: wooden shelves lined with handcrafted stoneware and framed art hung on the walls. Potted plants gave the restaurant a sense of intimacy and closeness. Unlike a kitschy diner where loud kitchen noises and a rushed atmosphere prevailed, Pestle & Mortar invited its guests to get cozy and stay a while.

Koa was not alone.

The guy with the man bun who I had seen at the school was with him, dressed in a queerly articulative, artsy fashion, a contrast to Koa's subdued layers of protection—a familiar beige wool cardigan over several earth-toned patterned shirts.

I faltered at finding the two of them together but moved my feet and approached when Koa glanced up and found me at the door. So, this wasn't an intimate lunch date. He'd brought reinforcements. A quiet disappointment pierced my chest. Thinking back, Koa hadn't quite answered my inquiry about his dating life during our last visit. Was this guy a boyfriend? The vibe said yes.

The stranger noticed Koa's inattention and followed his gaze, his face splitting into a wide grin.

"Hey," I said to Koa when I got to the table. I pulled out a seat across from them and sat cautiously, flashing my attention to the other guy and holding out a hand. "Hi. We haven't met. Jersey Reid." Then I noticed my paint-flecked fingers and chuckled. "Sorry, I'm a mess. I was painting and didn't have time to clean up. It's dry. I swear."

Unflinching, the man shook, his fingers long and dainty, hands softer than they had any right to be. "Niles Edwidge. It's nice to meet you."

"He's a coworker," Koa explained.

"A friend," Niles corrected, nudging Koa's side. "I've heard so much about you."

"You have?" Boggled, I flipped my attention between the two.

"He hasn't. Niles is presumptuous and arrogant. He's drawn conclusions based on paltry evidence. Ignore him. He insisted on being here."

"Isn't he delightful?" Niles rested a hand on the back of Koa's chair in a familiar fashion as he leaned back. "What are you painting?"

"My parents' house. Fixing it up to sell."

Koa hadn't taken his eyes off me, and his undivided attention stole my focus from the superfluous man at his side. Layers and layers of clothing. Layers and layers of mystery. My childhood friend was as unreadable that afternoon as he'd been in our youth.

"It's good to see you again," I said. "I didn't expect your text."

Koa scanned my paint-stained shirt. "I should have called sooner. Apologies. I ran out of time."

"No, he ran out of courage," Niles corrected. "It was like pulling teeth to get him to agree to this. The poor guy dropped everything and raced over here covered in paint to see you. What does that tell you?"

Koa cleared his throat and spoke to Niles. "Perhaps you could find us menus."

"Of course." Niles did as he was asked, leaving Koa and me alone, but not without sending a subtle wink in my direction.

When he was gone, Koa mumbled, "I'm sorry I didn't give you more notice."

"It's fine. Why am I here, Koa?"

"It's Niles's opinion that our reconnecting would be good for me. Since he is a relentless pest and finds humor in prying into my affairs, it was easier to agree than to continuously battle him on the subject."

"Flattering." I glanced at the far side of the room where Niles was chatting and laughing with a full figured, silver-haired woman in an apron. "Who's Niles?"

"I told you. A coworker." Koa cut his gaze to the table, breaking eye contact for the first time since I'd walked in.

"Try again."

Koa sighed. "An ex with far too much interest in my personal life. We're... friends."

The woman handed Niles a stack of menus. My time was running out. If this meeting had been forced on Koa, I wanted nothing to do with it.

"Before your *friend* gets back, answer honestly. Would you prefer I end this here and now? I can make an excuse and leave if you don't want to be here. I would never have pushed."

"I know you wouldn't." Quieter, he added, "You never did."

"Well?"

A pained expression crossed Koa's face. He stared intently at the table's surface, hands half covered by the cardigan's sleeves, fingers twisting and twining together. Before Niles returned, Koa lifted his wary amber eyes and reached across the table, taking hold of my wrist as he whispered, "Please stay."

And what could I do? In that moment, Koa wasn't a forty-four-year-old, unreadable man. He was an eleven-year-old boy reaching out to me in the dark, begging me to stay by his side and fight the demons only he could see.

I'd stayed then, and I would stay now.

14

Jersey

CAMP KAWARTHA 1990

The guys hated Koa. He was the strange kid who wandered alone in the woods and talked to himself. He wouldn't play archery or capture the flag, choosing to read under a tree instead, and the counselors treated him like he was made of glass. We all knew he had to take medicine, and Justin said he overheard it was because Koa was schizo. I didn't know if it was true. Justin liked attention and lied a lot. But I'd seen the blank fits so many times, I wondered.

We didn't play together during the day, and our nighttime escapes were limited. When we did sneak out, it was like living in a whole different world. Koa was different with me, excitable and imaginative, and we had fun together, provided I was careful about how we played. No more bad guys and bandits. I did everything I could not to scare him.

On random nights, Koa cried in his sleep, waking our entire cabin. Crying at eleven years old was bad, and he suffered the consequences.

One morning in our second week of camp, Koa peed the bed, which was way worse. Not a single person let him live it down. News spread like the plague, and even the six-year-olds on the other side of camp made fun of him.

Koa's peculiarities made it hard to be his friend during the daytime. I risked being an outcast. When the guys decided to make Koa's life a living hell, I did my best to redirect their attention or defend him. It didn't always work, so too often, I stood by and watched it happen, my heart twisted in a knot.

Justin stole his toothbrush and dropped it down the outhouse toilet.

Bruce smeared mud on the back of Koa's shorts, so it looked like he'd shit himself.

Peter spread rumors that Koa's mom and dad were brother and sister, which was why he wasn't right in the head.

Daniel used words like faggot and retard—until the counselors got mad and threatened to send him home.

If Koa was affected by the nasty names, rude comments, and pranks, he didn't show it. He spent his days trapped in his own world, seemingly content playing in the forest or reading his books. It was as though he lived in a fairy-tale land or another dimension.

More times than not, I wondered why I felt so defensive inside. Why my friends' unkindness prickled my nerves. So what if I gave him a bracelet and promised I wouldn't be mean. That was a year ago. It didn't count anymore, did it?

But something inside my brain prevented me from bullying him like everyone else. Something drove me to sneak out at night and play with him in the woods or crawl inside our log for long chats.

One rainy afternoon, we were stuck inside the rec building where the air was sticky, and it smelled like damp socks and Bruce's farts.

Arts and crafts had been set up, along with quiet board games. Randy encouraged kids to join him in circle activities, which were dumb and babyish. The younger boys gravitated to his corner of the room while the rest of us horsed around, itching to get back outside and run.

Rainy days at camp sucked.

The guys and I had gathered at the craft table, but none of us were making anything. Justin rolled spitballs and launched them with a plastic straw at Koa, who sat against the wall nearby, nose in a book. Even when a wet, chewed wad of paper slapped him in the knee, he didn't react. Bruce snorted and tore more paper for Justin. Together, they chewed new ammo. The next ball flew and landed in Koa's hair, where it stayed. Koa didn't flinch.

"Knock it off," I said to Justin. "He doesn't even care. Let's make something."

"Crafts are gay," Peter said.

"You're gay," I returned. It was the ultimate comeback, and the others laughed.

Eventually, they got bored of Koa and moved on to an aggressive game of snakes and ladders, which was why a short time later, when Koa slipped out the door and into the rainy afternoon, I was the only one who noticed.

Where was he going? He hadn't asked permission to leave, but none of the counselors seemed to have registered his absence. Somedays, it was like Koa was invisible to the adults. So much of our bullying went under their radar, and it made me wish they would open their eyes and pay attention.

Pretending I needed a bathroom break—which meant a short jaunt across the field to the outhouses—I quit the current game and checked in with Randy to be sure it was okay before I left. He told me to be fast.

I told him I had a raging poop forming. He laughed and insisted I take my time.

I slipped out into the dreary day and scanned the open field, catching sight of Koa as he vanished down the path to the lake. Head down against the weather, I raced after him. Rain splattered my face regardless and soaked through my shirt. It felt good after being stuck in a stuffy building for so long.

I caught up with Koa in time to see him fling his paperback in a grand arc into the water. My jaw hit the floor, and I faltered a few feet from the boulder at the lake's edge where he was perched. The splash was barely perceptible; the thunderous rain pattering against the water drowned it out. I scanned the area where the book had landed but didn't see it. Billions of rain dimples and ripples from the wind marred the lake's surface.

Koa turned and startled at finding me there. His face streamed water. It dripped from his nose and off his chin. It plastered his hair to his forehead. The thin cotton shirt he wore was see-through and glued to his frame. I fared no better. Even my running shoes were full up.

"Why did you do that?" I had to shout to be heard. His actions confounded me. Koa loved reading. He was always with his nose in a book.

"I hated it. It's a stupid story, and I don't want to read it anymore."

It made no sense. That wasn't a reason to throw a book in the lake. "But... What book was it?"

"*Lord of the Flies*. They killed Piggy."

"Who?" I'd never heard of the book and didn't know who Piggy was.

"The mean boys. The ones like you and your friends. They killed him, and I don't want to read books where people die."

A stab of hurt pierced my heart at hearing Koa categorize me as a bully equal to Bruce, Justin, Daniel, and Peter, but I didn't know how to address the comment, so I went with what felt easier.

"You could have just stopped reading it if you hated it. You didn't have to throw it in the lake." A snort of laughter escaped me, and I pinched my lips together. "I mean, that was kinda dramatic."

Koa crossed his gangly arms around his midsection. "You don't understand. My grandfather will make me finish it at home if I don't finish it here. But if I lose it or tell him someone stole it, maybe I'll never have to read it again."

I didn't tell him his grandfather could easily buy a new copy. Koa wasn't stupid, and I was sure he'd figured that out already.

"Man, if I threw all the books I hated in the lake, it wouldn't be a lake anymore. It would be a mountain." I snorted again, but Koa didn't even crack a smile.

"Why did you follow me?" he asked.

I shrugged. I couldn't have answered if I wanted to.

Koa glanced along the path at my back. "Are they coming too?"

"No."

"You aren't really my friend." He held up his arm where the bracelet I'd made him hung sodden from his thin wrist. "This was a lie."

"No, it wasn't. I don't call you names like them."

"You don't play with me. You only like me during our nighttime adventures when the other boys aren't around to see us together."

That was true, and I didn't know how to respond. It didn't feel good to be called out, but Koa would never understand how hard it was to be his friend and not get shunned.

We stared at one another for a long time before I approached the boulder and climbed up beside him, peering out across the lake. The dock was to our left, a half dozen canoes tied to posts, bobbing in the restless water. The sky was close, a heavy burden of clouds hanging low enough the world shrank under their assault. I turned my face to the heavens and closed my eyes, letting the world shower down on me.

No wildlife stirred. The trees sagged, sodden with the weight of rain. Noise surrounded us, a thunderous pattering, hitting the water, the rocks, and the shore.

"I'm here now," I said. "Does that count?"

"How come you're here?"

"I don't know. I wanted to know what you were doing. I don't hate you. Do you want me to go?"

Koa hugged himself and said nothing, following my gaze across the lake. All our differences washed away, and we were simply two boys again. I didn't care if Koa was different. Sometimes, I felt different too. Since he hadn't told me to leave, I stayed.

"Want to go for a swim?" I asked.

I expected him to say no or give me a funny look, but Koa shrugged. "Okay."

We stripped to our underwear—pointlessly since we couldn't get wetter—and jumped into the water. It was warm and refreshing. We swam and laughed and splashed each other. I chased Koa, and he chased me. At one point, something bumped my shoulder, and I turned to find a sodden, floating copy of *Lord of the Flies*.

I pushed it beneath the surface before Koa could see it. Something about the book had upset him, and he seemed to have forgotten it. No sense in reopening the old wound.

The more we played, the more Koa laughed. The more he laughed, the happier I got.

After a time, we swam ashore and sat on the boulder beside our clothes. When I asked if Koa wanted to try sneaking out again at midnight to play Tom and Huck in the dark, he told me sure. When I asked how come his grandfather made him read books he didn't like, he shrugged and got lost in his head.

I stopped asking questions.

After a time, Koa said, "Everyone's going to die someday. You can't stop it."

"I know."

"Does it scare you?"

"Yeah. A little. What about you?"

"No. I can't wait to die."

I squirmed, unsure where to put myself or how to respond.

"What do you think happens after we die?" Koa asked.

"Um... I guess we go to heaven."

"My grandfather says the same. I don't believe in god. I think when you're dead, you're dead."

I chewed my lip and picked at a scab on my knee. The conversation was too weird and complex for my eleven-year-old brain, and I would have rather talked about pirates and treasures like we usually did. Death was not something I liked to think about.

Eventually, we dressed and wandered back to the rec hall. The guys didn't ask why I'd been gone so long, but Randy noticed how wet Koa and I were and told us to go change.

The heavy rain hadn't let up, so sneaking out was a no-go. The downpour gave our cabin ambient background noise. So when Koa cried in his sleep that night, no one woke up. I slept on the top bunk and heard it all.

I feared his nightmare would make him pee the bed again, so carefully, quietly, I scaled the back end of our bunk and sat on the edge of his mattress. It was too hot in the cabin, so we all slept in our underwear. Koa was sprawled on top of his sleeping bag, hair stuck to his sweaty forehead, a sheen coating his lanky body. I shook his shoulder until he woke with a start, flipping over in a frantic hurry to see who was there. Huge, terrified eyes stared at me in the dark. My eyes were as adjusted to night as they were going to get, and Koa's pale face seemed to glow. Silver tear tracks lined his cheeks, and his breathing was hitched and raspy.

"You're crying," I said when Koa continued to blink in confusion. "Were you having a nightmare?"

He nodded and glanced around the quiet cabin at all the unmoving bodies lost in their dreamlands. Koa must have registered no one else was awake and looked back warily.

"What were you dreaming about?" I asked.

His lower lip trembled. "They shouldn't have killed Piggy. I hate that book."

"Oh. Good thing it's at the bottom of the lake now."

Koa nodded.

"Sorry I woke you. I didn't want you to pee the bed again."

In a panic, Koa fumbled a hand over the front of his underwear. Relief flooded his face.

Since I'd saved him from shame and his nightmare was gone, I figured I might as well go back to my bunk and try to sleep, but when I moved to go, Koa's shaky fingers wrapped around my wrist. "Please stay," he said, his voice meek.

He trembled, teeth chattering, but it wasn't cold. Worried someone would catch me talking to Koa in the middle of the night, I checked the sleeping bodies around the room. No one had stirred. The rain pounded the tin roof of the cabin.

"Okay. For a minute."

Koa moved over, and I lay down. Like I'd done in the log, I wrapped an arm around him, offering comfort like my mom did to me when I had a bad dream. It seemed like the right thing to do. Koa buried his face against my arm. His damp cheek told me he was still crying. His shaking eventually calmed. His breathing evened out. In no time, he was fast asleep.

I didn't know what to do. If the guys caught me like this, I'd be shunned forever. They would call us faggots. It would be my hair full of spitballs and my pants covered in mud.

But I didn't move. Holding Koa kindled a warmth deep, deep inside my belly. It was like the soft kiss of butterfly wings. Strange, not in a bad way, but in a terrifying and exhilarating way.

I stayed like that for an hour. Only when my eyelids grew heavy, and I feared falling asleep did I go back to my bed.

Three more times that summer, I woke Koa from nightmares before his cries alerted the rest of the cabin. All three times, he clung to my hand and whimpered, "Please stay."

And I did.

Each time, the butterflies multiplied.

15

Koa

PRESENT DAY

"Please stay," I whispered before Niles returned. Jersey's warm skin under my fingers was not the same as it had been years ago on the bottom bunk in the dark of cabin eight. The skin of his wrist was coarser with age, covered in dark hair, and flecked with specs of paint. The bones underneath were denser, no longer in the growing stages of youth.

The unsureness left Jersey. His gaze softened. He nodded, shoulders settling, body molding to the chair, no longer cusping the edge of flight.

I released my hold as Niles returned with two menus, not three. He pushed one in front of me and the other in front of Jersey. "Turns out I can't stick around. You two fine gentlemen are on your own. It was lovely to meet you, Jersey. If you're in the neighborhood, Timber Creek Academy is having its spring concert at the end of the month. You should swing by. My students are exceptional. Do you like classical music?" Niles didn't wait for Jersey to respond. He clapped my shoulder. "Either way, Koa has all the details. Hopefully, I'll see you around."

Bending, Niles pecked a kiss on my temple and added too low for Jersey to hear, "Try not to be morose. He's a definite looker. If you don't scoop him up, I might."

Folding his coat over an arm, Niles bowed out with a smug grin and a wink. Strolling away, he kept his shoulders back and his chin high. Jersey watched him go, turning back when the bistro's door fell shut.

He touched his temple. "Your ex is awfully chummy."

"It's his default setting." *A direct contrast to my inaffection*, but I didn't add that. "You'll have to excuse him. Niles has the wrong idea."

I opened the menu and browsed even though I knew what I was ordering. I'd had a hunch Niles was going to abandon me. The whole thing was a setup, and he would hear my opinion on the matter on Monday.

"Wrong idea? If he's trying to win you back, he probably shouldn't have left me alone with you."

I huffed. The notion of Niles trying to win me back was comical. "No. That's not what I meant. Niles has got it in his head that you're an old childhood crush and that we—"

"I *am* an old childhood crush." The smile on Jersey's face was boyish. "You tried to kiss me, remember?"

"Distinctly. An action I regret, considering what followed."

The smile faltered.

Dammit. Admitting the foibles of my past wasn't how I wanted to start this lunch date. I would have preferred they stayed buried. We'd discussed them once. We certainly didn't need another go-round. The past was in the past.

But such was life.

Such was Niles.

"Regardless, my nosy ex is unaware of our history and thought it would be beneficial for me to... rekindle a friendship with you. He likely thinks our meeting might stir up old romantic feelings or something. He's whimsical and sentimental. Musicians. I swear, it's ingrained in their DNA. Anyhow, I agreed to meet with you again."

I closed the menu and set it aside. "You'll have to forgive me if this whole encounter is awkward. I'm not adept at making or being friends with people. I'm used to being alone. Aside from teaching, I struggle to be social. Ask Niles. It drives him mad. The world and I don't mesh. We never have."

Jersey's smile was back. He had specks of paint on the coarse hairs of his trim beard. "Sounds exactly like the boy I knew."

"Worse. Believe me."

"Not possible. Koa, you were the most solitary child at camp. The only person you associated with outside of me was Huck. And he wasn't real. He's not still kicking around, is he?"

I got the sense Jersey was only partly joking.

"No." My cheeks warmed, and I searched for Fern, Pestle & Mortar's jovial and aging owner. Niles must have asked her to kindly leave us alone for a bit.

"I was kidding."

"No, you weren't. You wanted to know if I was still that unstable kid from camp."

And I was. Partly.

When Jersey looked at me, he saw a child. He saw the boy who talked to imaginary friends and wet his pants when the dreams got bad. Would he be able to separate the boy from the man? Sure, my bladder control was no longer an issue, the nightmares had abated years ago, and Huck had been replaced by Rask, but I was still the same troubled soul deep inside. Detached. Unapproachable. Morose, as Niles tended to put it. I still carried a darkness within that would never go away. My problems might have matured with age, but they were still there and would be until I died. I wasn't any less of an outcast.

Jersey added his menu to mine and reached for my hand. I wanted to pull away, but something in the touch was grounding. I hadn't been gifted with thick bone structure or sturdy muscles. My frame was willowy and frail. Growing up, I'd felt vapor-thin and often pretended no one could see me. With little to no meat on my bones, I suffered from perpetually chilly fingers and toes.

"I never cared how different you were all those years ago, and I don't care now. I would love to rekindle a friendship. Most of my childhood memories have turned to dust, but our days at camp are so vivid it's as though they happened yesterday."

"And those are positive memories?"

Jersey chuckled. "Yeah, why?"

"Odd. For most people, good memories fade. It's the damaging ones that remain with more clarity. Time won't erase them, and they live inside us, slowly poisoning us to death."

"I thought Niles told you not to be morose."

"I don't think you were meant to hear that."

Another soft laugh. "All right. Look. I can stay, and we can get to know each other as adults, or I can go. This isn't up to your buddy, Niles. It's up to you. I don't like that he might have pushed you into it."

"He didn't. Push is the wrong word. Niles strongly encouraged it, and I value his opinion."

"Okay. So I'm staying?"

I stared into Jersey's soft denim-colored eyes, so earnest, hopeful, and full of life. So much like the boy who had rescued me time after time at camp. The boy I'd kissed. The boy who had rejected me.

"Stay, but don't set high expectations. As Niles likes to say, I'm an acquired taste, and most people don't acquire it. You may never warm up to me as I am now."

"Koa, I warmed up to you when I was eleven years old and you threw *Lord of the Flies* into the lake."

I chuckled at the memory. "You called me dramatic."

Jersey disconnected our hands and fell back in his seat, laughing. "I repeat. You threw a book into the lake because you didn't like where the plot went."

"I regret that. As an English teacher, I'm appalled and ashamed of my treatment of classic literature. I'm a little more desensitized now. Piggy's death is quite symbolic in a literary sense."

"I'm guessing your grandfather bought you a new copy?"

"Turned out he had another on the bookshelf." After beating me with it until I couldn't sit down for three days, I'd been forced to read it out loud. Every page. But I kept those extra details to myself.

"Do you still hate it?"

"My views have since changed."

Jersey chuckled. Fern appeared from the back of the restaurant and came to our table, asking if we were ready to order. On my suggestion, Jersey asked for a Reuben, the same as me. The coffee was palatable, so I ordered a specific Arabic blend that suited my particular tastes. Jersey copied.

Alone again, we stared at one another. We had history, but a chasm of years between the past and the present needed to be filled. I wasn't sure how to begin. My ineptness must have shown, and Jersey took the reins.

"So, when did you and Niles date?"

"You seem awfully concerned about my love life."

He scratched at a burn mark on the table's surface. "Curious is all. Never mind. What do you like to do in your free time?"

I touched his hand, stilling the motion and grabbing his attention. When he glanced up, I said, "Niles ended it between us two years ago."

"He ended it? I would have thought it was the other way around. He's... very affectionate toward you."

"That's Niles."

"Why did he end it?"

I pulled my hand back, folding my fingers together. "It's complicated. I couldn't give him what he needed."

Fern arrived with our coffees, and I wrapped my hands around the steaming mug, absorbing its heat. "And you? You told me about your divorce, but that was ages ago. Is there anyone in your life?"

"Not recently. Middle-aged dating is not all it's cracked up to be. I don't have it in me to hang out at bars or clubs, and most nights, I'm all too happy to crash on the couch with bad TV. There are dating apps nowadays, but I haven't had much luck in that department either."

"How is it the famous hockey player doesn't have women lined up at his door?"

Jersey laughed, the skin beside his eyes creasing. "You're funny. My fame, if you can call it that, died fifteen years ago. I'm no one special. Nothing but a washed-up has-been."

"So hockey fans don't follow you around, begging for autographs."

"Nope. They never did. When I go out, mostly no one even recognizes me. It's a rarity if someone connects my face with the twenty-year-old hockey player I used to be. Besides, I was background noise in a sea of superstars. I didn't even qualify as an influencer for commercials or anything."

"I think you're being modest. You played professional hockey. That's not nothing. Do you know how many kids dream of turning pro?"

"I do. I was one of them. No one tells you what it means and how fast the dream can be ripped away." Something passed in Jersey's eyes, and I got the sense I was poking at an old painful wound. He played it off well, remaining humble, but the hurt in his core bled to the surface.

I changed the subject, backtracking to his other question. "I've never followed sports. Don't watch TV at all, in fact. It's all pointless drivel. I read, write, play music—poorly—and put all the energy I have left into teaching the next generation to think—a task that has grown more concerning over the years. Social media is slowly rotting the brains of our youth."

"So I shouldn't look you up on Facebook?"

"You won't find me."

"Noted." Jersey sipped his coffee. "You always did like to read. At camp, your nose was always in a book."

"The world was unkind. I found escape in literature. It's the one gratitude I have when it comes to my grandfather. He gifted me an appreciation for the written word."

Jersey ran a hand over his beard and balanced his chin in an up-turned palm. Sorrow peered back at me. "The world really was unkind to you, wasn't it?"

"I won't discuss the past, Jersey. Kindly leave it, or I'll walk out the door."

"Fair enough. Can I ask something personal?"

I nodded but cut my gaze to the counter, hoping to see Fern with our lunch. He'd had his warning, and I wasn't bluffing.

"Is your grandfather still in your life?"

"He's in a nursing home full of cancer."

"I'm sorry."

I glanced back. "For what?"

"For... your grandfather's poor health."

"You're not responsible. Cancer is indiscriminate, and we all have to die eventually. Unless we take our own lives, we don't get much of a choice about how it happens."

Jersey didn't seem to know what to say to that.

I heard Niles in my head, telling me to lighten up.

Our lunch arrived shortly after my unfiltered comment had caused a swell of silence between us.

We ate.

Jersey talked about his job as a physiotherapist and life in the big city. He talked about various sports injuries he'd seen over the years. When I asked about his accident on the ice, he explained.

"I played defenseman. Are you familiar with positions in hockey?"

"No."

"Basically, my job entailed stopping the other team from scoring in our goal. Well, I was deep in our zone, doing my job, and I took a nasty hit. Before I landed on the ice, I heard this loud pop. No idea it came from me until I tried to get back on my feet. Torn ACL. The pain in my knee was intense. I managed to get myself off the ice but knew it was bad. Had to undergo surgery. Twice actually. If I had been ten years younger, I may have bounced right back, but as it stood, my body was resistant to healing. Even today, when I go too hard on the treadmill or overexert my knee, I get an ache, making me hobble like an old man."

"Sounds painful."

"It was, but it hurt my pride more than anything, especially when the new season rolled around, and I still wasn't strong enough to play. Add in the fact that I got addicted to pain meds, and my life imploded."

The topic was heavy, and since I knew what it was like trudging through a swamp of ugly, I tried a new angle.

When I asked how painting the house was going, he shared about the slow progress, including the long list of repairs he had yet to make.

Another difficult subject. It seemed I wasn't alone in misery. Jersey had accumulated plenty of his own.

He asked about my classes, and I tried to explain how I combined classic literature and philosophy. He understood neither, and I caught him nodding along and agreeing for the sake of it, a blank expression in his eyes.

We had nothing in common, and the conversation grew quiet.

When our meal ended, Jersey refused to let me pay.

In the parking lot, we stood between our two vehicles with an awkward air of indecision floating between us. Lunch had proven a truth I'd long known. Jersey and I weren't compatible as friends or anything else. We were night and day. A long-standing jock and a book nerd.

Since I wasn't one for games or beating around the bush, I decided to be blunt.

"I'm sorry this didn't work out. Thank you for lunch. I'm really sorry about your parents, and I hope you get everything worked out."

"Wait. What are you saying?"

I glanced toward the road. The afternoon traffic on Lansdown was steady. People moved about their day and lives, indifferent to those around them. "I figured it was obvious."

"What was obvious? I'm confused. You'll need to spell it out. I thought we had a nice lunch, and you were open to the prospect of… friendship."

But he said the word like it was a substitution for another.

"What's the point, Jersey?"

"The point?"

I motioned between us. "We aren't the same. In fact, we couldn't be more opposite. That's always been true, hasn't it? Sure, we formed a somewhat tremulous friendship as children, but we aren't kids anymore. Our interests don't align. Our lives are different. What's the point? What is there to gain? Are we building a friendship? Are we... rekindling a romance that never existed? I hope you realize how inane the notion would be. Are we—"

"Stop." Jersey's boyish smile creased his eyes, and he tucked his thumbs into the front pockets of his jeans. His tattoos caught the sunlight—colorful flowers in bloom among other black and white designs. Their density and complexity drew the eye, and I'd spent all of lunch trying not to stare or ask questions. Tattoos were personal.

"You speak like a literary professor," he said. "Has anyone ever told you that?"

Niles had, but I chose to stay quiet and waited for Jersey to say what he had to say.

He stepped into my bubble and lowered his voice. "I disagree."

"With what part?"

"All of it. The romance between us, although juvenile and immature, *did* exist. And if you can't reflect back and see it, you aren't as smart as you think. And I don't feel like the notion of revisiting it would be inane. People don't have to be alike to get along. They don't need shared interests or hobbies. Sometimes, it's their differences that make the relationship better. So what is the point? The point is, I had strong feelings for you as a child, and upon discovering those letters and seeing you again, I realized those feelings are still there. Still alive. I've always been drawn to you, Koa. I couldn't explain it then and can't explain it now, but that's the truth. If you don't want to consider reexploring our youthful romance as adults, I would be satisfied to rediscover a friendship. We can learn about each other again, dig deeper, and find the things we have in common because I'm sure they exist. All I know is when you texted and asked me to join you for lunch, I nearly imploded with excitement, and life has been pretty dreary this past month."

Through Jersey's speech, I stared at the asphalt parking lot between us. Before I could formulate a response or think about how I could possibly explain the sheer disappointment he would feel when he got to know me better and discovered I was empty of emotions, a shell of a man, he closed the gap and drew my face up with warm hands cradling my jaw.

"Don't dismiss this before we give it a shot. Think about it."

"I don't know how to do this, Jersey. In the end, I will only hurt you."

"I'm a pretty tough guy." His gaze fell to my mouth and lingered. "I was scared of what transpired between us at fourteen and ran. But I'm not afraid anymore. I know who I am, and I don't want to close this door just because we have nothing in common. That's an excuse."

Jersey pressed his lips to mine. His beard rasped my chin as his warm mouth took me in.

I closed my eyes as the earth beneath my feet shifted.

His tongue brushed lightly against my lower lip, kindling heat in my belly. A long-dormant part of my soul stirred, and I was frightened. I was comfortable feeling dead inside, but with his warm hands, sure touch, and confidence, Jersey wanted to bring me back to life.

But I didn't know how to live in this world. I didn't know how to feel or hope, and I certainly didn't know how to love.

I rested my hands on his chest and didn't quite push him away, but he got the hint and ended the kiss. Jersey remained in my bubble, his mouth hovering a hairsbreadth from mine. "You're trembling."

I was, but I couldn't draw attention to it. I couldn't agree or disagree or express the turmoil his return had caused. I'd spent my entire adult life embracing the sheer redundancy of it, not caring about anything, going through the motions, and distancing myself from people and situations.

It was easier.

And then Jersey came back, and with one kiss, my tenuous control slipped, and I was falling.

He stroked my cheek with the rough edge of his thumb. "You have my number. Think about what I said."

With one last soft kiss, a whisper against my lips, and one last lingering look into my eyes, Jersey released me, got into his too-big Jeep, and drove away.

I stood alone in the empty parking lot at Pestle & Mortar, staggered, confused, and with my long-dead heart thumping with new life behind my ribs.

I wasn't equipped to deal with any of this.

But a quiet voice inside me urged me to try.

16

Jersey

The following three weeks consisted of short text conversations between Koa and me. He would present what he considered a justifiable reason why we couldn't pursue a relationship and/or friendship, and I countered it. He started with arguments I'd already disputed, but I happily reiterated my opinion.

Koa: We have nothing in common.

Jersey: It gives us more things to talk about.

Three days passed in silence before he tried a different angle.

Koa: I have a diagnosed inability to connect with people. Do you want a doctor's note? I can get one.

Jersey: Haha. We connected perfectly fine over lunch the other day and never had an issue as kids. Plus, your ability to share those details helps me understand you better, so thank you for sharing.

Koa: *groans* You sound like my therapist.

Several more days passed. I was at the office, finishing up paperwork, when he tried again.

Koa: I will not share my past with you.

Jersey: I've never asked and respect if there are things you can't tell me.

Days went by.

One evening, after smacking my thumb with a hammer during banister repairs, as I was nursing my wound with an ice pack and shot of bourbon, my phone chimed with Koa's latest argument.

Koa: You can do far better than me. I'm damaged goods.

Jersey: We all have scars.

Then, a few days after that.

Koa: My work schedule leaves me terribly busy. I don't have time to dedicate to building new friendships.

Jersey: Now you're making excuses. Besides, don't the summer holidays start at the end of June?

It was the last Monday in May, three weeks and two days since I'd kissed him in the parking lot at Pestle & Mortar when Koa broke.

Koa: Niles's spring concert is this Friday night. Would you like to attend with me?

I smiled at the message as I stood outside the therapy room, a patient waiting on the other side of the door. I typed a quick reply.

Jersey: I'd be honored.

⤝

The concert was at seven, so I rescheduled my last two appointments on Friday afternoon so I could get away from the office with enough time to race home, change, and drive to Timber Creek Academy. Koa and I planned to meet at the school. He'd turned down my offer to pick him up, explaining he was staying after class to help Niles organize the affair.

I pulled into the school parking lot at six thirty. With the bustle, I had to drive around twice to find a spot big enough to accommodate the Gladiator. Dozens of parents spilled out of cars, arriving to see their children perform. Several students gathered in the courtyard, socializing and watching the commotion.

The concert was to take place in the school auditorium. I didn't know where it was, so I followed the crowd, listening to the buzz of proud parents discussing their genius children and their futures.

Koa had promised to meet me in the foyer at quarter to seven. I made my way there and found a spot near the wall to linger as the flow of parents continued through the double doors into the auditorium.

It had been a long time since I'd been inside a high school. Albeit, Timber Creek was no ordinary school. It was an elite academy, and its prestige showed. Plaques of students' achievements lined the walls, showing past scholarship winners, honors students, and specialty awards for insanely high accomplishments. Framed newspaper clippings talked about those who had gone on to make a difference in the world.

I scanned a few articles, feeling small and unimportant in comparison. These kids were brilliant. They became specialized surgeons and researchers. They discovered cures for diseases or wrote for influential magazines about topics I couldn't begin to understand. One article talked about a former student, Dr. Calvin Gerbert, a nuclear physicist, who had been hired by one of the top research hospitals in the country to take charge of their nuclear medicine department. A girl named Kassie Valdai, who had also earned a Ph.D., was making strides in some kind of gene study.

Koa appeared beside me as I puzzled over the next article in line. "You made it."

"I did." I motioned at the wall of honors. "Christ, these kids are smart. I can't understand half of these article write-ups. The words are too big. Me and my B average wouldn't have made it a day here."

"They aren't all successful. A handful make something of themselves, and the rest drown under the pressures of university. Sex, drugs, and no more parental guidance is a bad mix. A recipe for disaster in many."

Abandoning the newspaper clippings, I turned to face Koa for the first time, taking him in.

He meekly smiled, tight, tense, and uncertain. "Hello, Jersey."

"Hey. You look incredible."

"You flatter me."

"It's true. I've wanted to say it since the day I showed up at your house."

The cable-knit sweater was absent. In its place, Koa wore a brown tweed jacket and matching vest, a pale-blue checkered shirt underneath, and a brown tie. Paired with dark jeans and a leather belt, he looked every inch the high school English teacher. The soft waves of his hair were gelled and orderly, falling in an easy sweep to the side over his forehead. Long-buried secrets lived behind his amber eyes, mixed with a hint of nervous energy today.

Koa touched the front of his vest self-consciously. "I didn't dress up or anything. This is how I came to work this morning."

"Well, I guess you always look incredible then." I winked, and Koa cut his gaze to the double doors of the auditorium.

"Thank you." He cleared his throat and offered a smile and wave to a student who raced by.

"Have you ever attended a high school musical performance?" he asked.

"No. So far as I know, Derby isn't a band kid. I believe he plays on a few sports teams, but I've never been invited to watch. Will it be terrible? I know our concert band in high school was frightening, but this place is for gifted students, isn't it?"

Koa returned his attention to me, a tiny smirk pulling at the corner of his mouth. "They're not bad. Niles is a stickler for perfection. He works them hard. If they're horrible, which is unlikely, we'll refrain from telling him, deal? Trust me, he'll be insufferable otherwise."

"Deal."

A man and woman interrupted, saying hi to Koa, commending his teaching, and commenting on the content of the unit his class had recently finished. Koa thanked them but didn't encourage further engagement, letting the parents talk their fill and move on. The reservation he portrayed was not strictly for me. It seemed he was like that with everyone.

Once the man and woman headed inside the auditorium, Koa turned an apologetic look in my direction. "I'm sorry. The parents have little contact with us outside our monthly phone calls to discuss progress reports or our biannual parent-teacher night. At events like this, they tend to swarm."

"No worries. I'll happily share you."

He gestured to the doors. "If we hide, they won't bother us. Shall we?"

"Lead the way."

I followed Koa as he guided us through the double doors and to the back row of gradient seating. Most of the students' friends and family occupied the front half of the auditorium, so the rear was mostly vacant. We sat dead center, side by side, the armrest providing an awkward barrier I could have done without.

I scanned the stage where risers had been positioned in a half-moon along the back. Chairs and music stands sat at intervals, some on the lower level, others above, enough to accommodate at least thirty musicians.

The timpani and other percussion instruments had a spot behind the chairs to the left. A shiny black grand piano waited down front on the right.

"Are you familiar with classical music?" Koa asked, his leg bumping mine when he angled his body toward me.

"I'm about as familiar with classical music as I am with classic literature, which we both know starts and ends with *The Adventures of Tom Sawyer*."

Koa chuckled. "Fair enough. I shan't bore you with specifics then."

"Shan't? Do people say that? You're cute. Please do bore me with specifics. What do I need to know before delving into a spring concert?" Adjusting, I leaned closer to Koa, keeping our legs pressed together. Balancing my chin on an upturned palm, elbow on the armrest, I grinned, aiming for playfulness. "And remember, I'm not scholarly, so go easy."

I earned a shy smile and sensed Koa didn't give them out freely. "The concert band has four pieces they're playing tonight. It will be interspersed with solos and duets. You can expect to hear Vivaldi, Bach, Debussy, Mozart, Tchaikovsky, and more. Have I lost you yet? Those are the bigger names, and I should hope they're familiar."

"So far so good. You start naming composition titles, and I'll probably glaze over."

"Noted. Although I'm sure many of them will be familiar to the ear." Koa glanced at the stage, nodding to the grand piano. "What you should know is Niles is a bit of a diva. His concerts start and end with his own piano solos. He likes to ensure the parents are aware their children are being taught by an accomplished musician."

"Kind of arrogant."

Koa hummed acknowledgement. "True, but he's sore about the fact that he never acquired a Ph.D. It makes him unnecessarily defensive, especially with the parents. To be fair, several written complaints to the school board concerning his qualifications have been made. The parents feel they are paying for a superior education for their children and should, therefore, get the most qualified educators. The thing is, Niles is the best they're going to find anywhere. They just can't see past credentials."

We sat silently for a while, listening to the buzz of conversations and watching the influx of parents rushing to find last-minute seats.

Koa sat stiffly, but his leg remained nestled against mine. Not once had he attempted to move it. It was something. Recalling his adamant attempts to derail this friendship—or whatever we were calling it—I trod carefully, keeping things light.

"Thank you for inviting me. I know you have reservations about this"—I gestured between us—"but I'm glad you're giving it a chance."

Koa glanced at his hands, where they were folded in his lap. "I haven't agreed to date you, Jersey. I've merely agreed not to shut you out of my life."

"Good enough for me."

"I don't have anything to offer. Nothing worthwhile anyway."

"How about you let me be the judge of that."

"Very well."

"Did you get a chance to grab dinner earlier?"

"No. Niles and I were too busy setting up."

"Can I offer to take you out when this is over?"

Koa stared from his hands to the stage, fine creases appearing on his forehead. "Are you suggesting a date?"

"Yes, but if that doesn't suit you, we can call it a meal between old friends."

He turned, gaze sweeping my face. "Okay. It can be a date, provided you don't set your expectations too high. I'll disappoint you."

"You keep saying that, but I doubt it."

"And I'm not putting out."

I snorted, and the corner of Koa's lip twitched.

"Will that be an issue?" he asked, amusement still on the surface.

I was about to respond, about to reach out and brush aside a stray piece of hair that had fallen over his forehead, when the lights dimmed.

"We'll revisit that," I whispered.

Koa smirked and turned to the stage.

The momentum of our conversation might have been lost due to the commencement of the concert, but his words and the tiny taste of future possibilities stayed with me all throughout.

A spotlight came up, and Niles appeared in its center. He was sharply dressed and full of mirth.

"Good evening. It's wonderful to see so many faces tonight. Nothing brings me joy like our annual spring concert. These young men and women have worked hard all winter and are eager to take to the stage and show off their accomplishments. I won't hold them up too long. A few quick reminders. If you could please ensure your cell phones are silenced or turned off, it would be much appreciated. Nothing throws off the mood more than your cleverly selected ringtone. Also, in accordance with school policy, we ask that you not record the concert this evening.

"There will be a short intermission a little over the halfway mark, during which time we will have students in the lobby, serving refreshments. We ask that you please refrain from bringing food or drink into the auditorium itself." Leaning into the microphone, he whisper-added, "Our custodial staff will have a fit."

The audience laughed.

"Now, without further ado, let's begin."

Niles moved to the grand piano, the spotlight following. He sat, back straight, fingers poised over the ivories, chin high. A held breath hung in the air for a beat before he began.

I may not have known the first thing about classical music, but I could recognize talent when I saw it, and Niles was exceptional. His fingers danced with grace, confidence, and ease. The room swelled with crisp notes, captivating everyone.

I stole a glance at Koa, who watched and listened with a faraway look in his eyes. The music gained pace with a sudden crescendo before falling back into a lumbering, haunting melody. It whispered to the audience, seeping into the cracks and pores of every person present. It was impossible not to feel the deep, resonating tones on a cellular level.

Niles's entire body swayed and moved with the long, flowing sentences. He was lost to the music he created; eyes closed as he played whatever piece it was by heart. I turned my attention back to Koa and monitored his reactions, curious about his feelings toward his ex. The distant, glazed expression remained, and I got the sense Koa wasn't hearing the music any longer and was trapped in one of those blank fits I used to see in childhood.

Concerned, I moved my hand to his thigh and squeezed. He startled, inhaling sharply, then snapped back to the present. He didn't object to the touch or pull away. Glancing at me in the dark, he offered a sorrowful smile. It cut deep. It spoke of wounds buried under ancient scars, ones he hid from the world. The broken boy from Camp Kawartha wasn't gone. He lived inside the grown-up version of Koa, carefully concealed but still very much alive. The broken boy trusted no one. He'd lost faith in humanity long ago.

I hadn't understood his troubles in our youth, but as an adult who had seen horrors on the news, who'd read countless articles about the war in the Middle East, about inner-city murders, campus rapes, and child abuse. I could imagine what Koa might have suffered. Whatever it was, it was bad.

Koa settled in his seat and remained present as Niles finished his solo with a flourish. The man stood and bowed as people respectfully clapped. The concert band took to the stage next, and there was a commotion as they got situated with their instruments and music. Niles stood in the conductor's role up front, motioning to his students as they got organized.

Koa leaned in and whispered, "The first piece they're going to play is Vivaldi. 'Spring.' It's part of *The Four Seasons*."

"Never heard of it."

Koa bumped his shoulder into mine. "Yes, you have. Just wait."

He was right. As they began and the familiar tune filled the air, I grinned. In fact, I knew it well enough I could have hummed along.

"Told you," Koa said, still glued to my side, still whispering close enough to my ear I could feel the warmth of his breath.

I squeezed his knee in acknowledgment, keeping my hand in place, wondering what he might do if I offered a light caress. I didn't.

The band played another piece, something Koa called 'Triumphant Fanfare,' not something I recognized, before the solos began. Most sounded decent. A few tripped up. Niles accompanied a flute player on the piano. Throughout the concert, Koa continued to lean against me, allowing my hand to remain on his thigh. After a time, I caved and stroked a thumb over his knee, a tiny nudge forward to see how he'd react.

Again, he didn't object or move away.

I closed my eyes and let the music wrap around me. Koa sat close enough that I caught his scent each time I inhaled. Wool, candle wax, and a hint of almonds. He smelled like an old library, like solitude and loneliness.

I'd been alone for many years, and although there was a thirty-year gap between Camp Kawartha and now, time hadn't changed how Koa made me feel. I had always been drawn to him. These feelings weren't new, but they were more mature, more recognizable, and I couldn't dismiss them.

Intermission came and went. Niles briefly appeared in the foyer and was thrilled to see I'd come. Upon hearing about Koa's invitation, he grew smug and self-satisfied, like it had been his doing all along. Niles didn't linger, informing us he had wild students backstage, riding waves of adrenaline, and who would fast lose control of themselves if he didn't instill order.

The second half of the concert was shorter but no less engaging. Koa put distance between us, and I never found the right moment to rest my hand on his leg again.

After Niles played the closing piece and the event ended, I waited as Koa spoke with a few parents and checked in with his ex to be sure he didn't need help packing things up. He returned a short time later and announced we were good to go.

"So, dinner?" I asked.

"I could eat. Thoughts?"

I wasn't familiar with the Timber Creek area, so I suggested somewhere I knew well. "Do you eat fish and chips? It's not classy, but I know a mom-and-pop joint in Lakefield. Won't find better."

"Sure."

"They don't have much of a dining area, but we could get takeout and go to my parents' house. It's empty, but I haven't gotten rid of the patio set around the back yet. It's a nice evening. We could eat outside."

Koa agreed, albeit he wore the same mask of reluctance he'd worn at the bistro a month ago. He'd agreed to this date, but he didn't trust it.

We drove separately, meeting at the old-fashioned seafood restaurant on Water Street along the Otonabee River. It was one of the few places where you could order decent fish and chips. Nautical Nibbles had been around since my childhood and was a spot my family had frequented often. Dad used to have a habit of stopping there on our way home from games or late practices, and I would eat my weight in fish bites and french fries.

Koa and I ordered the standard two-piece meals with chips and coleslaw, and once they were ready—wrapped in newspaper and boxed like they'd been doing for thirty years—we took the food back to my parents' house.

17

Koa

Jersey led us into the empty belly of the house. Without furniture, the cavernous space echoed. He walked with familiarity through a living room, down a hall, and into another area, all without hitting a switch to illuminate the way. Since the sun had gone down, casting the world and house into a void of darkness, only the faint streetlights shining through the uncovered windows guided us.

It was gloomy, and I thought of Grandfather's house and how I'd been putting off packing his belongings and selling them. How the mere thought of returning to that prison gave me hives. Escapees usually didn't look fondly on returning to their cells. Jersey's experience seemed to differ. He appeared to take comfort in soaking up the past and instead was having trouble letting go of the nostalgia.

Off the kitchen, beyond a sliding door, sat the backyard and patio. The stones were crooked and uneven, weatherworn and cracked. The grass grew long. Jersey put his food down on a rickety plastic side table, tugged a second chair loose from a stack near the wall, and placed it beside the one already out. Then he lit a few strings of imitation crepe lanterns. The colorful globes hung from wires between poles surrounding the perimeter of the patio. They filled the backyard with soft light, throwing puddles of red, gold, blue, and green across the ground.

I sat, and Jersey joined me. "I haven't touched the backyard yet. Can't bring myself to do it. Still gotta clean up the gardens, go through the shed, and probably cut the grass. Fix these." He stamped a foot, indicating the cracked stones beneath us. "It's the last thing on the list, but I'm dragging my feet. The rest of the house is done, and I've even spoken with a Realtor, but I haven't given her the go-ahead to show the place yet."

"You grew up here?" I glanced around, but no matter how hard I tried, I couldn't see the yard through the eyes of a child. I couldn't envision games, toys, and climbers. Hell, I couldn't remember what it was like to be a child at all, to have those youthful experiences, to know such freedom. Those innocent years had been torn away before I'd had a chance to grow a single memory. The most prominent thing I remembered was summer camp, but that hadn't happened until I was ten.

"I did. Spent many years in this yard. Broke my arm right over there when I was six." He indicated a garden bed circling the perimeter of the yard. "Fell off a friend's pogo stick into the rocky barrier." He sighed. "Used to help Mom plant flowers in the spring, cut the grass for Dad all summer, rake the leaves in the fall, and skate all winter."

"Skate? Back here?"

"Yep. Dad built a rink every year. Dead center, from fence to fence and all the way to the maple in back." He gestured. "My friends would be here from the time school let out until their moms called to have them sent home for dinner. Then after, they'd be back, and we'd skate some more. My mom would make hot chocolate when we needed a break, and we whined when it was time for bed. I practically lived out here all winter."

"Sounds memorable."

"It was, and god help me, Koa. I don't know how to let it go."

My reactive comeback was to tell Jersey there was no god to help him, but he wasn't Niles, and I didn't want to get into great philosophical debates when I was supposed to be enjoying a date night. I was still baffled I'd agreed to go out after the concert.

The connection we'd made in the auditorium came back to me. Jersey's hand on my knee, tugging me away from the ledge inside my mind. Niles's sorrowful music had caught me off guard and drawn me to the precipice as it had done on more than one occasion. Leaning against Jersey's side, inhaling the fresh scent of his skin, and absorbing the warmth and solidity of his body against mine had grounded me the same way it had done many moons ago.

Jersey unwrapped his fish and chips, finding plastic cutlery in the takeout bag. He dug in, so I did the same. We went through the squeeze packs of tartar sauce in no time, chuckling when we both made a grab for the last one. Jersey let me have it, using ketchup instead.

Nightlife stirred all around us. Lakefield was a quiet, secluded town. It reminded me of the Timber Creek campus after dark. I couldn't hear traffic or the bustle of city noise. The air was crisp and clean without pollution. Even Peterborough was not immune to the corruption of an urban environment, so the escape that evening was nice.

Straining, my ears picked up a boat horn in the distance, a creaky tree moaning in the wind, branches rubbing together, and crickets somewhere nearby, singing their chirruping songs at each other. The symphony of chirps reminded me of an incident at camp, and I smiled inwardly at the memory.

"Remember Peter's cricket collection?" I glanced at Jersey, who laughed.

"Oh my god, I forgot all about that."

It had been one of the few times the boys in the cabin had treated me like an equal. The calamity had been too great for divides. We had become united in chaos. Banded brothers working together on a mission.

"How many do you reckon there were?" I asked.

Jersey popped a fry into his mouth as he tipped his head back with a grin, thinking and chewing. "Shit. I don't know. The guys and I spent all day collecting them in that field of Indian grass beyond the archery grounds. My legs were cut to shit when we finished. I had a rash for a week after. Couldn't stop scratching. The shoebox was full to bursting, though. Had to be three or four dozen."

Three or four dozen crickets. That sounded about right.

Peter and Bruce had built a cricket homestead during arts and crafts using a shoebox. By the time they finished, it contained several rooms and various levels. Then, the boys had filled it with as many crickets as they could find, but they hadn't secured the lid before hiding it under their bunk that night. Somehow, when the moon was high and the campers had long ago burrowed in their sleeping bags, the orchestra had gotten loose.

"Randy was not impressed," I said.

"Well, as a teacher, can you blame him? At three o'clock in the morning, he had a cabin full of eleven-year-old boys chasing down dozens of crickets with flashlights."

I laughed. "The noise. The whole cabin was chirping. It was loud enough that I remember wanting to cover my ears."

"If Justin hadn't screamed bloody murder, the racket of them all would have woken us eventually."

"They attacked him while he slept."

"They didn't," Jersey said, "but they did crawl all over him. Must have smelled good or something."

"I would have screamed too."

For once, it hadn't been me waking up the whole cabin with cries of terror, but I'd happily joined in the hunt to recapture as many crickets as we could find. Randy had made Peter throw them outside, but they were wily insects, and far too many evaded us.

"I think we encountered random fugitives hiding under the bunks for the rest of the summer."

Jersey chuckled softly at the memory. "Randy was so pissed. Those damn things never shut up either."

"Probably why he didn't come back the following year."

Jersey agreed.

We ate more of our meal, the chirruping of crickets in the distance making us both smile.

"How about the time that kid Andrew got hit in the face with the soccer ball and his nose exploded," Jersey said. "Remember that? How it gushed blood all down the front of his shirt. When Darwin saw, he freaked out, thinking the kid had knocked all his teeth out or something and he was going to get sued."

I recalled it all too clearly. I never played sports with the other boys, but I often sat on the sidelines with a book and watched. Andrew's blood had been everywhere, and it had triggered me into a bad episode.

Jersey waited expectantly for me to respond to the memory, something he recalled with great amusement. I nodded, unable to look him in the eyes. "I remember."

He registered my unease, paused with a bite of fish halfway to his mouth, and seemed to play back through the reel of time to figure out where he'd gone wrong. It clicked, and he lowered his hand. "Shit. I forgot. You freaked out."

"It was nothing."

"It was not nothing. You…"

"It was nothing. I was a mess back then. Easily triggered into… episodes. You didn't live my life, Jersey. I don't expect you to recall those details. To you, it was a humorous accident."

"You had a bad night that night."

I stared at my food. "If it's all the same, I'd rather not discuss it."

"Okay."

It had been yet another night Jersey had lain by my side, keeping the demons at bay.

For the second time that night, I stepped away from the ledge in my mind, unwilling to be drawn into the darkness of my past. I drew up other memories from camp, better memories, and we reminisced over the next hour.

About the time a boy named Oliver had fallen out of the canoe when he'd leaned too far over the edge to admire a water snake. Oliver had freaked out, certain he was about to meet his demise by snake bite or venom, even though the reptile had been frightened off by his flailing.

About the time I had tied Jersey to a tree with a skipping rope, pretending he was a pirate and I'd captured him, then panicking when I couldn't undo my skillfully tied knots to let him free.

About the time our cabin had put on a concert around the bonfire, and we'd worn our underwear on our heads as part of our costume as we sang camp songs and played air guitar. We were thirteen, and I'd been less shunned that year. Jersey had made sure of it.

Our bond had grown exponentially by then.

Not once did we touch on the endless quiet afternoons we'd spent curled up in a hollow log, side by side, heads close as we talked about everything and nothing.

Not once did we discuss the dozens of times Jersey had saved me from nightmares, lying beside me in the dark and holding me until I felt calm enough to sleep.

Not once did those lingering looks and unnecessary touches in the last year of camp come into the conversation. Nor the day I'd tried to kiss him or his reaction.

"I still have your bracelet," I said when the conversation lulled.

"You do?"

"In a box at home with a few other camp mementos."

"I can't believe you kept it."

I'd been staring across the backyard, but I turned and met Jersey's eyes. "I believed in your promises."

A wash of red light from one of the lanterns pooled around his chair and caught the side of Jersey's face, touching his beard and making it glow auburn.

I saw blood.

I heard screaming.

I blinked, and it was gone.

"They were big promises for a young kid," he said. "I did my best."

"I don't fault you."

"I'll make it up to you."

I could only smile, but the tension remained. I looked across the yard again. I didn't like how the scarlet light touched him. I didn't like how precariously balanced I was between the past and present.

Too much reminiscing was dangerous.

It was getting late, and the more serious tone I'd injected into the moment felt like a mistake.

"I should head out. Rask will need to be fed, and I have papers to mark."

"It's Friday."

"And it will take all weekend to get through them."

Jersey didn't protest. He told me to leave the takeout mess, and he would tidy it later, then he escorted me through the cavernous house and out the front door. My Audi was on the road. I hit the fob to auto-start it and turned to Jersey.

"Thank you for accompanying me to the concert."

"Thank you for inviting me and agreeing to have dinner afterward."

"It was nice."

We stared at one another, and I found myself unable to retreat yet unwilling to do something about the tension that had been building between us all night. In my mind's eye, I saw the catastrophe on the horizon. I heard the frustration in Jersey's tone some day in the future because I was too closed off, too distant.

Then I saw the boy. The boy who, without knowing it, had rescued me from myself long ago at camp. The boy with friends who had bullied and teased. The boy who wasn't always kind but who took care of me anyhow.

The boy I'd once loved.

Until he left me too.

Then I'd shattered.

All those roaring thoughts hit me instantly, and Jersey had no idea of their tumultuous impact, how they unbalanced, unsteadied, and disrupted my equilibrium.

He reached for my hand, and I let him take it. His thumb massaged mine as he peered at me in the dark, seeing everything and nothing.

Jersey was taller by an inch or so, but it wasn't enough to make a huge difference.

"Thank you," I said again, circling back to the beginning, unsure what else to say.

"I want to kiss you goodnight, but I don't want to overstep. I didn't ask last time, but I'm asking this time."

For all I struggled to understand where any of this could possibly land us, I couldn't say no. This was Jersey, and I had wanted his kisses since I was fourteen. "I would be all right with that."

But he didn't close the gap. Using the backs of his fingers, he brushed the hair from my forehead as he read the expression on my face. "You're troubled."

"I'm still coming to terms with the idea of you being back in my life, and I'm preparing for this, whatever it is, to prove to be as pointless as everything else. It's unsustainable, Jersey. You'll see."

"That's dreary."

"Niles prefers the term morose. I know, and I can't change it. I fear you're woefully unprepared for the likes of me, so it's not liable to last. You'll realize soon enough how disastrous this is."

Jersey smiled, his eyes creasing. "You have a truly fatalistic approach to life."

I chuckled. "Not you too. I swear, I'm going to put you and Niles in a classroom and give you both a lesson on fatalism. That's not what this is. You misunderstand me."

He squeezed my hand, stepped closer, and lowered his voice. "I'm here when you're ready to explain it, but I get the sense these qualities you allude to are worse in your head."

"They're not. Trust me. Niles left because I couldn't give him what he needed."

"Sex?"

A short laugh escaped me. "What? Where did you get that idea?"

Jersey shrugged. "You said you wouldn't put out tonight, but is that a forever thing? Is that why Niles gave up? I'll be honest, I'm not sure I could wait indefinitely on something like that, but I'm all right if you need time."

Jersey was joking, but a hint of concern tainted the question.

"Relax. I'm not sex adverse, but I have standards, and they include not putting out on a first date."

"Second date?"

I gave him a look. "You're incorrigible. I thought you were going to kiss me."

"I am."

And he did.

Strong, slightly callused hands took my face and drew me in. Jersey's warm, pliable mouth descended on mine. Firm. Controlling. The essence of a man who knew who he was and what he wanted. I envied him.

Closing my eyes, I savored the connection, searching for those tendrils, that barely perceptible spark of life his kiss had given me the last time we'd come together like this at the bistro.

And I found it.

That time, when Jersey's tongue grazed my lower lip, I invited him in for more. His taste, the gentle, caressing way he advanced, consumed me. It was as though Jersey alone could draw me from the shadowy world where I lived into a place full of sunshine, color, and promise.

But what would I do in that world?

It wasn't real. The illusion was a hormonal reaction, a bone-deep yearning for a pleasure I often denied myself. The physical aspects of a relationship had never been the issue. The human body—for the most part—was hardwired with a desire for sexual contact.

It was the layers of emotional bonding where I failed. It was building a connection, falling in love, and believing in tomorrow that was impossible. Jersey and I could kiss all night, and I could break my rule and let him take me to bed, but it wouldn't create meaning in a meaningless world. It wouldn't create hope where there was none to be had.

My inability to form attachments would still exist in the morning.

And when Jersey realized how I operated and understood I could no longer love him like I had as a boy, he would leave too.

The kiss naturally ended. Jersey hovered near my mouth, touching my face, our breathing wispy and labored.

"Can we do this again?" he asked. "Have another date?"

"Yes... but give me time to... process."

"But you'll text me, right?"

"I will."

"I'll hold you to that. I'm not letting go."

"Okay."

"I promise."

He planted one last kiss on the corner of my mouth before stepping back. The moment he released me, an acute chill entered my system. The desolate world where I lived swept back in around my feet and dragged me away to the shadows. The moment of pleasure and escape had ended.

I left, and Jersey watched me go, standing in the dark by the front door outside an empty house that had once belonged to his parents. As I drove home, I wondered what life might have been like had things not turned out the way they had.

It was not a thought process I allowed myself often, but the first boy I'd ever loved was back in town, seeking a romance we'd never been able to realize as children. I wondered, if I'd grown up differently, might we have had a fighting chance?

As it stood, I had my doubts.

18

Jersey

CAMP KAWARTHA 1991

Someone brought a cap gun to camp this year. The counselors didn't know. The boy, eleven, a year younger than us, brought it out during free time on the second week we were there and pretended to shoot people. The gun was plastic and had an orange tip. It didn't look real, but the bangs were loud, and we all got into it, acting the part of victims, falling to our deaths or taking cover so we wouldn't get hit.

It was a riot.

Until it wasn't.

Koa lost his shit.

First, we heard him scream. Then, before anyone could stop him, he ran at the boy with the gun and tackled him to the ground. Koa wasn't playing. We realized that when the punches flew. He aimed for the boy's face, hitting him once, twice, three times. Blood smeared the boy's lips. He cried and tried to shove Koa off. Declan, our cabin leader, managed to tug him free, but then Koa turned his aggression on Declan.

It was wild. Every boy in camp watched with stunned curiosity.

Koa thrashed.

Kicked.

Screamed.

Headbutted.

Cursed.

Bit.

Pulled hair.

Then he broke down.

Uncontrollable, wracking sobs enveloped his entire body as he crawled away to the edge of the forest.

Koa trembled.

Keened.

Cried for his mom.

Snot bubbles formed in his nose.

His body shook like he was having a seizure.

Everyone was afraid of him. Even the counselors.

No one knew what to do.

It took four grown-ups over an hour to calm him down. By then, Koa was locked in a blank fit, arms and legs limp, eyes glazed, and he wouldn't come out. He was sweating, drooling, and unresponsive.

They called his grandfather and sent him home.

There were still two weeks of camp left, and I worried about him the entire time. When I got home in August, I wrote him four letters in a row, asking if he was okay.

He didn't respond until November.

Koa never talked about the incident with the cap gun. It was like it had never happened.

19

Jersey

PRESENT DAY

Jersey: I don't know the first thing about gardening. I've lived in an apartment in Toronto for over a decade. How do I know what's a weed?

Koa: Unless it comes in a pot with instructions on a tag, I can't help you. I hire landscapers.

&

Koa: Who are considered the fathers of existentialism?

Jersey: ??? Should I know this?

Koa: Well, not Milton. MILTON! I can't begin to wrap my head around this. I don't even teach Milton. His work is too theologically complex for teenagers. The verse and syntax alone are too hard to understand. Do these kids absorb nothing? Am I wasting my time?

Jersey: I don't know who Milton is.

Koa: Seriously? John Milton. Paradise Lost.

Jersey: ???

Koa: Ugh, never mind. It's too much.

Jersey: Marking papers, I assume?

Koa: Dying a small death.

Jersey: So what's the right answer?

Koa: Kierkegaard and Nietzsche, but I'd have given partial credit for Dostoyevsky or Sartre or even several other minor influencers. Good grief. Milton. I'm going to crawl into a hole and cry.

Jersey: I don't know any of these names.

Koa: I have a headache.

Jersey: I disappoint you, don't I?

No response.

❧

Jersey: I was thinking of reading a book. Any suggestions?

No response.

Jersey: You're the literary teacher. What can you recommend?

No response.

Jersey: I feel like people who read are smarter. Like books wake up your brain or something.

No response.

Jersey: Koa?

Koa: I can't process this question. It hurts too much.

Jersey: Lol, how come?

No response.

Jersey: I bought one of the top ten thrillers of the year. Found it on a staff rec table at the bookstore. The girl working said it was "Totally creepy, dude." Wish me luck.

*Koa: *head desk**

Jersey: Lol

~❧

Jersey: Dandelions are the bane of my existence.

  Koa: Hire someone. Save yourself an ulcer.

  Jersey: They are the head lice of lawns.

  Koa: You listen as well as my students.

  Jersey: They spread like lies and rumors.

  Koa: You're as mature as my students too.

  Jersey: Do you remember that thing we did with dandelions where we flicked the head off, saying, "Mama had a baby, and her head popped off?"

No response.

~❧

Jersey: Turned down three offers today.

  Koa: Lowballs?

  Jersey: No.

  Koa: What was wrong with them?

  Jersey: Nothing... just can't do it yet.

~❧

Koa: I hate War and Peace.

  Jersey: Never read it.

  Koa: It was great the first two times. I have huge respect for Tolstoy. One of my favorite Russian authors (after Dostoyevsky of course), but at this point, I'd use this special edition as toilet paper and not feel bad about it.

Jersey: Ouch. What did it ever do to you?

No response.

Jersey: You could always throw it in the lake.

Koa: Lol. I might just do that.

⸺ 🦤

Jersey: So...

Koa: ???

Jersey: It's been three weeks since I've seen you.

Koa: And?

Jersey: And I know you're busy getting ready for exams, but do you want to grab lunch or coffee sometime? We're long overdue for date number two, and I kind of miss you. Am I allowed to say that?

No response.

Jersey: There's a cinema in Peterborough, isn't there? We could catch a movie.

No response.

Jersey: I could scrounge up tickets to a baseball game or something. You'd have to come my way.

Jersey: Wait. You don't like sports. Never mind. Thoughts?

No response.

Jersey: It would be low-key. A relaxed date. No expectations. I promise. We don't have to call it a date if you don't want to. I'd just like to see you again.

Jersey: Koa?

Koa: Sure. I'd like that too.

20

Jersey

I pulled into the parking lot at Timber Lake Academy on a Friday afternoon in late June. Exams started the following week. Koa had objected to the timing of our second date—I was officially allowed to call it that—but I figured he could do with a break.

He'd promised to stay in touch, and our text conversations, although brief and stilted at times, had been steady for the past few weeks. When he'd made no effort to advance us beyond the written words, I'd taken the initiative and invited him out. However, *what* was on the agenda that evening was a mystery. We hadn't decided what we were doing.

I was early. School was still in, and the grounds at the academy were quiet.

The blast of air-conditioned air pumping from the vents in the Gladiator felt good. Instead of staying hidden and enjoying the reprieve, I shut down the Jeep and wandered to the courtyard, planting myself on a wooden bench under the protection of a few stoic evergreens.

An uninhibited sun hung high in the western sky, baking the earth with its early summer heat. It was a few degrees cooler under the trees, their shade a welcome relief. Cicadas sounded in abundance. Their ticking and high-pitched musical whine filled the air. The woodchip path underfoot, leading from the school to the benches and off in various directions, was worn from foot traffic. Spears of sharp and brilliantly green grass covered the campus like a blanket, except where it refused to grow under the evergreens. A scattering of pine cones reminded me of camp, as did the pungent scent of sap and earth.

Timber Creek's location was peaceful. I could see why Koa had decided to take the job at the secluded academy instead of at a busy university. The sheer congestion and bustle of the city was enough to raise anyone's blood pressure.

The bell rang, marking the end of the school day, and I watched as the teens scattered like cockroaches from a burning building, their energy high on a Friday afternoon, especially with only a week left in the school year. A few passersby acknowledged the strange man on the bench, but no one said anything as they flew off to their dorms or to find their friends.

The rush abated to a trickle, and then I was alone again, the distant sound of teenage voices fading. Koa knew where to find me. I'd texted before leaving Toronto. I'd texted again when I'd arrived.

He hadn't responded, but that was typical. Over the past few weeks, I'd gotten used to Koa's habit of inserting long pauses between responses. Besides, he was likely too busy teaching.

Twenty minutes after the bell, a familiar man exited the main building and clocked me on the bench before offering a smile and wave. Niles approached with a confident strut, shirt sleeves rolled, hair tied back, and a smile on his face. He had the air of a musician. Artsy folks vibed differently than the rest of the world.

"Mr. Reid," he said as he got closer.

"Doctor... Shit. I don't remember your last name. Hello, Niles."

"It's Edwidge, and I haven't earned the title doctor, but thank you."

Oh right. Koa had explained as much.

Niles sat, angling his body to face me, draping an arm over the back of the bench. "So, date night number two. Impressive. How hard did you have to work for that?"

"Not too hard."

"His quirks haven't scared you off yet?"

I chuckled. "Hard to do since I've known about them for years."

"Right, right. Summer camp friends turned pen pals, am I right?"

"We are."

"It took a pry bar to get that much out of him."

That didn't surprise me.

"It's a cute story. And here you are after all these years." Niles clucked his tongue.

"Here I am."

"Where are you two heading?"

"No clue yet. We haven't decided."

Niles chuckled. "Typical. Koa doesn't like going out. Crowds and people make him uncomfortable. He's much more content with quiet dates at home or somewhere secluded."

"Noted."

"Can I ask you something?" Niles's stance was casual, but an edge of concern tainted the question. Was this going to be a jealous ex moment? But hadn't Koa said Niles was the one who'd ended it between them?

"Sure. Ask away."

Niles scanned me. "Do you know?"

"Know?" I stared blankly for several beats, uncomprehending, before the gears clicked. "Oh. About his past?"

"Yes."

"No. Do you?" My blood tingled with a shot of adrenaline. I'd told Koa I would never ask. I'd told him it didn't matter, but if Niles knew and..."

"No. God no. No one does. I was curious how close you two were."

"Not too close anymore. But even as kids, he didn't share that stuff."

"No. I imagine not."

"Spit it out, Niles. I can tell you have more to say."

Niles peered across the parking lot for a long moment before glancing back. "I don't mean to sound bitter or to give a lecture, but I'm compelled to speak. Be careful with him. Koa likes you. I knew right away you two shared something... special. Learning who you were to him, seeing the letter you sent, and how he reacted was the first time I had ever seen a spark of anything resembling life in Koa's eyes. If he's reluctant with you, it's because you pose a threat."

"Whoa. A threat? What the hell does that mean?"

"Koa doesn't let anyone in because the closer people are, the bigger the risk to his secret. And whatever that secret is, whatever he shields so dearly from the world, it's a ticking time bomb. If you detonate it, I'm not sure he'll be able to find his way back."

"Do you artsy people always talk in metaphors?"

"I'm serious."

I frowned. "I'm not following."

Niles's smile disappeared. "Koa's very closed off, and I'm not saying you shouldn't try to open him up. God knows I've tried and failed a hundred times. What I mean is, and yes, follow the metaphor, there is a locked door deep inside him, containing something... dark and ominous. Something painful beyond belief. I don't know what it is. All I know is, whatever lives behind that door was something Koa locked away when he was eight years old. It is the reason he moved in with his grandfather—a vile and abusive man.

"Did you know Koa will talk freely about his violent grandfather, but he won't go near that door inside his head? That door scares him more than the man who raised him. And that's saying something. If you brush up against it, try to unlock it, dismantle it, or break it down, I fear it could... it could send him away for good. It could make Koa completely unreachable.

"He lives on a separate plane of existence from you and me. He's already hard to access on a good day. Don't make it worse. Please listen. This isn't jealousy talking. I know he can never love me, but I will *always* love him, and I will be destroyed if you break him more than he's already been broken. It's taken me *years* to find a way to connect with him, to bring him back into this world, if only as a shadow. He smiles now. He laughs if the mood is right. I'm just... please be kind. Find patience, or don't do this at all. He will frustrate you, and..."

Niles glanced down at the bench between us, forehead creasing. The pleading tone burned the lining of my belly. His words coiled in my intestines and flooded my veins. It hurt to hear someone vocalize something I'd known my whole life.

"He will frustrate me and... and what?" I prompted.

"And don't be shocked when he can't love you either. I'm not sure he's capable anymore. I think those emotions were severed in childhood. He'll give you what he can, but it may not be enough."

"I'm not you."

Niles offered a wan smile. "No, you aren't."

I wanted to argue that Koa and I had a different bond. I wanted to object to all the labels and assumptions Niles had used when describing him. I wanted to dispute the notion that Koa couldn't love. Yes, he could. He'd loved me at fourteen. He'd said so.

But I knew better. Fourteen was a lifetime ago. Childhood infatuation was nothing compared to the real emotional responses of adulthood. Love at fourteen was an illusion. A concept too complex to be understood.

Mostly, I wanted to call Niles out for being a possessive asshole, but that would be unfair. I didn't sense jealousy in him at all. He was protecting a friend. A wounded, damaged man he loved dearly.

And who was I but a stranger who yearned to rekindle an old childhood romance.

I had a lot to say but no words to express myself.

At camp all those years ago, I'd been oddly protective of Koa, and those feelings hadn't gone away. They had slumbered, gone dormant, but they had reawakened.

And here was a man who felt the same.

A door clattered at the back exit of the school. Niles and I glanced over as Koa wandered out into the sunlight. He squinted, shielding his eyes against the midafternoon assault as he scanned the parking lot. When he saw the Gladiator, he turned and found us on the bench in the courtyard.

"Please," Niles said as Koa approached. "Don't hurt him worse than he's already been hurt."

"I have no intention to."

Niles turned to me and spoke quietly. "Thank you." Then he rose and met Koa halfway down the cedar chip path, kissing his cheek in the familiar way they had. "Enjoy your date."

Before walking away, Niles glanced back. We shared a silent conversation, and he was off.

Koa stood before me as layered as ever, including the knitted cardigan. He hugged himself in a way I was quickly learning was typical.

"Aren't you hot?" I asked, tugging at the sweater's hem.

"No. It's cold in the building. They had central air installed three years ago, and whoever is in charge of the controls must be in late menopause because I swear the windows are frosting from the inside."

Koa peered after Niles, who had taken a path beyond the parking lot and was nearly out of sight. "Should I ask why you two are colluding?"

"It was nothing. Niles wanted to give me a friendly warning not to shake before opening."

"Unusual metaphor."

"English wasn't my subject, but you folks at this top-end academy seem to like them."

I earned a soft smile before Koa moved to take Niles's abandoned spot on the bench. "How's the highly acclaimed thriller you're reading?"

"Is that sarcasm?"

"No. I'm deeply curious."

"It's riveting. I'm only on chapter two."

"Didn't you start it two weeks ago?"

"Is that criticism?"

"Not at all. It's a concern."

I laughed. "The book's almost three hundred pages long, you know. Give me time."

"Glad I didn't suggest you read *The Count of Monty Cristo*."

"You gave me no suggestions. Why? Is that a good one?"

"Coined as the quintessential tale of revenge. Alexandre Dumas. Over twelve hundred pages. I read it when I was seventeen. Took me four days. I've revisited it often."

"Christ, that would take me ten years."

Koa's attention drifted to a group of students crossing the courtyard. One of them glanced up, noticed us, and waved. "Hi, Dr. Burgard."

Koa waved back. Once they had passed, he turned to me. "Care to stroll the grounds? I could give you a tour."

"Sure. And we can decide what we're doing today."

We hadn't made solid plans. I'd hinted at a late lunch, dinner, or a movie, but Koa hadn't given me a finite answer, constantly deflecting. With Niles's revelation ringing in my ears, I understood why now.

We followed the cedar path as it weaved through the school grounds. Koa pointed out several buildings, identifying them as we went.

"That's the boys' dormitory. Beyond its walls, lives disorder, an entire warehouse stock of Axe body spray, and about three hundred and ten pairs of mismatched socks and dirty underwear. I'm grateful beyond belief they don't demand teachers take any responsibility for the students' care. They hire people for those duties. The girls' dormitory is on the other side over there."

Koa paused. "The monolithic building in the middle"—a garish stone structure with carved and crumbling statues along its roofline—"contains the dining hall, the lounge, an after-school area, a study hall, a second library, and some administrative offices."

We took a path around the south end of the main school, and Koa nodded to another prolific structure. "That's the main library. Half of it's being restored, so it's under construction. Hence the need for a minor library in the common building."

Scaffolding climbed the west side of the main library, and a large tarpaulin covered several windows.

As I'd suspected, the newer building I'd seen on my first visit turned out to be an administration building.

Once we finished the grand tour of the exterior property, Koa took us inside the main schoolhouse and showed me to his classroom on the second floor. The classic style desks, blackboard, lead paned windows, and vintage architecture gave it a historic vibe. Koa's classroom was a testament to what he taught. Posters with famous book quotes hung on the walls. The faces of long-dead men stared back at me from busts. Hundreds of books cluttered the endless line of shelves, all titles I would never have touched as a teenager—and likely not as an adult either.

I picked one of the thicker books from the shelf, reading the title out loud. "*The Complete Works of William Shakespeare.*" Blowing out my cheeks, I shook my head. "No, thank you. Never understood a word that man wrote. Gibberish." I waved it at Koa. "I had a teacher in high school who wouldn't let us use the *Coles Notes* to decipher this crap either. Made us suffer. You aren't that teacher, are you?"

"I am." Koa smirked and plucked a different book—equally thick—from the shelf, thumbing through it once before showing me the cover. *The Complete Works of Edgar Allan Poe.* "How about this one?" he asked. "Any history reading Poe?"

"'Quoth the Raven, Nevermore?'" I cringed. "That's it. That's all I've got."

"Correct, but I fear continuing to test your knowledge."

"I fear it too." I returned the Shakespeare book and strolled around the room, reading spines on other books and quotes from the posters.

Koa sat on the edge of his desk, watching me. It wasn't as cold as he claimed inside, but he held fast to the swaddled sweater.

Did I make him nervous? Or was it like Niles had suggested? Was Koa literally holding himself together day in and day out? Holding that door shut against the world? It broke my heart if that was the case.

"You must think I'm a real dummy," I said after puzzling over a poster with a quote by Mary Shelley. "I've never even read *Frankenstein*. Saw the movie once. I probably wouldn't understand the book. Classics are beyond me."

"*Frankenstein* is quite digestible. You might enjoy it. And you're not, as you called yourself, a dummy. Like I tell my students, we are each, in our own way, unique. We cannot all contribute the same gifts to the world, or life would be dull and lopsided. In that vein, we all see through a different lens. The goal is not to peer through the spyglass of another, but to interpret our own view and share that perspective in the best way we know how."

"You really say that to your students? I'm not even sure I understood it."

"Every year in about October, someone comes to me and says they want to drop my class because they don't think they're smart enough to interpret classic literature. I don't need them to always get it right or understand every passage. They don't have to possess the skill of reading between the lines or be able to decode everything by Keats or Byron—and I can see the blank look on your face."

I chuckled. "Big names, I assume?"

"Yes. What I want is for my students to use their minds. To bend, think, and discover what the words on the page mean *to them*. It's especially important when we explore philosophy. So long as they're willing to be vulnerable and openly talk about their opinions, perspectives, and feelings, they can't be wrong and won't fail my class."

"And what about you?"

"What about me?"

"Do you openly share your opinions, perspectives, and feelings?"

"To a degree. Some of what I feel is too complex and personal for students. I write about them instead."

"Would you share your thoughts with a potential date?"

The coy smile Koa wore on rare occasions felt like a win. "When you're ready to discuss philosophy, Mr. Reid, you let me know."

"Yikes. I'll put it on the back burner for now. Sounds like a heavy topic, and we're supposed to be having a date today. Speaking of. Any idea what you want to do? I made some suggestions, but you haven't given me any feedback."

Koa pushed off the desk. "We aren't finished with our tour. Come on. Let me show you the lake."

And again, he deflected.

⋅⟨⋆

We took the cedar path through the courtyard. At a fork, Koa angled away from the main campus and headed along a trail that sloped downward through denser trees. I could hear the restless water in the distance, but it wasn't yet visible.

In no time, the path opened up, and we emerged onto a dirt service road that ran along the edge of an embankment. The lake sloshed against a rocky shoreline. To the north, several houses sat along the water's edge, following its slight bend. They were carbon copies of one another. Pale beige siding, chimneys, covered verandas, and docks with small fishing boats tied to pilings. The sun glistened off their water-facing windows, cutting like glass against my retinas and making me squint.

This section of the river was narrow. On the opposite shore, more waterside homes teetered on the sloping embankment, evenly spaced with grassy fields in between. A woman weeded a garden. A man pushed a lawnmower. Two children, no more than five or six years old, with pants rolled to their ankles, balanced on rocks with fishing nets slung over their shoulders. Their guardian read a book nearby. Someone's laundry line flapped in the breeze.

We crossed to the water's edge and peered at the purling flow of the rippling lake as it moved around obstacles, sloshing and banging against nearby docks. Seagulls dipped and dived in the cloudless sky. A few floated lazily downstream, drifting on the current.

It was peaceful. Serene.

"What lake is this?" I asked, tipping my face to the sky and letting the sun's heat wash over me. I already knew, but I was hoping to provoke conversation. Koa was quiet and withdrawn, staring across the lake but not seeing it.

"Chemong. It joins Buckhom Lake farther north and runs parallel to Pigeon Lake to the west. They're small bodies of water. Decent fishing, I'm told. Do you fish? I mean, beyond what we did at camp."

I chuckled. "The most we caught at camp were sunfish. I'm not sure that counts."

"It doesn't. Those poor things. They suffered."

"Do you remember that guy named Martin? He was in Heckler's group. Or was his name Melvin? God, I don't remember anymore. He hooked a catfish but couldn't get the damn thing off his line. Tore his hands to shreds. Cried like a baby."

Koa cringed and nodded. "It was awful, and your friends were unkind."

"They always were. But no, I haven't fished much since then. Never had the patience for it. Or the time. You?"

"No. It's inhumane. Hypocritical thinking, I know. I love to eat fish, but I don't want to see or be responsible for killing a living creature. If I think about it too much, I'd likely turn vegetarian."

That didn't surprise me. Koa had always been sensitive in that way. He had avoided fishing at camp, had a deep aversion to archery, and there was the reaction he'd had to Andrew's bloody nose, not to mention the book that had landed in the lake because the boy in it had been killed.

Violence, gore, and death were triggers for Koa. I needed to consciously remember that and stop rehashing those parts of the past that upset him.

We wandered for a short time along the embankment, the warm breeze drying the sweat along my brow. I couldn't understand how Koa still wore the sweater. Sure, it was cooler by the water, but the temperature was still easily twenty-six degrees or more.

"Are you opposed to a homecooked meal?" The question came out of nowhere. Koa's gaze was locked on the horizon, face expressionless when he asked.

"No. It sounds lovely, so long as I'm not responsible for making it, because that would be scary. One star. Do not recommend."

Koa smiled. "I like cooking. There's something therapeutic about it. Restaurants are busy and loud on Friday evenings. I'd prefer to avoid such chaos. I don't go out much, Jersey. That's why I haven't answered you. I'm not a fan of TV or movies either, so the cinema doesn't hold any appeal. Honestly, I don't enjoy being around too many people. But... I wanted to agree to this date, so I thought maybe I could cook for us."

"It sounds incredible." And private, which was okay with me. I'd spent enough of my years in the spotlight among crowds. With the onset of middle age, quiet nights at home attracted me more and more.

"Where do your feelings lie with Greek food?" he asked.

"Definitely pro-Greek. What were you thinking?"

"Lamb? Eggplant? I make an incredible moussaka."

"Yes, and yes. There are few things I won't eat. Sign me up."

Koa nodded, and some of the tension left his shoulders. "Perfect."

A small fishing boat bobbed in the distance. Koa's gaze seemed locked there, but his mind was far away. I watched his expression, wishing I could read his complicated thoughts and not wanting to rush him. He appeared content. At peace. Calmer than the first few times we'd met. Although he was distant, I didn't get the sense this was a blank fit like I'd seen during the concert or multiple times in our youth. Koa, it seemed, processed every ounce of his life in a rigid, structured way. Internally. Privately.

Niles's warning surfaced, and an ache grew behind my ribs as I considered why Koa needed to process, why he struggled with crowds and people and emotions in general. How bad was bad? I feared it was a level I could never imagine. The boy I'd known at camp had been a mess. The man before me, deep down, might not be much better.

After a long while, Koa blinked out of his daze and turned to me with a cautious smile. "Shall we?"

The way the sun glimmered in his hair and whispered along the curve of his face caught me unaware. Koa had always possessed a quiet beauty. A softness. It had always made him seem fragile. Under the kiss of the sun, beside the gently flowing water, as he hugged his sweater tight around his middle, I had the sudden urge to protect him. From the world. From evils I might never understand. From his own mind if necessary.

"Not yet." I stepped closer and brushed the hair off his forehead, letting the silky strands ride the edges of my fingers. His skin was warm under my palm as I cradled his face.

Eyes searching, an unhidden reluctance surfaced.

"I want to start this second date off right."

"Are you getting fresh with me, Mr. Reid?"

"I certainly am, Dr. Burgard." I leaned in and kissed him softly yet with an urgency to soothe his troubled mind and soul.

Every time I tasted Koa, my blood rushed faster through my veins. Time vanished. The years melted away. I was fourteen again, but all the confusing, mangled thoughts I could never explain or express were gone. For once, I could comfort the boy who'd touched my heart with his fragility, the boy with a passion for books and a penchant for adventure. The boy who had trusted me.

For once, I was brave and certain I could conquer the world.

For once, I wasn't afraid to give Koa what he'd been looking for back then. Friendship. Comfort. Protection.

Even love.

21

Koa

SPRING 1992

Dear Huck,

I don't know if I'm going to camp this year. Grandfather said he's undecided. I want to go. I know last year was bad, but it won't be bad again. I told him as much, but he didn't believe me. He told me to stop pestering, and he'd think about it. If I don't go, will you still write letters to me? I like getting your letters. They make me feel less alone. You're my only friend. I'm still homeschooled, and so I rarely see other boys.

Did I tell you I have a doctor? I think I did. I can't remember. Anyhow, she's the kind that works on messed-up heads like mine. I'm not schizo like Bruce says. I just store a lot of bad stuff up there, and it won't go away. The doctor changed my medicine again, and I'm calmer now. I don't think I'll have those episodes anymore. Her name is Dr. Pickering. She's a nice lady, except when she wants me to share stuff I don't want to share. I told her if I talk about the bad stuff, then it will never go away. She doesn't agree. Anyhow, she thinks camp is good for me, so she's going to help me convince Grandfather to let me go. She said I need to do things healthy young boys do. She said it helps me adjust to the world, and I need to make friends.

Grandfather doesn't get it. He thinks he can make me better without her, but the court said I have to go to the doctor until she says I can stop. Dr. Pickering says I'm not ready to stop. Maybe never. That sucks.

I wish I could live at camp forever. I don't even care if people make fun of me. I would live there even if it snowed. I'd sleep in our tree like a hibernating bear. I like it at camp because you're there, and you make me feel safe. You help me stop the nightmares when they come.

I have to go. Grandfather is yelling for me to go downstairs.

Your best friend, Tom Sawyer

Dear Tom Sawyer,

Dude! You have to come to camp. Who will help me look for pirate treasure? Did I tell you Bruce and I had a major fight after you left last year? He kept calling you schizo, so I punched him right in the face. Made his lip bleed. I got in trouble, but I don't care. He was talking shit about you, calling you other nasty names too, so he deserved it. Justin agreed. Justin doesn't hate you. He said if you come next year, we can make our own club and not let Bruce join. I don't know about Peter and Daniel.

Ever since you left last year, I've been worried about you. I'm glad you have a doctor that helps with your head stuff. I have bad stuff in my head sometimes too. Like, I worry I'll get hurt and not get on the travel team in the fall, and all my hockey dreams turn to shit. Or I worry I'll miss blocking a game-winning goal, and everyone will blame me for the loss. Sometimes, I have bad dreams about it too. Hopefully the new medicine will make you better. What's wrong with your head? Is it just *the bad thoughts, or do you have depression? My mom says my aunt has depression, and it's an imbalance in her brain. She takes medicine for it and sees a head doctor too. I'm sorry if you have depression. It sounds awful.*

If you don't come to camp, I will definitely still write letters. But you have to come. It won't be the same without you.

Huck the Pirate Hunter and Bandit Slayer (I slay them with my hockey stick)

⚓

Dear Huck,

Grandfather said I can go! I hope you get this letter quickly. Camp is in three weeks. We're leaving early to drop me off because Grandfather has an appointment in the afternoon that day, so I'll meet you in our secret spot. Come and find me. I'll wait for you there.

Did I tell you I got a new piano for my birthday? Grandfather said thirteen was special and it deserved a special present. I'm going to have to practice harder now and get even better. Grandfather said I have no more excuses for playing bad. I wish he'd bought me a BMX instead. There's a boy down the street who has one, and I see him out riding it all the time. I don't know him. He's not my friend, but I haven't had a bike since I was eight. I used to like riding it. I wonder what happened to my old bike. Do you have a bike? Can you do tricks? The boy down the road can ride with no hands. He can also pop a wheelie. That looks cool. I want to try that, but I need a bike first. Stupid piano. What kid wants a piano?

Anyhow, see you at camp, Tom Sawyer.

PS. Don't forget my book.

PSS. I don't have depression.

PSSS. I'll save you the top bunk.

⟿

I lay perfectly still inside the hollowed-out tree trunk, watching a chipmunk scamper around a few feet away. The creature didn't know I was there, but it stilled every so often, perking up like it had heard something. Its teeny nose sniffed the air as it stood on its hind legs.

The arrival of other kids to camp was nothing more than a faint commotion far off beyond the trees. Squeals of delight. Laughter. Shouts of excitement. The first day was always a bustle of energy. After Grandfather had dropped me off, I'd selected a bottom bunk in the thirteen-year-old boys' cabin, always in the corner. I unrolled my sleeping bag on top—no mattress pad this year since I hadn't wet the bed in months—then put my knapsack on the upper bunk to save it for Jersey.

Our leader that year was a guy named Mikey. He was new and didn't know about my problems until Grandfather told him. I didn't like how Mikey looked at me after that, but he faked a smile and told me we should lock up my medicine in the staff building. We walked together to put it away, and Mikey told me he had just turned twenty and had a girlfriend in college. He asked if I had a girlfriend yet, and I said no. How was I supposed to get a girlfriend when I never left the house and did school at home?

Besides, I didn't care about having a girlfriend.

Once my medicine was put away, Mikey told me it was my job to remind him to give it to me daily. Since I didn't want my head to mess up again, I would be sure to remember.

While I waited for Jersey inside our log, I thought about what he might look like and wondered if he'd changed much since last summer.

Would his hair be longer? Shorter? Would he be taller? Would his freckles still be the same? I hadn't changed much. At least not that I could tell. I was still scrawny and had a baby face. I thought a lot about Jersey over the winter, often seeing him inside my head. I liked closing my eyes and pretending he was with me. Sometimes, we talked, and I imagined his side of the conversation. Sometimes, the other Huck came back and joined us—not often. Only if I was extra sad or feeling alone.

The chipmunk scurried off among the brush and ferns, and I couldn't see him anymore. I waited, chin propped on my upturned hands, elbows digging into the dusty remains of the disintegrating trunk innards. Maybe I had grown bigger. Either that or the trunk had grown smaller during the winter.

An army of ants entertained me for a while, and I listened to a woodpecker hammering a tree nearby. No matter how hard I searched the branches overhead, I couldn't find him.

A short time later, crunching leaves and snapping sticks announced the arrival of someone. I grinned. Jersey had never been good at stealth. It sounded like he was trying to sneak up on me, but I heard him loud and clear. I covered my mouth so I wouldn't laugh out loud and slowed my breathing.

He inched closer.

Closer.

It was him. It had to be. Who else knew about our secret spot?

A moment later, he jumped into view, shouting, "Boo!"

But I wasn't scared, and I burst out laughing.

Jersey laughed too.

It had been more than a year, and Jersey did look different. Older. He didn't turn thirteen until August, but anyone comparing us would have thought he had a year or two on me. His hair was messy and longish. His skin was tanned, even though summer had only just begun. He was broader, thicker limbed. Brawny. I knew he played sports, which was obvious in how he carried himself. Athletes had a look.

And the biggest difference of all was the white plaster cast on his left arm. It covered his wrist, part of his fingers, and went to his elbow.

"Oh no! You broke your arm." In his letter, he said it was one of his fears because it could ruin his hockey.

Jersey's smile told another story. He waved the covered appendage in the air. "It's nothing. It's just my wrist. No big deal. The doctor said it should be healed by hockey tryouts."

"How did you do it?"

"Did a ramp jump with my skateboard. Didn't nail the landing. Crashed hard. It was wicked awesome though. I heard the bone snap."

"Eww."

"It hurt, but I didn't cry."

Crying when you were almost thirteen would have been mortifying. I still cried—a lot—but I tried not to when people were watching. I didn't want to be tagged as a baby.

Jersey's eyes crinkled like they always did when he was happy. "Move over," he said, dropping to his knees. "I want to come in."

"There's not much room."

"So? We'll squish."

The tree had definitely shrunk, but we didn't care. We burrowed deeper than usual, inching back as far as we could go so not even the sun, where it bled through the canopy of leaves, could find us.

Jersey struggled to find a comfortable place to put his bulky cast. He said it hurt a bit when he leaned on it, so he kept squirming and moving.

"Did you take the top bunk?" I asked.

"Yep. I forgot your book again."

"Again. Your memory sucks. Did you read it?"

"Not yet... Ouch. Stupid arm." He angled his body sideways. Our knees bumped. "I'm, like, halfway or something."

I wasn't sure Jersey would ever finish it. It had taken him years to get that far. I'd read a hundred books since then.

"Have you met Huck yet?"

"Yeah. Once. You didn't tell me he's a homeless kid."

"So? Huck's cool. It's not his fault. His dad's a drunk."

Jersey rested his casted arm on top of me. We were squished in the log so tight it was comical, arms and legs crunched together. Jersey headbutted me, laughing. "I missed you."

My belly fluttered with his words. "I missed you too."

"You're gonna stay the whole time, right?"

"I'm going to try."

He moved his injured arm, sticking out a pinky. "Promise me?"

I pinky shook and said, "Promise."

"Promises are for forever."

"I know." I couldn't stop smiling and showed him I still wore his bracelet.

Jersey's face was so close to mine that I saw every crease and divot. I could smell Jersey's sun-kissed skin and feel its warmth bleed through my thin T-shirt. Coldness sometimes lived inside me, even on the hottest summer days, but when I was with Jersey, he made the shivers disappear.

"Are your friends here?" I asked.

"Bruce is, but I'm not talking to him." Jersey playfully headbutted me again, a smile stretching from ear to ear.

I headbutted him back, and he copied. We goofed around like that for a while, then Jersey groaned and shifted to his back, taking up all the space, but it looked like he was struggling to find a comfortable way to lie down with his arm.

With Jersey on his back, it forced me to lie half on top of him. Where else was I supposed to go?

In the past, during the nights when my dreams woke me, I'd lain against Jersey for comfort, and he never seemed to mind. But those were secret times when I was not okay in the head, and he'd comforted me. This wasn't one of those times, and I was afraid if I got too close, he might call me a fag and push me away.

Mikey's words rang in my ears. *Do you have a girlfriend?* No, but sometimes I wished I had a boyfriend, and I wished even more that his name was Jersey. I knew what that meant, but I hadn't told anyone.

"Lie down. Stop squirming," he said.

When I couldn't find enough courage, Jersey tugged me against him. I giggled when I landed awkwardly, sprawled halfway across him. "I think our log is too small for us."

"It's our lair. We can't abandon it. We have to make it work."

I stopped fighting and settled. I didn't rest my leg over his or wrap an arm around him. I kept tight to my side of the log and wished my heart would calm down. I put my head on Jersey's shoulder since it had nowhere else to go. He didn't complain. He kept his good arm folded behind his head and the one with the cast resting on his chest.

I liked being close to Jersey. I liked the way he smelled and the way my skin came alive in his presence. The noises inside my head both calmed and went crazy in a different way. The bad stuff was always more manageable when Jersey was around. Sometimes, I wished I could be with him forever.

He still didn't know about my past. I wouldn't ever tell him. Grandfather said it was best to stay quiet. Telling could mean the TV and newspaper people might come back, and they had been awful.

I had two secrets now. The second one was both bigger and smaller than the first. Grandfather didn't know I liked boys and not girls. No one did. It scared me a little, but not like the first secret. It also excited me, making Pop Rocks explode in my belly. Like now with Jersey.

If Jersey didn't mind being this close to me, maybe he had the same second secret as I did. Maybe he liked lying against me too. It was his idea, wasn't it? Did it make his belly swoop the way it did mine?

I didn't tell him how I felt. I couldn't. I lay still and soaked up the feelings instead.

The birds sang in the trees, the woodpecker went to town, and it sounded like messy classical music all around us. Jersey talked about the last hockey season and how he couldn't wait for tryouts for the next. He talked about school—we would both be starting grade eight in September. And he talked about wanting to lift weights like this kid he knew in high school who was majorly buff and played hockey.

"Then no one would get past me. I'd be a brick wall."

When he told me about a girl he liked in his class, the coldness that always lived inside me returned. Her name was Abigail. Jersey said she was super pretty. Blonde hair that curled all the way down her back. Pretty blue eyes and long lashes.

"She plays girls basketball," he said.

Grade eight meant they'd have their first dance at his school, and he hoped and prayed she'd dance with him. "Like, to a slow song. How cool would that be?"

Jersey said he was going to ask her out to a movie. He'd never been on a date. He said he wanted to kiss her. He said a boy in his class had kissed a girl before and told him it was the best thing ever.

Like Mikey, Jersey asked if I had a girlfriend.

I said no.

He asked if I knew any hot girls.

I said no.

He asked if I'd kissed anyone before.

I said no.

He asked if I'd been on a date.

I said no.

I didn't want to be inside the log anymore. I didn't want to feel Jersey's warm body against me. But when I told him we should go back, he trapped me in his casted arm and said, "Not yet, Tom. We need to make a plan for this summer."

The arm stayed around me. Like a hug I wasn't sure I wanted anymore.

I was confused.

Maybe Jersey was too.

All that summer, I stayed confused. Jersey kept his promise. He and Bruce didn't talk. Justin accepted me warily. Peter took Bruce's side, and Daniel didn't attend camp.

We canoed together—Jersey wasn't allowed to swim. We caught frogs at the pond—he had to wear a plastic bag on his cast so it didn't get damaged. And Jersey always sat beside me during bonfires, close enough our legs touched. He dragged me back to our log time and again just so we could lie there and chat, and since the space was small, it meant we had to lay close. Super close.

I didn't have as many nightmares—not with the meds I took—but a few times, Jersey snuck down from the top bunk when everyone was asleep, and we lay side by side, whispering into the night.

During one of those nighttime chats, Jersey fell asleep in my bed. I studied his slack face, knowing I should wake him up. His lips were parted, and I stared at them, wondering what it would be like to touch them with mine. Wondering if he would taste as good as he smelled. I almost did it. I almost pressed our mouths together. Our noses were almost touching. It wouldn't take much. His breath fanned my chin. If I moved a fraction closer, his breath would be on my mouth, and we would be kissing.

But I didn't dare. If Jersey woke up, he might get mad. He might not stay my friend, and he was the only friend I had.

So I let him sleep awhile and imagined it a hundred different ways instead—which was dangerous since it made my whole body wake up with tingles.

Jersey startled awake on his own a short time later. I smiled at him in the dark. He grinned back.

"I better go to bed."

"Okay."

But he didn't move. His smile changed. The look he wore was serious. Questioning. The fingers poking out of his cast brushed mine, and I didn't pull away. He didn't take my hand, but we touched like that for a long time. Once, and only once, Jersey's attention moved to my mouth, and I wondered if he might be thinking the same thing as me.

He didn't kiss me, but I thought maybe he wanted to.

Maybe he'd forgotten about Abigail.

Jersey went back to bed then, and he didn't spend another night beside me after that. I think whatever happened inside his head scared him away.

22

Koa

PRESENT DAY

Cooking, like reading and journaling, gave me comfort. The mathematical concepts involved. The methodical rhythm of it. The way it stimulated various senses at once. It was rewarding and one of the few things I took pleasure in. Cooking for another person was oddly satisfying, and I'd pondered extensively how such a response was innately human. It fulfilled a fundamental nurturing component scientists believed was ingrained into our species. It made my existence in a meaningless world feel less alien.

I'd never shared that with anyone. Not even Niles, who had always enjoyed my meals.

Jersey took to the same stool where he'd sat the first time he was over. Hoping he would accept my invitation for a quieter evening, I'd tidied the accumulation of novels and other debris from the island, ensuring nothing personal was lying about like it had been previously.

"I have a Brunello di Montalcino to go with dinner." I indicated the bottle of wine as I located the corkscrew in a drawer. "But it needs time to breathe before we can drink it. Can I make you a cocktail starter? Maybe a negroni?"

"I'm not sure what that is, but sure. Whatever you're having is fine."

"You're not one for cocktails, I assume?" The cork popped, and I waved the bottle under my nose, inhaling. "Or wine?"

"Busted. I mostly gravitate to beer. Does that make me a Neanderthal?"

"No, but beer wouldn't pair with the meal."

"I'm not too sophisticated when it comes to alcohol, I'm afraid. Still painfully twenty-one at heart, happy with cheap beer or vodka coolers. But I'll gladly participate with whatever the appropriate adult beverage is you're serving."

I smirked. "Negroni it is."

I set the wine aside to breathe while I collected the ingredients to make our cocktails.

Jersey sipped it hesitantly when I sat it before him, shifting the curling garnish of orange rind aside with a finger. He moved the liquid around his mouth before swallowing, considered, licked his lips, then sipped again.

"And?" I asked, waiting for the verdict.

"What's in it?"

"Gin, vermouth, and Campari."

"It's not bad. Strong." But that didn't stop him from having a third, heftier mouthful.

"Should I cut you off at one?"

"I guess that depends on where you intend this date to end. If I can't drive home, you'll need to put me up in your bed."

"I have a couch."

"What fun is there in that?"

I hummed and made a point of scanning and judging the entire package that was Jersey Reid. "I guess we'll see."

He snorted, shaking his head at my assessment. "You're a hard sell, Dr. Burgard. You could do worse than my forty-four-year-old ass, you know."

"Perhaps."

And since flirting wasn't my forte, I found some nice background music—classical piano—and set to work on dinner, seasoning the lamb and preparing moussaka in a casserole dish.

Jersey offered to help, but I turned him down. Drink in hand, he moved in beside me and watched instead, leaning against the counter. I wasn't used to having an audience, and his presence so close to my elbow was distracting.

"Where'd you learn to cook?" he asked as I sliced and salted the eggplant.

"Self-taught. I'm passionate about decent food, but eating out at worthwhile restaurants adds up over time. It's not a difficult skill so long as you apply patience and can read a recipe."

"Ah, it must be the patience part where I fail."

"Are you sure? I hear you're not much of a reader."

"You're a funny man now. I see how it is."

I smirked. "You don't cook?"

"Simple stuff. Spaghetti, steak, anything that doesn't require too much prep or ingredients. I can barbecue the hell out of most meats. I can fry an egg and boil a potato. That's about where I cap out. When I played hockey, eating out was all I did. We were always on the road, or the intensity of our practice schedule meant there wasn't time for anything but takeout."

"But you haven't played in over a decade."

Jersey chuckled. "Can't teach an old dog new tricks, I guess. I get by."

"Excuses." We chatted about our favorite foods while I stirred, mixed, and prepared the moussaka. It was a complicated dish but worth the effort. I was pleased to hear Jersey's palate was so diverse. I had an interest in cultural dishes and was eager to have someone to try them out on.

"How's your drink?" I asked as I put the finishing touches on the moussaka and checked the temperature of the oven before sliding it inside.

"Gone."

"And your head?"

"Not buzzing yet."

"Good. You can make us another." I gestured to the bottles I'd left out. With instructions, Jersey was more than capable. Although his orange curls left much to be desired. I teased him when he set my glass down.

The lamb and moussaka would need time to cook, so I invited Jersey into the library. We sat together on the couch, bodies angled toward one another, knees touching. His presence in my house and life was incongruous with all I believed. It upset the harmony I'd learned to live with, yet I couldn't seem to turn him off or disconnect the way I'd done before he'd resurfaced.

It concerned me. Disconnecting had been a means of survival for so long that I feared the incapacitation of the reflex.

Isolation was familiar. Jersey was not.

I sipped my drink and closed my eyes, seeking balance in a maelstrom that had battered me raw for as long as I could remember. Jersey left me to my thoughts, which I appreciated. It was something I'd had to teach Niles. He was a talker and often invaded my peace.

Words, as they often did, came to me out of nowhere. Had I been alone, I'd have written them down in a journal. As it stood, I spoke them out loud. "Like shadows, my sorrows lie at my feet. Chained and bound. An infinite defeat. Stretching long, bleeding pools of sadness. I weep, unable to get free. For if thy heart knew such pain, you shan't share my woes. You'd fight. You'd tell me, son, remember, shadows cannot exist without light."

I opened my eyes and found Jersey regarding me with a tender fascination.

"That's beautiful. Tremendously sad but beautiful. Who wrote it?"

I stared into my tumbler, at the orange liquid, slipping like oil around the melting cubes of ice, refracting the light. "A once torment-ed man."

"Is he still?"

"At times. It's why he struggles with this." I gestured between us.

Jersey touched my knee, thumb stroking ever so delicately. "Does he want to talk about it?"

"No. He wants nothing more than to forget."

"Okay. If he changes his mind..."

I met Jersey's gaze. Being with him wouldn't fix anything. It wouldn't erase the past. It wouldn't break the bonds that held me captive. It wouldn't change the future. All that was, and all that was yet to be, was forever black and tainted. Spoiled.

"I wish..." *I wish I could feel*, but the words stuck in my throat.

"You wish?" Jersey prompted.

"I wish..." I shuffled and cleared my throat. "I wish I could like marmalade." I plucked the orange rind from my glass, sucked the residual liquor from its flesh, and set it aside. "I use rinds for garnish, but for whatever reason, ingesting them triggers my gag reflex. They're bitter."

Jersey grinned, and I was glad he accepted the diversion from the inadvertent morose direction we'd been headed.

"I wish I had a thesaurus inside my head so I could sound smarter when talking to you," Jersey said.

"I don't judge you."

"I judge myself. I feel stupid."

"You're not." I set my drink aside and glanced at where Jersey's hand rested on my knee. Using a finger, I traced the prominent veins on the back of his hand. "I wish I had manlier hands like you." I displayed one, palm down. "Mine are too soft. I'd call them musician's hands, but I hardly consider myself a musician."

Jersey pressed his palm to mine. The size difference was jarring. His fingers were thicker, his skin rougher. The bones beneath weren't delicate like mine. "You have a writer's hands." He weaved our fingers together and kissed my knuckles. "I noticed that the first time you invited me over. You have a callus here." He touched the spot where my pencil rested when I wrote.

"Hardly a callus. More of a divot."

"You're an artist. Artists need more dexterity."

"I still wish they were manlier."

"I wish you would read me more of your poetry."

I chuckled. "I wish you wouldn't ask that of me."

"I wish you weren't embarrassed by it."

"It's not embarrassment. Much of my work is deeply personal."

Jersey released my hand, tenderly touched my face, and brushed the hair off my forehead. "I wish to know you on a deeply personal level, Koa. I hope someday you feel safe enough to share it with me."

"I wish it were that simple," I said, quieter.

"And why isn't it?"

I couldn't explain who I was. The depths were beyond comprehension. "I wish…" I leaned into his touch, absorbing the warmth of his palm against my cheek as I closed my eyes. "I wish I was better at this."

"You're doing fine."

"My head is all over the place."

"Stay with me. Right here. In this room. Nothing else matters."

Could I make that true? It seemed impossible.

"I wish you would kiss me," I whispered.

Jersey's lips found mine. I kept my eyes closed and pretended I *was* fine. I pretended, for a moment, that I could exist in Jersey's world and be the man he wanted me to be. I wanted it to be that simple. I wanted it to matter—the kiss, the connection, *him*. I wanted to feel alive and understand all the things I'd been missing in life.

I didn't want the gaping distance anymore, but I couldn't shed the protective cocoon I'd built so long ago. I couldn't breathe without pain. I couldn't exist without torment. So, I detached. I stayed far away from it all.

The past consumed me. The future eluded me. And the present was untrustworthy.

It was safer to exist in nothing. *As* nothing.

Jersey's careful advancement spoke of respect and concern. He didn't deepen the kiss until I encouraged it. He didn't touch my body until I touched his first. Part of me wanted to surrender, tell him to take me to bed. I yearned to feel alive, to peel free the rotting carcass from around my soul.

It hadn't worked with Niles. No matter how many times we shared a bed, I had felt nothing more than the base pleasure of a fleeting orgasm. If Niles, my lover for over a year and my best friend, couldn't breathe life into me, what hope did Jersey have?

What hope did anyone?

The kiss naturally ended, but Jersey didn't move away.

"You taste delicious." He stroked my cheek. The hand lingering on my leg drifted higher, and my interest in that regard was piqued. I wanted him to keep going and stop at the same time. I wanted the pressure of his touch, the feel of his body against me, and I wanted him to leave me alone in the dark where it was safe.

Undecided, I said instead, "I should check dinner."

He didn't protest. Jersey followed me into the kitchen, hovering nearby. I knew the lamb wouldn't be done, but I made a show of inspecting both it and the moussaka before announcing they needed more time. I set the alarm on the oven for another thirty minutes.

"Another drink?" Jersey asked when I stalled.

"How about wine? It'll be ready."

He agreed, and I poured two glasses before setting to work on making a Greek salad to go with our dinner. It was a distraction. "Are you okay with black olives and feta?"

"Absolutely."

"Cucumbers? Tomatoes?"

"Yes, and yes."

"Red onion?"

Jersey chuckled. "Add it all in."

As I scooped a few olives from a jar, Jersey slipped an arm around my waist and plucked one from the cutting board. He held it to my lips, and I smiled, letting him feed me the salty drupe. When my tongue grazed his thumb, he hummed and pressed the hard line of his body against my back, immediately snagging another.

"Do it again." He presented the olive, his words hot and heavy by my ear.

"You're incorrigible."

But I ate it in the same fashion as before, erotically swiping my tongue against his thumb.

A rumble vibrated through Jersey's chest and into my back. He rocked his hips forward, pressing a distinct swell of arousal against my backside.

When he tried to steal a third olive, I batted his hand away. "Enough. There'll be none left for the salad."

"Don't care."

"I do. Be a gentleman."

Jersey remained glued to my back, hands secured to my hips, groin subtly moving, pressing against my ass while I finished making the salad. Occasionally, he trailed his nose along my temple, his gusting breath warm by my ear. More than once, he skated his lips down the line of my neck, and when I tipped my head to the side, he burrowed his face in the crease at my shoulder, kissing, licking, and sucking the exposed skin.

The attention thrummed through my body, tingling pleasantly in my groin.

At this rate, dinner would be a wash.

It took effort not to abandon the food prep and drag Jersey upstairs. It had been a long time since I'd found pleasure in another man, and my blood was electrified at the prospect.

When the salad was finished, I shifted it aside and turned in Jersey's arms. He pressed me against the counter and descended on my mouth. The kiss was more aggressive than on the couch. His direction intent. His interest unmistakable—it pressed unapologetically against my thigh.

I snuck a hand under his shirt, seeking skin, unable to push him away.

"How long do we have?" he said into the kiss.

"Not long enough."

"You underestimate me. Let me taste you, Koa. Let me give you pleasure."

I couldn't find the words to say no. In retrospect, maybe I didn't want to. Hot lust sizzled and accumulated in my center. It radiated through my veins. It took me prisoner, and I wanted Jersey's mouth on me.

When I didn't protest, he unbuttoned my pants and slipped a hand inside, fumbling then fondling purposefully. I couldn't think, and the reprieve from my incessantly tormented mind was a relief I couldn't express. I rode the wave, moving with him, thrusting into his awkward but gratifying touch, applying more pressure.

Jersey moved his hand beneath my underwear and found flesh. Hard, aching flesh. The attention sang through my body, rippling from head to toe.

A noise escaped me—part moan, part whimper—as I focused on the new sensation. On the warm hand against my hard length. On Jersey's strength and insistence. On the push and pull. On the buzz, the gentle hum tingling through every cell, reminding me I wasn't dead inside.

Jersey's beard rasped my chin as he kissed me deeper, our tongues dueling and tangoing. Fighting and dancing. I drifted on a cloud, far, far away, my feet no longer touching the ground. I was somewhere else, somewhere far away from the pain and emptiness, and I never wanted to return.

When Jersey broke the kiss, he peered deep into my eyes, asking without words for permission to take it further.

I nodded, and he pushed my pants down as he sank to his knees.

His mouth engulfed me, and I was gone again. In another atmosphere. In another dimension. I was a man untouched by tragedy. A man without a past. Without memories, pain, and sorrow.

For those few blissful minutes, I was alive.

I grasped the counter's edge, clinging as my knees trembled. His tongue wove circles around my shaft. His throat clamped down, squeezing and wringing every ounce of pleasure from my body. I didn't open my eyes. I feared crashing back to earth and losing these few minutes of reprieve.

Jersey sucked me down again and again. He skillfully fondled my testicles. He raked his nails over my quivering thighs. At one point, he gently prodded my hole with a wet finger. Somewhere on the edges of my mind, I registered him coming up for air.

He rasped, "Fuck, you taste good."

Then he was on me again, and the strings of my sanity pulled taut. How far away could I go? How long was the ride? And when I reached the end of this blissful journey, would I still be in one piece?

I came unexpectedly. Without knowing how precariously close to the edge Jersey had taken me, I fell over without warning. Like cresting the peak of a roller coaster, the sudden dip in my belly caught me off guard. I cried out. I sought Jersey's head and tangled my fingers in his hair for purchase. Hanging on.

Hanging on.

Hanging on.

My feet came to rest on the ground again, and I slumped depleted against him as he rose to his feet. Jersey wrapped his arms around me and said nothing, allowing me to conquer the aftershocks alone.

Was I alive? Was I in one piece?

Had I transformed into someone else?

A timer beeped, and the moment shattered. I was me again. I lifted my head from Jersey's shoulder and saw amusement and satisfaction staring back at me. He arched a brow in silent question.

The incessant beep of the alarm mangled my thoughts, and I couldn't process the scene. I couldn't figure out how to feel—or if I felt anything at all.

"Excuse me." I gently moved Jersey out of my space to fix my pants and shut off the noise.

The floor undulated. I was a boat on rough seas. Unmoored. Disoriented.

This world didn't want me. It persisted in its effort to eject me.

In the silence that followed, I leaned against the counter, trying to find balance. Jersey moved in behind me—it was how it had all begun—and whispered cautiously, carefully, "Are you okay?"

"It was unexpected."

Was it?

"But are you okay?"

"Yes. Thank you." I didn't have other words. I should. For all I could bleed my heart onto a paper with ink and write prose as I unburdened my soul, I was bereft of explanation when speaking out loud. "Dinner's ready."

I shrugged Jersey off, unable to let him pass through the gates between me and the rest of the world.

He moved, and I busied myself, finding plates and cutlery, unable to turn around, knowing I would see the same look in his eyes that Niles had given me for over a year.

Hurt.

I'd warned them both. No matter how badly I wanted things to be different, they couldn't be.

23

Jersey

Koa went out of his way not to look at me as he plated the food and topped off our wine. We ate at the island without conversing for several long minutes. I used the time to process his response to the blowjob, to watch him, to read between the lines—which proved difficult.

He'd walled himself off worse than usual.

Was this what Niles had meant? This emotional distance? Was Koa unable to acknowledge what had transpired? Had it meant nothing?

Koa had enjoyed the blowjob. He couldn't deny it. I'd felt his pleasure. I'd heard the soft noises he'd made. He'd wanted to receive as much as I'd wanted to give.

"This is delicious," I said, hoping to bring him around and show him I wasn't hung up on his indifference.

If he needed time, I wouldn't push. I might not have patience when cooking food or reading books, but I would have patience for Koa, knowing his struggles to connect with people.

Koa cautiously peered over his plate. "Thank you. I enjoy Greek food, particularly lamb."

"I can't remember the last time I had it."

"Really? I make it often. In winter, I have a recipe for this lovely lamb and orzo soup. I'll be sure to call you next time it's on the menu."

I smiled. "I'd like that."

Koa ducked his chin and ate, still tense and unreadable.

The moussaka was creamy and rich yet delicate and perfectly seasoned. The salad, with its sharp dressing and fresh ingredients, provided a flawless contrast. The lamb was tender and juicy.

I needed to get us back on stable ground.

"Okay. We should get a few nagging things out of the way before we move this date night forward." I injected playfulness into the words, but Koa turned a wary glance in my direction.

"Meaning?"

"Pineapple on pizza. Yes or no?"

His frown melted away, replaced by a soft smile as he cut another piece of lamb. "Absolutely not. I like pineapple and pizza, but they don't belong together."

"*Phew*. Good answer. I was worried. Toilet paper. Does it hang over the top or dangle in behind?"

Koa laughed with a quizzical expression. "I'm not sure I've paid attention."

"Oh, you have. Maybe you do it subconsciously, but I guarantee you always hang it the same way."

"I'd have to check then. Are you saying there's a right way and a wrong way to hang toilet paper?"

"I am. And it's a dealbreaker. We'll leave that one for now."

"Considering I'm indifferent to the matter, I might be swayed to change my practices if I'm incorrectly hanging my toilet paper."

"I'll keep that in mind. Very courteous of you. Now, when you cut a sandwich, do you do it on an angle, so you have two triangles, or do you slice it into mirroring rectangles?"

"I don't cut a sandwich. I eat it whole."

I cringed and shook my head. "I don't know. This is going downhill."

Amused, Koa eyed me. "How about this one?" he asked. "Do you button then zip or zip then button?"

"Button then zip. Honestly, who would do it the other way? That's just weird. Mayo on french fries?"

"Never."

"Ketchup?"

"I can do without. Do you fold socks or roll them together in a ball?"

"Neither. I toss them into the top drawer willy-nilly and scramble to find matches every day."

Koa's laugh was beautiful. "So, are we compatible, Mr. Reid?"

"I think so. Blessedly different in many ways, but it should work."

Koa stared ponderously from the other side of the island, sipping his wine. "You say *blessedly*. All right. This one is more serious and has proven to have a marked impact on relationships of all kinds. We should get it out of the way early. Do you believe in god?"

"Wow. Go big or go home, huh?"

"It's important. Well?"

"I don't know. I don't *not* believe. I'm not a fan of organized religion, but I have faith. I haven't been to church since I was a kid. I don't pray, and I have no intention of forcing my feelings on others. They are mine and mine alone."

Koa hummed and worked on his meal.

"Did I pass the test?"

"It was a good answer."

"How about you?"

"Atheist."

I had assumed.

"And I take issue with people force-feeding me religion," he added.

"Noted. Won't happen."

"Good."

After our meal, Koa collected the dishes and set them aside before retrieving a sticky dessert from a container in the fridge. He put two pieces on plates and set one in front of me. "Baklava. I'm afraid it's store-bought, but you can't have Greek food without a proper Greek dessert, and the bakery we have in town does a fine job."

I picked up my fork to dig in, but Koa stopped me. "Ah-ah-ah. A moment. We require a digestif."

"A what?"

"An after-dinner cocktail. Hang on." Koa spent a minute working at the counter. Whatever he was doing involved alcohol from his impressively stocked liquor cabinet and the fancy coffee machine. It gurgled and whirred and scented the air with its heavenly brew. He poured ingredients into a silver flask, added ice, and spent a minute shaking it.

When he brought two martini glasses to the island, rims dusted with powdered chocolate and a sprinkle of coffee dust on the lightly foamed surface, I grinned. "What do we have here?"

"Mocha espresso martinis. They're exquisite. Trust me. And they pair wonderfully with baklava."

I sipped the offering and groaned, letting the concoction of flavors dance across my tongue before swallowing. "Wow. This is incredible. I need one of these bad boys every morning with breakfast." I licked powdered chocolate from my lips and had another drink.

Koa smirked. "It would make for an interesting day."

We enjoyed our desserts and martinis. Between the predinner cocktails, the full bottle of wine we'd emptied, and the digestif, my blood was warm, and I had more than a gentle buzz.

We retired into the library with two fresh martinis when we were done. Koa didn't join me on the couch but sat at the piano. "Do you mind?" he asked.

"Please."

"I'm not nearly as skilled as Niles, but I can bang out a few tunes."

Koa was modest. His skill was beyond reproach—and he'd had as many drinks as me that evening. The song was moody and dark, full of sorrow and pain. I didn't recognize the piece, but I recognized the anguish with which he let the music flow through him. Every note was carefully expressed, poignant and purposeful.

He played with his eyes closed, and I took the private moment to study his face. He was naked and raw, bleeding his heart through his fingers, allowing me a peek through the window to his soul.

I was taken away by the music. It hurt on a level I couldn't describe, and those urges I'd felt before to protect and keep Koa safe from an unjust world raged forward.

He was the boy I'd once known. He was the man who didn't want to let me in. He was mystery personified.

But most of all, he was wounded, lost, and broken, adrift in a world I might never be a part of. Niles had warned me, and I saw it now.

Koa stopped when he blundered a section. He scowled at the piano as though the fault was in the instrument, not his fingers.

"What was that called?" I asked, voice quiet so as not to shatter the fragility of the moment.

"'Nocturnes no. 2.' Chopin."

"It was beautiful."

He didn't respond to the compliment and retrieved his martini glass from the side table and joined me on the couch.

"You're better than you give yourself credit for," I said.

"Thank you. It's... a healthy means of expressing myself, according to my therapist. I find it more frustrating than healing, but she insists I continue to play."

"You're in therapy?"

Koa huffed. "For my whole life, Jersey. But you knew that already. Please don't act ignorant. It doesn't suit you."

"I knew you were in therapy as a kid."

"I still see someone once a month."

"That's good, right?"

"It is what it is. I think we're at an impasse, my doctor and me. My visits do nothing but cushion her retirement in my opinion. We're long past making progress."

I wasn't sure what to say to that. It was unsafe territory, and I knew better than to pick a scab.

Koa sipped his mocha espresso martini, a faraway look in his eyes. When he side-eyed me, I asked, "What are you thinking?"

"Will you stay tonight?"

"You've fed me enough alcohol, driving wouldn't be wise, but do you want me here?"

A long pause ensued before Koa nodded. "Yes. I'd like it very much."

"I wasn't sure you would after earlier. You seemed... unsatisfied."

Koa frowned, appearing ashamed or frustrated, I wasn't sure which. "I enjoyed the exchange."

"Good to know. I did too. I'd love to stay."

"You'll share my bed?"

"I'd be honored."

But the night was still young, and Koa didn't seem ready to transition to other things.

We chatted about music and how his grandfather had forced him to take lessons growing up. He told me he was tone deaf, and although it didn't mean he couldn't read and play notes or understand the written language on a score, his ability to progress into composition was severely hampered. Ad-libbing was an impossibility. He memorized the notes on a page but could never learn to play by ear.

When I requested it, he entertained me with the violin. His skill was astounding. I would never have guessed he had a musical handicap that prevented him from distinguishing different tones of musical pitch. I told him as much when he finished. Again, he bashfully blew off the compliment.

His cat, Rask, joined us at one point, curling up on the couch at Koa's feet. Koa petted him and explained he was named after his favorite book character from Dostoyevsky's *Crime and Punishment*.

"Raskolnikov," Koa said.

"Raskal..." I rattled my head. "That's a mouthful."

"His full name is Rodion Romanovich Raskolnikov."

"I can't even pronounce that. You poor thing," I said to the cat.

Koa chuckled. "Welcome to Russian literature."

"I thought Huck was your favorite book character."

Koa turned introspective. "He was, but I outgrew Huck a long time ago."

I could understand that. When I'd reread *The Adventures of Tom Sawyer* recently, it had struck me as juvenile. Curious about this Russian dude who was Koa's new favorite character, I made a mental note to look up *Crime and Punishment* in my free time.

The night grew quiet, and conversation slowly flittered away. The martinis were gone, the wine bottle empty, and neither of us was reaching for more to drink.

"It's after eleven," Koa informed me. "Shall we go to bed?"

"If you're ready."

Koa shut down the house, fed the cat, and we climbed to the second floor. His house was old but beautifully restored. Natural wood with intricate carpentry you never saw anymore. Wide baseboards, gorgeous trim, and stunning architecture. The floors creaked, but I could hardly blame them. Even I creaked in my old age—the cranky knee had never liked stairs.

He showed me the upstairs bathroom, found a newly packaged toothbrush, and then directed me to the bedroom when I was done. I didn't have anything to sleep in and was having trouble reading the room.

Koa didn't give me a sign and scrambled about, turning down the bed, drawing the curtains over the long window on the eastern and southern walls, and avoiding eye contact.

There was a distinct disconnect between us. I felt it but didn't know how to erase it. When he shut off the bedside light and came to me in the dark, I surrendered. I let Koa undress me like a lover. I returned the affection when he kissed me passionately and encouraged me to touch him like I had earlier in the evening. We used the language of hands and mouths. No words.

We undressed one another while standing, hands fumbling with buttons, breaking the kiss only when necessary.

On the bed, naked, we explored each other with silent touches. I wanted the light on so I could see all of him sprawled out beneath me, but I got the sense the barrier he'd erected was intentional.

Koa's hands were all over me. He mapped my broad chest, followed the curve of my ribs to my back, and traced the length of my spine. Delicate, like he was playing an instrument. Like he was reading Braille. The tone changed. His nails bit into the round globes of my ass, drawing me nearer as he arched his hips off the bed.

I chuckled and went with it.

He was hard when he rocked against me, and I groaned, gyrating, matching his moves, seeking that pleasure I'd been yearning for all evening—the one only half-realized in the kitchen before dinner.

Beneath the fresh mint flavor of toothpaste, I tasted Koa. Pure, honest, troubled Koa. And maybe it was my imagination, or maybe it was wishful thinking, but I would swear I remembered it from a time long ago when a fourteen-year-old boy had dared to kiss me at camp, and I'd pushed him away.

Koa's tongue sought mine. His teeth nipped playfully at my lower lip, drawing it into his mouth, where he sucked ever so gently. I felt the pull in my groin and hissed, "Fuck, Koa."

He did it again, and I pressed against him with purpose, grinding our lengths together, rutting like I was eighteen again but unable to help it.

Alight with lust and tingling with desire, I did all I could not to go too fast, remembering the blankness he returned earlier after I'd pleasured him in the kitchen, fearing its return. I let Koa be in control.

Apart from the odd noises of pleasure, he was a quiet lover. Whispered pleas of my name floated between us on occasion when our lips parted, but nothing more. I found his throat with my tongue and teeth, and Koa tipped his head back, giving me access to explore. Taking my time, I did exactly that. There was no rush. We had all night.

I rasped my tongue along the faint scruff on his jaw. I peppered kisses down strained neck tendons to his collarbones. I buried my nose in his soft chest hair, inhaling and brushing my lips over his nipples one at a time before moving on.

Taking the path down his sternum, I tasted his navel, the arch of his hips, the crease at his thigh. I urged him to let his legs fall to the side, and I fitted myself between them and swallowed his cock again, yearning to have his flavor back in my mouth.

Koa gasped and buried his fingers in my hair as I worked him slowly and purposefully. His reaction was better than earlier. Less inhibited. He moved his hips, moaned, and whispered my name over and over, thrusting and pulling my hair. His legs trembled. Before he cusped the edge and came, he encouraged me up the bed, and we kissed again.

He wrapped a hand around me and stroked, and I gripped the blankets beneath me as the power of his touch slowly undid me. I shuddered and gasped. "Koa... Jesus... So good."

"There are condoms in the drawer," he said against my mouth.

"You want that?" I had hoped, but I wasn't about to presume.

"Yes."

I found the supplies where he indicated and returned, bracketing him with my knees and placing a hand on either side of his head, peering down at him in the dark, again wishing for light. Shadows were thick. I could barely make out Koa's expression and desperately wished to read his face so I knew how to proceed. So I knew if he was enjoying this as much as me or going through the motions because it was expected. But Koa wore darkness like a mask. He hid behind it.

He clung to my waist, dragging me against him until I had him pressed to the bed. "I like the weight of you on top of me. It feels good."

Using his feet, he stroked along my calves, then hooked his ankles at my lower back and ground his erection between the tight fit of our bodies.

"Are you waiting for something?" he asked.

"No." *Yes. Kind of.* But I thought I understood what he wanted.

We kissed again, frotting, grinding, and building friction. The pleasure mounted and tingled in my lower belly. I could have come like that and been happy, but Koa had asked for more, and I intended on delivering.

I shifted, found the lube, and used it to coat my fingers. Koa snagged my wrist and guided the hand between his legs.

There was no question anymore.

I took him down my throat again as I explored his hole, working a digit inside. He moaned and shivered, pressing against the intrusion, welcoming it. His nails bit into my flesh as I drew his pleasure out, inching him closer to orgasm without letting him get there.

"Enough," he breathed. "Please, Jersey... I'll be finished before you properly start."

I chuckled, easing up. "Can't have that."

I couldn't find the condom. It was too dark. We laughed and felt around until Koa located the foil-wrapped package. In a heartbeat, I was hovering over him again, foreheads touching, lips ghosting, breaths mingling.

"Are you okay?" I was still unable to read him.

"Stop delaying."

It wasn't an answer, but I heeded the advice.

It had been a long, long time since I'd been with a guy. After Christine, there had been a few, but for whatever reason, I gravitated to women. Koa had always been the exception. At thirteen, fourteen, and now. He'd called to me then, and the pull I felt today was equally magnetic and impossible to ignore.

When I entered him, the pressure and intensity stole my breath. I ground my teeth and tried to make my quads stop jittering. They refused to listen. My entire body was alight and vibrating. Screaming for more.

But I wouldn't rush.

Koa tugged me into a harsh kiss, and all my senses drifted away. I kissed him back with the same ferocity as we moved together. We kissed until my lips were raw and every nerve was a live wire, sparking and zapping electricity over my skin.

It was hard to pay attention to Koa's reactions when my body was so fueled with need and begging for release. He was with me. He was kissing me back. I told myself it was enough. He was an adult. He would know his limits and boundaries. He'd wanted this. He'd asked for it.

Soft noises of pleasure danced in my ears, and I savored them.

When I was sure the end was near, as I cusped the point of no return, Koa tapped my arm. "Wait. Stop. Off for a sec."

I pulled out, unsure what was happening, but it wasn't serious. Koa rolled to his hands and knees and peered back at me. "Okay."

I didn't ask questions. I entered him again, and the slow waltz we'd been dancing came to an end. There was urgency with the new position, a desperation to reach our peaks. Koa stroked himself, face buried in a pillow as he met every thrust. I chased my orgasm while clinging to his hips. I couldn't hold off much longer.

When Koa cried with pleasure, I ensured he rode it all the way to the end. My orgasm swiftly followed, and the sudden crash back to earth was intense. I collapsed against Koa's back, breathing ragged, heart jackrabbiting out of control. He wasn't faring much better. Our skin was slick from exertion.

When I pulled out and landed beside him on the bed, we didn't speak for a long time. I wasn't sure what to say, and the sense of disconnect I'd felt when we'd entered his bedroom was back. Even without seeing his face clearly, I knew Koa wasn't with me.

He was far, far away. In another dimension. On another planet. Untouchable. Unreachable. Unreadable.

"Hey." I searched for his hand but found his arm instead and rubbed it. I inched closer so I could hopefully see him better.

Nose to nose, like too many nights at camp when I'd been unable to acknowledge my feelings. "Are you okay?"

"I'm lying in a puddle."

I chuckled. "We should clean up."

He pulled away and left the room.

Only as I listened to the water run in the bathroom did I realize he hadn't answered my question.

Again.

24

Jersey

After cleaning up, I fell asleep quickly. Between a solid orgasm and the cocktail of drinks flowing through my system, it was inevitable. Koa had let me enclose him in my arms, but I wasn't sure it was what he wanted. In the dark, I couldn't read him. When I awoke several hours later, he wasn't in bed.

The clock on the side table said it was after four in the morning. I listened, thinking he'd snuck off to use the bathroom, but the house was silent. The longer I waited, straining to hear anything to indicate where he'd gone, the more convinced I was that Koa wasn't returning.

When had he left?

Had he slept at all?

I fumbled in the dark for my underwear and shuffled to the hallway, making my way to the stairs. The only sound was the creaking boards as I descended, and there wasn't much to do about that. When I reached the bottom, a faint whiff of coffee lingered in the air. I aimed for the kitchen, but it was dark, moonlight from the window shining off the countertops. I followed the hallway to the library and found Koa at an aged wooden desk, a shaded lamp illuminating the area around him but not much more.

Focused on writing, reading glasses perched on the end of his nose, Koa didn't notice me. Rask sat on his knee, and he absently petted the animal as he scribbled now and then in what seemed to be a thick journal. I stood in the doorway, yawning as I took in the scene. Soft classical music played from somewhere, barely audible and melancholic.

At one point, Koa stopped writing, sipped from the stoneware mug beside him, and glanced at the cat. "I don't care what you think. I'm telling you how it is with me. The illusion. We've discussed it before."

I frowned.

Koa went on. "I hear you, but what is happiness? Truly." He paused as though waiting for a response, then continued as though he'd gotten one. "Exactly. And fundamentally, it's subjective. What makes one happy doesn't necessarily make another feel the same." Another pause. "Yes, I realize that's the point. But I don't buy into that philosophy."

Koa scowled at the animal. "I am not. I admit some of his ideas are noteworthy, and... don't interrupt. I'm entitled to my opinion. Happiness doesn't make life worth living. Period. It changes nothing. Happy, or sad, or indifferent, life ends the same. We're not discussing this further. Be quiet, and let me write."

He returned to his notebook.

My heart pinched.

As a child, Koa had retained an imaginary friend for years longer than was healthy. I wasn't sure when Huck had finally been put to rest. Koa had been careful to hide the boy's existence—or nonexistence, as it were—the last few years we'd been at camp, but I'd caught him talking to Huck on occasion, even at fourteen. Maybe Huck had never gone away. It seemed a part of the make-believe boy lived on in Rask.

And what that meant for Koa's mental health about split me in two. I'd never understood the sheer severity of what he might have gone through as a child, and I wasn't sure I could comprehend it as an adult. What sort of tragedy did it take to break a person so thoroughly that they invented companions for conversation and company? How deep was Koa's loneliness?

Only then did I contemplate the words he'd spoken. *Happiness doesn't make life worth living. Period. It changes nothing. Happy, or sad, or indifferent, life ends the same.*

I let him resume writing as I backed out the door and retreated down the hall. When I approached the library the second time, I ensured he heard me coming. Yawning and groaning with sleepiness, I collapsed heavily against the archway. "There you are. You're up early."

Koa peered up, removed his glasses, and set them aside. He offered a shadow of a smile. "Good morning." Rask jumped down from his lap and slinked away.

"Is it? In my world, this isn't even close to morning."

Koa chuckled. "My days typically start around four. I like the predawn quiet. Can I make you a coffee?"

"Not yet." I wandered into the room and sat on the edge of an armchair near the desk, facing him. "What are you writing?"

He closed the leather-bound book, setting his pen on top. "Journaling. It's supposed to help this." He motioned at his head.

"Is it me?"

"I'm sorry?"

"Am I the reason your head's"—I made the same motion—"doing whatever it's doing?"

"Oh. No... Yes. Partly. Believe me, there are a lot more layers involved."

And I knew he didn't want to talk about it when he cut his gaze to the journal.

"So your typical day begins at four a.m.? Yuck."

Another soft chuckle. "Often."

"And what do you do this early in the morning?"

"Drink coffee. Sit outside if it's nice. I write. I think. If words don't come to me, I focus on advancing my curriculum or marking papers."

"How hard might it be to convince you to return to bed?"

"I couldn't sleep more if I wanted to."

"I'm not asking you to sleep, Koa."

His smile turned coy. "In that case, not hard at all."

⁎

Koa and I didn't have another date night until early July. Exams and report cards busied his life, and he couldn't spare the time. I respected his crazy work schedule but wondered if he didn't use it as an excuse. If he needed time to process, I would give him time.

Our text messages remained brief exchanges, but at least they were regular.

I never brought up what I'd witnessed in the library that morning, but it stayed with me like a bruise that wouldn't heal. If I thought about it, the ache was unbearable. Part of me wanted to talk to Niles, but another part of me thought it wasn't fair to Koa to share something that was likely deeply personal and could potentially embarrass him.

So I kept it to myself.

It was early July when he invited me for dinner again. School was out for the summer, and he seemed far more relaxed. It was during that second dinner that I started to pick up on the tiny nuances of Koa's personality I'd missed. Things that had changed since childhood.

At camp, as a boy, Koa had clung to me. He'd sought me out and stuck close to my side—especially in the last two years.

As an adult, this was no longer the case. Koa was the definition of introverted. Although he seemed to enjoy my company, he didn't cling to the idea of us having a relationship. It didn't seem to excite him like it did me. He likely would have been just as happy alone.

After another night in his bed, sensing a strange disconnect between us, I concluded that Koa didn't know how to have a relationship. He fumbled along well enough to hide it, but the signs were glaring.

He never initiated sex, but he never turned it down—and he seemed to enjoy himself. He didn't reach out affectionately to touch me or hold my hand—unless I broke the ice and did it first, in which case he played his part by reciprocating. We talked plenty, but where emotions were concerned, Koa backed off. He couldn't express himself with feelings. Everything in his world was a nonissue. Nothing mattered.

And there was always a distance between us. It was as though I couldn't reach him even when he sat beside me on the couch or lay in my arms in bed.

He was there, but he wasn't.

I hated it and wondered if this was what had driven Niles away.

Koa's presence in the relationship was missing.

Koa excelled at conversation, although he often—unintentionally, I believed—steered us down darker paths. When that happened, he pulled back and sank into himself as though annoyed he'd taken us there. He could talk books, and food, and music all night. Those were the few times I saw him truly engaged. I dare say happy. So, although I didn't speak the language of arts and literature, I encouraged those topics if only to see the lighter side of him emerge. If only to see him smile.

It was an evening in mid-July, a third or fourth date, as we sat outdoors, the sun going down, drinking wine with a fancy French name I couldn't remember, when Koa queried, "Did you ever ask Abigail on a date?"

It took me a full minute to remember who Abigail was, and I laughed. "No. Wow, I forgot all about her. She went out with a guy named Keller instead, and they *dated*"—I used air quotes—"until tenth grade or something. I'd long moved on by then."

Koa and I sat side by side on the low wooden fence that cut across the property line, dividing Koa's yard from the land next door. Koa's house backed onto a cemetery that had gone to seed. The grounds were overgrown with trees. The ancient stones, like jagged teeth, no longer stood tall. The timeworn monuments were cracked, leaning tiredly in most cases, growing soft green moss over their surfaces. Their inscriptions were no longer legible.

Koa had told me the cemetery wasn't in use anymore. They had run out of room to bury new people in the 1920s. It had been given over to the earth, and he hadn't seen a groundskeeper in years.

In the distance, a crumbling white church stood sentinel. The windows were boarded up, and the steeple was rusty and home to at least three bird's nests—as though guarding the structure against an unpredictable world.

The cemetery was peaceful yet stirred odd emotions in me when I considered how often Koa claimed to sit outside. Was this what he stared at all the time? What kind of thoughts would arise viewing a decrepit cemetery day in and day out? Did he walk the grounds? Koa had a bleak outlook on life, and he often spoke of death like it was nothing more than a trip to the grocery store.

"So Abigail wasn't your first kiss then?" He ran a finger around the lip of his wine glass and stuck the digit in his mouth, peering sidelong at me as he asked.

"You were my first kiss, Koa."

"I don't count. I took from you what you weren't willing to give."

"Bullshit. I wanted it. I just wasn't ready to admit it."

"Hence the unwillingness. Therefore, I don't count. Who was your first kiss?" He sipped his wine, gaze drifting to a mausoleum in the distance. Ivy grew up its side, covering the pitted stone walls.

"My *second* kiss was a girl named Geneva, and I was sixteen before it happened. We dated as only high school kids know how, and no, I never got into her pants—as much as I wanted to. As much as I lied and told everyone I had."

Koa chuckled, and I bumped him with my shoulder, upsetting the wine in his glass.

"How about you?" I asked.

"I was in university. First year. I guess that made me eighteen. I don't know his name. It wasn't important. I don't think I ever asked for it."

"Oh come off it. Who was he?"

Koa shook his head. "I'm serious. I really don't know. He used to eye me obsessively at the library when I was studying. Never said a word. Walked by my table over and over. We exchanged a few smiles. I sensed his interest. I wasn't stupid. One evening, I made a point of walking past him on my way out and slipped him a note with my dorm number on it. He showed up an hour later, and I got a lot of firsts out of the way."

"How terribly naughty of you."

Koa chuckled.

"And you never asked for his name?"

"No. It didn't matter. I was more curious about what I'd been miss-ing out on, and I had no interest in it becoming anything permanent."

"And?"

"And what?"

"How was it?"

"Not all that satisfying, to be honest. He was a... wet kisser."

I laughed. "What does that mean?"

"Too much saliva. I think he was eager to impress and failed by trying to eat my face off. And, for the record, there is such thing as a bad blowjob."

"Oh, I've been there a few times."

Koa grew quiet and distant. I wondered if he was back there or if he was remembering other moments, other nameless men. Had there been many? I didn't ask. I was getting used to those times when Koa retreated inside his head and his brain took him on a journey I wasn't privy to. It wasn't like in childhood when he had a blank fit. These days, Koa came back quickly and without much effort, but I still lost him now and again.

"Does your grandfather know you're gay?" I asked. "Is that why you two don't get along?"

Koa had spoken sporadically about the aging man in the nursing home. I knew he visited him on a schedule and hated every second of it. Their relationship was poor, and I knew enough to know Koa had suffered under his hand growing up. The man was never Papa or Grandpa. He had always been *Grandfather*. And those stories never had an accompanying smile.

Koa drank deeply from his wine glass, setting it on his knee when finished. "He's known since I was a teenager. Rather, he presumed. I never confirmed it. My grandfather force-fed me religion growing up. He was especially interested in those passages that claim to be against homosexuality. I was forced to read them aloud. I protested once and only once, and he smacked me with his Bible and reminded me god didn't like faggots."

Koa's cheeks were flush—from anger or drink, I wasn't sure. On a handful of occasions, he had openly admitted his grandfather was an old-school authoritarian. He believed in physically disciplining a child when they misbehaved. He would smack Koa around if he got lippy, used a ruler on his fingers if he made a mistake playing piano, and forced him to sit up all night reading texts aloud, ignoring the child's incessant yawning and making him start again if he mispronounced words.

Koa cared little for the man, and it showed.

He'd gone quiet again, gaze locked somewhere in the distance, but I wasn't sure he was seeing the world around him.

"Why did you end up living with him?" I knew it was a question I shouldn't voice and regretted it the second it left my mouth.

Koa blinked back to the present. "I had no other family." He stared into his empty wine glass. "Please change the subject. You're treading close to territory you promised you wouldn't."

I let it go.

The sun set, and Koa invited me inside.

His introverted life meant we didn't go out much. He occasionally came to my apartment but seemed more comfortable on his own turf. Through July and into August, we spent every weekend together. We talked endlessly, had lunch at quiet diners, and walked the Otonabee River, which cut through the eastern side of Peterborough. Koa played music, read me poetry—which I didn't understand—and we reminisced about camp—the good memories.

I still hadn't sold my parents' house and had turned down every offer brought to the table—even the better ones. I had no mind for it and eventually told the Realtor to remove the listing.

Koa and I walked through the cemetery some evenings, hand in hand, chatting like a proper couple. The disconnect was always there, an ominous shadow preventing us from growing closer. He talked disturbingly about death, explaining his personal belief that humans were essentially no more important than the algae in the ocean. Our lives were without purpose, he said. The nature of good and evil were merely constructs derived from humans to bring order into a meaningless existence.

Koa spoke of things that went far over my head. About philosophers whose thinking he agreed with or disagreed with. About the essence of his own philosophical beliefs, which I could barely follow. He showed me a book he'd written, but when I tried to read it, I got lost in the first three pages. He was an intelligent man, and some days, I felt stupid in his presence.

But Koa ruminated often, and I quickly learned he wasn't seeking my opinion. He was simply talking out loud. He didn't need a debate partner. He needed someone to listen.

So I listened.

And I worried.

And I fought the cavernous gap between us, wishing I could find a way to close it.

By mid-August, I'd not connected any better with Koa than the first night I stayed over. He was present in the relationship, and he wasn't. He enjoyed sex, but he always left me feeling alone after, even when he snuggled up against me and fell asleep.

Koa gave me his mind. Koa gave me his body.

But I couldn't get near his heart.

And the worst part was I had fallen back in love with him. Only it was grown-up love, not the love of youth.

And I wasn't sure he could return it.

I thought of my conversation with Niles back in June, about the door Koa had locked in childhood. I wondered if the things that made Koa human had been locked behind that door and if he knew how to access it anymore.

It seemed like Koa pretended to care, but he was so indifferent to the world around him it frightened me.

25

Jersey

The summer was coming to an end. Koa was neck-deep in curriculum preparation, and it was getting harder and harder to convince him to take a break, but I'd planned a night out, something I hoped he would enjoy, and although wary of venturing anywhere public, he'd agreed. His skepticism was high when I wouldn't tell him where we were going. The moment I told him to bring his cardigan because it might be chilly, I seemed to lose his trust. The August weather was sweltering, but he donned the wool sweater over his T-shirt and wrapped it tightly around his middle for protection.

After making a few phone calls, I'd connected with the manager of Peterborough's OHL team, a guy named Bently Hogan. I wasn't opposed to throwing my name and career stats around when it served a purpose, and the guy nearly lost his shit when he heard he had a retired pro player in town. We'd chatted for over an hour on the phone, and when I told him why I'd called, he was more than happy to accommodate my request.

It was off-season, but Bently had explained how the team's coach was already running drills with the players most evenings on the freshly poured rink at the arena. When I pulled into the parking lot outside the massive concrete building, Koa shifted in his seat, facing me. I felt the heat of his gaze and the questions he had yet to speak.

"Trust me."

"Are we here for a hockey game?"

"I wouldn't do that to you. I know how you feel about crowds. Besides, it's way too early in the season. I was surprised the ice was down, to be honest."

"Why are we here?" Koa scanned the lot, likely noting we weren't alone. Several cars were parked near the back entrance.

"I reserved us some ice time. Don't worry. This lot will be heading out soon." I nodded at the congestion.

"I don't understand."

I parked away from the other vehicles and killed the engine, shifting to face Koa. "I thought we could enjoy a private skate. Just us. No one else." I shrugged. "Maybe it's dumb, but I thought... I was trying to come up with a creative date. We can leave."

Creases formed on Koa's forehead, and for a second, I thought he would tell me exactly that. "I don't know how to skate. I've never been on ice."

Leaning over the console, I cupped the back of Koa's neck and drew him toward me, pecking a light kiss on his worried brow. "I figured. I'll teach you. If you'll let me."

"I'll fall."

"Maybe, but I'll do my best to ensure it doesn't happen." *Like in life*, I wanted to add, but that took enormous trust, and Koa wasn't ready to believe in the power of love yet. Baby steps.

"I don't own skates."

"I rented some."

"Oh. What about your knee?" He glanced at the location of the old injury.

I kissed him again on the mouth. "Now you're looking for excuses. It will be fine. It only gets cranky if I overdo it."

"You limp when you get out of bed in the morning."

"I'm forty-five now. It's called morning stiffness and not the good kind."

I earned a small laugh. "You're incorrigible."

"Always. So what do you say?"

With a tentative smile on his face and one last lingering look at the building, Koa submitted. "Okay. But no laughing at me."

"I would never."

"Promise?"

I held up a pinky, and Koa, although clearly thinking I was ridiculous, hooked his baby finger with mine.

We headed inside. The echoey and familiar noises of hockey drills filled the air. A sharp whistle, the thud of someone hitting the boards, the slap of sticks on the ice. A blade grinding to a halt. Men's voices.

Worse, the scents of an arena assaulted me; a slight chemical odor from the artificial ice, musty dressing rooms, rubber flooring, and hints of Zamboni fuel. Cold air brushed my cheeks, a drastic contrast from the muggy outdoors.

My chest ached.

What I didn't tell Koa was that it had been about twelve years since I'd been on the ice. The verdict from the doctor back in the day had destroyed me, and although I'd given it my all after I was deemed healed enough to play, I struggled. When my team officially dropped me, I packed my skates away and hadn't laced them up since.

It was almost too much. It was almost me who turned us around and left.

I took Koa by the hand as we descended the tiered rows of bleachers to floor level, sitting near the team's box. The coach was wrapping up. The players had gathered to listen to him speak. I couldn't hear what he was saying, but I'd listened to enough coaches in my day, so I could guess.

My eyes stung with the nostalgia of it. The yearning to be part of the game again was as fresh as ever. I'd given my life to hockey. From the time I was old enough to skate until I'd been cut down and told it was over.

Life could change on a dime, and riding the wave out of the slump wasn't always easy.

I didn't realize I was squeezing Koa's hand too tight until he bumped my shoulder, speaking softly by my ear. "Are you okay? You're tense."

"Yeah. It's... harder than I expected."

Koa, perceptive as always, glanced at the players and back. "When's the last time you went to an arena with the intent of going on the ice?"

I tried to smile, but my cheeks weren't having it, and my throat thickened, making talking difficult. "Way, way too long."

Koa scooted closer and leaned his head on my shoulder. He cradled my hand between both of his. For Koa, it was a big step. Displays of emotion made him uncomfortable. His automatic response was usually to change the flow of conversation or leave the room until it was over. Koa recognizing I was having a hard time and offering support was monumental. Instead of getting distant, he drew closer.

Baby steps.

I was starting to have hope.

The players slowly dispersed, and Coach Jarvis, having noticed us, waved as he approached the boards near where we sat. "You Reid?"

"That's me."

The man scanned me as though looking for the player I once was and not finding him. "All yours. Hogan left some skates here in the box." He gestured. "I'll be up in the old bugger's office for a bit. Let me know when you're done, and I'll lock up."

"Thanks. I appreciate it."

Jarvis grunted and was about to turn away when I stood and offered a hand to shake. He obliged, reluctantly, eyeing Koa over my shoulder.

Unlike the team manager, Jarvis wasn't in awe of my hockey career, or maybe he sensed something he didn't like between Koa and me. That was fine, so long as he left us alone, I didn't give a shit. I never cared to be anyone's hero, and if the guy was a homophobe, he could kiss my ass.

Once the team had vanished to the changerooms, I took Koa to the box and found the skates Bently Hogan had reserved for us. Koa followed my instructions for putting them on, ensuring the laces were tight, but when he tried to stand, he wobbled and landed back on his ass on the bench.

"I fear this will not go well," he said, ruminating at the blades under his feet. "If I break my neck—"

"You won't. I've got you." I held out a hand, and Koa used it to get to his feet once again, still wobbly.

Ensuring Koa had a firm hold of the boards, I opened the gate and stepped onto the ice for the first time in twelve years. The feeling of it under my blades was indescribable. I skated a few feet away, cut a sharp stop, and then swerved back and forth to regain the feel of a skill that had once been second nature. Once I was confident I hadn't lost the ability, I returned to Koa.

His expression was one of awe and skepticism. "You make it look easy."

"Like riding a bike. Come on. It's fun."

"Fun is reading in my chair at home."

"You have to get out on occasion."

He hummed but took my hand, squeezing with a death grip, and stepped tentatively onto the ice one foot at a time.

I grinned. "There you go."

"I'm terrified of moving."

"I won't let you fall. Use the edge of the blade to push the ice away at an angle. One foot then the other."

Koa tried as I skated backward, keeping a firm hold of his waist to balance him. After some fumbling and three near falls, he got the hang of it. The short staccato movements were more steps than slides, but he was moving and grinning, so I wasn't about to correct him on his first attempt.

We did a round of the rink. Koa's attention remained on his feet, fingers digging into my arms. Slowly, he grew more confident and managed to glance up from time to time and meet my eyes.

"How are you doing?" I asked.

"It's... I'm skating. I can't believe I'm skating." He laughed, and Koa didn't laugh often. For that brief moment, he was a kid again, and it felt like a win. Like I'd given him something good for a change. Something he could file away with the handful of other positive memories he had—which I knew were few and far between.

We continued in circles until I thought Koa was comfortable enough. I moved in beside him. Looking less confident, Koa trailed one hand along the boards while holding mine with the other. But we managed a few rounds without crashing and falling, and his smile never broke.

"I can't believe you did this for a living. I always thought hockey players needed sticks to keep themselves upright."

I snorted. "Who told you that?"

"I'm not sure I remember."

"Well, I assure you, I was quite proficient in my day."

"You miss it, don't you?"

"Yes. Terribly. I'm not sure I've ever learned who I am without hockey. It defined me for so long. Once that chapter in my life ended, the rest of the pages were blank."

"I can't imagine losing your career overnight. It would be devastating. But you know, your struggles afterward... the drug addiction, the anger, the way you fell into a pit of despair. It was warranted. I know you blame yourself, but you shouldn't. You did the best with what you were given. Sometimes that's all that matters."

Spoken like a man who had been in therapy his whole life.

I shifted to skate backward again, moving in front of Koa, holding his hands in mine, and dragging him along. "You know, I could say the same thing to you."

His smile dimmed. "It's not the same."

"Why not?"

"It just isn't."

We skated in silence, both of us ruminating. Koa drifted like he often did, and I didn't have the strength to draw him back into the light. My own past haunted me. Instead, I tugged him against my body and whispered, "Just glide. I've got you," into his ear.

He rested his head on my shoulder, and I took us around the rink several more times. I wished for so many things in that moment. I wished I had the power to erase the past—or rewrite it. I wished I could help Koa believe in a brighter tomorrow—but to do that, I realized I needed to believe in it too.

When Koa complained his feet hurt, I guided him to the box, and we unlaced our skates and sat for a while on the bench.

"Did you have fun?" I asked.

"I did. Thank you. I'm sorry to be so ignorant about hockey. I'm sure you'd prefer to be with someone you could watch games with and banter about bad plays."

"I don't wish for anyone else, Koa. Only you."

"You could teach me. This winter, when the season starts."

I chuckled. "You would hate every second of it."

"Likely."

"But I appreciate what you're trying to do."

I stared out at the ice, unable to suggest we leave, stuck in limbo, reminiscing over my hockey days and wondering who I was at the end of it all.

Koa took my hand and squeezed. "I wish I knew how to offer you comfort. I recognize you're hurting, but... I'm not qualified to offer advice. Not really. But I guess if I've learned anything over the years, it's that we can't change the past. We can only learn how to live with it."

"Have you learned how to live with yours?"

Koa wore a thousand-yard stare like he was looking through the years to a time long ago. "Sometimes, I think I have. Other times... not so much."

"I think it's why I can't sell the house. I've already lost everything important to me. Hockey. My parents. My son. If I sell the house, it's like saying goodbye to all the good memories too."

"Niles would say you need to find happiness in the now. Find a reason to wake up every day. A reason to be alive."

"Sounds like you've been told that a time or two."

Koa nodded. "He's preached at me plenty. I'm offering you his advice, but I've never bought into it."

I didn't say anything. We were falling into that dark philosophical hole we skirted too often, and I knew where those conversations led. We were supposed to be having a nice night out, and my mood had plummeted.

"Would you like to join me at a café for a hot chocolate?"

Koa's smile returned. "I would. That sounds lovely."

26

Koa

School began on a Tuesday, as always. The day after Labor Day. It was chaotic, and I left Timber Creek with a headache, driving straight to the nursing home for my biweekly visit with Grandfather.

Jersey had texted during last period, but I had yet to get back to him. Commencing a new semester would likely reduce our time together, and I'd experienced a quiet regret. Spending the summer with Jersey had been a nice change of routine. I'd enjoyed it more than I expected. More than I was willing to admit. Enough I'd shared about my new relationship with Dr. Kent during our last appointment—a regrettable mistake.

She'd pressed the issue, but I'd refused to play her game. When asked if I could identify the feelings and emotions that had arisen as a result of dating Jersey, I'd stared out the window and changed the subject.

It didn't stop her pursuit of answers.

When asked how engaging in a relationship again made me feel, I'd lied and said it made me feel nothing.

When Dr. Kent persisted, questioning why I'd decided to date at all if I felt nothing for the man, I'd mentally checked out, a skill I'd mastered as a teenager.

I'd learned young that I was permitted to have personal thoughts, and I didn't always have to share them.

My mind had been on display for one doctor or another for as long as I could remember, and it grew tiresome having my life exposed and my very nature constantly under the microscope.

The check-in process at the nursing home was quick and easy. I signed my name, grabbed a visitor's badge, and rode the elevator to the third floor as I responded to Jersey's text, asking how my first day had gone.

Koa: Potential is high. I won't hold my breath. I've been fooled before. The age of cell phones and social media is rotting the brains of our youth.

Jersey: Lol. Call me when you get home?

Koa: Aren't you at work?

Jersey: Got off early.

Part of me wanted to invite Jersey for dinner, but an hour and a half was a long drive for a couple of hours of entertainment, and we both worked the following day. I agreed to call him later and pocketed my phone.

Before entering Grandfather's room, I closed my eyes and took a deep breath.

The dying man slept. He didn't stir at my arrival. He rarely did anymore. The cancer had ravaged him whole, and I wasn't sure how he still lived. The body he inhabited was bone covered with a transparent layer of tissue paper skin. His sunken eyes didn't open anymore, even when he was awake.

A wheezing inhale followed by a rattling exhale filled the room at even intervals, and I watched as his concave chest rose and fell, rose and fell. The cannula had slipped from his nose, so I adjusted it.

I tried to care but couldn't. I tried to summon emotions or at least identify them, as Dr. Kent was so fond of saying. But there weren't any. No sadness. No guilt. No joy. No frustration. No anger. No fear. Nothing. I was a husk, no different than the man in the bed. A vessel of slowly dying organs that would one day stop working as well.

What difference would tears make?

I sat on the vacant chair and opened the bedside table, removing the worn tome from within. I found the page where I'd left off and read aloud, eager to do my duty and be done with it.

The dying man stirred and turned his head at my voice. My name came out in a questioning rasp. "Koa?"

I ignored it and continued to read. It was the only gift I could give, and mostly because books had been the only thing to keep me alive for the past four decades. I read as much for me as for the dying man.

He listened. The changed rhythm of his breathing was the only indication he was awake. I didn't stumble or pause. I pronounced every name with precision, every syllable, putting emphasis as the Russians did on certain vowels. I injected proper emotion as I'd been taught. I gave the characters voices and personalities, remembering the sting of the ruler across my knuckles. I'd been trained like a whipped dog to do my duty, and there I was, despite everything, chasing a bone that had forever dangled out of reach.

The dying man wouldn't see the end of the book. Not this time. *War and Peace* would victimize him as it had many within her pages.

But for today, I read.

Grandfather listened.

When Darnel arrived with a dinner tray an hour later, he offered me a sympathetic smile. I thanked him, and he left for a moment so I could say goodbye. Since Grandfather could no longer feed himself, Darnel would return when I left and spoon the pureed mush between Grandfather's shriveled lips, keeping him alive another day despite his body's insistence to quit.

"I'm stopping. Your food is here." I put the book away and stared at the dying man in the bed.

I waited.

Perhaps he would forget.

Perhaps his mind had rotted away.

Perhaps...

But no. He reached with a bony, trembling hand, seeking blindly. I took it like I always did. His grip was weak, hands cold and frail. If I clung too tightly, they might crumble to dust.

Silence prevailed.

Grandfather groaned and moved his lips. Sounds emerged, but they didn't form words. I would not pray for him or with him. If he could no longer give voice to his god, then he could think the words instead. If his god existed, he would listen and understand.

I waited.

Grandfather sputtered. Sticky white foam gathered at the corners of his mouth. His trembling hand tried to squeeze mine, but his strength was gone. If he'd been healthy, I'd have probably earned a smack for my insolence.

But he wasn't.

So be it.

A few minutes passed before he managed to throw my hand off with as much aggression as he could muster, saying something I could only surmise was meant to be an insult.

It didn't matter. Praying wouldn't save him. If he truly believed in the afterlife, wouldn't his god know what he was trying to say? Besides, if he believed in the afterlife, his god wouldn't want my prayers.

I stood. "I'll see you Thursday."

He didn't respond.

I left without looking back.

But I wouldn't see him on Thursday.

Grandfather died the following morning.

I was reviewing our first unit of study with my senior literature students, Shakespeare—I always began the year with Shakespeare—when Annette Mandel, Timber Creek's secretary, interrupted, knocking on the open classroom door.

She gave an apologetic smile and waved me over, handing me a slip of paper. "The nursing home called. They want you to call back immediately."

"We've been over this. There's no need to interrupt—"

"I know, but the lady seemed adamant this time. She said right away."

They always seemed adamant to Annette. I tucked the folded paper into a pocket without looking at it. I didn't need the home's number. She knew that too but always wrote it down regardless.

"I'll call them on my lunch break. Thank you."

"Koa." She touched my arm. "They said right away. They said it was important."

"Yes, but I'm teaching. It can wait." And the home always said it was important, but I didn't point that out.

Something in Annette's face made me give up the fight.

"Fine." I instructed a boy named Derik to go to the front of the class and take charge. "I want you to work together to come up with a list of five Shakespeare plays you want to study this year. No arguing. You're seniors. Find a diplomatic means of addressing the problem. And keep your volume down. I'll be back in a moment."

"I can watch them," Annette offered.

"They're fine." I paced down the hall a short way, but Annette lingered at my classroom door. It was the beginning of the year. Students were still riding the summertime high and would quickly get rambunctious without a teacher in earshot, so I supposed she thought her presence would help them stay organized.

The call ended quickly. Once I connected with the nurses' station on the third floor, Dotty, the head nurse working the day shift, informed me Grandfather had passed away. She explained how, in accordance with his instructions, his body would be moved to the Gaslow Funeral Home that afternoon.

"Do you have any questions?" she asked.

"No."

"I'm terribly sorry for your loss, Mr. Burgard."

I thanked her and hung up, sliding my cell phone back into my pocket.

So that was that. Grandfather was gone. Cancer had won. We all knew it would.

When I turned to head back to my classroom, my feet wouldn't budge. Something strange coursed through me like I'd been injected with a numbing agent. Every muscle seized, and no matter how great my force of will, I couldn't unstick my shoes from the floor.

For a moment, my entire body felt petrified, and I was certain I would remain in that spot, in the corridor, for eternity. Confused, I took a second to evaluate. What was this feeling? Shock? But I'd been expecting his death for a long time. I searched for remorse. I searched for sadness. I searched for guilt, anger, or even pleasure. I found nothing. Nothing but a strange thickness in my blood, preventing me from moving, preventing my lungs from expanding and contracting as they normally would.

The man who'd raised me, who'd disciplined me without mercy, who'd stripped me of every remaining thread of humanity I'd possessed was gone.

And I didn't care.

I didn't care.

"I don't care." Saying it aloud helped.

"I don't care. I don't care. I. Don't. Care."

The odd sensation passed quickly with my new resolve.

I returned to the classroom, the brain fog I carried everywhere I went a bit thicker than usual, but nothing I couldn't handle.

I went to move past Annette, but she stopped me with a soft touch to my arm, lowering her voice. "Is everything okay? The lady on the phone sounded... distraught."

"Everything is fine. My grandfather passed is all. Excuse me."

I removed my arm from her hold and left Annette slack-jawed and confused in the hallway.

Derik had done well. A list of eight plays awaited my approval on the blackboard. "Eight isn't five. I'll need to have a word with Dr. Allan and see what he's teaching you in math." The students laughed. "It looks like we need to dwindle this list down some. Everyone take out a scrap piece of paper."

Annette remained in the doorway a long time, watching with a hand over her mouth and a crease in her brow.

I ignored her.

I moved on.

The lunch bell rang at eleven forty-five. The classroom emptied at lightning speed, everyone eager to fill their growling bellies. As I copied the information I needed from the blackboard into my planner, Niles appeared at the door, rapping gently with a knuckle.

I glanced up and away again as quickly. He wore a serious expression, and I knew without asking someone had sent him. Someone had told.

"What are you doing?" he asked, venturing into the room.

"Making a list so I can move forward with my curriculum. You see this?" I gestured to the blackboard, tapping the play title on the bottom of the list. "This is the first time in more than six years they've chosen *Othello*. It's exciting. Finally, something different. I'll probably start with it."

"Koa."

I wouldn't look at him and continued writing in my planner. "*Romeo and Juliet* is always a given. Same with *Hamlet* and *King Lear*. *Macbeth* is a guarantee. Every year, the students choose the popular ones, but *Othello?* That's a treat. I look forward to it. It was one of Shakespeare's top plays, but oddly enough, it's rarely chosen."

"Koa." Niles's shadow fell over my notebook, and he removed the pen from my hand, nudging my shoulder so I would stand upright and face him.

"What?" I injected a touch of irritation into my tone, hoping it would warn him off. Niles had no qualms about stepping over lines he wasn't invited to cross or delving into topics I didn't want to discuss. It had been an ongoing issue in our relationship and bled into our friendship.

Pulling an attitude never worked before, and it didn't work now.

"Go home." My friend wore a mask of sorrow.

"Why? It's noon. I have two more classes to teach after lunch and—"

"Go home," he said gentler, rubbing my arm. The touch didn't feel good, and I pulled out of his reach, hugging the limb to my body. I didn't want to be comforted, caressed, or reassured. I wanted to stay on the outskirts of the world where I'd lived my whole life. It was safer. Quieter.

I wished I had my cardigan, but it was at home. The weather was still stifling, and after our trip to the arena the other day, I'd hung it in the hall closet. I needed it. Its reassurance. Its protection.

"The man who raised you has passed away, Koa, and you have things to take care of. You don't need to be here. Annette called in a sub for this afternoon. Go home and take care of you."

"There is nothing wrong with me, and I have nothing to take care of. Grandfather organized everything on his own. The funeral home has their instructions, and I can show up or not. It makes no difference. I've chosen not to go. I have things to do here. Excuse me."

When I tried to retrieve my pen, Niles wouldn't let me have it. Against my will, he drew me into his arms and hugged me so tight I couldn't get free. But he knew I wouldn't try.

It wasn't worth the fight. What did it matter? I could stand there and argue with Niles or let him have his way. I could fight tooth and nail, stay and teach my afternoon classes, and try to make everyone on staff see how much of a nonissue Grandfather's death was, but they wouldn't understand. I could speak until I was blue in the face, but it would change nothing.

Submission was easier.

"Go home," Niles said by my ear. "I don't care if you call the funeral home or open a bottle of wine, get drunk, and write morose poetry. Go spend time with your thoughts. It's a lot to process. Get away from here."

"And if I don't want to?"

"Do it anyway. And call out tomorrow too. Take the week."

"Now you're being ridiculous."

"Call Dr. Kent, and—"

"Absolutely not."

"Koa, you need to face this with—"

"Don't patronize me. The man meant nothing to me, and you know it."

"Fine. Then go home and toast his death. Save me a glass, and I'll come by when I get off later. We can celebrate together."

"No. I'd rather be alone."

"Then be alone." He squeezed me tighter and kissed my temple before releasing me. I'd learned long ago the power of surrender. The power of Niles Edwidge. It had nothing to do with weakness and more to do with indifference. If I didn't care one way or the other, it was easiest to let him have his way. It closed the issue faster than arguing.

So I went home.

I did not call the funeral home.

I didn't call Jersey or respond to his text later that night.

I talked to Rask, drank expensive wine, and wrote morose poetry, as Niles had suggested. It poured out of me. Unstoppable. Unforgiving.

The wine was a bad idea. It deepened the ever-present fog. It amplified the nothingness.

The world became a giant sensory deprivation tank, and I floated there, unable to think, unable to feel, unable to process.

Words spilled out of me onto paper, ink smearing under my fast-moving hand. Its context was a toxic and grisly stream of consciousness, ugly and perverse. I didn't understand it or know where it originated, but there it was. I destroyed each page the second I filled them, tearing them from the journal and crumpling them. The balls of discarded paper filled the waste basket and my desk.

I couldn't stop writing. The words ate me alive. Caustic yet soothing. Beautiful yet ugly. Necessary. I purged. I bled onto the paper.

Night came. The darkness that lived deep in my soul stirred and woke. It had been slowly gaining power all day. I'd felt it and could no longer hold the door shut. My strength was depleted.

The horrors I had avoided for years breathed down my neck and whispered in my ear. They flashed across my retinas like waking dreams.

The rotting poison I'd locked away decades ago seeped through the cracks and bubbled to the surface. It crawled through my veins. It curled around my lungs and heart and wormed its way through the narrow channels of my brain.

For the first time in many years, I was back there. In that house. Hiding from the monster.

Running for my life.

Unable to escape.

27

Jersey

Koa had gone silent, and it nagged at me. Our texts were regular enough that I could anticipate them daily. Usually I initiated the conversation, but he always responded. I hadn't heard from him since Tuesday night. The six texts I'd sent on Wednesday had gone unanswered. The call I'd placed that morning went to voicemail.

Between clients, I checked my phone again. Nothing. It was nearing four on Thursday afternoon. Classes would be out for the day. Koa had no excuse for ignoring me, so his silence was concerning. I sent another text, asking him to at least check in so I didn't worry, and then pocketed my phone as I made plans to drive to Peterborough after work.

My next patient was a college-level basketball player with a bad knee who had recently undergone surgery. Surgery for an athlete was never good, but at nineteen, he had a high chance of a full recovery, unlike I'd had at thirty. I read the guy's chart while standing in the hallway, reminding myself of our progress and what therapy techniques we were working on.

Before I could open the door, my pocket buzzed with an incoming phone call.

"Finally." I scrambled to answer, seeing Koa's name on the screen. "Hello? Where the hell have you been? Are you okay?"

"Hi. Jersey? It's Niles. Do you have a minute?"

Niles? On Koa's phone? My stomach dropped.

"Is everything okay? Where's Koa?"

"He's here. Can't you hear him?"

In the background, someone played piano. It wasn't the melancholy Chopin Koa had demonstrated for me a few times over the summer. Whatever score he'd gotten a hold of was angry and violent. The abrupt, fast pounding of notes, although precise and intentional, radiated something caustic and aggressive through the phone.

Coming from Koa, it made no sense.

"What's going on? I've been calling and texting for two days. He hasn't—"

"His grandfather died, and... I can't reach him. I've lost him, Jersey. I don't know what's going on. He won't call the doctor. He won't talk to me except to yell at me to get out and leave him alone. He's... beyond approach. He's had moments of instability in the past, but I've never seen him this bad. Can you come? If you can't talk him down, I'm calling an ambulance."

"An ambulance? Christ." I scrubbed a hand over my beard and spun in place before staring at the door separating me from my client. I had another scheduled after him. "I need a couple of hours. I'm at work, and I can't leave. I can be there for six thirty or seven. Will you wait?"

"I'll stay with him until then." The enraged music continued in the background, growing louder and faster as Koa reached a certain part of the piece. Niles sighed. "Sorry to call while you're working."

"I'm glad you did. I'll be there as soon as I can."

I disconnected the call and stood for a long minute, processing. Koa's episodes from our camp days came back to me. Specifically, the one where he'd attacked another boy and had been sent home. In those days, when something or someone threw Koa over the edge, it was hard to get him back. The following year, he'd told me he was better. He'd told me he had medicine because his brain was sick.

I'd never understood the full implication of that statement at the time.

As a child, I'd always assumed medicine made sicknesses go away. If a kid got an ear infection, the antibiotics eliminated it. What I hadn't comprehended in my youth was the lifelong effects of mental health illnesses. What Koa dealt with—whatever it was—was a forever deal, and once again, his barely stable mind had been pushed beyond its limits.

I had a feeling that didn't happen as often anymore, but when it did, it was catastrophic.

I finished the day queasy with worry, leaving paperwork behind so I could hit the road and get to Peterborough. I arrived at a quarter to seven and parked on the road since Niles's vehicle occupied the driveway behind Koa's Audi.

Standing on the porch, I heard the same aggressive piano music coming from inside. It had been hours, and he was still at it. Unlike earlier on the phone, the music had grown sloppy, his mistakes glaring. I knocked but let myself in, figuring it would go unheard over the racket.

Niles met me in the front hallway and offered a wane smile. "Prepare thyself, my friend. The battlefield is messy, and the odds are not in our favor."

I chuckled. "What do I need to know?"

"He's... toeing the line of self-injurious. I tried to stop him, but I was afraid he'd physically throw me out the door."

"Self-injurious how?"

Niles didn't explain and hitched his chin, indicating I should follow him into the library.

Koa sat on the piano bench, wrapped in the cardigan I hadn't seen since our skating date, his face a picture of concentration, cheeks pink, hair in disarray. His focus was on a spread of sheet music, his fingers dancing stiffly and aggressively over the ivories.

He stumbled, fingers slipping on the keys. Stopping, he made fists with both hands, flipped them knuckles down, and smacked them repeatedly against the top edge of the piano—hard enough I flinched. Hard enough there was no way it wouldn't hurt.

"Again," Koa said through gritted teeth.

And he played.

"Jesus."

"It's been going on for hours. His knuckles on his right hand are already bleeding, and he won't stop. His hands are going to be a mess."

"What the hell is he doing?"

"Disciplining himself for making mistakes. But the more he does it, the worse his playing. It's a vicious cycle. They're going to swell like balloons at this rate."

Speechless, all I could do was watch the horror show as Koa played—poorly—then smacked his knuckles on the piano as punishment, screaming, "Again!"

I wanted to collapse and cry. I wanted to yank him away from the instrument and wrap my arms around him so he'd stop. I wanted to find a way to reach the innermost part of him he shared with no one so maybe I could understand the pain he carried around with him like a shadow.

A fire burned in the fireplace. It was much too early in the season for such things, and the room was stifling. Koa's hairline was sweat-drenched, and I couldn't fathom how hot he must be wrapped in a cardigan, sitting a few feet from the roaring flames.

I didn't know what to do.

Niles turned to me, lowering his voice. "Unless you can talk some sense into him, I'm calling an ambulance. They'll lock him up, and he'll be pissed, but this isn't right. This is a breakdown, and I don't know about you, but I'm not qualified to handle it. He needs professional help."

Niles was right, but I wasn't ready to give up. Not yet. "Give me a few minutes." I didn't know what I was planning, nor did I think I could offer any special words to calm Koa down. If Niles, his longtime friend and ex-lover, couldn't reach him, what hope did I have?

I didn't start by approaching Koa. I aimed for the stairs to the second floor. Niles called after me, "Where are you going?"

In the bathroom, I rooted through the medicine cabinet, finding a veritable pharmacy of prescription medication. I figured I might. No one has a lifelong relationship with a therapist and doesn't have a drug or two on hand to show for it. Especially Koa, who'd been in active therapy for as long as I'd known him.

I read the labels one after another, their contents barely pronounceable, and I was familiar with a lot of drugs in my line of work. I wasn't sure what half of them were for, and based on the fact that all of them were full, I wondered if Koa bothered taking them at all.

But I found what I was looking for. Xanax.

I returned to the library, where Koa was busy reorganizing the sheet music, laying the next few pages on top of the ones he finished playing. Without contemplating my approach or the consequences, I sat on the bench beside him and closed the fallboard.

Koa stilled. It was like I'd powered him down with the simple action. The only part of him that moved was his chest with his rapid breathing.

He didn't look at me. His gaze remained fixed at a spot in the middle distance, hands curled and cradled loosely against his sweater. "What are you doing here? I didn't invite you."

"Niles called. He told me you weren't feeling well."

"I'm fine." A shudder radiated through him, and he lifted a hand, examining it. He stuck a bleeding knuckle into his mouth, then shook it like it stung, staring at it again as though amazed at the damage. They were red and inflamed, battered like he'd been punching a brick wall for hours, and I worried he might have cracked bones.

I studied him and couldn't find the person I'd spent the summer with. The intelligent, sophisticated man I'd fallen in love with, the man with a passion for literature and melancholy music, was gone. In his place, I discovered the broken boy from camp. The one who couldn't figure out how to be like the other children. The one with a secret he held so tight to his chest it was slowly destroying him.

Koa had retreated further inside his head than usual, and I couldn't imagine what he saw. I glanced at Niles and asked him to find a glass of water. He skipped out of the room as I turned back to Koa.

"I know you can hear me. I know you're listening. You don't have to talk. You don't have to tell me what's eating you. I know it's bad. I know there's a lot going on in your head right now, but you're scaring

Niles. He wants to send you to the hospital, and I know you don't want that. Something really rotten has moved in upstairs, hasn't it?"

I brushed Koa's sweaty hair from his forehead. He didn't move away or flinch. "And I bet it doesn't feel good. I also know it's hard to make it stop sometimes. It happened at camp when we were little, more than once. One time, it was so bad they had to send you home, and I hated it. I wanted to be there for you, just like I do now.

"A long time ago, you told me taking medicine made your head better. I think it would help what's happening right now."

Niles cautiously handed me the glass of water and backed off. I set the bottle of Xanax on the fallboard. Koa focused on it. Staring. Not moving.

"You don't have to feel this way, Koa. You must be exhausted. It's okay to take a break from it all."

His vacant stare remained stuck on the pill bottle, but I waited. I knew his gears were spinning. After a few minutes of quiet contemplation, he picked it up and fumbled to open it with his swollen hands. He helped himself to a single pill.

I felt like I'd won the war, but in truth, I'd one a single battle. It was something.

I offered him the water, and he drank the whole thing, hand trembling enough that I feared he might drop it.

Handing back the empty glass, he stood and wrapped the cardigan around his middle as he stepped out from behind the bench. He was unsteady, but I didn't reach for him.

Koa glanced from me to Niles and back. "I'm going to bed. You can all stop worrying now. I'll be fine."

Without looking back, he left the room.

We listened as he climbed the creaky stairs. When a door on the second floor shut, Niles asked, "What did you give him?"

"Xanax. He'll sleep."

"He's got a full bottle of wine in him."

"Then he'll sleep well."

Niles collapsed on the couch, kicking his feet out and covering his face with his hands. "I'm spent. I've been here for hours. I can't believe you walk in, and in five minutes he's better."

"He's not better."

"You know what I mean. He stopped playing. I couldn't get him away from the damn piano."

I spent a second at the fireplace, smothering the flames the best I could before sitting in Koa's favorite reading chair. "What happened?"

"He cracked. I don't know. Yesterday, after he got the news, I could barely get him to go home. Today, he's... I've never seen him like this."

"I have. Kind of. It was different. As a kid, he'd have episodes at camp. Usually, something triggered it. Violence, blood... a cap gun once. That was the worst. Archery. He would either detach or lose his shit completely. He beat a kid up once."

"Koa?" Niles stared with astonishment. "No way."

"Yes. Attacked him. Punched him bloody. It took several counselors to get him off. No one could calm him down."

"So this was like an adult version of a tantrum, you think?"

"Maybe." Although that explanation didn't sit right either. It was an episode. I didn't have a better word for it.

"I don't get it," Niles said. "He's always acted indifferent toward his grandfather."

"He hates his grandfather."

"I wouldn't say that. Hate is a strong emotion, and Koa rarely expresses strong emotions of any kind." Niles shifted upright on the couch and tucked a leg under his ass, facing me. "You must see that."

"I do, but it doesn't mean he doesn't feel them."

Niles narrowed his eyes, staring unpleasantly. The ex and the current boyfriend. I knew what he was thinking. Had Koa opened up to me? Had he let himself be vulnerable? How on earth had I walked in and calmed him down in under five minutes when Niles, his longtime best friend, hadn't been able to make a dent?

I had to give the poor man something. He was important to Koa too, and I couldn't pretend he wasn't. We were both riding in the same boat on the same tumultuous ocean. We were both being rocked by the same waves. We were both trying to rescue a man who, some days, I thought would prefer to drown.

"He's distant with me too," I said. "I can't seem to... It's like we don't live in the same world."

"I know that feeling."

"He knows how to play the relationship game, but there's nothing behind it."

Niles's eyes glistened, and he looked away. "I know. It killed me when I couldn't bring him around. Make him see that..." Niles trailed off.

"I know," I whispered. "I have to ask... Is he suicidal?"

Niles flinched at the question, gaze jerking back around. I'd listened to Koa talk about death more than once, and it had unsettled me.

"No."

"How can you be so sure?"

Niles considered. "Because... because you have to care to be suicidal, and Koa has always been indifferent."

"Doesn't that make him more apt?"

"No. People who take their own lives usually feel trapped in a world causing them excruciating pain. They can't handle it anymore, and death is a release from that pain. An escape."

"Koa *is* in pain. Don't you see that?"

"No. Koa is indifferent. He doesn't care about anything. Past, present, future. None of it matters to him. He doesn't feel rejected by the world. He doesn't care one way or the other. He merely exists because it is what's done. What happens happens according to him."

"I'm not sure I agree."

Niles shrugged. "I don't think he's suicidal. I doubt it's ever crossed his mind. Koa's views on life and death aren't like yours or mine. Life is as meaningless as death to him, so there would be no point in suicide. Don't you understand? Haven't you listened to his philosophies?"

I had. Koa tried to explain his views several times, but I couldn't wrap my brain around them. I didn't understand how Niles could be so sure. Everything about Koa screamed high-risk.

"It won't change," Niles said, butting into my musing.

"I'm sorry?"

"The gap you feel. The distance. It won't change. He doesn't know how to connect with people. Not deeply. Not emotionally. Therapy has not helped in that regard, and love is a concept Koa will never understand."

"I don't believe that."

Niles's smile was sad. "I was there once too. Ambitious. Eager to show him what he was missing. It will eat you alive if you let it." Niles stood and glanced around the room. "Good luck, Jersey. I hope I'm wrong. I hope you can reach him. I'm going to head home. He isn't required to be back until next week. The funeral is tomorrow morning at ten. Try to convince him to go. I think it would be good for him."

"I won't force it."

Niles nodded. "Let me know if he's planning to attend. I'll be sure to make an appearance."

He left me sitting by the smoldering fireplace, sweating, heart twisted, and stomach full of lead.

Alone, I wandered Koa's library. His desk was a mess of torn and balled papers, journals lying open, and pens scattered. Pages filled with writing stared up at me. An empty glass of wine left a ring on the blotter, a deep burgundy stain. I didn't invade his privacy and read what he'd left unattended. It wouldn't have been fair. Koa had been in a state of unraveling, and no matter my curiosity, I wouldn't overstep unless invited. His writing was deeply personal. That much I knew.

I made some calls, rescheduling and canceling appointments for the following day. I'd originally planned to head home that night, but I didn't feel comfortable leaving Koa alone, no matter what Niles said.

His episode concerned me. I was out of my league, pretending to know more than I did. Xanax and a good night's sleep was one thing, but Koa might still need to explore the hospital option if he wasn't more stable come morning.

Maybe I could convince him to call the doctor.

Rask found me and rubbed against my legs, purring softly, then meowing loudly when I ignored him. I found a can of cat food in the kitchen and shut down Koa's house before heading upstairs. Koa was asleep on top of the covers, wrapped in his cardigan, knees tucked against his chest. He was a forty-five-year-old man trapped in a nightmare more than three decades in the making, and in the wash of moonlight glowing from the window, he had the presence of a child.

And I didn't know if he could ever break free of those bonds.

As he slept, I turned on the bedside light to examine his hands. They were no longer bleeding, but swelling and bruising had set in. He would be lucky if he could bend his fingers by morning. Deciding they didn't need doctoring, I nudged him awake. Groggy and incoherent, he didn't put up a fight and let me undress him and tuck him into bed properly.

I used the washroom and shut off the light before crawling in beside him. Even in his coma-like state, Koa immediately moved into my arms, resting his head on my chest, tucking it under my chin, and wrapping an arm securely around my middle. It was the same way he'd lain on me at camp all those years ago when I'd saved him from nightmares. I'd secretly loved it then, and I openly loved it now.

If only I could fight the demons for him and give him a break.

I stroked his hair as he slept, burying my nose in the tangled mess and inhaling. He smelled like Koa—like a library, like candlewax, like pain, sadness, and a bone-weary loneliness I might never be able to conquer. It was far too early for bed, so I lay awake, thinking and wishing I had answers, wondering at this path I'd ended up on and how life was unpredictable.

Koa may not believe in god, but I wondered if fate had guided me back to him when he needed me most. If my parents hadn't died, I wouldn't have been back at the house. If I hadn't returned to the house, I would have never found those letters.

It was nearly four when he stirred. I woke instantly, having barely coasted the edges of sleep all night.

"Hey." I snagged his hand as he sat on the edge of the bed, aiming to escape.

"Sleep. I'm fine. I need coffee and a toothbrush. Not in that order."

I chuckled. "Can I join you?"

"It's four a.m."

"And I'm awake."

He turned to face me in the dark. "Why are you here? Don't you work today?"

"I took a long weekend. Thought maybe you needed me instead."

He turned away again, buried his face in his palms, rested his elbows on his knees, and sighed. My eyes adjusted to the dark, and I made out the defeated bow of his bare back and the knobs of his spine.

I traced a hand down its curve and scooted closer to kiss his shoulder, wanting to draw him back down into my arms and hold him until all the hurt went away. An impossible feat.

"Did Niles call you?" he asked, words muffled.

"Yes."

"I figured. Why is my head pounding?"

"He said you'd gone through at least one bottle of wine, possibly more. I gave you a Xanax before you went to bed."

"Dangerous mix."

"It was necessary."

Koa didn't disagree, groaned, and got up. He shuffled around in the dark, finding something to wear—underwear, a T-shirt, and the cardigan. When he closed himself in the upstairs bathroom, I went down to the kitchen to start coffee. I'd had several lessons over the summer on how to work the fancy machine and knew the precise settings and type of grind Koa liked when making his brew.

He joined me as a second mug filled. I placed his coffee on the island when he sat, wrapping his sweater securely around him like armor.

"Thank you."

I'd lit a few of his scented candles, avoiding the harsher overhead lights and keeping the room dim and tranquil. I'd even put on soft classical music because I knew Koa liked it in the early morning, and I hoped it would keep him calm.

Koa examined his hands, flexing them the best he could and wincing when the swelling pulled his skin taut and restricted motion.

"Anything broken?" I asked.

"No."

"Do you remember last night?"

"Yes. Vividly." He wrapped his injured hands around the warm mug. "I'm sorry you witnessed that. I'm ashamed."

"Don't be. I'm sorry about your grandfather. I didn't know until Niles told me."

Koa sipped his coffee, not acknowledging the remark.

"Will you go to the funeral today?" I asked.

"No. My presence is unnecessary."

I didn't push it. Whatever Niles thought, Koa was a grown man who could make his own decisions, and maybe the funeral risked setting him off again.

"What's on the agenda?"

"Nothing since I'm not to return to work until next week. I'd have been better off occupied."

I disagreed but kept my opinion to myself.

We drank coffee across from one another, Koa lost in his head, me doing all I could to see beyond his thick walls. The fearful incident of the previous evening lost its urgency and significance in the calm of a new day. Koa made no more mention of it, and I was hard-pressed to bring it up.

He showered while I made breakfast—I was not as skilled in the kitchen, but he didn't care—and we ate in relative quiet. After breakfast, I took a turn in the bathroom and returned to find him organizing his desk in the library.

He had dressed in layers, the cardigan on top.

"Do you need more coffee?" I asked from the doorway.

"No, thank you."

Koa smoothed out the crumpled balls of paper he'd picked off the floor and read them, grimacing before tearing them to shreds and discarding them in a waste basket. He read through a few pages in the open journals before closing them and stacking them to one side.

"You were busy last night."

"I suppose. None of it is fit for human consumption. My ninth graders could produce better."

"I'm sure that's not true."

He glared over the top of his reading glasses, the look saying, *you have no idea*.

And I didn't, so I let it go.

Koa continued to tidy up while I gave him space. When he finished, he collapsed in his desk chair and pushed his glasses on top of his head. Rask appeared, and he invited the cat onto his knee. I wondered if he would have preferred to chat with the animal but dismissed it. Rask soaked up the attention while Koa remained distant.

"Will you call the doctor?" I asked.

"No. I have an appointment next week. I won't get in sooner. It's fine. You needn't worry, Jersey. I've spent my entire life in a state. This isn't new. Again, I apologize you had to witness it. These things happen. Please don't be alarmed."

But I was alarmed because these things, as he called them, weren't normal.

Rask jumped down and found a spot to sleep on Koa's favorite chair. The man looked lost without the feline for company. A glazed, far-off look came to his eyes. I was losing him again. If he went too far away, I might not be able to pull him back.

I approached carefully, sitting on the edge of the desk and drawing Koa between my legs.

I removed his glasses, setting them aside. "Have I ever told you how sexy those glasses are?"

He snorted derisively. "They're a mark of age. I hate them."

Cupping his face, I urged him to look at me. "Do you know what?"

"What?" His voice was thin.

I threaded my fingers through his soft hair, pushing it back off his forehead. "I love you."

Sorrow crossed Koa's face before he looked down at his swollen hands. "Jersey—"

"I know you struggle with that concept, and I don't expect you to say it back, but I wanted you to know you aren't alone in this big nasty world. You have people fighting for you. People who care deeply for you, and I'm one of them."

"Thank you, but I will always be alone in this big nasty world."

I kissed the top of his head, but I couldn't encourage him to look at me again. "You're wrong this time. I may never understand how hard it is to be you and the battles you fight every day, but I'll be here in whatever capacity you'll have me. I won't give up on you."

"You will."

"I won't."

He leaned in, resting his head against my sternum, and let me stroke his hair. Niles was wrong. Koa wasn't incapable of feeling emotions. If I had to guess, he felt them so strongly that he didn't know how to handle them most days. I believed he was starved for love. At some point, and I might never know why or how, he'd lost his parents. The grandfather who had taken him in was not a suitable replacement and had beaten and molded Koa to fit his expectations.

As children, Koa and I had connected, and when, at fourteen, he'd reached out and tried to love me, I'd rejected him.

Niles had put in a great effort, and I didn't fault the man, but he too had given up.

If Koa never figured out how to love me back, I would accept it. But I would not walk out again. I would not fail him.

"How about we go for an early morning walk? Get some fresh air."

28

Koa

It was barely seven, but the sun was up, and the day was bright and beautiful. The pastel blue sky, cloudless and open, seemed endless, like it went on forever. I could breathe easier and was glad for Jersey's suggestion.

The residual effects of Xanax lingered, making my limbs heavy and mouth dry. I didn't usually medicate. I hated the way it made me feel, and over the years, I'd significantly reduced the number of pills I took on a daily basis. My doctor didn't like it, but she didn't have to. It was my life and my choice. The only person who had to live with the consequences was me. Last night had been a whirlwind, and I'd lost control. Jersey was right to offer me Xanax.

I insisted on a stroll through the cemetery behind the house. It likely wouldn't have been Jersey's first choice, but he agreed. When he tried to take my hand, I pulled away. I wasn't ready for contact. My insides were still liquid, and vulnerability was an issue I couldn't quite shake. I needed a few minutes on my own to stabilize.

He didn't object.

Summer clung to the land. The leaves were still a bright and vibrant green, dancing in the breeze, oblivious to their imminent ruin haunting the next corner. The temperature, although crisper in the early morning, was rising fast. The grass sparkled with dew. My sweater was too much, but I couldn't think of shedding it. It gave me a sense of security I couldn't explain. Without it, my wounds would be open to the world, and the last thing I needed was to invite infection into my already infected soul.

Jersey wore cargo shorts and a tee. He must have thought I was ridiculous to bundle in so many layers, but how was I supposed to explain the impossible? How else could I hold myself together?

I wandered in silence, staying a few feet ahead, pausing on occasion to puzzle the writing on a crumbling headstone. Most of them were illegible. Jersey kept pace behind me, like a shadow or a guardian. I should have hated him for assuming I needed protection, but I didn't.

At the whitewashed church, I paused as I had many times before to contemplate its relevance. Its meaning. So many people found peace and serenity in prayer. Grandfather had. But the whole concept of religion and faith made no sense. I couldn't pretend to believe in a higher power. It offered me no comfort.

Jersey came up beside me, and we stood shoulder to shoulder. He said nothing, and I appreciated it. His silence was a gift Niles had never been able to give. Although, I was sure Jersey had as many questions as my ex. As many concerns.

The cross at the church's peak was rusted and crooked, growing nests. A morning bird perched on its crossbeam, fluffing its feathers, chittering and singing to himself. A hymn? Praying maybe? The bird had more serenity than me.

"My mother prayed in vain on the day she died." My voice was thin, barely audible. I didn't know I was speaking until the words fell from my mouth and hung in the air. I'd never told anyone. Even my therapists hadn't gotten all the details. "She screamed and cried and begged for her life. She asked god to protect her. To save her."

I turned to Jersey, challengingly. "He didn't because he isn't real, and before you argue and say that god works in mysterious ways and my mother is in a better place or whatever nonsense I've heard a thousand times, I don't believe any of it. The fact is, our existence on this planet is insignificant. There is no after. There is only now. We are an embodiment of cells that have come into being quite by accident. We weren't created from stardust. There is no good or evil. No right or wrong. Nothing we do or say matters. The end result is always the same. We live. We die. And in a thousand years, if humans are still crawling around on this miserable planet, they will still live and die as we did."

Jersey held my glare without backing down. When I finished talking, he took my hand. The ache through my knuckles was profound, but he was gentle. "So... if that's the case, shouldn't we make the most of our time? If this is all there is, why not make it worthwhile?"

"You mean create happiness?"

"Why not? It's the only thing we have the power to do. Why not treasure these moments? Take joy in what we can."

I smiled and brushed a hand over Jersey's shorn beard. It was soft under my fingers. Warm. Comforting in a way I couldn't express aloud. "You're more philosophical than you think, Mr. Reid."

"Hardly. I'm pretty black and white, but it makes sense to me. We don't have to live in misery just because it means nothing to be here. We can choose happiness."

I sobered, glancing back at the church. The bird was gone. The structure was nothing more than a skeletal frame, slowly fading to dust. "I don't know how to be happy."

"I don't believe that. Lots of things make you happy. Books. Music—when you aren't punishing yourself for making mistakes." He caressed the top of my wounded hand with a thumb. "Good coffee. Cooking makes you happy. Stop me if I'm wrong."

But he wasn't, so I stayed silent.

"There has to be more."

"Teaching," I said quietly.

"See?"

"Writing."

"What else?"

I thought but couldn't come up with more, so I shook my head.

Jersey brought his mouth to my ear. "How about good sex?"

I smirked. "I suppose that's enjoyable too."

"Strolls through the cemetery?"

"No." I glanced at the decrepit church. Windows boarded over. Paint peeling. A century's worth of dust and grime held it together. "This place feeds my melancholy. It helps me think straight. It reminds me... how pointless it all is."

"In that case, we need to stop coming here." He said it jokingly, but I was sure he meant it.

Jersey tugged my hand. We walked on. Deep in an overgrown section, along a worn path and under a sprawl of scented evergreens, was a bench. Its crossbeams were rotting, but it still functioned to hold two grown men when they had to rest their legs.

We sat among the dead. Squirrels rustled in the undergrowth, and the wind sang through the trees. If I closed my eyes, the sounds and smells of nature brought me back to my camp days. Those few summers contained my entire childhood. The only positive memories I had happened at Camp Kawartha—and many of them were tainted.

Jersey didn't push me to talk, and I was grateful. Part of me wanted to tell him everything, the whole ugly truth of my past, but I didn't know how. It felt dangerous. Risky. If I let it out, I might not be able to pack it away again. I had a profound fear of losing control and winding up hospitalized. If the previous night was any indicator, I was already skating the edge of sanity.

"Obviously, you've pieced together that I experienced tragedy as a child."

"Yes." He rubbed my leg soothingly and lovingly.

"I can't talk about it. Sometimes, I want to, but I'm not sure how to... let it out without losing myself. It's taken a long time to... come to terms with things. I'm barely stable. If you think last night was bad, talking about the rest of it could be a thousand times worse. I'm afraid they would lock me up and throw away the key."

"I doubt that, but I respect your decision."

I stared at Jersey's hand methodically stroking my leg. "My grandfather's death was enough to upset my equilibrium. Everything came at once. I didn't expect it. The... memories surged forward, and... I couldn't escape them. You don't know what it's like to live a real nightmare and never be able to wake from it. It's... I couldn't... Yesterday, I..."

Jersey waited while I fumbled for the right words.

"I was stuck in a loop. Reliving it. Running. Hiding. Fighting... I'm not making sense."

"Just talk. Say whatever you need to say. Get it out."

"I can't," I whispered. "It's too much, Jersey. I can't."

Jersey wrapped an arm around me, drawing me against his side. "Then don't. Either way, I'm not going anywhere. You've got me for as long as you'll have me."

We stayed like that for a long time. The sun rose higher, warming the earth and drying the dew. The dead slept on. The irony was never lost on me how I could feel more alive in a cemetery than anywhere else on the planet. A place of death. In a spot where both ends of the spectrum met.

"If I had never kissed you at camp, would you be here now?" I asked.

"Yes."

"That was definitive."

"It's a no-brainer. We had a connection, Koa. I was a confused kid back then. Even if you hadn't made a move, I'd have had the same reaction finding those letters because I was halfway in love with you even then. I just didn't understand what I felt."

"If it means anything, there was no halfway for me. I was a four-teen-year-old boy head over heels, terrified of that summer ending and never seeing you again."

"And I ruined it."

"No. I learned a valuable lesson that day. Don't kiss boys you aren't sure feel the same way."

Jersey chuckled and held me tighter. Silence prevailed. I felt calmer for the first time since getting that phone call from the nursing home.

"Could you ever love me again?" Jersey asked, his voice a tentative whisper.

"I don't know, but I want to try. Be patient with me."

"I'm not going anywhere."

29

Jersey

CAMP KAWARTHA 1993

A somber blanket had been draped over Camp Kawartha. It happened at the end of every July. Most kids were affected, but we fourteen-year-olds had it worse. It was our last year, and some of us had been attending camp since we were six-year-old babies. It was stupid they didn't run a program for older teenagers, but whatever.

I had no clue what I'd do with myself next summer. Dad said I would have football camp to worry about since I would undoubtedly make the high school team, but football wasn't half as thrilling as hockey, and I couldn't make myself care.

Camp wrapped up the following day, and everyone was in shut-down mode. Counselors assigned duties, and there was no more fun to be had. Koa and I had volunteered to clean up the equipment shed. I figured it would be a simple job, but it was trashed.

I spun, scanning the mess, unsure where to begin. Over the past month, kids had rip-roared in and out of the building, taking what they wanted and never returning them to their proper place.

"Where do we start?" I asked, more to get Koa talking than anything.

Koa was quieter than usual. It had been a strange month. Bruce and Daniel hadn't come—too cool for camp, I assumed. Justin was there, but everything was different. Our gang had dissolved. New alliances had formed, but they weren't as strong. Being the oldest cabin, we had a lot more privileges. A lot more freedom. We were junior leaders with the younger kids, organizing games and bossing them around.

When we weren't involved in stupid kid stuff, our cabin leader let us do our own thing. A lot of the guys liked fishing or canoeing, but mostly, people would goof-off, not really playing anymore since we were too big for that. We indulged in a lot of smack talk and conversations about girls. Fourteen-year-old boys had wild imaginations in that department. Big dreams, overinflated libidos, and no experience. Lots of high school predictions were thrown into the mix since we were all headed that way in September. It was the cusp of a new age for most of us. We were teenagers, mini-adults, ready to conquer the world.

Koa often sat with us but said little. He'd mastered the art of blending into the background. Being homeschooled meant he didn't share the same experiences or excitements over the next phase of life. It was all the same to him. No one made fun of him anymore, but no one paid him attention either, except for me. Koa and I had become friends outside of camp too. Our pen pal letters were frequent, and despite our obvious differences, I was drawn to him in a way I couldn't explain.

"Let's wind the nets first so we don't trip on them," Koa suggested.

The badminton nets lay sprawled on the floor in a tangled heap. Birdies and rackets were twisted and knotted among them. It alone would be a chore. We sat on the cement floor of the shed under a blaze of overhead fluorescents and began.

Koa was focused, as always, and I couldn't help stealing glances when he wasn't looking. He always seemed sad, like he was being crushed by the world—especially when camp was ending—so every time I made him laugh, it felt like scoring the winning goal in a playoff game. His laugh made me lightheaded. It was a drug, and I was addicted.

I tugged a birdie free from the net, put it on my head like a cone hat, and waited for Koa to notice. It was dumb, but I tried to be extra goofy for him. I liked it when he noticed me. I liked it when he paid me attention. Alone in the shed, it felt like our own private island. The rest of the campers were off doing their own cleanup chores.

It took a few minutes before Koa looked up, but he didn't miss the new accessory, and I earned a snort. Koa was small for his age. It was a good thing he didn't like sports. He would be flattened on the field in a second. But his smile was larger-than-life. It took up so much space I sometimes thought it ate the oxygen from the air which made it hard to breathe.

"What?" I asked, looking around like I had no clue what had made him laugh. "Is something wrong?"

"You're an idiot."

I modeled my new hat, posing Vogue-like. "You don't like it? I think you're jealous. Here, I have one for you too." I crawled over the tangled net and placed a birdie on his head, twisting it once so the tiny plastic ends snagged his hair, and it wouldn't fall off. "There. Now you're an idiot too."

He giggle-snorted again at my ridiculousness, and I felt like I'd won a million bucks.

We worked on the net wearing our make-shift hats, trying not to giggle. It was stupid, but I didn't care. When mine fell off, Koa crawled over and replaced it. At one point, I had three birdies stacked high on my head. I felt like a clown.

Koa and I had escaped many times that summer to our hollow log. We didn't fit inside anymore—unless we wanted to squish together—so we hung out on top, sitting side by side, legs pressed together as we shredded leaves, peeled sticks, and talked about anything and everything.

I talked about hockey, school, girls I thought were hot—because girls had become as important as hockey in my teenage life—and comic books. Koa often explained about an adventure story he was writing, seeking feedback and inventing the plot as he went along, wanting to know what I thought. He spoke of his studies—which were far beyond my understanding—his music lessons—which he hated—and his dream of going to a big university someday because he wanted to be a teacher.

It was our private time, and even though we had nothing in common, I soaked up every second. It was our last summer together, and knowing it was ending and we might not see each other again made my stomach feel oily and sick. I'd been trying to figure out how we could visit each other outside of camp when we lived so far apart.

"Do you think your grandfather would drive you to Lakefield sometime so we can hang out?" I asked. "You could come for a weekend. Mom wouldn't care."

Koa shook his head as he rolled the net around the post part that stuck into the ground. "He doesn't let me play with friends during schooltime."

"Not even on weekends?"

"No."

"But that's dumb. You're a kid. Don't you get a break?"

Koa shrugged. The birdie had slipped sideways on his head, threatening to fall. I knew Koa lived in Oshawa, so it was a long way to go for a one-day visit.

"What if my dad brought me to your house?"

"I'm not allowed friends over."

"Ever?" It seemed unfathomable.

Koa didn't respond and carried the net to a steel shelf along the wall of the shed and placed it on top. I collected the badminton rackets while he found a mesh bag and went around scooping up the birdies.

He plucked the three from on top of my head, smirking as he stuffed them away. "No more hats," he said. "Game over."

Game over for real. What did he mean he couldn't have friends? Koa was hard to figure out sometimes. He said little but was thinking all the time.

He stuck the birdie bag on the shelf. We tackled the endless spread of balls next. Koa collected them, and I tossed them from across the room into the huge wooden crate along the back wall. I wasn't a basketball star, but I pretended, whooping and cheering when I made a basket.

If I missed or the ball bounced off the rim, Koa raced after it so I could try again. He cheered along with me, and his praise made me feel larger-than-life, better even than when my hockey coach congratulated me on a decent play. Was I showing off? Definitely. Did I understand why? Not at the time.

The parachute gave us trouble. It was bigger than the shed, too big for the two of us to properly fold, and we ended up forgetting our duties and building an indoor tent fort instead, pinning the edges down under equipment bags and draping it dome-like over lower shelves until we had a decent cave.

We sat under the parachute, the red, green, yellow, and blue color swatches filtering the overhead light and casting a rainbow spectrum over our faces. Koa grinned at our creation, and I smiled because he smiled.

The space was small, and our knees touched, but neither of us moved. No big deal. We always sat with our knees touching. I didn't know when it had become a thing, but it was—on the hollow log in the woods, on the dock at the lake while we fished, during evening bonfires, and even at random times when we hung out with the other kids, sitting under the poplar trees, chatting about our futures.

Koa didn't have nightmares as much anymore, but I still snuck down to his bunk after our cabin was asleep so we could whisper. It felt devious and wrong, but lying with him in the dark, our voices hushed, our noses almost touching, was exhilarating.

Our parachute hideout felt the same.

Private.

Sneaky.

Like we were on another planet and rules didn't apply.

"Will you keep writing to me?" Koa asked, twisting a shoelace around a finger until it turned purple, not meeting my eyes.

"Of course I will, and when I'm sixteen and get my license, I'll drive to your house and pick you up. Screw your grandfather. He can't tell you what to do. We can go out or something. Like to a movie or the arcade. Somewhere cool. Maybe we can go cruising for girls. They like guys who have cars." I didn't know for a fact, but it sounded right. I'd heard stories of guys making it to third base with girls in the backseat of their cars. I didn't know for sure what third base was—outside of baseball—but I knew it was good.

Koa nodded somberly, and it bothered me he wasn't more excited.

"But I'll always write to you. We're pen pals. We have been since we were kids. Why would that change?"

"Because camp's over. You'll be busy at high school and probably forget about me."

I touched the knotted bracelet on his arm, the one I'd given him years ago. He still wore it even though it was stained and faded, some of the ends frayed. It didn't smell great either, like pond water or sour milk, but it made me happy to see it on his wrist every year.

"What did I tell you? Promises are for forever, remember?"

Koa smiled. "I remember."

"You'll always be my friend."

"Okay."

I wanted to tell him I would miss him, but it sounded weird, so I didn't. He was sullen, and I wanted to make him laugh again, but the birdies were outside the parachute cave, and I didn't have anything on hand as a replacement. My wits failed me, and his gloominess was contagious. I didn't want camp to be over either. I didn't want to never see Koa again.

"You can send me pieces of your story to read. Like when you finish a new chapter or something. One day it will be a book. If you publish it, you'll be famous."

"I won't be famous. It's not that good.

"I think it's awesome. You'll be a best-selling author someday. I know it. Then you won't care about me anymore. You'll have an awesome life and live in a mansion and eat caviar or something. Date supermodels." I laughed, but Koa grew quiet. I sensed he was upset.

"What's wrong?" Nothing about Koa was ever simple or straight-forward. He was complex to the point I couldn't always understand him. What I thought was funny didn't always hit the same for him.

"This is wrong." He pressed the heels of his palms against his eyes and leaned forward. Was he crying?

"What? I don't understand."

Koa waved a hand, encompassing his surroundings. No tears, but his cheeks were flush, and I didn't think it was the parachute coloring them. "This," he said louder. "Everything. It all sucks. Life sucks. People suck. None of it matters, Jersey. Don't you get it? Who cares how many books I read or at what level? Who cares if I write a famous novel, get rich, and live in a mansion? And I don't care about stupid supermodels, okay? Who cares if I can someday play 'La Campanella' on the piano? It doesn't matter if I become a teacher, a doctor, or a garbage man. I could live in a cardboard box and drink sewer water. Don't you get it?"

He trembled with rage.

"No."

"We're all gonna die the same. Even the rich and famous. Even the serial killers in prison. Even the supermodels. We are all doomed to the same fate. Did you know humans aren't any more special than the algae in the ocean? We are exactly the same. Just because we're an intelligent species doesn't mean we get a free ticket to forever. We still die. Camp was the best fun of my life, and you are the best friend I've ever had, but now it's over. The end. Done. So what was the point? Where did this fun get me? Nowhere. It gave me memories that will never go away, and all they'll do is make me sad. I have enough stupid memories I hate. I don't need more. All camp did was show me that everything ends. Everything. Nothing lasts forever."

Koa often went on tangents so serious and dark I struggled to follow. At fourteen, the thing I worried about most was if my lucky underwear was clean when I had a game or if I could form a complete sentence and not sound stupid when talking to the girl across the street who was two years older than me.

Not Koa. Koa went deep. Far deeper than I could fathom.

There was a kid on my hockey team whose sister was in high school. She was considered goth. I didn't know exactly what that meant, but she wore black clothes, black makeup, and always talked about death. She listened to what my mom would call the devil's music.

Sometimes, Koa gave me those same impressions, and I never knew what to say. Knowing how easily he could slip into rages and blank fits, I worried about setting him off. I knew our last day at camp would be ruined if he didn't relax.

I shuffled until I sat in front of him. When he looked up, cheeks bright red, a world of hurt stared back at me. I leaned our foreheads together like we did at night in the dark, only this time, I could see the swirling amber in his eyes. I could make out the tiny marks on his skin.

"I promise I won't stop writing," I said.

"Okay."

"I promise when I'm sixteen, we will go for joyrides in my car. Fuck your grandfather."

He smiled. "Okay."

"I promise to be your best friend forever, even if we don't see each other for a long time."

"Okay."

"Can you promise me something?"

"What?"

"Can you promise to try not to be sad all the time? I can't always be there to make you smile, but I hate it when you're not happy."

His bottom lip quivered, but he nodded.

"Promises are for forever, Koa. You can't say yes unless you mean it."

"I know. I'll try."

I touched his bracelet, feeling the tiny knots under my finger. It turned into holding his hand, and I wasn't sure what I was doing, but I knew Koa needed to be comforted. Everything was inside out and backward. My blood felt funny. My stomach kept swooshing. I was dizzy like after a head rush.

Koa reached for my other hand, and we connected there too.

It was warm in the equipment shed under the parachute. Our breathing had made the air thick. My hair stuck to my head and sweat tickled down my spine under my shirt. The moment felt serious, and I was both terrified and excited for some reason. I couldn't move.

The next thing I knew, Koa's lips were pressed to mine, soft and warm. I was on fire, and the flames burned over my skin all the way down to my groin. Koa was kissing me, and at first, I thought, *holy crap, this is what kissing feels like*. Then, in a flash, my brain screamed, *Koa is a boy. What the fuck is wrong with you? Kissing him makes you a faggot.*

I shoved him away so hard he fell against the side of the parachute, which tugged the end loose on my side, and the whole thing collapsed. I couldn't breathe and was trapped under a nylon skin that wanted to keep me in place. Nothing about this was fun anymore, and I scrambled to get out, knocking things off shelves in my haste, cursing enough my mother would have threatened me with soap. Angry words fell unfiltered from my mouth. I called Koa every nasty name the gang had been calling him since day one.

When I managed to break free, I ran.

I ran and ran and ran and ran and ran....

I couldn't get away from the feelings inside me. The burning. The tingling. The head rush.

I ran more.

Harder, faster, longer.

And I would continue to run for another half dozen years before I realized I couldn't outrun this thing. It was part of me.

But Koa was long gone by then, and I'd broken my promise.

30

Jersey

PRESENT DAY

We got back to the house around ten. Somewhere, his grandfather's funeral was in full swing, but Koa didn't acknowledge it. It was as though the man who had raised him from boyhood never existed. Koa was restless, moving about the house but unable to settle or focus on tasks.

I wasn't sure how to help. Koa had a lot going on inside, and the few nuggets of his history given to me in the cemetery were already more than I'd ever expected to get. I'd pieced together that his mother had been killed, and Koa, an eight-year-old boy, had witnessed the ordeal. How else would he know she'd prayed and begged to god? But what was it Koa had survived? What had he seen? What had he experienced? The circumstances surrounding her death were as blurry as ever. Was his father involved? Had Koa known or lived with a father figure previously? Many kids were raised by single parents, so it wasn't out of the question.

I couldn't ask. I'd promised.

I encouraged Koa to find a book and lay with me on the couch. We often spent time like that, him reading, me watching videos on my phone—hockey news, draft prospects, scores, replays, player stats, anything I could find because I would never be able to let go of the game.

But Koa couldn't lie still. Even a book didn't hold the power to contain him. His mind was too busy. Instead, he made endless loops of the library, pacing, lost in thought. I made him coffee and a sandwich at noon and convinced him to sit and eat. By midafternoon, Koa didn't know where to put himself. When I convinced him to try reading again, he fell asleep in my arms. I was no expert, but I thought the Herculean effort of holding himself together had worn him out. I wasn't stupid. Koa was on the verge of cracking and doing all he could to stay in one piece.

At some point, lack of proper sleep snuck up on me, and I joined him in slumber.

I woke sometime later to lips against mine, a body pressing me to the couch. Hands explored under my T-shirt, rooting through my chest hair on an expedition to a destination I was equally eager to visit. I kissed Koa back, savoring the soft press of his mouth, the firm line of his erection against my thigh, and the high level of yearning and desperation in his unspoken words. I clung to his hips, dragging him closer, arching against him as I hummed. "Mm...Nap time over?"

"Yes."

What a way to wake up.

I didn't want to open my eyes. I feared the distance that would separate us. I feared the walls he'd built so long ago that kept the world at bay. I feared never being able to break them down. In the dark, behind my closed lids, I could pretend he was with me. All of him.

Heart and soul. I could make believe it wasn't merely a burbling need to be satisfied. It was an act of love, a connection shared by two people who had lost the means of verbalizing their emotions because they ran too deep to be expressed any other way.

I feared I would see the truth if I opened my eyes.

Midafternoon meant slow and lazy. We weren't in a hurry. Nothing was urgent. Time was not a thing to be worried over. Koa's touch over my abdomen raised goose bumps and elevated my thirst for more. His fingers brushed my pebbled nipples, and I groaned against his mouth, pulling his lower half against me harder, rutting and encouraging the gradual build of pleasure.

He found the button on my shorts and undid them, slipping down the couch and taking me into his mouth. I tore a hand through my hair, hissed, and cursed. "Christ, Koa... Jesus... That's... so good."

He came off and said, "There is no god. Your obsession with cursing his name during sex is boggling. Leave him out of the bedroom, would you?"

I chuckled, still refusing to open my eyes as I blindly searched for Koa's head and shoved him back down. "Shut up and do your thing. I'll curse the good lord's name all I want."

I felt Koa smile around my length as he sucked me down again. Then I forgot my name because who could think straight when getting their cock sucked? It didn't take long before I surrendered to my desire to see what was going on and opened my eyes, peering down at Koa as he drew out my pleasure.

His hair hung in a curtain over his face, blocking my view. He was quiet but focused. Koa was a master of his art, a wise student of study and perfection. His skills reflected his personality.

He must have sensed the attention and peered up. Liquid amber rings, swallowed up by overblown pupils. Tortured as always, but beyond the surface, hidden from almost everyone, was a man who needed to learn to feel safe again in a world that had been unkind.

I touched his cheek, pushed his hair aside, and encouraged him to stop, to come back to me, to kiss me like he had when I'd woken. I would find a way to bridge this distance. Somehow. I would love him no matter what. Prove life wasn't without joy and happiness. Show him it was worth living.

I rid him of his many layers as our mouths remained fused. Naked wasn't my goal, but goddammit, he had too many clothes on. Koa chuckled when I said as much, calling me a heathen when I cursed the lord's name again.

When I found skin, I audibly sighed. "I knew you were under there somewhere."

"Your determination knows no bounds."

I ran my hands over his sides. "I like exploring your nakedness. Sue me."

His hair fanned my face. "I happen to enjoy yours as well."

I stroked him, and his lips parted with a tiny gasp. "You agreed earlier. Good sex makes you happy."

"It does."

"I plan to make you very happy right now."

His smile was a hook, and it snagged my heart, reeling me into his orbit. I pushed his pants the rest of the way down, and he toed them off. Mine were already gone, lost in a tangled mess on the floor.

"Condoms," he said. "They're upstairs."

"Do we need them?"

A pinch pulled between Koa's brows. "You want to go without?"

"Only if you're on board. It's been a while since I was with anyone else. Can't say I've been actively playing the field for a long time. My last test was a green bill of health."

And I need you to see how serious I am, but I kept those thoughts to myself. I planned to keep my promise this time.

"Niles was the last... Sorry. I'm sure you're sick of that reminder."

I shrugged. "I've come to terms with it."

"I had a negative test when we parted ways. There's been no one since."

"So? I guess the question is, am I a fling?"

"Those days are far behind me."

"Good." I took his face between my palms. "Are you with me?"

"I'm trying," he whispered.

"Do you want to get a condom?"

"No."

We kissed again, and I held Koa close, needing him to feel safe and protected. The heat had simmered some, but finding our way back didn't take long. The couch wasn't a great spot for getting frisky. Two grown men—one with a cranky knee—and not enough room to move around meant some creativity was necessary.

Koa didn't flip. He'd made that clear over the summer, and I was fine with that. It didn't matter to me either way so long as both parties were happy. At one point, I ended up sitting with Koa straddling my lap. Spit was nature's lubricant, and men had been using it for centuries, so I wasn't about to shatter the moment a second time so one of us could find the manufactured crap in a plastic bottle upstairs in the bedroom.

Fuck that.

Koa didn't complain, and with him on top, he had all the control.

I didn't let him bury his face in my shoulder. I didn't let him close his eyes and hide—as much as I'd done the same thing at the beginning of this encounter.

I encouraged him to look me in the eyes so he could feel the love I had for him. I wanted to inject it into his veins. I wanted to engrave it into his skin as a permanent reminder in case he ever doubted my conviction. I wanted to find a way to fuse our souls so he understood he would never be alone again. There was good to be had. Happiness. And I would spend the rest of my life proving it to him if I had to.

Koa rode me, slow and steady, but there was a struggle in his amber eyes. He wanted to pull away. He wanted to hide, but I kept him there. I grounded him. In the end, he kissed me thoroughly and intently, his only means of escaping eye contact.

I allowed it.

Not a single part of him went unexplored. I mapped his skin and worshiped every inch with my mouth and hands. When our lips fused, when Koa whispered my name, I took him in hand and stroked him through to the end.

Only then did I take my pleasure.

After, having Koa in my arms, face buried in my neck, hot, panting breath against my skin as he trembled—with aftereffects or the overwhelming fear of exposure I didn't know—was what I treasured most.

I held him tight for a long time, and he let me. I wasn't sure if we'd made progress.

"I love you," I said as I brushed the sweaty hairs along his neckline and followed the path of his spine to his ass.

He didn't say it back, but he did squeeze me tighter.

⋘

Koa was calmer the rest of the weekend. Niles stopped by on Saturday, and Koa invited him to join us for dinner—a creamy lemon chicken piccata. Wine was a given, but Koa was a bit of a connoisseur when it came to pairing drinks with meals, so it wasn't a surprise. Niles spoke the same language, and I faked it, happily guzzling whatever Koa put in front of me.

Was it weird sharing space with Koa's ex? Sometimes, especially when they seemed to have a lot more in common, but I could also appreciate their friendship. Koa didn't connect well with anyone, and Niles's presence seemed to give him comfort. When I couldn't always be around, I felt better knowing someone he trusted was nearby if he needed to talk.

On Sunday, I had to head home, but before I left, Koa took me into the library and pulled a wooden box from a top shelf on the bookcase. From within, he retrieved the knotted friendship bracelet I'd made him years ago.

"Oh my god. You weren't kidding. You still have it."

Handing it over, he asked, "Can you put it on me?" No eye contact. Body rigid.

"Of course." I took it and turned it around in my hands, examining it. The threads were discolored and worn, the lines and tension uneven. Numerous mistakes stood out, and I laughed. It was so poorly crafted. As a kid, I'd thought it was perfect.

Koa had to have noticed the flaws, but he must not have cared. It was the symbology that mattered, and when I considered what this bracelet had once meant, it made me sad. It represented the promises I'd broken, and I hated myself for it, even though no one would blame a scared fourteen-year-old for not knowing who they were.

"Are you sure?" My enthusiasm waned.

"Please."

"When I gave you this—"

"You promised to always be my friend, and you've come back into my life. The hiatus in between is understandable. I want to wear it again."

I didn't protest his decision. When he offered his wrist, I did my best to tie the strings tight. It was too small, and I struggled to get it done up. The remaining threads didn't leave me much to work with. It ended up tight enough it pinched Koa's arm. He saw it but said nothing.

"Thank you." He traced a finger over the faded colored stripes.

I tipped his chin so he would look me in the eye. "Does it help?"

His throat bobbed. "Maybe. I hope so."

We didn't see each other until the following weekend, but we texted and spoke frequently on the phone. Koa had returned to work, and the conversation focused mainly on his curriculum and the plans he had for the school year.

When I asked how he was doing on a more personal level, he grew quiet. Koa shared about his grandfather's house, wondering if there was a company he could hire to empty and clean it. When I asked why he wouldn't do it on his own—having recently tackled my parents' house—he told me he wanted nothing to do with the place.

The price tag for such endeavors turned out to be expensive. The conversation in that regard ended. Koa refused to address it. His grandfather was part of his past, indirectly connected to another part he wished not to discuss. Walls. Boundaries. Blockades.

The ordeal of the previous weekend, his fury at the piano, and the requirement of drugs to calm him down weighed heavily on us both. I tiptoed carefully, wishing he would open up and stop holding a lifetime's worth of pain inside.

I thought often of the worn bracelet I'd put on his arm, and when I arrived Friday evening and found he wasn't wearing it, my heart broke. I didn't ask why, but I hoped it was because it was too uncomfortable and not because he'd given up. Not because it was yet another reminder of something painful.

Koa

Allowing my students twenty minutes at the end of last period every Friday so they could catch up on homework before the weekend was a gift for them and me, a tradition that had been going on since I'd started teaching over a decade ago. It gave me quiet time for reflection, and lately, I'd needed it.

Grandfather's passing had upset my equilibrium, and three weeks later, I was still feeling its residual effects. But Jersey's presence in my life had overthrown my sanity and wreaked havoc on my nerves. I yearned to be with him, but every time we were together, it was a battle to hold on. My fingers scrabbled for purchase on a ledge where I dangled over a bottomless pit. I existed in a permanent state of uncertainty, ready to fall.

I didn't know how to keep him, but if I didn't sort myself out, he would walk away like Niles.

My journal writing had grown murkier. My poems held a gloomy tone even I couldn't deny. The choices I made for personal reading were beyond morose. Niles would have much to say if he knew. I was a sinking ship in a sea of boiling tar. Land seemed farther away than ever. Navigating life had never been so challenging—or lonely. It was easier when I didn't care about anything, but Jersey came back into my life, and I could no longer claim indifference.

I felt things I didn't know how to feel. Things I didn't know how to process or express.

I'd never learned to live amongst the living. I'd only known how to stalk the outskirts of life while looking in. A specter. A shadow. Crossing this invisible barrier was a feat, and I had no skills to draw on.

I didn't understand the obstacle course, so I didn't know how to succeed.

I'd failed with Niles, but I didn't want to fail with Jersey. If he walked out of my life, I wasn't sure I'd survive. It would be another grave for my mind to tend. Another loss at my expense. Life could be bitter, and cold, and hateful. How come no one else saw it?

I didn't know how to give myself completely to anyone. I didn't know how to unlock the chains around my soul without it shattering into a billion shards.

When I'd mentioned my current struggles to my doctor at our appointment the previous week, she had turned the question back on me like she always did, like I was somehow in possession of the answers when, in fact, I was lost. It was unhelpful and frustrating. I told her as much, raising my voice, which was unlike me. She'd smiled as though my temper was amusing.

I'd left the appointment angry and couldn't remember ever having done that before.

When Jersey had seen me without the bracelet the previous week-end, I'd read the defeat in his eyes. His pain had radiated and filled the room. Not once had he brought it up, but in bed, he unconsciously traced a finger around my wrist where it belonged.

Guilt had eaten me alive ever since.

It was why the moment he'd left Sunday afternoon, I'd finagled a solution, digging up a long safety pin so I could connect the ends without it cutting into my skin. I'd spent the rest of the week staring at it, revisiting the past, wondering about the future.

It was quite likely the first time in my life I'd dared to hope.

Under the droning buzz of students studying, unable to concentrate on marking papers, I ran a finger under the knotted bracelet, looping it around my wrist over and over as I stared at the faded colors, hearing the words of a young boy so long ago, making promises of forever.

So many conversations churned inside my brain. Ones from decades before, others more recent. Some I'd had with students, others I'd had with Niles or Jersey. My doctor's words and smirk ate at me.

A common theme presented itself.

Happiness. When would I accept happiness into my life?

I'd taught philosophy for years and always dismissed the notion.

What was happiness anyway? And could it be, at its core, the meaning of life?

"Dr. Burgard?" Hailey Tomlin called my name, waving a hand in the air.

"Yes, Miss Tomlin."

"I don't understand this."

"Bring it over."

I welcomed the distraction. Shakespeare had been confusing students for as long as teachers had been adding it to the curriculum. Hailey wasn't the first, and she wouldn't be the last. She was a bright student, always rooting deeper into her studies and applying herself with vigor.

We worked through the assigned passage one line at a time, discussing the wording and structure and deciphering what the author was trying to say.

"But it bugs me because, like, it doesn't flow well, you know? I spend so much time puzzling its meaning, but I can't connect it to the story or characters. I lose the emotion of the play."

"Not everything can be understood on a first read or at surface level. Sometimes, it takes going over passages more than once to get to the marrow of what the author is trying to say. A lot of classics are like that. Every time you read them, you find more meaning. You need to have patience. If you try to force it, it won't happen. Let your brain relax and take in what it can, feel it, and process it."

"Okay." She read the section quietly in her head, then glanced up when finished.

"Now read it again. Out loud this time. You understand the words. Now, let's find the deeper meaning."

She read it again. We discussed it. Then again. More discussions. By the fourth or fifth time, the difficult passage flowed off her tongue with ease, and the meaning sank in. She tackled the next section while sitting beside me, but I let her be the teacher. I let her take the reins. We worked until the bell rang, announcing the end of class and the beginning of the weekend.

"Do you understand the process now?"

"I do. And I feel it."

"And every time you read it, you'll feel more and more and more."

Hailey raced back to her desk to pack up. The kids flowed out the door like someone had announced free ice cream in the cafeteria. The silence in their absence was deafening. It swelled and engulfed me. It hummed in my ears.

I tidied my desk, head spinning around questions I had no answers to, a burning need to understand life like never before, and floundering like every philosopher since the dawn of time.

At one point, I stilled, my words to Hailey coming back to me. Could it be that simple? Was I rushing to understand something on a surface level without digesting it first? Was my impatience a barrier?

Jersey worked late and wouldn't be in town for several more hours, so with my thoughts in a tangle, I wandered to the music room in search of Niles, knowing he stayed late Friday afternoons for choir practice.

I found him at his desk, a dozen kids running around the vast music room, goofing off before practice. The noise was moderately dampened by the soundproof ceiling tiles.

"Master Edwidge," I said, breaking into his concentration as I approached. His classroom was rowdy enough that he hadn't registered my arrival.

His head snapped up, and he grinned. "Dr. Burgard. A pleasure as always."

"Can I steal you for a minute?"

"Absolutely. Give me a second to round this bunch up." He whistled sharply, and the chatter quieted. "Vince. On the piano, if you please. Run scales for warmup, then practice the chorus we worked on last week. I'll be back in five. I need a coffee, or I'll never survive you bunch. Anyone who misbehaves will be singing a solo of my choosing before we leave tonight."

A decent threat since most teens hated being called out.

Niles and I strolled across campus to the cafeteria. I had no idea why he would subject himself to their subpar coffee. It was barely palatable first thing in the morning when it was fresh, never mind at the end of the day.

He bumped my shoulder as we walked. "What's on your mind, cocoa bean?"

I chuckled. "You haven't called me that in ages."

"Probably shouldn't call you it now. Pet names might not go over well with your new beau, and I already get the feeling he isn't fond of me."

"He likes you fine." My smile faded. Thinking of Jersey caused my chest to tighten.

The cloudy afternoon threatened rain, but for late September, it was warm. Regardless, I hugged my cardigan around me and sighed. "I have a serious question, and please don't coddle me. Be honest."

"I always am."

I stopped walking and faced him. "How could I have fixed us?"

Niles's brow creased. "What do you mean?"

"You know what I mean."

Niles raked his teeth over his bottom lip, glancing across the field to the main building we'd left behind. "We've talked about this plenty. You know the answer."

"You loved me, and I couldn't love you back. I know. But... what does that mean? At its core. What was it I did that made you feel unloved. What wasn't I giving you? Truly. I don't know if I understand. We had good conversations. We share the same likes and dislikes. There was never an issue in the bedroom. Please."

Niles chuckled and tipped his head to the sky. Several strands of hair had fallen from its bun, and he'd tucked them behind his ear as he met my eyes again. "Is this because of Jersey?"

"Of course it is. I'm going to lose him too, and..."

"And?"

"And... I don't want to."

Niles studied me. "Do you love him?"

"I'm not sure if I know how. I'm not sure I know what it means."

Niles's face was a picture of anguish. I'd hurt him. He'd tried endlessly to be who I needed, and I'd been unable to give back even an ounce. But unlike with Jersey, I'd never felt the urge to fight. Our end had been inevitable from the start.

"Christ, Koa."

"All you people need to stop cursing a nonexistent deity. It drives me nuts."

Niles chuckled, but it was a sad sound. "I can't explain love to you."

"Why not?"

"Because it's not something you define. It's something you feel. In here." He rapped his chest over his heart.

"Try. Please."

He sighed and spent a long minute staring into the distance. "Love means giving yourself to someone completely. It's a bonding of emotions. A feeling of protectiveness. It's about trust, affection, and respect. It's... allowing yourself to be vulnerable. Exposing your heart and knowing the other person will keep it safe."

Niles brushed the backs of his fingers along my temple. "It's about sharing your beautiful mind." He touched my chest. "And your damaged soul with someone else. If you can't let that person in, if you always keep them at arm's length, the distance between you will turn toxic. It will eat at your relationship until there is nothing left."

"Like it did with us?"

Niles smiled sadly. "Yes."

"I'm sorry I couldn't love you."

"It's okay." He dropped his hand and stepped back, putting a bit of distance between us. Again, his gaze wandered elsewhere. "I'll find someone someday."

"Anyone would be lucky to have you."

Niles returned his attention to me. "And you. If Jersey is your person, then I truly believe you'll wake up and find a way to take down those walls one day. You'll be ready. But, a word of advice. Don't wait too long. Forever isn't guaranteed."

Niles took my hand and squeezed. "Go home. Enjoy your weekend."

He kissed my temple before wandering toward the cafeteria, leaving me alone with my thoughts. I didn't go home. I took the path to the lake and sat on the rocky embankment for over an hour. Misery had always been my companion, but did it have to be?

Could I find joy in a world that had left me jaded?

Could I learn to live instead of merely existing?

Could I learn to love?

Could I let go of the past and stop letting it control me?

I didn't know if it was possible, but I wanted to try.

≼

Jersey arrived at seven. Usually, we enjoyed a late dinner together, something I prepared, but that evening, I redirected him out the door, announcing we were going to a restaurant instead. He didn't argue when I insisted on taking the Audi, but I did earn an odd look when I pulled onto the highway and left Peterborough altogether, heading back the way he'd come.

"Can I ask where we're going?"

"There's a new Somalian restaurant in Oshawa that Niles said does an excellent goat dish. Ever had goat?"

"Can't say I have, but Oshawa? That's almost an hour. Why so far away?"

"I wanted to try their menu."

A lie. My stomach was so queasy I wasn't sure I'd be able to eat.

Jersey's gaze burned the side of my face, but I didn't take my eyes off the road. Venturing to my hometown had been eating at me all afternoon, but I'd fought against every vibrating nerve and screaming protest from my brain telling me not to do this.

Dinner at a restaurant was a diversion, and Jersey had pieced that much together, but he didn't know why.

Niles's warning clung to me. *Don't wait too long. Forever isn't guaranteed.* I knew what I had to do, but it was making me sick thinking about it. I'd almost taken a Xanax before we left, but I needed to be the one to drive, and I couldn't drive while medicated. So, I fought to stay calm. I pushed back against the door in my mind, wanting to open.

Jersey touched the bracelet on my wrist, startling me. He didn't say anything, but I sensed his relief. When he weaved our fingers together and held me tight, the pressure in my chest lessened.

It was after eight before we arrived at the restaurant. The quiet dining area meant we were seated right away. After placing our orders—wasalad, a goat shoulder dish with roasted vegetables and chappati—Jersey took my hands over the table. His thumbs gently massaged away the tension.

"Why are we here, Koa?"

My insides sloshed as I stared at our connection. I wanted to run, but where would I go? I'd been running my whole life, afraid to face the past, afraid to live in the present, unwilling to accept I could have a positive future.

"I need to collect something from my grandfather's house before the cleaning company starts."

"You hired someone?"

"Yes. I shopped around and found a cheaper price. He left me money. I'm using it. I refuse to do it myself. I can't."

"Okay. So you have some possessions you need to pick up?"

"No. It's..." The words got stuck in my throat. "It's... Yes, I suppose." An easier answer than trying to explain. "I didn't want to go alone."

Jersey squeezed my hands. "No problem."

Our food arrived, and we ate. It was decent, and Jersey diverted the conversation to *Crime and Punishment*. "That book is a crime, and reading it is a punishment."

I laughed. "I'll pretend you didn't just say that. It's my most treasured book. Russian literature is a challenge, but you learn to appreciate it. Dostoyevsky's a big first step when venturing into classics. He's a favorite of mine, but still. If you wanted to try Russian literature, I'd have suggested a short story. *White Nights,* maybe. He wrote that. Or *The Death of Ivan Ilyich*. Tolstoy. Love that one too. An exploration of mortality."

"Sounds awful."

I smirked. "It's quite good. Or you could try—"

"Forget it. No more classics. I don't have the mind for them. That *Crime and Punishment* book was a cliff, and I dive-bombed to the rocky crater below, smashing all my intelligence on the ground in a messy pile of mutilated brain."

"Look at you being poetic."

Jersey chuckled. "It's going bye-bye. I'll never finish it. I'm going back to *Sports Illustrated* magazines. Far more comprehensible."

"You should try some classic science fiction."

"Koa."

"I'm just saying. Expand your mind."

"We are not the same."

We weren't, and oddly enough, it had never mattered. Even as kids, our differences never bothered us. Jersey was athletic and outgoing. I was bookish and introverted.

"The Timber Creek Bears are playing their first game next Friday," I said. "Home field advantage. Want to watch?"

Jersey's eyes widened. "Are you inviting me to a football game?"

"I am. High school football. So long as you don't mind the amateur aspect, it could be fun. I don't understand a thing about it, but I'm sure you won't mind explaining the rules."

Jersey chuckled. "I don't mind at all."

"Coach Blain will probably die of shock to see me out there."

"You'll have to introduce me."

"I will."

After dinner, we wandered back to the Audi hand in hand. Before Jersey got in, he kissed my cheek. His silent support was grounding. I drove the familiar streets of Oshawa until I got to my old neighborhood. Grandfather's house was a split-level, brick-and-siding combo. He'd gone into the home three years ago, and I'd paid someone to clean twice a month.

He'd told me to sell it, but I'd avoided having anything to do with it until now, putting off the inevitable for as long as possible.

I parked in the driveway and turned off the car, staring at the shadowy windows—ominous eyes in the dark. The sun had set long ago, and a single porch light illuminated the front stoop. It was on a timer, set to turn on at nightfall, giving the illusion someone was home.

I was sure the neighbors weren't fooled at this point. No one had been home for years.

I didn't move to get out of the car, and Jersey never questioned me.

Memories flooded my brain. The door rattled. Somehow, I managed to hold it together.

"I left the summer I turned eighteen, right after finishing high school. I got into Western, won a few scholarships, and moved to London the first chance I got. I never came back. Not for a holiday or a summer vacation. Never. I lost touch with my grandfather until the call came telling me he had cancer and was moving into a nursing home. School became my life back then. My saving grace. Then, work kept me busy. I didn't want to revisit the past, and even though he wasn't the worst part of it, his cruelty left its mark."

The shadowy interior of the car made it easier to talk. The leather of the steering wheel creaked under my palms as I worked on my shaking nerves.

"I never knew my grandmother. She died long before I was born. My mother was in her early twenties, I believe. My father didn't speak to his parents, so they were never in my life. When I was... When everything happened, and I was left alone, Grandfather was the only family I had. Neither of my parents had siblings. Grandfather refused to let child services put me in foster care, but he didn't know how to raise a kid. He grew up in a different age. Women reared children, and men worked, so he was out of his element. It was a... poor situation. We clashed. His entire focus was to ensure I was properly educated, to the point he forgot to let me be a child. I was severely traumatized when I arrived, but his answer to that was to tell me to get over it. Move on. Be a man. Pray if I needed comfort because he wouldn't give it to me. Death was part of life. It was god's will."

I took the keys from the ignition and faced Jersey. His face was in shadow, but I registered the pain in his eyes. "I don't want to go in there. If I could hire a crane to flatten this place, I would. But there is something in the basement I need to get."

"Okay." He took my hand and laced our fingers.

"When I find what I'm looking for, I'm going to give it to you, and I need you to promise me something."

"Anything."

"Take it home. It will contain all the answers you've been asking yourself for a long time."

I didn't know if Jersey, like Niles, had tried to research my past. If so, he would have failed. The reporters at the time would not leave Grandfather and me alone, so Grandfather had relocated us to Oshawa and changed my last name. It was the best thing he'd ever done for me. He'd given me anonymity in an unkind world more interested in slandering an eight-year-old's name than empathizing with what he'd been through.

My story was lost in the void, and only with the right hints and clues could anyone connect me to the horrors of the past. It was the only reason I'd survived this long.

"When you're done with the box, I want you to destroy it. Burn whatever's inside. I lived it. I don't need the reminder. I can't promise I'll be able to talk about it, but at least you'll know the whole ugly truth."

Jersey's eyes glistened. Their pale denim color was lost in the dark. His grip on mine was painful, and I wasn't sure who was holding up who.

"You don't have to do this," he said.

"I do."

I found Grandfather's keys, and Jersey followed me inside, one hand on my lower back the entire time, never breaking contact.

The too-close walls, the furniture, and the scent all threw me back in time. Memories pressed in from all sides, and I had to push them away as I aimed for the basement. I watched where I was going, but I refused to see. I shut down. I turned off. Numb to the bone, I moved automatically, knowing where to go, needing to get in and out as fast as possible.

Nothing remained of my old life except one box. It contained no mementos, pictures, nostalgic toys, or keepsakes. My parents' house had been a crime scene for months. By the time the police had released it, my grandfather and I had vanished from the public eye, and he'd hired someone to take care of getting rid of everything that remained. My parents' life insurance, the money from the house sale, and all remaining financial accumulation had been put into an account, held in trust until my eighteenth birthday. The money had helped me escape Grandfather's house and establish my own life.

The box contained dated newspapers, magazine articles, police reports, and everything else my grandfather had managed to collect about the incident. Why he thought it was necessary, I might never know. But he'd gathered it all. He'd stored it away. Perhaps he thought I would want it one day. I couldn't pretend to understand how the man's mind functioned. We had never been on the same wavelength.

If he grieved for his daughter, my mother, I never saw it.

Regardless, I knew the box existed. It had haunted me growing up. The monster from my dreams, from my past, lived inside the box in the basement under the stairs, always stalking me, never dying. No matter how many times I saw his death behind my eyes, he was always there.

Finally, I could slay the demon. Destroy the evidence. Burn it to the ground.

Would it be enough, or would I see his face in my dreams for the rest of my life?

The box took no time to locate, and I put it directly into Jersey's arms. Without missing a beat or pausing to look around, I hustled back up the stairs and outside. The crisp fall air hit my lungs, and I drank it up like I'd spent too much time underwater and was finally able to breathe.

Hunched over, hands on my knees, I closed my eyes as the world spun, and my ears rang.

Jersey's hand landed on my back, and he rubbed gentle circles, never saying a word. The comforting touch was enough.

We drove back to Peterborough in silence—Jersey with likely a hundred and one questions on the tip of his tongue, and me debating if I'd done the right thing.

Niles's words spun in my brain. It wasn't too late. I would find a way to break down this wall. I would give Jersey all I could. It had to be enough.

At the house, I encouraged him to put the box in the Gladiator. I didn't want it anywhere near me.

He hesitated, cradling it in his arms. "Are you sure about this?"

My brain screamed no, but my mouth said, "Yes."

"I can burn it and never look inside if you'd prefer. You don't need to share this with me if you don't want to."

"But I do. I want us to work. I want to stop feeling trapped in my own head. It's about trust, Jersey. It's about learning to be vulnerable." I stared at the box, unable to touch it. "This is all of me. This is who I am."

"And you're giving it to me?"

"Yes."

When Jersey brushed the backs of his fingers over my cheek, I realized I was crying. When was the last time tears had found my eyes?

I couldn't remember. My insides shook, and I wrapped my cardigan around me tighter. Jersey threaded his fingers through my hair and drew me in for a long kiss.

"You are more than a box of horrors. I hope you know that."

"It's my foundation. It's what made me into the man I am today."

"I love that man," he said, his voice a whisper against my mouth. "I love him heart and soul. Whether you share this or not, that won't change."

But it had to help. I thought maybe, *maybe*, I could close this gap. I could erase the distance. I held Jersey's face, digging my fingers into his soft beard, clinging for dear life like I'd unfairly done as a child.

The words came out thick when I spoke. "A long time ago, a scared, traumatized boy dared to dream about happiness. He dared to love his best and only friend in the world. It didn't work out. The boy was a hopeless case back then."

"He wasn't."

"He was. He still is most days. His best friend left without a word, and the boy spent years lost and unsure of how to fit into a cruel world that didn't want him. The boy and his best friend grew up apart, but the friend returned after many years, telling the boy he was wrong to leave. Telling the boy he loved him. I want to be happy, Jersey, but I'm not sure I know how."

"I'll teach you."

"First, take this box home and read its contents. You might decide I truly am a hopeless case."

"I won't."

"You might."

"I won't. I promise."

"Careful. Promises are for forever."

Jersey smiled against my mouth. "I know."

And he kissed me again. I squeezed my eyes closed against the burn of more tears. This would either destroy me completely or set me free.

32

Jersey

I got home late Sunday evening and set the sealed box on the round kitchen table. The apartment wasn't big, so the box's presence seemed to swallow up every inch of free space. Whatever was in it was bigger than me, more enormous, more strenuous than all my life experiences combined. My life had its fair share of messiness, but my hockey accident, subsequent addiction, Christine taking Derby and leaving me high and dry, and then losing my parents in a tragic car crash somehow felt minor compared to what I knew I would find in Koa's past.

On the drive home, I'd told myself a hundred times to throw it away sealed. I didn't need to know what kind of trauma had the power to destroy a person so thoroughly.

But Koa had given me a piece of him. The most private piece imaginable. The one he had coveted and protected his entire life. The one he had given to no one. It was the key to the door he'd locked years ago.

And he wanted me to open it. He was inviting me inside.

Why? Because he knew there was no other way of tearing down the walls he'd built. Koa was telling me he loved me in the only way he knew how. The darkness and distance might prevail, there may be no getting away from it, but Koa wanted me to know he trusted me.

I opened a beer and sat, staring at the box, imagining the worst. It was unmarked, plain brown cardboard. For all I knew, he might have grabbed the wrong one, and it would contain his grandfather's stamp collection.

No. Koa hadn't hesitated. In the basement, he'd known exactly where to go. Whatever was inside had likely haunted him for years.

I drank the beer and found another cold one in the fridge. The pale ale went down easy, and I waited for it to dampen my nerves. I needed a cushion before taking this path.

What would I find? How badly would it hurt?

Whatever Koa's secret, it would ruin my night's sleep. I would suffer at work in the morning. Koa had asked me not to talk about it. He'd made me promise to destroy the contents when I was done. Would I be able to keep that promise?

Nausea filled my belly.

"Fuck me." I set the beer down and drew the box forward. "Am I doing this?"

The empty apartment didn't answer, but my heart responded with a kick and a punch.

"Fine." I pulled the edge of the packing tape, breaking the seal. It was old and disintegrated under my careful ministration. I had to remove it in pieces.

The box's flaps fell open, and I stalled.

It took another beer and a half before I could peek inside.

It was mostly empty. A few old newspapers. A handful of torn, glossy pages from a magazine or two. A thick brown folder labeled

with block letters, *Yates, October 1986*. The word *COPY* was stamped
on the front. In the opposite corner was a single word and a name.
Homicide-Det. Hanover. Timeworn pages stuck out of the folder at
odd angles. The frayed seam suggested it had been opened and closed
a thousand times.

Yates.

Koa Yates? Or was it the last name of the person who'd done the
killing?

Only one way to find out.

I removed the folder and set it aside. The newspapers had been
bundled and rolled, secured with a thick elastic band. I removed them
from the box as well and tugged the elastic free, flattening the stack
the best I could, which was next to impossible, considering they had
probably been stuck like that for more than three decades.

The collection of newspapers came from various cities. St.
Catharine's, Hamilton, and London primarily. The top three were
dated October 4th, 1986. The headlines were the same, but the wording varied.

St. Catharine's Teen (14) Goes on Killing Rampage.

Mother and Father Shot to Death by Teenage Son.

Troubled Teen Murders Family.

Numb, I chose the *London Free Press* and read the article.

*Early yesterday morning, a fourteen-year-old St. Catharine's teen
went on a killing rampage, murdering his mother and father before
going after his eight-year-old brother. The teen was said to have used a
hunting rifle that was supposedly kept in a locked cabinet in the family's
garage. How he acquired the key is unknown.*

*The police claim to have found evidence of a struggle in the attached
two-car garage where forty-four-year-old Lawry Yates was found dead
beside the family's Camry with a single gunshot wound to the head. It*

is believed Lawry might have seen what was happening and tried to intervene before it was too late. Forty-two-year-old Elise Yates, the teen's mother, was found dead in the Yates's kitchen, shot once in the stomach and a second time in the head.

It is assumed that the teenager immediately went after his younger brother, who the police believe tried to hide on the second floor of the house during the chaos, knowing he was in danger. Evidence of gunfire was found in the ceiling and walls on the second floor, indicating the teen might have tried to scare the brother out of hiding or shot after him as he ran.

No one knows for sure what transpired inside the house yesterday morning. The traumatized eight-year-old isn't speaking to the police or medical professionals at this time, but it is speculated that he might have surprised his older brother at one point, attacking him in an effort to get away and save himself. It is believed the two struggled at the top of the stairs, where the teen gunman fell or was pushed. The older boy was knocked unconscious, and the younger child was able to find a phone and call for help.

The teenage gunman died later that evening in hospital of severe head trauma.

It's unknown at this time what caused the St. Catharine's teen to embark on this heartbreaking act of brutality. Friends and neighbors alike are shocked and grief-stricken, wondering at the tragedy that has touched their small town...

The words blurred, and I had to grip the side of the table so I wouldn't slide off the chair. I went back to the top of the page, reading it again, seeing the words yet not absorbing them. How was this real? I'd heard and read about outrageous acts of violence over the years: school shootings, a man who drove down a sidewalk in downtown Toronto mowing people down, knifings, brutal assaults that left multiple casualties. But they had always felt like fiction. They had never touched me or my family. This was different. This involved the man I loved.

When he was nothing more than an eight-year-old boy.

Jesus, Koa. How?

My blood ran cold. I read the article in the Hamilton paper and the one in the St. Catharine's paper. They all told the same story. More papers had been bundled in the pile, covering the weeks that followed. The teenager was eventually named. I guess dead murderers lost their rights to privacy, or someone had leaked it to the press, and the papers didn't care about lawsuits.

Augustus (Gus) Yates.

If one boy's name was leaked, I knew the other would have been too. Maybe Koa's name never showed up in the newspapers, but that meant shit when it came to the media. In a small town, people talked. Everyone knew everyone. A person couldn't remain anonymous.

And Koa had likely suffered—as a victim and as the one who'd killed his brother. Would he have been hailed a hero? Knowing the way people were, there would always be someone who would slander his name. Accuse him of being no better than his murdering brother.

I pulled the brown folder toward me. The police report. Interviews. Extensive details. Photographs I didn't need to see. Why had Koa's grandfather requested this? To what purpose?

I read it all, detaching from the worst of it, slapping the photographs face down on the table's surface when I couldn't bear to see their horrors. It would have been easier to pack everything away in the box and dump it in the lake, but if Koa had lived through this and wanted me to know all there was to know, I had to walk this path, if only so I could understand his nightmare.

Koa had witnessed or at least been in the house when his older brother had shot and killed his parents. He had listened to his mother's screaming and pleading to god to save her. He'd heard the gunshots. The silence that would have followed.

Worse.

Koa had been hunted by his brother, knowing his fate would be the same if he was found. Whatever had transpired on the landing of the second floor, the story was never made clear—interviewing a traumatized eight-year-old boy had proven to be difficult. Whatever had happened, Koa, in a state of fear, shock, rage, or merely in self-defense, had pushed his brother down the stairs and killed him.

He'd killed his brother. It was only then sinking in.

"Jesus," I breathed. "Holy fucking Christ."

I stared at the spread of articles over the kitchen table. It wasn't a movie. It was real life. Koa's life. How had he ever moved forward? How had he survived?

Everything I'd witnessed at camp made sense. His strong dislike for archery. His repulsion for blood and refusal to play hunting games in the woods. The cap gun and Koa's attack on the boy who'd shot it. Even throwing *Lord of the Flies* into the lake.

The endless nightmares and bed-wetting.

The blank fits that took hold and wouldn't let him go.

His ongoing need for an imaginary friend. Someone he could control. Someone who would listen. Someone who made him feel safe.

It all made sense.

Even today, Koa's obsession with death was understandable. His separation from the world. His inability to connect with people. The morose poetry and music. No god. No meaning to life. It was all a waste of time in his eyes. Nothing mattered.

He might have grown into a functioning adult with a respectable career, but he'd never truly healed. How could he? How could anyone?

I needed another beer.

I sat up all night with the articles and police report, reading them, thinking, with my stomach in a knot. Twice, I almost got in my car and drove to Peterborough, but out of respect, knowing Koa needed his space, I didn't.

At long past three in the morning, I sent Koa a text.

Jersey: I love you, Tom Sawyer. That won't ever change.

I wasn't surprised when he texted back right away. Knowing I possessed his innermost secrets must have made it impossible to sleep.

Koa: I love you, Huck.

And I had no doubt.

None. At. All.

≪≋

It was a long week. Every day dragged, and all I wanted was to drive to Peterborough and see Koa. I wanted to hold him in my arms and never let go. The shooting was decades ago, but to me, it was fresh, and the fear it caused was inescapable. I had turned forty-five over the summer, a middle-aged man, and I was terrified by what I'd read.

How had an eight-year-old boy survived it?

Since I didn't have a fireplace or a backyard pit in my city apartment, I had to get creative when it came to destroying the box and its contents. Shredding it wasn't good enough. On Thursday, after a miserable day at work—I hadn't been sleeping well—I drove an hour to a provincial park, paid for a day pass, and then found a deserted campsite. I sat on a rotted picnic bench under a canopy of trees with leaves that had yet to change color and burned every single page from the box, and then I burned the box itself.

I snapped a picture with my phone and sent it to Koa, so he knew it was gone.

I didn't get a response, but that was okay. I hadn't expected one.

Long after the evidence was ash, I sat. At one point, I buried my face in my palms and cried. For a boy who had never had a chance to be a child. For a family shattered. For my son, who hated me and wouldn't take my calls. For my parents, whose house I couldn't seem to let go of.

For the man I'd loved all my life.

Grief hurt, but it also cleansed the soul. Hours later, when I left the campground, I felt lighter. Life would go on, and maybe Koa was right. Maybe there was nothing more out there. Maybe we were algae in an ocean. But I firmly believed we could make the best of the time we'd been given. We could make our own happiness.

The following day after work, I set out on a mission. An idea had struck in the middle of the night, and I was determined to make it happen. Koa had given me something, and I wanted to give him something in return.

It took a while to find what I wanted, but when I did, I was pleased and couldn't wait to see him on the weekend.

33

Koa

An odd peace settled over me after getting Jersey's text sometime in the night between Sunday and Monday morning, several hours after I handed him the key to my troubled heart. The contents of the box, of my whole dreadful life, were no longer a secret.

Jersey knew everything, and he was still texting.

Still there.

Still loving me.

The ground hadn't cracked open, and the nightmares had stayed away. All week, with an emergency Xanax in my pocket, I waited for the annihilation of my mind, for the people in the white truck to show up and take me away. But things were calm upstairs, calmer than they'd been in a long time.

My doctor's knowing smile from the other week appeared in my head over and over, and I finally understood what it meant. She had seen emotions in me for the first time. Instead of my usual passivity, she had witnessed fear, impatience, and frustration. I had opened up and given myself permission to feel and express things. It was the most progress we'd made in decades.

I'd spent the entirety of my life with the top button of my shirt too tight. Who knew that all I had to do to be comfortable was unbutton it?

Niles noticed the change on Thursday afternoon. He had band practice, ever rehearsing for one concert or another—this time, it was Christmas—and I lingered, accompanying the class on the piano, something I rarely did since I never felt skilled enough to join.

It made Niles smile, which made me smile—except when he treated me like a student and gave me a hard time about missing an entrance or flubbing the rhythm.

He waved his hands in the air more than once, stopping the class, and with a dramatic groan, said, "You're all terrible. You most of all." He glared playfully in my direction.

The students laughed, but we continued. Rehearsal ended up less serious than usual since I wasn't skilled at sight-reading, and the band members had been playing these pieces for weeks. Determined to prove myself worthy, I swore to join them for every practice until Christmas.

When the rehearsal ended and the kids filed out, Niles pulled out a violin.

"Play with me?"

We tinkered with a few duets, familiar pieces we'd been toying with for years. Niles could pick up any instrument and any piece of music and master it in ten seconds. My skills were nothing in comparison, but I kept up, even when he insisted on combing through a filing cabinet and finding new music to try.

If I flubbed a part, Niles went off on his own, playing solo until I caught up. Mindlessly, he would count me back in. During difficult sections, when my fingers wouldn't cooperate, Niles adjusted the tempo to suit my needs.

Regardless of my countless errors, I had no inclination to punish myself. My grandfather's stern voice was a distant hum, no longer screaming in my ears. Perhaps it made me an evil person, but his death had brought peace to my life. The dark cloud of his existence no longer hung over me. The sun warmed my face.

After some Mozart, we played Schubert, then Debussy, before meandering into some favorites by Beethoven. When my fingers tripped over the keys for the five-millionth time, I laughed and gave up.

Niles finished the song alone, lowered the violin, and tipped his head to the side. "Something's different with you."

I stared at my best friend, recognizing the endless patience he'd had with me over the years. A surge of emotion raced through my veins. Without him, I would have had no one. I never would have called Jersey. I never would have fought this hard.

I loved Niles—valued him to the very depths of my soul—but it would never be the same love I had for Jersey.

"I'm taking your advice."

"Oh? What advice was that? God knows I'm a wealth of information."

"There is no god, and your ego has been far overworked today. Let it rest."

Niles chuckled and placed the violin aside. "What advice?"

"I'm learning to be vulnerable. Learning to trust."

"And?"

"And I'm... I'm ready to take down some walls." I stared at the ivories, thinking about Jersey, my past, and my grandfather. "I want to learn how to be happy."

Niles moved onto the bench beside me and ran a finger along the keys. He bumped our shoulders. "I think that's valiant."

"I told Jersey."

I didn't have to clarify the essence of what I'd revealed, and maybe it would hurt Niles to know I'd confided in someone else and not him, but such was life. Perhaps someday I would share with him too.

"Good for you. I think that's great. Healing. It will help, Koa."

"You're not mad?"

"About being second best to your hockey star? Nah. So long as he treats you well."

I smiled and rocked into him, bumping his shoulder back. "Are you jealous?"

"Of course I am." Niles sobered. "I'll always wonder why it couldn't have been me."

"You haven't lost me."

"I know. If anything, I have more of you now than I ever did before, and I have Jersey to thank for that, so..." He shrugged.

I tinkled a few keys, my stomach stirring with oily sludge. "I'll tell you someday too, Niles. I promise, but I'm not ready yet."

"And if you're never ready, that's okay." He took my hand and kissed the top. "Play with me?"

"Always."

So we played. Piano duets never worked for us. Niles was a bench hog and a showman, always invading my space. He tended to play his part and mine simultaneously, slinking a hand between my arms and shooing me away, but it was all in fun.

We laughed and played for another hour until he'd succeeded in shoving me off the end of the bench and went solo.

Niles insisted on taking me out to eat, and while we enjoyed sandwiches and soup at the bistro, a text from Jersey came through. No words. He'd attached a single photograph. A bonfire stared back at me. Lost in the flames was a familiar cardboard box.

I stared at it for a long time, my meal forgotten. Peace was real, and it bloomed in my chest, making it easier to breathe for the first time in almost forty years.

Niles leaned over the table to see what had captured my attention. "What is it?"

I set my phone down and smiled. "A new beginning."

⚜

Naturally, I was nervous about Jersey's arrival Friday evening. He knew every ugly detail about my past. Although our chats flowed as they typically did throughout the week, the foundation of our relationship had changed. He couldn't help but look at me differently. What would he see? A victim? A murderer?

I wanted to be none of those things.

I wanted to be me.

Jersey texted when he left Toronto, and I busied myself making dinner. Cooking had always been a solid distraction from my runaway thoughts. The evening menu included rosemary pork roast, turnip au gratin, and twice-baked brussels sprouts. Soft music helped calm me, and I made myself a mojito, which Jersey would have called a pregame warmup. He could catch up when he arrived. The art of pairing drinks with food was not a skill in Jersey's repertoire, but he drank whatever I placed in his hand without complaint. A food and drink connoisseur he was not.

While dinner cooked, I deposited myself at my desk, found my glasses, and opened a journal, scribbling random thoughts while my brain relaxed and woke up. My compositions had been tumultuous this past week. A direct reflection of my agitated brain. In the end, my head was too tangled to write, so I wandered my library instead, tracing a finger along familiar spines of books I'd read enough times to quote.

Words of long-dead authors had always riveted me. The problems of yesteryear weren't any different than they were in our modern world. The questions people asked were the same. The soul, if one believed in such things, was unchanging.

Dostoyevsky had always been a personal favorite. I connected to his explorations of mortality and life. His insight and portrayal of humanity was powerful. In the famous chapter of *The Brothers Kara-mazov*, one I made my students read year after year, he was quoted as saying, *The mystery of human existence lies not in just staying alive, but in finding something to live for.*

I'd studied, analyzed, and picked that chapter apart more times over the years than I could count. Maybe he was onto something. Had I finally found something to live for? Could I stop merely existing?

I moved on to my collection of Albert Camus, another author whose philosophies I'd studied to death, argued, and reworked into something more agreeable to my disagreeable system. Absurdism was... absurd. I loved its foundational essence, but I'd always fought Camus's beliefs—enough that it drove Niles mad. One of Camus's notorious sayings came to me. *You will never be happy if you continue to search for what happiness consists of. You will never live if you are looking for the meaning of life.*

The paradox he suggested had never been clearer. And for the first time in all the years I'd studied the man's work, I agreed.

Had I stopped for five seconds and listened to my literary heroes, maybe I'd have solved the conundrum of my paltry existence long ago. But I'd stubbornly persisted in arguing my point, denying happiness, and refusing to apply any sort of meaning to life. I'd been content in my misery.

Had I been wrong?

Could I change my thinking and find peace for once?

A knock at the door announced Jersey's arrival. I wandered to the front hall, cocktail hugged between hands, a nervous jitter racing through my veins, and met him as he entered. All it took was Jersey's smile to know everything would be okay.

He removed my drink, set it aside, and engulfed me in his arms. We stayed like that for a long time, the unspoken words hanging in the air around us. *I know,* they said. *I know, and it's all right.*

After a time, Jersey pulled back, still smiling behind his short beard. "Hey."

"Hey."

"I missed you."

"Did you?"

"God yes."

"There is no—"

He leaned in and kissed me before I could finish the sentence, and I laughed against his mouth.

"Dinner's almost ready," I said when we parted.

"It smells great."

"Cocktail?" I picked up my discarded glass and displayed it.

"What are we drinking?"

"Mojitos for a starter and wine with dinner."

"Sounds fabulous."

A beer would have been equally fabulous for Jersey, but such was life. We had little in common, but our differences gave our relationship flavor. We were never short on conversation.

I made Jersey a drink, but instead of sitting, he hung near the counter and watched, his gaze stripping me bare—and not in the way I preferred. He was searching my soul, picking at the wound under my skin, deciding how to proceed. I wasn't sure if he found what he was looking for, but the analysis ended, and I breathed a sigh of relief.

Since dinner needed more time, we sipped our drinks and shared about our week. Not a word was spoken about the box and all Jersey had learned about my life. I was glad, having feared he might bring it up or want to discuss it despite my request.

At one point, while sitting on the couch, he trailed a finger over the dingy bracelet on my wrist, reverently stroking the worn knots. He'd given it to me a lifetime ago, but its symbology meant everything.

We shared a smile.

"I called my son last night," Jersey said when the conversation lulled.

"Oh wow. Really?"

"Yep. He didn't want to talk to me, but I made Christine put him on the phone. It was horribly one-sided at first, but he came around. We talked for over an hour. He's been playing hockey, I guess. At school. I had no idea." Jersey's smile was strained. "I offered to take him to a game, and he was all over it. Then I couldn't shut him up. We're having lunch next week, and I'm gonna call a buddy of mine and get tickets to something local."

I recognized the mixture of joy and relief on Jersey's face. His relationship with his son, Derby, was a sore spot he rarely talked about.

"I'm happy for you."

"You did this."

"Me?"

He nodded and stared into his tumbler. "Life's too short. We can either let the past stain our lives or forge ahead and make a brighter future." He took my hand and squeezed. "Thank you."

I wasn't sure what to say. I was the man who had let the past sink him like a stone in the lake. But Jersey saw past all those toils and troubles and recognized my small effort to find the surface again.

We ate dinner, drank wine, and chatted. It was easy. Comfortable. Peaceful.

After, Jersey insisted on sitting outside. The back fence had become our spot. We'd spent endless evenings watching the sun go down and enjoying each other's company. Fall was slowly taking over, and the nights were cooler. Soon, the leaves would change color and blanket the earth. Winter would settle, bringing with it a quietness I had always treasured.

The sun had gone down ages ago, but regardless, we sat on the wooden fence in the yard overlooking the cemetery. Under the canopy of trees, the headstones and church were nothing more than silhouettes. Stars filled the sky. A crescent moon climbed to its apex.

I closed my eyes and breathed serenity into my lungs until Jersey's words drew me back to the present.

"I have something for you."

He handed me a small, gift-wrapped box.

"What is this?" My birthday was long past, and Christmas was still a way off.

"Open it."

His expression gave no clue as to what was inside. I undid the wrapping and found a plain rectangular box underneath. Wedging the lid off, I uncovered a tri-wrap leather bracelet. Three layers: one braided, one beaded, and one with a punched design on the smooth surface. All three joined together at a black matted clasp.

I stared at it, then at Jersey. "I don't understand."

He didn't respond. Shifting on the fence, he took my wrist and unclasped the pin holding the worn and knotted bracelet he'd made for me decades ago on my arm. He set it aside. From the box, he withdrew the new one and put it on.

"It's not a friendship bracelet this time, but a promise bracelet. A little sturdier and a lot more grown up. It fits better too, and this one is more binding." He took my hand and weaved our fingers together.

"Jersey—"

"Listen. This one doesn't represent the promises of a child. It represents the promises of a grown man. I will *always* stand by your side in whatever capacity you need me. I love you, Koa. I think I always have, but I'm not walking away this time."

I cradled his face between my palms. "I may not always know how to express it. I may shelter myself from the world or pull back at times for self-preservation, but I do love you, Jersey, and I'll work hard to ensure you always know that. Please be patient with me."

"Always." He kissed me, and I felt whole and complete for the first time in my life.

Epilogue

JERSEY

Fall turned to winter, and life drastically changed. I sold my parents' house in November. After watching Koa sign his grandfather's house over to a young family, I found the courage to let go as well. Enjoying a final beer in the backyard where I'd grown up, I cried for the years lost to anger and drug addiction. I cried for my parents, wishing I'd had one more day to apologize for the mess I'd become. To tell them I loved them.

On a positive note, I'd developed a relationship with my son. We'd bonded over hockey, and he'd invited me to a few of his high school games. However, any advice I tried to impart earned me a teenage-worthy eye roll I was only now getting used to. Derby had opened up and accepted his father back into his life. He talked about video games and girls he was crushing on. He told me about the bands he liked and the movies he'd watched at the theater. We laughed, shared, and joked like father and son should, which warmed me inside and out.

Christine was happy to hear I was dating again and had said as much one evening when I dropped Derby off. She wanted to know about Koa and invited me in for coffee. We'd talked for over an hour, and I made strides in repairing that relationship too.

But the biggest change was my living arrangements. In mid-November, I gave my notice at the apartment and moved to Peterborough to live with Koa. Three days a week, I commuted to the city and the clinic, where I'd reduced my hours to part-time. To make up the difference, I'd taken a coaching position with the Peterborough minor hockey team after their coach had up and quit at the beginning of the season. The phone call from the team manager, offering me a job had thrown me for a loop. The pay wasn't great, but it was enough compensation for my missed hours at the clinic, and I was thrilled to get back into the game.

Koa's and my relationship had blossomed. Although there were plenty of times when he seemed untouchable and distant, lost in the past, he smiled more, and I never doubted his love. He might never fully heal from the trauma of his youth, but he'd come a long way. The sun shone down on him, and he did all he could to soak up its light and shed the darkness.

He made a point of finding the precious moments in life that brought him joy. Niles had even convinced him to accompany the band for the annual Christmas concert, which was where I was headed that evening.

Leaving the clinic at five, I had enough time to drive home, change, and race to the school for their seven-thirty concert.

I'd invited Derby to join me, but he'd told me it sounded lame. When I'd explained it would be a good time to meet the guy his father was dating, he'd called it extra lame. Teenagers. I still wasn't used to the attitude.

Since I was plenty familiar with the school and auditorium, I didn't need a guide to show me the way. I'd met a few of Koa's colleagues and had developed a friendship with Timber Creek's football coach, Blain Rivers. When I'd offered to give him a hand on the field, he'd been over the moon. Hockey and football were nowhere near the same sport, but Coach Blain was convinced I was a superstar because I'd gone pro a hundred years ago. We occasionally shared beers and talked sports, something I couldn't do with Koa. It was nice.

The auditorium was packed and shining with Christmas garb. Poinsettias lined the stage. I found a seat in the back row where Koa and I had sat during the spring concert in what felt like a lifetime ago.

The show opened the same way, with Niles giving a speech and showing off his superior skill on the piano. The man was a bit egotistical. When I'd pointed it out to Koa, he'd laughed and said it was a cover. Niles suffered from low self-esteem, so he worked his strengths where he could.

Once the concert band took to the stage, Koa sat on the piano bench, sharply dressed in a black suit and snappy red tie. I grinned, knowing he was nervous. Koa was still hard on himself about his playing, unable to see his own worth, but he'd grown more confident, and I loved seeing him up there on stage.

Reading glasses perched on the end of his nose, he accompanied the band through several Christmas pieces, and he was brilliant. When they finished, a trumpet player waved a hand at Koa, insisting he stand and take a bow.

After the concert, I took him for hot chocolate, and we strolled the streets of Peterborough, admiring the Christmas lights. We'd organized a small gathering for the holiday. Koa planned to cook a feast. Derby and his new girlfriend were joining us, along with Niles.

Niles was the closest thing Koa had to family, and I appreciated the man more every day. He'd done a lot for Koa over the years, and I valued him. I still saw hurt and sadness in Niles's eyes when he looked at Koa. Niles had loved him once, likely still did, and watching his best friend rediscover life without him had to be both gratifying and heartbreaking. I hoped he would find someone special someday. He had a lot to offer and deserved someone who could love him back.

In bed that night, Koa and I made love, and he was right there with me, staring into my eyes the whole time, present, emotions on the surface. I knew at times he wanted to hide, but he didn't. For as hard as it was, he let himself be seen.

I rocked inside him, kissed the corner of his mouth, and whispered how much I loved him. I laced our fingers together on the pillow above his head, the slight rise of the leather bracelet pressing against my skin. Its meaning had become powerful to Koa. He never took it off, and I often caught him staring at it while sitting at his desk amid term papers or while writing in his journal. When he played piano, it was in front of him, a constant reminder that I wasn't going anywhere.

I'd promised him forever, and I meant it.

Koa didn't often tell me he loved me—the words were hard for him to express—but I saw it in his eyes every day. As I sank into his body again and again, it was there, looking up at me, and I soaked it in, treasuring it.

We never talked about his past or about his life growing up in the aftermath of such a tragedy. Those terrible times had been laid to rest. Maybe we would never revisit them, and that was okay. But if he was ever ready to venture down that road, I would hold his hand and keep him steady.

The following morning, the sun shone brightly, warming the half-frozen world. Bundled up, we took thermoses of exquisite coffee and a thick blanket to the back fence, where we sat and peered among the frosted headstones of the cemetery. Winter birds hopped and sang among the bare branches of the trees. A lone deer wandered through the pines, staring at us once with its ears perked before running off.

Koa leaned his head on my shoulder, his soft hair brushing my cheek. I pecked a kiss on his crown.

"Thank you," he said into the quiet winter morning.

"For what?"

"Giving me back my life."

Need more angst?

The Devil Inside

Their love was innocent and pure...
Until they were forced to believe differently.
Until they were brutally schooled on the "right" way to love.

Oakland is not gay.

Jameson is not gay.

Being gay is wrong. It is immoral. It is a sickness they must fight. It is the devil inside that needs to be purged.

At least that's what they've been conditioned to believe.

They've spent years trudging through the wreckage left behind after eight months in conversion therapy as teenagers.

When their lives collide again fifteen years later, the denial they've lived with for years gets harder and harder to fight.

They loved each other once. Can two broken men find a way to love each other again?

-ᰔ-

Love Me Whole

Twenty-eight-year-old Oryn Patterson isn't like other people. Being an extremely shy social introvert is only part of the problem. Oryn has dissociative identity disorder. He may look like a normal man on the outside, but spend five minutes with him, and his daily struggles begin to show.

Oryn shares his life and headspace with five distinctively different alters. Reed, a protective, very straight jock. Cohen, a flamboyantly gay 19-year-old who is a social butterfly. Cove, a self-destructive terror, whose past haunts him. Theo, an asexual man of little emotion, whose focus is on maintaining order. And Rain, a five-year-old child whose only concern is Batman.

Vaughn Sinclair is stuck in a rut. When his job doesn't offer the same thrill it once did, he decides it's time to mix-up his stagnant, boring routine. Little does he know, the man he meets during an impromptu decision to return to college is anything but ordinary.

Vaughn's heart defies logic, and he finds himself falling in love with this strange new man. But how can you love someone who isn't always themself? It may not be easy, but Vaughn is determined to try.

More Nicky James

Valor & Doyle Series

Department Rivals (prequel)

Temporary Partner

Elusive Relations

Unstable Connections

Inevitable Disclosure

Defying Logic

Disrupted Engagement

Matrimonial Merriment

Shadowy Solutions

Invisible Scars

Skeletons in the Closet

Hometown Jasper Series

Clashing Hearts

Confused Hearts

Forgetful Hearts

Concealed Hearts

Rail Riders

End of the Line

Lost at the Crossing

Catching Out

On the Fly

Death Row Chronicles

Inside

Outside

Trials of Fear

Owl's Slumber

Shades of Darkness

Touch of Love

Fearless (A companion novel)

Lost in a Moment

Cravings of the Heart

Heal With You

A Very Merry Krewmas (Trials of Fear Special)

Fear Niblets

Rigger's Decision

Slater's Silence

Healing Hearts Series

No Regrets

New Beginnings: Abel's Journey

The Escape: Soren's Saga

Lost Soul: AJ's Burden

Taboo

Sinfully Mine

Secrets & Lies

End Scene

Risk Takers

Rule Breakers

Historical

Until the End of Time

Made in the USA
Middletown, DE
01 March 2024

50661972R00217